Whisper on the Wind

Whisper on the Wind

Maureen Lang

TYNDALE HOUSE PUBLISHERS, INC., CAROL STREAM, ILLINOIS

Visit Tyndale's exciting Web site at www.tyndale.com.

Check out the latest about Maureen Lang at www.maureenlang.com.

TYNDALE and Tyndale's quill logo are registered trademarks of Tyndale House Publishers, Inc.

Whisper on the Wind

Designed by Beth Sparkman

Edited by Sarah Mason

Published in association with the literary agency of WordServe Literary Group, Ltd., 10152 S. Knoll Circle, Highlands Ranch, CO 80130.

Scripture quotations are taken from the *Holy Bible*, King James Version.

ISBN-13: 978-1-61664-796-4

Printed in the United States of America

To my husband, *Neil*, whose wit and wisdom have inspired me and whose integrity is the model on which so many of my noblest characters are based. To my daughter, Torie, who never tires of "talking writing." And to my two boys, who allow me to write, even during the day.

Finally, of course, to the memory of those many real-life heroes of Belgium who bravely produced *La Libre Belgique* during the German occupation of World War I.

*O*nce there was a young man who came of age just as war erupted, a war reaching farther than the world had ever known. His country, his home, his parents, his very future—all were threatened by an enemy whose power stretched wide. He shared only one belief with his oppressors: that the written word is the immortality of speech. Because of the oppression, he could not roar as they did, but found a way to join a whisper so incessant that even his enemies stopped to listen. . . .

Prologue

August 1914

Louvain, Belgium

Edward Kirkland kicked through the ashes, staring at the black dust as if seeing what it had been just yesterday: his home. All that was left was a pile of charred ruins amid the shell of the hotel his father had managed. And there, not far in the distance, was the university. He could see the vestiges of the library from here, with nothing but rubble in between. Compliments of the German Imperial Army. There wasn't a thing Edward or all of Belgium could have done to stop it. Not that they hadn't tried, but a mouse couldn't fight an eagle.

Edward turned to leave. He shouldn't be out anyway, with German soldiers still roaming the streets, keeping the peace they'd broken with their arrival. He needed to return to his mother and brother in hiding at the church.

Something on the ground glimmered in the faint afternoon light. Though he stopped to investigate, scraping away fragments with the tip of his shoe, Edward knew nothing of value was left. Before they set the fire, the Germans had carried anything of worth out to a waiting cart to be shipped to Germany as spoils of war.

Then he saw the rose and a flash of silver light. With a lump in his throat, Edward bent and picked up the picture frame. He saw that the glass was broken and most of the photo burned away . . . except for the middle, where a shard held it intact. And there, smiling as if the world were a happy place, was Isa Lassone's face.

Isa, his mother's young charge, who'd fled with her parents before the invasion. She was safely ensconced in peaceful, prosperous America. She had both her parents, both her silly, selfish parents, while his father lay dead and the remains of their home smoldered.

The picture might have fallen without the glass holding it down. Bracing the photo in one hand, with the other he brushed away the broken pieces. He should let it go, let it join the wreckage of his home.

But Edward's thumb pressed it back into place, firmly within his grip.

Slipping the frame into the pocket of his coat, he made his way through the brightening streets. The ground was strewn with debris—bricks, glass, even a stinking dead horse here and there, the carcass oozing under the early August sun. Half the city was gone, along with Edward's father. Shooting and looting had lasted all night, but he'd had to see the hotel and university himself before he'd believe that they, too, had succumbed to the fires.

Something inside told Edward he should pray, reach out to God to help him face this day. That was what his father would have done, what he would have wanted his son to do.

Edward turned up the collar of his coat against an ash-laden breeze and walked away, trying not to think at all.

"Halt!"

Edward did so because to refuse a soldier's orders was to be shot. He'd seen it done.

"You will come with me," came the awkward command, followed by a firmer, *"Es ist ein Befehl!"*

Edward raised his hands, sorry for only one thing: his death would multiply his mother's grief.

Part One

SEPTEMBER 1916

1

SCOPE OF WAR BROADENS

Rumania joins Allied Powers with hopes of shortening the war

Germany has declared war in response, claiming Rumania disgracefully broke treaties with Austria-Hungary and Germany. The Allied Powers, at the forefront including France, Britain, and Russia, welcome additional men and arms. They remind the world which country was the first to break a treaty when Germany marched into Belgium in direct defiance of an agreement to respect Belgium's neutrality should international strife begin.

Fifteen nations are now at war.

La Libre Belgique

"Oh, God," Isa Lassone whispered, "You've seen me this far; don't let me start doubting now."

A few cool raindrops fell on her upturned face, blending with the warm tears on her cheeks. Where *was* her new guide? The one she'd left on the Holland side of the border had said she needed only to crawl through a culvert, then worm her way ten feet to the right, and there he would be.

Crickets chirped, and from behind her she heard water trickle from the foul-smelling culvert through which she'd just crept. Some of the smell clung to her shoes and the bottom of her peasant's skirt, but it was Belgian dirt, so she wouldn't complain. The prayer and the contents of her satchel reminded her why she was here, in this Belgian frontier the occupying German army strove to keep empty. For almost two years Isa had plotted, saved, worked, and defied everyone she knew—all to get to this very spot.

Then she heard it—the chirrup she'd been taught to listen for. Her guide had whistled it until Isa could pick out the cadence from any other.

She edged upward to see better, still hidden in the tall grass of the meadow. The scant mist cooled her cheeks, joining the oil and ash she'd been given to camouflage the whiteness of her skin. She must have grown used to its unpleasant odor, coupled with the scent she had picked up in the culvert, because now she could smell only grass. Twigs and dirt clung to her hands and clothes, but she didn't care. She, Isabelle Lassone, who'd once bedecked the cover of the *Ladies' Home Journal* with a group of other young American socialites, now crawled like a snake across a remote, soggy Belgian field. She must reach that sound.

Uneven ground and the things she'd hidden under her cloak and skirt slowed her crawl. Her wrist twisted inside a hole—no doubt the entrance to some creature's home—and she nearly fell flat before scuttling onward again. Nothing would stop her now, not after all she'd been through to get this far, not after everything she'd given up.

Then her frantic belly dash ended. The tall grass hid everything but the path she left behind, and suddenly she hit something—or rather, someone.

"Say nothing." She barely heard the words from the broad-shouldered figure. He was dressed as she was, in simple, dark clothing, to escape notice of the few guards left to enforce the job their wire fencing now did along the border. Isa could not see his face. His hair was covered by a cap, and his skin, like hers, had been smeared with ash.

Keeping low, the guide scurried ahead, and Isa had all she could do to follow. Sweat seeped from pores suffocated beneath her clothes. She ignored rocks that poked her hands and knees, spiky grass slapping her face, dirt kicked up into her eyes by the toe of her guide's boot.

He stopped without warning and her face nearly hit his sole.

In the darkness she could not see far ahead, but she realized they'd come to a fence of barbed wire. A moment ago she had been sweating, but now she shivered. The electric fences she'd been warned about . . . where bodies were sometimes trapped, left for the vultures and as a grim warning to those like her.

Her guide raised a hand to silence whatever words she might have uttered. Then he reached for something—a canvas—hidden in the grass, pulling it away from what lay beneath. Isa could barely make out the round shape of a motor tire. He took a cloth from under his shirt and slipped it beneath the fence where the ground dipped. With deft quickness, he hoisted the wire up with the tire, only rubber touching the fencing. Then he motioned for her to go through.

Isa hesitated. Not long ago she would have thought anyone crazy for telling tales of the things she'd found herself doing lately, things she'd nearly convinced her brother, Charles, she was capable of handling despite his urgent warnings.

She took the precious satchel from her back and tossed it through the opening, then followed with ease, even padded as she was with more secret goods beneath her rough clothing. Her guide's touch startled her. Looking back, she saw him hold the bottom of her soiled cotton skirt so it would touch nothing but rubber. Then he passed through too. He strapped the tire and its canvas to his back while she slipped her satchel in place.

Clouds that had barely sprinkled earlier suddenly released a steady rainfall. Isa's heart soared heavenward even as countless droplets fell to earth. She'd made it! Surely it would've been impossible to pass those electrified wires in this sort of rain, but God had held it off. It was just one more blessing, one more confirmation that she'd done the right thing, no matter what Charles and everyone else thought.

Soon her guide stopped again and pulled the tire from his back, stuffing it deep within the cover of a bush. Then he continued, still pulling himself along like a frog with two broken legs. Isa followed even as the journey went on farther and took longer than she'd expected.

She hadn't realized she would have to crawl through half of Belgium to get to the nearest village. Tension and fatigue soon stiffened her limbs, adding weight to the packets she carried.

She heard no sound other than her own uneven breathing. She should welcome the silence—surely it was better than the sound of marching, booted feet or a motorcar rumbling over the terrain. Despite the triumph she'd felt just moments ago, her fear returned. They hid with good reason. Somewhere out there German soldiers carried guns they wouldn't hesitate to use against two people caught on the border, where citizens were *verboten*.

"Let me have your satchel," her guide whispered over his shoulder.

Isa pulled it from her back, keeping her eye on it all the while. He flipped it open. She knew what he would find: a single change of clothes, a purse with exactly fifty francs inside, a small loaf of bread—dark bread, the kind she was told they made on this side of the blockades—plus her small New Testament and a diary. And her flute. Most especially, her flute.

"What is this book?" His voice was hushed, raspy.

"A Bible."

"No, the other one. What is it?"

"It's *mine*."

"What is it doing in this satchel?"

"I—I wanted to bring it."

"What have you written in here?"

Instantly flushed with embarrassment, she was glad that he couldn't see her face any better than she could see his under the cover of darkness. No one would ever read the words written in that diary, not even the person to whom she'd written each and every one. Well, perhaps one day he might, if they grew old together. If he let her grow old at his side.

"It's personal."

He thrust it toward her. "Get rid of it."

"I will not!"

"Then I will." He bolted from belly to knees, hurling the little book far beyond reach. It was gone in the night, splashing into a body of water that no doubt fed into the culvert she knew too well.

Isa rose to her knees as the object of her gaze vanished in the blackness. The pages that securely held each intimate thought, each dream, each hope for her future—gone. Every page a visit with the man she loved, now forever lost.

"How dare you! You had no right."

The guide ignored her as he resumed the scuttle forward.

Fury pushed Isa now. That diary had meant more to her than this dark figure could know. When at last he stopped and stood beneath the low branches of a forest to scrape the wild heath off his clothes, Isa circled to confront him.

At that moment the clouds parted enough to allow a bit of moonlight to illuminate them. And there he was, in glorious detail—older, somehow, and thinner, but the black brows, the perfectly straight nose, the square jaw, and the eyes that with a single look could toss aside every sensible thought she might have. The very man about whom—and *to* whom—that diary had been written.

Her heart skipped wildly, rage abandoned. "Edward!"

All he offered was confused scrutiny, a glance taking her in from head to foot. She took off her hat and her blonde hair tumbled to her shoulders. In the dim light he might not be able to see the blue of her eyes, but surely he saw her familiar smile, the shape of her face, and the welcome that sprang from the deepest part of her.

The look on his face changed from confusion to recognition. Then astonishment.

"Isa?"

She threw herself toward him, and he received her as she dreamed he might one day, with his strong arms enveloping her, his face smiling a welcome. His eyes, if only she could see them better in the darkness, must be warm and happy. She longed for him to kiss her and raised her face, but there the dream ended. He pushed her away to arm's length.

If there had been any warmth in his eyes a moment ago, it was gone now, replaced by something not nearly as pleasant.

"What are you *doing* here? I thought it was a fool's mission to bring somebody in. A girl, no less. And it's you, of all people!"

She offered a smile. "Well, hello to you too, Edward. After more than two years I'd expected you to be happy to see me. A guide was supposed to take me *to* you; no one told me it would *be* you."

"We'll retrace right now, young lady." He took one of her hands and moved away so easily that he must have believed she would follow.

"I'm not going anywhere, except home. If you knew what I've been through to get here, you wouldn't even suggest such an absurd notion."

"Absurd? Let me give you the definition of the word, Isa. *Absurd* is smuggling someone *into* a country occupied by the German army, *into* a starving prison camp. Do you know how many people have been killed here? Is the rest of the world so fooled by the Germans that you don't even know?"

"Edward, I'm sure no one on the outside knows everything that's going on, except maybe Charles. He was in France, caught behind the lines. And now he's working with the British, not far from where you were born. In Folkestone."

"Your brother? Working? Now there's a new concept. He should have talked you out of coming here."

Isa wouldn't admit just how hard Charles had tried. "I found my guide through him. Mr. Gourard—"

"Gourard! He was here—he was with us the day my father was shot."

"Oh, Edward." She leaned into him. "He told me your father was killed." Tears filled her eyes, an apparently endless supply since she'd been told the news. "I'm so sorry."

He pushed her away, but not before she saw his brows dip as if to hide the pain in his eyes. "Look, we can't stand here and argue. The rain was working with us to keep the sentries away, but if we have to go through that fence when it's this wet, we'd better go *now* before it gets worse. We've got to keep moving."

"I'm not going back." If he knew her at all, he would recognize the tone that always came with getting her way.

He stood still a long moment, looking one direction, then the other, finally stooping to pick up her satchel—now lighter with the absence of one small diary—and heading back to the grassland.

She grabbed his arm. "No, Edward! I won't go. I—I'll do anything to stay. I've been through too much to give up now."

He turned on her then, with a look on his face she'd never seen before—and his was a face she'd studied, memorized, dreamed of, since she was seven and he twelve. That the war had aged him was obvious, and yet he was still Edward.

He dropped the satchel to clutch both of her arms. "Do you think I'll let you walk into a death camp? That's what Belgium is, even your precious Brussels. Go back home, Isa. Your parents got you out. Before all this. Why would you be foolish enough to come back?"

"I came because of you—you and your family. And because *this* is my home."

His grip loosened, then tightened again. He brought his face close, and Isa's pulse pounded at her temples. But there was no romance in his eyes. They were so crazed she couldn't look away if she wanted to.

"Isa," he said, low, "I'm asking you to go back."

Her heart sped. "Only if you come out with me," she whispered. Then, because that seemed to reveal too much and yet not enough, she added, "After we get your mother and Jonah."

He dropped his hands and turned away, facing the grassland instead of the trees.

She could tell him what she had hidden inside her flute; surely that would change his mind about the wisdom of her actions. But something held her back. If she gave it to him now, he might simply accept the flute but return her to the border anyway. No, she wouldn't reveal her secret. Not yet.

Isa picked up her satchel and started walking—deeper into Belgium, away from the grassland, into the wood that no doubt served a nearby village. Beneath her skirt and blouse, the other goods she carried tightened her clothes so she could barely breathe, but she didn't stop. She didn't even look back.

Before long she heard Edward's footfall behind her. At first they did not speak, and Isa didn't care. Her journey had ended the moment she saw his face. This was where she'd longed to be. She'd prayed her way across the Atlantic, escaped the wrath of her brother and all those he worked with. Days of persuasion led to downright begging, until she'd tried going around them and contacted Brand

Whitlock, the American ambassador to Belgium, to arrange her passage home to Brussels.

But her begging had accomplished nothing.

Yet her journey had not ended there, thanks to the whispered advice of a clerk who worked in Folkestone with her brother. When Charles went off on an errand, another man approached her and spoke the name of a guide who started Isa on the final leg of her journey to Edward's side.

"We're coming to the village road," Edward said flatly. "I was told your papers would give your name as Anna Feldson from Brussels, which match mine as John Feldson. We are cousins, and I am bringing you home from visiting our sick grandmother in Turnhout. There is a German sentry on the other side of this village, and we'll no doubt be stopped. There won't be anyone on the street at this hour, which is a good thing because even the locals won't trust us. Nobody likes strangers anymore, especially this close to the border. So if we do see anybody, keep to yourself and don't say a word."

She nodded. A few minutes later the trees parted and she saw shadows of buildings ahead. The rain had let up to a drizzle again, and the moon peeked out to give them a bit of light. She wasn't soaked through but knew a wind would send a chill, especially now that the anxiety of crawling through the underbrush was behind them.

Edward stopped. "I'm only going to ask once more, Isa, and then I'll not ask again." Now he turned to look directly into her eyes. "We have enough darkness left to make it safely. Let me take you back to the border."

"I can't," she whispered. When the crease between his eyes deepened, she said, "This is where I belong, Edward. It must be where God wants me, or I never would have succeeded."

"God." He nearly snorted the word before he turned from her and started walking again toward the village.

"Yes!" She hurried to catch up. "If I told you all the ways He's protected me so I could get this far, you wouldn't doubt me."

Edward turned on her. "I refuse to hear it, Isa. God's not in Belgium anymore; you'll find that out for yourself soon enough."

His words stung. God had used Edward to show her His love to begin with, and she knew *He* wasn't about to let Edward go. Had Edward let go of God, then? When? And *why*, when he must need God more than ever if things here were harder than she had imagined?

They walked through the quiet village without incident, the soft leather soles of their wet shoes soundless on the cobbles. The village was so like many others of Belgium: a few small homes made of familiar brick, a stone church with its tall bell tower, and a windmill to grind grain into flour. So different from the frame homes or sprawling businesses Isa had left behind in New York, but so dear that she wanted to smile as deeply as Edward frowned.

At the other end of the narrow village street, there was indeed a German officer stationed on the road. Isa's heart thudded so loudly in her ears she wondered if she would be able to hear over it, or if the soldier would hear it too.

But he said nothing, not a word, at least not to her. He looked at them, looked at their papers, then asked Edward in rather bad French why they were traveling so early in the morning, having come so far from Turnhout already.

Edward replied that the steam tram was unreliable but that they hoped to reach the next village in time to catch it anyway.

The soldier waved them through.

"That was easier than I expected," Isa whispered once they were well away.

"Don't underestimate other soldiers based on that one. A suspicious one with a rifle can do as he pleases."

But Isa was too relieved to be gloomy. "Amazing how I can still understand you through your clenched jaw, Edward."

Edward didn't look at her. "We have to be in Geel in less than an hour if we expect to make the tram."

They made their way in silence, under sporadic drizzle and meagerly emerging sunlight. When at last they came to the next town, it was quiet until they reached the tram station, where soldiers outnumbered civilians. So many soldiers did what the rain couldn't: dampened Isa's spirits.

She had a fair understanding of German, but she could barely keep up. Not that she needed to; the soldiers ignored her, speaking of mundane things to one another, hardly worthy of interest. She prayed it would stay that way, that she and Edward would be invisible to each and every armed soldier.

A commotion erupted from the front of the platform. German commands, a snicker here and there. Silence from the civilians.

A man not much older than Edward was forced at gunpoint to open the packet he carried, to remove his coat and hat, even his shoes. A soldier patted him from shoulder to ankle.

Isa could barely watch and wanted more than anything to turn away. To run away. She told herself to look elsewhere, to allow the victim that much dignity, but was transfixed by the sight of such a personal invasion. Her throat tightened so that she couldn't swallow, could barely breathe. She couldn't possibly withstand such a search, and not just for modesty's sake. "Edward . . ."

"Keep your eyes down and don't say a word."

"But—"

"Quiet."

A tram entered the station and the man was allowed to board, everyone else soon following. Edward nudged Isa and they took seats.

The secret goods beneath Isa's cloak and clothing clung to her skin, as if each sheet, each letter were as eager as she not to be noticed. She feared the slightest move would sound a rustle. Carefully, slowly, she stuffed her satchel beneath the seat, wanting to take comfort that it had escaped notice. If her flute was looked at with any scrutiny . . . She couldn't bear to think of it.

The vehicle rumbled along far slower than the pace of Isa's heartbeat. She wanted the luxury of looking out at the land she loved, the fields and the villages, the rooftops and steeples, the mills and the farms, but her stomach didn't allow her eyes to enjoy any of it. At each stop a few soldiers departed, but new ones joined them. She tried not to study what went on, at least not conspicuously, but longed to learn how the soldiers chose which civilians to search. It appeared entirely random. More men were searched, but women weren't spared. One holding a baby was made to unswathe her child, who screamed and squirmed when jostled from its secure hold.

Isa did as Edward told her, kept quiet, eyes cast downward or upon the passing landscape that under any other circumstances would have been like a gift from the finest art palette. One hour, then two. After the third she could stand it no longer. Surely they were near their destination? But she had no idea how far Louvain might be at the rate they were going with so many stops and searches. No doubt they could travel more safely by foot without losing much time.

Six times she nearly spoke, to urge Edward to take her out of this tram. Six times she held back. But one more search and she could resist her impulses no more.

"I—I must get off the tram, Edward. I'm sick."

"Sick?"

"Yes, I must get away from—" She wanted to say *away from the soldiers* but dared not in case any of them spoke French and overheard. "I must get away from this awful tram. The stop and go is making me ill."

"Another hour. Surely you can last?"

She shook her head even as from the edge of her vision she saw a soldier looking her way. *How do you not look guilty when you're completely, utterly, culpable?*

Isa stood as the tram came to a slow stop at the next intersection. She kept her back to the soldiers, jumping to the ground just as soon as it was safe to do so. Then, without waiting for Edward, she walked forward as if she knew exactly where she was going.

She walked a block, well out of sight from the disappearing tram. There she stood . . . not amid one of the lovely villages, with their ancient way of life so quaintly preserved and appreciated. Instead, she found herself at the end of a row of destruction. Crumbling homes, demolished shops. Burned ruins of a town she once knew. Aerschot, where she'd dined and laughed and dreamed of walking the street with Edward's hand in hers.

A moment later Edward's shadow joined hers. "Are you positively mad?"

"We're in Aerschot?" she asked, barely hearing his question.

"Obviously. And several hours' walk from Brussels. Do you know how ridiculous that was? We don't need any complications, Isa."

She faced him. "Your contact didn't tell you what I'd be carrying, did he?"

Suspicion took the place of the anger on his face. "What?"

"Well," she began slowly, "I would try to show you, but among other things, I'm afraid I'd never get everything back in place."

He let out what she could only call a disgusted sigh as he ran a hand through his dark hair—hair that seemed thinner and yet sprang instantly back into place, symmetrical waves that framed his forehead, covered his ears. He needed a haircut, but she found she liked the way he looked too much to think of changing anything, even the length of his hair.

"Isa, Isa," he said, shaking his head all the while. "I should make you take out every scrap and burn it right here and now. Do you know what could have happened if you'd been searched on that tram?"

"Which is why we're no longer on it."

"You might have warned me!"

"I tried!"

He paced away, then turned to stand nearly nose-to-nose with her again. Not exactly the stance she'd dreamed of when she'd imagined him at such close proximity, but it sent her pulse racing anyway.

"You could have been shot. Do you know that? Shot."

She nodded. "They warned me."

His brows rose and his mouth dropped open. "Then why did you agree to the risk?"

"Gourard told me there are no newspapers, no information at all about what the rest of the world is doing to try to save Belgium and end this war. How have you lived so long without knowing what's going on? I have the best portions of a couple of recent newspapers. And I have letters, too. Letters from soldiers. Don't their families deserve to know they're all right?"

"It doesn't matter what I think. Gourard shouldn't have taken your life so lightly or trusted such things to a young, naive child."

"Child! I'm perfectly capable of deciding what risks I will or won't take. I'm the one to decide what I will or won't do for Belgium."

"It was bad enough for you to come back, but to bring contraband—it's beyond foolish."

"Edward, don't be angry with me. I'll deliver the letters and then be done with it if you like, if it's too dangerous for us. But I won't abandon what I brought with me."

"I don't care about the risk for me. I've done so many things the Germans could shoot me for that one more thing doesn't matter. It's you. Maybe the Germans wouldn't shoot you—being just a girl—but who knows?"

"I'm not —" . . . *just a girl.* But she didn't bother with the words. She doubted they'd convince him.

She looked away, embarrassed. All she could think of when she agreed to smuggle the letters was how desperately she had wanted news of him and how other families cut off from their loved ones must be desperate too. She couldn't have refused to take a chance with the letters and lived with herself. "I agreed to take the risk for the same reasons you've taken so many. Your mother and father didn't teach values only to you and Jonah, you know."

He emitted something between a moan and a laugh, then took her arm. "We're going somewhere for you to take out the letters. And the newspaper clips."

"But, Edward—"

He looked at her then, and she could see he was not to be argued with. "I'll carry them in my cloak. It won't be the first time."

MONSTER ARMORED CARS USED BY BRITISH IN CHARGE ON THE SOMME

Called "tanks" by those who've seen them, Allied soldiers themselves refer to these huge traveling fort machines as "Willies." Driven like motorcars but able to scale barbed wire, leap trenches, knock down houses, and snap off tree limbs, they are a formidable weapon indeed and will no doubt play an important role in the defeat of the Germans.

La Libre Belgique

They walked the rest of the afternoon, which to Isa was far preferable to sitting within searching distance of any German soldier. Until they came to a checkpoint they could not skirt.

"Put it together," the soldier said. "Play."

Sweat moistened Isa's palms as she looked at the pieces of her flute. Should she run? Not without the flute. And from a soldier with a gun?

She looked from the disassembled instrument to the German, feigning ignorance of his language.

"You . . . you play?" His attempt at French was barely decipherable.

She shook her head even while he shoved the pieces at her as if to convince her with his insistence. This soldier was as stubborn as a caricature in the American newspapers she'd left so far behind.

"You play the music," he demanded once more, in German again instead of his poor attempt at French.

She leaned away from him, taking a small step back, still shaking her head.

"*Ach . . . Dummkopf . . .*"

Better a free *Dummkopf* than an imprisoned flutist.

The soldier waved them away. Isa dared a peek at Edward, whose face was as emotionless as, she hoped, her own. If only he knew!

"This way," Edward said quietly once they were beyond sight of the guard station. She followed him off the road again, back into the bramble that had once been cultivated land.

"Is Genny in Louvain?" She'd wanted to ask details all day, but Edward was in such a sour mood she hadn't dared.

"We'll stop in Louvain because of what we're carrying, but my mother isn't there anymore."

"The Bardiou family is still in Louvain," she said. "I'm sure they will—"

He stopped so suddenly she nearly bumped into him. "No one is left, Isa. No one you knew, at any rate. Stop talking." Then he turned away from her, not even looking back to see if she could match his stride.

They walked at a steady pace, past farmhouses that looked empty, around motley crops. Mostly weeds grew in the fertile ground these days, with an occasional cluster of wheat, so different from what she remembered.

Isa had visited Louvain many times during the years she'd spent more time with Edward's family than her own, living in one of the best rooms their exclusive inn had to offer while Isa's parents often traveled. But as they entered the outskirts, her heart went heavy.

This was not the Louvain she knew. Where were the whitewashed brick homes and shops that had once lined the cobblestone street, the flowers that hung from each window, the gardens gracing every yard? Not a blade of color could be found, as if a massive paintbrush had drawn a swath of gray over the town. Entire blocks were burned to the ground; piles of brick and rubble stood crumbling where she'd once shopped and dined. She could tell by Edward's face that he'd grown used to the devastation, so she hid her horror.

She knew the university was burned, where both her father and brother had attended—and Edward, too, at only sixteen. Perhaps it had been destroyed on the same day Edward's hotel had burned, since it wasn't far. American headlines told about the university and its beloved library burning, but Gourard had told her about the hotel.

And St. Peter's, gone as well. How could they? But she knew that no matter how many of His churches the Germans burned to the ground, God wouldn't abandon Belgium, not when she needed Him most. Edward must be made to see that . . . somehow.

A smaller chapel still stood, one she'd never visited before. Edward stared at it and she knew that was their destination. At the top of the wide cement steps, open doors beckoned.

Soldiers lingered on a nearby corner, smoking and laughing despite the dinner hour.

"We'll round the block and come up behind the church." Edward's hand cupped her elbow so that even if she wanted to pause, she couldn't.

They cut through the alley between two shops still intact but abandoned: one a grocer with a torn awning flapping on a breeze and the other with a printer's logo in the window. Edward led the way to a back entrance of the modest, single-story chapel. Inside, colored light filtered through stained glass. A few people knelt in silent prayer at the altar, candles at each side lit as always in such chapels but perhaps more numerous than before the outbreak of war.

Isa had barely more than a glimpse of the altar as they passed through a hallway and down a narrow stairway leading to a tiled floor below. Downstairs they found several doors, all made of wood that, over the years, had absorbed the smell of incense. Edward went to one and tapped lightly.

A moment later a priest stood in the threshold. Bright dust flecks danced around the outline of his head like a halo, but until he held wide the door, Isa could see only the outline of a man wearing a cassock.

"Edward!" The priest was much older and barely taller than Isa, with a robust smile and the fair complexion of a Fleming, his sparse hair light and gray. "Come in; come in."

The private chamber offered nothing more than a simple pine desk, a narrow chair before it and a crucifix above two more equally uninviting chairs opposite the desk.

"And whom do we have here? I've not seen your face before, young lady."

"This is Isa Lassone, Father Liquori," Edward announced. "I'll be taking her to Brussels, but we have something to leave with you before we finish our trip."

"Oh? Edward?" He sounded cautious, but his smile never wavered despite his tone of voice. "Are you sure?"

Edward patted the cleric's shoulder and nodded his assurance. "I've known Isa since she was seven, Father. She's half-American by blood, but pure Belgian by choice."

"Ah." He looked her over again, this time with a renewed twinkle in his eye. "You and Edward, you are friends?"

Isa smiled. "Yes, very good friends."

Edward began opening his bulky shirt. "My mother is a servant of her parents—or used to be—"

"Edward! Your mother is no servant."

"Well, she was practically your nanny, wasn't she? That's a servant."

"My father is Belgian but my mother is American. My parents have always lived a rather . . . busy . . . lifestyle, but when they first brought me here, they stayed in Edward's hotel, until arrangements were made for us to move into a home in Brussels. That's how our families met. Whenever my parents were busy, off I'd go to Edward's wonderful hotel. His mother made it like a second home to me, which is why I wouldn't call her a servant. She's family."

"Uh-huh." Edward pulled letter after letter from his ever-flattening middle and more inner pockets than Isa had ever seen in a jacket. "Just ask Isa's mother if my mother was a servant or not, and she'll tell you the truth."

"Oh, Edward."

"She paid my mother, didn't she?"

"Why not? I ate her food; she sewed my clothes; she bought me books. Was she supposed to pay for that herself?"

The priest smiled. "I understand how you might be like siblings, then, fighting all the time."

Isa wanted to utter a hasty denial, assure the priest that Edward was anything but a brother to her, but a single glance told her that Edward hardly cared how their relationship was defined. He'd finished removing the letters he'd carried and was rebuttoning his shirt. All that was left were the two sets of newspaper clippings, one that Edward now held and the other still beneath Isa's skirt.

"We'll leave the room while you get the newspaper out," Edward said.

"No reason to leave." She reached into the waistband of her skirt and loosened the thick yarn. The paper dropped to the floor.

Before it had a chance to cool from the warmth of her skin,

Edward scooped it up and placed it, still folded, next to his own skin, replacing the letters he'd withdrawn.

"I thought you were going to leave everything here," she said. "Didn't you say this was as good as the secret depot I'd been instructed to use?"

"And so it is—for the letters. Father Liquori will know what to do with them."

"What about the newspapers? Where are we taking them?"

"*We* are not taking them anywhere. Father Liquori is taking *you* upstairs to wait until I return."

"But where are you going?"

The priest put a hand on hers. "Better not to know everything, little one. With these—" he waved his other hand over the letters— "you know enough."

Little one? How *could* he call her that, especially in front of Edward?

Edward watched the merchant behind the counter wrap a hefty fish in various layers of newspapers, precious smuggled ones neatly concealed within pages of the readily available German-run *La Belgique*. One simple word set apart the legal paper from the one Edward worked for: *La Libre Belgique*. One paper inspired and approved by the Germans, the other uncensored and worth risking his life for. *Libre*. Free. Dedicated to the day Belgium would be free again.

With a glance rather than money exchanged between customer and fishmonger, Edward made his way out the door. A little bell jingled his exit.

The headlines Isa had smuggled still lightened his heart—at least those he'd been able to glance at before handing them over to be wrapped with the other papers. *Allies Pound German Forces; Germany's Loss Put at 300,000; British Smash 7 Miles of Foe's Lines, Take 2,000 prisoners.* Those were the kind of headlines Belgians wanted to see! Not what the Germans printed every day, about sinking British warships and claiming victory at every turn.

The late afternoon sun shone brightly in the warm weather. Edward clutched the bundle beneath his arm. The train depot was a ten-minute walk, and he would barely make the drop time if he hoped to get this unexpected gift included in the current shipment.

Edward had never met the particular messenger he'd summoned through the fishmonger, and making his face known to yet another level in the various rings of communication was a risk. But it was one Edward couldn't help taking, with the newspaper clips so recent and encouraging.

Though he increased his pace, he held back from a trot. Any civilian setting a quick stride, especially one with a parcel, was like a flag waving at the nearest German sentry, demanding notice.

Few civilians but dozens of German soldiers gathered on the station platform. Travelers' identifications had to be checked, but Edward wasn't crossing the gate, so he would be spared that. Then he spotted his target: a man in a worn dark suit, complete with a red-tipped umbrella and a kerchief sticking rakishly from the coat's tattered breast pocket.

Edward approached the man casually and, without a hat to tip, bowed his head slightly, stopping nearby as if awaiting someone on the expected train. "Funny how it can rain in Louvain and stay dry in Aerschot, isn't it?"

The man, who had started to turn away, stilled. "Yes, and all the while it pours in Brussels."

They made the briefest eye contact before Edward turned away, going to a bench along the wall. He sat down, placing the fish beside him. A few moments later, as the train whistle sounded down the track, the other man sat.

Edward stood, leaving the fish behind.

The man took the wrapped fish and headed back to the edge of the platform just as the huge, black steam train came hissing to a halt. The news would find its proper way now, and with it, hope.

3

Verba volant, scripta manent—
Words pass, but writings remain. We seek in these pages
to be the mirror of a people united against the FOREIGNER,
to remind our fellow Belgians that though our homeland is
gagged under its oppressors, we are not, nor will we ever be,
defeated.

La Libre Belgique

"Wait here," Edward whispered. "Do not move until I come out."

Isa kept a retort to herself, offering only a nod. She was in the
vestibule of either a home or a closed business—it was hard to tell
which. He went inside the inner door and she looked around. Scant
moonlight shone through a tiny square window that was framed
with heavy wood and only large enough for a single pane of glass.
The entryway was stark, clean, void of furniture or adornment.

Like all the buildings they'd passed, this one had been shuttered and dark. She only knew they were in Lower Town, a Brussels
quarter unfamiliar to Isa. Edward had taken her down one sloping,
narrow alleyway after another, until she was certain she'd never find
her way out alone. Her family had always lived in Upper Town,
whose streets were far easier to manage. From various spots along

those fashionable avenues and boulevards she'd done little more than see the evening lights of Lower Town or, during the day, the rooftops nestled closely together. Most were tiled like those she'd seen in Spain; others were of tin, some of simple wood; and they were nearly all connected.

Now from within Lower Town she'd seen brick everywhere, closing in from all directions at twilight. Brick streets, brick buildings, brick steps leading to the little wooden doors that were tightly shut.

She leaned toward the inner door, straining to hear someone familiar, but the sounds were too quiet. Was this where Edward had been living since his family's hotel had burned? Was Genny here, just on the other side of the door? and Jonah? Isa longed to go inside but didn't dare. If it were only Edward's family inside, surely he would have brought her in.

Eventually the sound of voices died away and Isa sank to the floor. Finally, snug in her trust that Edward had brought her somewhere safe, she fell asleep.

⟡

"You should have brought her inside. Look, she's sleeping."

"A hard bed won't hurt her," Edward said to the woman at his side. "She's known nothing but the softest feather ticks most of her life. That's all changed now that she was foolish enough to come back."

"Bring her in and she can sleep upstairs. You shouldn't leave now anyway. Curfew started two hours ago."

"Our documents are good if we get stopped. We'll say the trams were late from Louvain because of so many stops at checkpoints. It happens every day."

"Oh, fine. Insulting the Germans for their policies will certainly endear you to them." She stroked the side of his face. "It'll be safer to stay. You know I'll worry."

Edward took her hand in his. "We're not carrying anything now except perfectly forged identification papers, Rosalie. What could happen?"

She laughed softly, leaning closer. "Any number of things."

"I'll see you in a few days. Go back inside before I wake her."

"I believe you worry more than I do. Are you so concerned about my safety? What does it matter if she sees me?"

"I told you, the fewer people who see a link between you and me, the better."

"You don't trust her, then?"

"She's not much more than a child, but an impetuous one and entirely too talkative. It's best for all of us not to exchange names or faces."

"Why, she's hardly a child, Edward!"

Edward glanced at Isa sleeping peacefully under a single beam of moonlight. Here was the girl Edward had known for years—and yet, she was different. The bones of her face were more defined, her neck somehow longer, her eyes larger. She was taller than the last time he'd seen her, yet she'd lost that gangly look. Perhaps because of the bulky peasant clothing. He realized he liked her better dressed in such a way; it removed her from the Isa he'd known, the one with the family so rich they hardly knew what to do with all that money.

Isa stirred and he turned from looking at her, all but pushing Rosalie back into her home. "Go inside, Rosalie. I'll see you soon." Then he closed the door.

By the time he faced Isa again, she'd scrambled to her feet, adjusting her clothing and slipping her cloak into place.

"Who was that?"

"No one you need to know."

"But—" She stopped before finishing her own statement, staring at him, her mouth agape. "Edward! You—your face!"

"Oh." He dared not go farther into the city without his Brussels identity firmly in place. Just having the disguise in place made him feel less like the Edward Kirkland, guilty of so many crimes against Germany, and more like the innocent man he portrayed himself to be. "Permit me to introduce myself. I am Nicholas van Esbjörn, a fifty-year-old businessman of Danish lineage. I have lived in Brussels most of my adult life—twenty-five, no, thirty years. And you are my niece now, still Anna Feldson. I hope you learn to answer to that name if a soldier sees your papers and calls you that, Anna."

"Oh, Edward." She shook her head. "I would hardly know you."

He knew Rosalie was the best. She had studied under the master himself, Lawrence Auber, the premier makeup artist at La Monnaie, the most famous opera house in Brussels—and, Brussels would argue, the best in all Europe. Perhaps it wasn't such a stretch to make him look older than his years, since the Germans had starved and beaten the youth out of him shortly after their arrival. Even since his return, what little food he ate never had a chance to soften the rough edges of his bones. But with Rosalie's artwork, his premature pallor now sported a line here and there, a touch of gray to his dark hair. Even his neck, if one looked close enough, was marred by new wrinkles that a man his real age of nearly twenty-three would not see for another score of years. He was, to look at him, past the age of a soldier on either side of the war.

"Better get used to it," he said as he led her outside and down the cobbled path. "This is how I live when I'm in Brussels."

"Where are we going?"

"To my mother."

"Oh! At last!"

A twinge of old jealousy teased Edward, something he hadn't felt since in knee pants. His mother, at least, would be happy to see Isa—happy but undoubtedly angry, too.

"But where, Edward?"

Edward slowed his pace when he noticed she barely kept up. "Right here in Brussels. Although," he added with a glance, "not in your Upper Town. She's with a Flemish woman along the Rue Haute in the Quartier des Marolles, not far below the German eye in the Palais de Justice."

"The Germans are in the Palais de Justice?"

He laughed at her naiveté. "They're everywhere, Isa."

They walked for some time, staying away from major intersections and keeping to narrow alleys. Edward didn't believe in unnecessary risk. He drew Isa with him to the shadows if he saw any of the Kaiser's soldiers or heard the clop of horses pulling a cart.

After a while Edward stopped before one of the buildings. He'd been here often enough in the past year or more since gaining his freedom—such as it was—but still he had to count the doors from the corner, they were all so much alike. Nothing adorned the structure, neither flower boxes nor welcome mat, not even shutters at the windows. Though swept clean, this home was stark and plain. Like all the others.

Edward pulled a key from his pocket and unlocked the door, then quietly let them into the small, dark parlor. The single common room in the house offered a sturdy, bare wood table, a cast-iron cookstove in the corner, and a freestanding cabinet laden with dishes. There was one bedroom on this level, belonging to Viole and her husband, an older Walloon couple who'd worked for Edward's parents when they'd begun managing the Hotel Cerise. Edward's mother and his brother, Jonah, used the two rooms upstairs. On the rare occasion Edward allowed himself to join them, he shared his younger brother's quarters.

"Everyone is asleep. You can rest right here in the parlor." He pointed toward a settee in front of the tall fireplace. "Come along, then; you can sleep a little before everyone rouses."

"All right."

He would have stepped past her, but she stopped him with a gentle touch to his arm. "Edward, wait. I wanted to—to thank you."

He grimaced and would have turned away, but she still held his arm.

"No, Edward, please listen. Will you sit with me? Here on the settee?"

He was tired and wanted to go to bed but found that sitting was too tempting to pass up.

"I know you think I've made a mistake in coming back, but even if you're right, what's done is done and I'm *glad* I'm here. I've longed to be here since the moment my parents forced me to leave." She sighed. "I was so young then, I didn't have a choice."

He wanted to tell her the passage of just over two years hardly counted toward aging her but didn't.

"Do you remember those days, Edward, just before the Germans came?"

He shrugged. He'd rather not recall. Yawning, he stretched out his legs and leaned back.

Isa shifted too, but to his dismay she leaned into him the way she used to when they were children. "There was so much going on, so much confusion. Everyone thought we'd be left alone, our little Belgium."

"As we should have been."

"Everyone was full of confusion and fear. . . ."

"And now only fear." He patted the hand that rested on his chest and for a moment felt every bit the age he was dressed to portray, so much older and wiser than this girl beside him.

"But none of us knew back then what would happen. We shouldn't have left so quickly."

"Why should your parents have stayed? Brussels was just a diversion for them, not a home."

"But not for me. Brussels *is* my home."

"So what? Do you think if you'd stayed you could have changed anything? Do you think you can change anything now? What good are you here, Isa?" She sat up with an open mouth, no doubt with a ready defense, but he raised a hand. "Let me answer my own question: None. None whatsoever. You're worse than that—you're a liability. Oh, there you go, with your eyes welling up and thinking I've insulted you. But be logical for once, will you? You're getting older now. Do you think anybody wants to be noticed by a German soldier? Least of all a woman, which you'll be someday."

"I think I already—"

"I haven't mentioned that we're dependent on charity for nearly every meal. No one works because to do so would be to work for the Germans. There are so few crops because they would go to feed the soldiers first anyway—*German* soldiers. Even if we wanted to work, because of the blockades there aren't any imports to keep our factories going, so what's the use? Passive resistance to the German regime allows us plenty of time to do nothing—nothing except avoid their presence, stick to ourselves, and await the day of liberation. If that day ever comes!"

"Oh, Edward, it will! Once America joins this war—"

"I didn't see any headlines about America wanting to be involved. If they haven't joined in by now, why should they *ever*? How many of their ships do the Germans have to sink?"

Isa looked from Edward to the glowing embers in the fireplace, but only for a moment. She nestled back beside him. "So, you must have had other smuggled newspapers. And you've been able to read them."

He had no intention of telling her how. He leaned back, closing his eyes. "Look, Isa, I've no wish to be harsh. But you don't realize you've jeopardized your life by coming back."

"I've come to help, Edward. Wait until you look inside my

satchel." He heard her stifle a yawn, which produced one in himself. He should go right up to bed this very moment.

But he was too comfortable to move.

"What's so important in the satchel?"

"I'll show you . . . later."

Then she yawned again.

And so did he.

"Who's there?"

Edward shook himself awake. "It's me, Mother."

Light was just starting to emerge from the window behind his mother at the foot of the stairs. Somehow he'd become entwined with Isa in his arms, and he shook her gently. "And . . . Isa."

"Oh! Edward, I'm always so happy to see . . . What did you say?"

"Edward?" Isa pulled herself away, and for a moment he nearly didn't want to let her go; she was so warm and the night had been chilly.

"Say hello to my mother."

Grogginess abandoned by them both, he watched Isa spring from the settee and pitch herself at his mother, the woman he knew Isa had spent more time with than her own mother. Edward stood, watching the reunion with reluctant satisfaction.

"Isa! Isa, my own little Isa. Oh, I sing praises to the Lord, seeing your face again."

They both laughed and cried, and Edward wanted to turn away, shake his head, or laugh and cry along with them. There were too few joys these days . . . although this shouldn't be one of them. She shouldn't have come.

"Am I dreaming?" Edward's mother held Isa tight, stroking her long, travel-ruffled golden hair. Then she held Isa at arm's length and looked at her. "Is it really you?"

"Oh, Genny!" Isa's voice tumbled like the tears falling from her face. "Now I know I've done the right thing."

"But what are you doing here? I thought your parents took you out of Belgium."

"They did."

"They've come *back*?"

Isa shook her head, and Edward spoke for her. "Only Isa."

"But how? And why? *Why?*"

"Oh, not you too, Genny? I came because I had to know you were safe. And in spite of what Edward thinks, I can help."

Genny pushed Isa's hair away from her face. "Seeing you has gladdened my heart, but Brussels is hardly a place for anyone to live these days."

"What's all the commotion?" The words were timid and roughed by bravado all at once, and Edward knew instantly the voice belonged to Albert. He made a better bellhop than house guard. "Who is in there?"

Hinges squeaked from the door to the first-floor bedroom, and a man peeked out. A moment later his wife stuck her head around the jamb too, her hair covered with a nightcap that resembled part of the maid's bonnet she'd worn in better days.

Edward's mother pulled Isa forward, holding up Isa's imprisoned hand like the winner of a prizefight. "Oh, Viole, it's my own Isa, come home!"

Viole opened the door fully then, and Albert stepped out as well. Their faces were hardly welcoming.

"Who is this daughter, Genny?" Albert asked.

Viole poked him with her elbow. "She is no daughter; she's that *fille hautaine* from Upper Town in Genny's care so long. Oh, beg pardon, *mademoiselle*. I meant to say—"

"That's all right," Isa said. That probably wasn't the first time she'd been called haughty, but it usually came from Edward himself. "I'm afraid I'm not welcomed by anyone."

His mother patted Isa's shoulder. "No one said you weren't welcome."

"Edward did."

Still a tattletale. He didn't reply. He wasn't going to take back a word, even if his mother might remind him about manners.

"He's only worried about you, dear," his mother said. "And so am I."

"I talked at great length with Gourard, and he told me what happened before he left."

"Gourard!" His mother repeated the name with surprise. "He escaped over the frontier to Holland more than a year ago. You spoke with him?"

"He helped me to get back into Belgium." She glanced at Edward. "He must have been the one to make sure it was you who guided me."

Edward didn't doubt it.

Albert cleared his throat. "I'll hear no more, *mademoiselle*. Whatever you are involved in isn't likely to be approved by the Germans, and I'll have no part of it."

"I'm not a spy, if that's what you're thinking."

Edward didn't mention that she'd smuggled in illegal newspapers and letters, making her every bit a spy according to the Germans.

"I want no trouble, do you understand? You're not blood to us—to Genny or to any of us—that we should all risk our lives protecting you."

Before the war no one would have spoken to Isa or any one of the hotel guests in such a tone. One by-product of the times that Edward didn't mind at all.

"But, Albert, she's nearly a daughter to me," Edward's mother said.

"Nearly isn't blood. I pray you've no plans to stay here. We've little enough to eat as it is and too little money to buy more."

Edward watched confusion reign on Isa's face, but it lasted no more than a moment. She pulled a perfect shield of composure over her flawless face. Her hair was askew and she was dressed in peasant's rags, but at that moment she was all Lassone: a wealthy heiress with her father's distant ties to Belgian royalty.

"I have no intention of inconveniencing you," she said. "At full light, I'll go home." She turned to Edward's mother. "I hope you know you are welcome to come with me."

Edward sighed at her proud announcement and spoke before his mother could reply. "How generous to offer your home. But do you know if *you're* welcome there?"

"What do you mean?"

"I mean that half the big houses in Quartier Léopold have been billeted with German soldiers for two years now or converted to hospitals. Yours is probably one of them."

"Oh . . . I hadn't thought of that." She looked his way again and her eyes flashed not with embarrassment but anger. He was used to her confidence—it came with money—but there was something new about that confidence, something . . . older. "I'm sure you believe I haven't thought of a great many things. But I have. I shall see Brand Whitlock tomorrow—or today. He'll set my papers in order, vouch for my residency, and have any Germans using my home removed for the length of my stay."

Edward said nothing, only exchanged a glance with his mother. Have a few Germans removed?

And what did she mean, for the length of her stay? Did she think that border was some sort of open highway, back and forth between Belgium and freedom?

Little fool. He just hoped whatever fracas she started wouldn't send too much attention their way.

4

Let us not forget the last proclamation of our beloved leader Burgomaster Max upon the arrival of our oppressors, to temporarily accept the sacrifices imposed upon us and patiently await the hour of reparation.

La Libre Belgique

Isa sat with a cup of steaming water in front of her. There was no tea, nor chocolate, nor coffee. She was told there was sometimes wild chicory to be had, but Genny said the taste was so awful they hardly pursued getting it. Pretending it was very weak tea, Isa sipped the hot water. The warmth felt good.

Viole and Albert had returned to their room, the door tightly shut. Isa knew they hoped she'd be gone once they emerged again, and she planned to do all she could to oblige.

She eyed her satchel on the table. Now was as good a time as any to show Edward and Genny what she'd brought. She reached inside for her flute and handed it to Edward.

"This is what you wanted to show me?"

"Oh, Isa, you brought your flute," Genny said. "There is so little happiness around these days, I'm sure we'd all love to hear you play."

"Not yet," Edward said, balancing the center in his palm. "There's something inside, isn't there? That's why you pretended you weren't the owner when that German asked you to play?"

Isa took the flute and stuck her finger in the end but couldn't reach what she sought.

"I think she needs a hairpin, Mother," Edward said. "Or two."

Genny went up the stairs, returning a moment later with a small silver box. Isa took out two pins, straightening and twisting them together. With caution and patience, she pulled out the hidden, tightly wound black material.

"What is it?" Genny asked.

The black velvet had been invisible through the holes of her flute, held securely between G# and C.

Genny gasped as Isa unfolded the velvet.

"There are eight diamonds, four emeralds, from rings my father gave me as birthday gifts. The diamonds aren't the same size, but even the smallest is the best quality our Congo supplies. I thought they would bring more value when trading for services."

"What services?" Edward asked suspiciously.

"It's why I came," she said. "I asked Gourard how I might bring all of you out of Belgium, across the frontier. He told me whom to contact and said these will be enough. I also have gold from the settings, melted down to little nuggets. They're sewn into my . . ." She paused with a shy glance toward Edward, looking quickly away as she finished. "Underthings. With as much cash as I could carry between the lining of my skirt and the cotton on the outside."

Edward leaned back in his chair, emitting a breath. "I don't know if I should be grateful or angry."

"Why should you be angry?"

He leaned forward again, folding his hands on the table. "Is there anything *else* you smuggled in without telling me? a codebook, maybe? plans to blow up the Kommandantur?"

Isa laughed. "You're too funny! Why should I have told you about the money and the gems? What would you have done differently to get them here?"

"You could have warned me about the flute," he said. "I almost threw the blasted thing in the river, along with that silly book of yours."

"My diary! Don't remind me."

"Oh, Edward, you didn't throw away Isa's diary?"

"I did. I know of at least two priests who've been killed for keeping a journal, and I wasn't about to join their ranks because of some silly sentimental rubbish."

"Don't call my diary rubbish!"

"Perhaps not—rubbish wouldn't send anyone to the firing squad. Did you happen to mention Gourard's name in that diary?"

She didn't answer.

"I can see you did. A connection to someone who's escaped over the frontier is automatic guilt in any German court."

Isa was about to protest when she caught the little shake of Genny's head. Clearly Genny thought this was one argument Isa could not win.

"How soon can we contact Gourard's network to help us leave? I have the name of a priest who will arrange for papers for the rest of you, passes to travel outside of Brussels." She glanced at Edward. "We don't need more than that, do we? You can guide all of us out the way you guided me in, can't you?"

"What about your loyalty to Belgium?" Edward asked. "That's all you've touted since I picked you up, how this is your home and you belong here."

"I meant every word, but I've always planned to use this treasure in the best way to benefit all of us. So when Belgium is its own again, there will still be Belgians to populate it."

"Well, at least you're talking sense." Edward eyed her. "Your plan might work."

"Good! How soon shall we leave?"

"I can talk to Father Clemenceau today."

"You—you already know Father Clemenceau?" Isa caught back more questions. "Of course, since Gourard arranged for you to be my guide, you must already know all of the connections between here and Holland."

"I know some," he said slowly.

Genny shook her head. "Those people are so dangerous. Albert has a healthy fear of it all. I wish you knew less than you do." She patted her son's forearm and then looked at Isa. "Now both of you know too much."

"I only know a few names," she said.

"Well, forget them," Genny advised. "As for escaping over the frontier, I don't—"

Taking up one of the diamonds, Edward interrupted his mother. "This much money will make the trip far less dangerous than you imagine, Mother. We can bribe every checkpoint guard between here and the border and walk right out."

"How can you be so sure? Greed is one thing, loyalty another."

Isa put an arm about Genny's shoulders. "Edward will make sure we're safe."

"I wouldn't agree to seeing you out if I didn't think you could safely escape, Mother," Edward said. "I wouldn't put your life—or Jonah's—in worse jeopardy than staying here."

"Not to mention your own life," Isa added. *Or mine*, but she didn't dwell on that omission just now.

Edward didn't look at her.

There was something heart-stopping in that simple act of avoidance.

"I will have Father Clemenccau talk to you," Edward said. "As soon as he sees the medium of exchange Isa's brought, he'll tell you how safe the journey could be. Will you talk to him?"

His mother nodded.

"Good." Edward twisted the velvet back around the gemstones, pushing them toward Isa. He stood. "Put these back where you had them, and by all means keep them safe. I'll tend to the arrangements."

Isa stood too, leaving the jewels on the table. "Wait."

He slowed but did not stop until he was at the door.

"You'll make arrangements for all of us, won't you, Edward? All of us?"

He placed a hand on the dark knob. But he didn't open the door, nor did he turn back to them. He stood still for a long, silent moment. "I'll make arrangements for you and my mother and Jonah."

"Then you might as well sit down," Isa said quietly. "What would be the use of spending all this on bribes just to turn around at the border?"

Edward faced her, his brows sinking. "I will arrange for you to leave as soon as possible, and you *will* go. But I'll stay behind."

"Now who's the fool for choosing Belgium over freedom?"

"Call me what you like. I cannot go."

"Then none of us will go," Genny broke in.

"That's fine with me," Isa said.

"Not with me." Edward retraced his last two steps, approaching his mother. "This is almost as foolish as Isa coming back in the first place. Although," he added with a glance her way, "seeing what she's returned with, I may have to recant some of what I've said. That only makes your refusal to go more foolish, Mother. She's done something extraordinary, something unbelievable. She's brought with her the means to get you out of this hell. Imagine eating a meal not provided by a soup kitchen. Imagine taking a walk anytime you please, in a garden—or wherever you like—without running into a German soldier. Imagine not fearing a night raid or

Germans ransacking your home. Imagine never again hearing the
sound of executions at Tir National. You *must* go, Mother!"

"You might as well give up, Edward," Isa told him. "She's not
giving in. And neither am I. If you stay, we all stay."

He touched his fingertips to his temples and rubbed as if to
erase pain. "This is outrageous. I can't . . . Listen, Mother." He put
his hands on her shoulders. "Jonah is nearly twelve years old. Who
knows how much longer this war will last? Before long we'll have to
spirit him away to keep him out of the work camps, unless he finds
a way out himself and joins the Allies on his own. I've heard some
soldiers are getting so young they're barely old enough to shave. If
you take him to safety now, you can spare him all of that."

"Yes, that's all true. And a good reason for you to let us all go by
leaving with us."

His lips tensed.

"You dress yourself like an old man to escape notice of the soldiers, but I know that's not the only reason. I know *you*, Edward. I
know how you were before the war, how you wanted to join, how
you argued with your father about it. Except for his good judgment
delaying you until it was too late, I'd have lost you by now. Somehow, though, someone else reached you. I may not know what you're
involved in, but I know you're fighting this war with every breath you
take. Not in a uniform, not with bullets, but you're fighting every
time you disappear from me. And that's why you won't go."

"It doesn't matter why, Mother. All that does matter is that Isa has
come with a way out. For you and for Jonah. Take it; *please* take it."

Genny closed her eyes. Isa put an arm around her shoulders,
effectively brushing Edward's hands aside. "Can't you see she wants
to go, Edward? But you must come too!"

He started to run his fingers through his hair, then pulled back,
as if remembering the dye that colored various strands gray. That
same hand started toward, then pulled back from his neck, too.

When he looked at Isa, the fatigue in his eyes almost matched the worn look of the false wrinkles on his skin. "If I tell you it would be safer for me if all of you were gone, would you listen then?"

"I don't understand," Isa said. "Surely you trust your own family?"

"It isn't a matter of trust," he said. "It's a matter of leverage. If I'm caught, they won't stop at punishing just me. They'll use whomever they please against me."

Genny sat on the nearest chair. She leaned back and closed her eyes for a long moment. When she opened them, she spoke softly. "Did you listen to what Isa said before about having come back because this is her home, about belonging here? Do you realize what it meant? She didn't mean Belgium or her fancy home here in Brussels. She meant *us*. You, Jonah, me. We're home to her, Edward. If we're here in Brussels, then we're home. If we go to Holland, then that is home, too. Home is wherever we all are—together. So if you choose to stay, then we'll call Brussels home for a while longer."

Edward looked from his mother to Isa, and she saw his silent plea for help. But she couldn't help him. Not this time.

"Edward," Isa whispered, "I know you think we don't understand all you've said about the danger, but it's you who doesn't understand. I know what it would be like for your mother if she left you behind, not knowing what will become of you. If this is hell, then that is too, of a different kind. Don't you see? A single day here is better than a thousand days over the border. A single day, if that's all we have. At least we're together. The way God put us."

Those were words she'd once written in her diary to him, words she'd only dreamed of saying to him aloud. She knew he thought it was only to keep their quasi-family together, but it didn't matter.

Edward turned away. Then he went out the door without saying anything more.

5

Let us respect the rules they impose upon us so long as they touch neither the liberty of our Christian consciences nor our patriotic dignity.

From a banned letter written by Cardinal Mercier
to pastors throughout Belgium, quoted on the
pages of La Libre Belgique

Isa stood in the American Legation parlor, having used her brightest smile, her wittiest wit, and her father's name to request Brand Whitlock's help in regaining ownership of her home. How many times had he and her father dined or played golf together? But so far nothing had penetrated Mr. Whitlock's obvious disapproval of her unexpected arrival back in Belgium.

"Well then, please instruct me as to how I shall go about getting the soldiers out of my home by my own effort. Shall I simply walk into my old vestibule, announce my ownership?"

"Isa, don't be ridiculous. You're purposely egging me on, aren't you?"

"Why, no. I'm just asking for advice. I thought you were here to protect the interests of Americans. If you can't help me, I'll have to do it myself. Who is in charge of the army in this city? Shall I go to see him?"

"Oh, I can just see the German general's face if you were to go to him. That would be a sight!"

"Then I shall go, and you can come along to see that face. What is his name?"

"Military Governor General Freiherr Moritz Ferdinand von Bissing. What do you intend to do? March right over to the Kommandantur and demand to see him?"

Isa frowned. "Have your fun. If you think I'm a fool, why don't you just say so?" She suddenly wanted to abandon all her bravado and have a good cry. So far nothing had gone the way she'd planned. Not even this, and she'd thought the ambassador would be on her side once he realized she'd returned in spite of his protest.

Whitlock stood to walk around his desk and sit on the edge closest to her. He even leaned down to take her hands in his. "Now, don't pout." Then, despite his hand patting, he glared. "You've put me in quite the spot, though. The Germans will smell a rat over your sudden appearance, no doubt about it."

"You'll do it, then? Get my home back for me?"

"No promises. I'll have to let them think you've been here all along, staying elsewhere. They'll wonder why you can't just stay wherever it is you've been staying, and I don't have a ready answer."

"It's my home, Mr. Whitlock! Isn't that reason enough?"

He uttered a humorless laugh. "I suggest you stay out of trouble, young lady, although it's trouble you're in already just by being here. Why don't you see Nell? She's at l'Orangerie in Ravenstein for the time being."

"No, no, I won't trouble your wife. I do have a place to stay, but not for long. I don't have a telephone, though, so I'll have to call on you for updates. Is that all right?"

"It'll have to be, won't it?"

She turned to leave, but before she'd reached the doorway, he called her back. "Isa, you do have your passport? papers?"

She raised her brows, hesitant to tell him about the papers she possessed that were so nearly legal. "I do have my passport—my own. And I have papers, too. . . ."

"Let me see them."

She pulled the identity form from her pocket but kept it too close for him to see the name Anna Feldson. "It's been scrutinized already. I'm fine in this regard. I keep my passport well hidden, always separated from this."

He held out his hand.

Slowly, she placed the paper in his open palm. He unfolded it, his brows lifting. "This is well done." Then he frowned anew. "I'll see about legitimate papers for you, too. Hopefully by tomorrow, but you must see my clerk for a photograph before you go. Now run along. I have a lot of work to do."

She walked once more toward the door, only to be called back again.

"Who is accompanying you?"

"No one."

He shook his head. "No escort, no gloves, no hat. What would your father say?"

"He might have said plenty, but he lost that right when he left Brussels, didn't he?"

Then she left his office, refusing to think of her parents. They were likely too busy to have noticed she'd even left home. She caught back the thought; it was too late to try convincing herself her parents deserved whatever worry she'd caused.

Anyway, the false pass in her hand had survived Whitlock's scrutiny and that filled her with confidence.

Isa headed to the heart of the city she loved. German uniforms abounded. Once-pristine parks were shut off to the public but used by German officers *and* their mounts—something never before allowed. Once-manicured trees, hedges, and lawns now grew untamed. Once-perfect gardens now sported weeds.

Armed military police patrolled the streets; guards stood at train stations. The only passengers on trams were soldiers. Few motorcars used the streets, and there was not a bicycle to be found.

Though her beloved city lay untouched by the cannonballs that had destroyed so many Belgian villages, Brussels was desecrated nonetheless.

Isa hid her disgust from the soldiers roaming the streets, but when she caught a glimpse of a civilian eyeing *her* with a scowl, she hurried on her way. Passive resistance must extend to refusing to read the German placards posted everywhere. She should have guessed as much. There were only so many ways to resist.

She found her way to Lower Town, where there were fewer placards and fewer soldiers. Fewer people were outside, and those who were ignored her, until a short shadow jumped into her path. "There you are!"

"Jonah!" She hugged him close.

At nearly twelve, he'd grown in the two years since she'd seen him. He had wavy dark hair like his older brother's and the merry green eyes of his mother. But his nose and mouth were his father's, and even as she welcomed that smile, the memory of Genny's husband reminded Isa of the hole his absence had left in her heart.

"Mother told me you came back during the night. I wish you'd have awakened me. I would've liked to see you first thing."

"Well, here I am, just a few hours later."

"But where did you go? Mother's not home; she went to wait in the lines to bring back bread with Miss Viole. I don't know where Albert is. And Edward's still gone. Mother said he'd be angry you left without him."

"But I'm back, safe and sound, so he has no reason, has he? And why aren't you in school?"

"No electricity today, so they sent us home. That's fine, if you ask me. None of my real teachers are there anymore anyway, and I don't like the German ones."

"But you must go to school, no matter what. Even the Germans value education."

"Well, I don't value what they have to teach, none of it."

She put an arm around his thin shoulders as they neared the door to Viole's home. "What if I told you there's a chance we might move to my old home in Upper Town? And you could go to school in that neighborhood? Perhaps they have Belgian teachers there."

"That would be fine . . . only . . ."

"Only what?"

"I've been by your old house, Isa. I don't think it's yours anymore."

She sighed. "Yes, I know about the soldiers. Hopefully they'll be moving soon."

"Out of Brussels?"

"Well, out of my house, anyway. And then we'll go and live there. You and your mother and Edward and me."

"Edward too?"

"Does that surprise you?"

By now they'd let themselves inside the modest home, which was dark even on an uncommonly sunny day due to so few small windows.

"It's only that he hasn't lived with us since he came back, so I'm wondering why he would now."

"Since he came back from where?"

Jonah's brows lifted. "Don't you know? The Germans took him, way back when they first came to Belgium."

"What do you mean, took him?"

He took her hand in his and led her to the table, directing her to sit as if she would need a steady chair beneath her. "They took him that day when they burned the hotel and the church and the university. Mother doesn't like me to talk about it—she said we should forget because God gave Edward back."

"But where did they take him? What happened?"

"We were hiding in the church and Edward went outside. He never returned. We didn't know what happened until the Germans brought all of us to the Rue de la Station . . . not so far from where our hotel used to be. We were made to stand, all huddled, and they added to our numbers all day long. They gathered people they found outside and made others leave their homes. We were tied with a rope all around us and couldn't sit—not for the whole day. I was too afraid even to be hungry. Do you know, sometimes the soldiers shot people just because they wanted to? And then they took men Edward's age and put them in a cart and sent them off. Mother kept telling me Edward hadn't been killed, that he'd only been taken. But we didn't know for sure—not until he came back, nearly dead, after working in Germany."

Isa's heart twisted at the horrors even little Jonah must have seen. Horrors Edward had lived. "But why didn't he stay with you after that?"

"Because Mother let the Germans think he died, just like the others who were sent home on that cart. Mr. Gourard brought Mother a death certificate and told us to say Edward was buried in a fresh grave by the church. It wasn't long after that Mr. Gourard went away. He was helping people like that. Against the Germans."

So Edward had more reasons than just smuggling people in and out of Belgium to flee German punishment.

"That's why Edward is someone else now," Jonah continued, "until the Germans leave. A man my father's age, so the Germans won't make him report every day like the others who are younger."

"Where does Edward live?"

"Here and there," Jonah said, without looking at her.

"What do you mean?"

"Only things we're not supposed to know."

"But things you know anyway?"

He fidgeted, standing near the table and twirling a fingertip on the smooth wood surface.

"Tell me, Jonah. You know I won't do anything to get Edward into trouble."

"I'm not worried about that. I'm worried about the trouble *I'll* be in if I tell you."

She laughed. "I won't say a word; I promise."

"Mother always says *promise* is a special word and I shouldn't go about using it—"

"Unless you really mean it," she finished. "I know. She told me the same thing. Covenants and promises. Like God made with us when He said He'd be with us always."

Without a word Jonah left the room, going up the stairs and returning moments later. In his hand was a folded piece of paper. "You won't forget your promise?"

"I won't forget."

Silently, he handed her the paper. Newsprint, lightweight but durable, plain black and white but clear, good-quality print, just a single page. At the top, in tall, bold letters she read, *La Libre Belgique.*

This was no normal newssheet despite its bold headline. The words stole her breath.

"Allies Attack from Sea to Verdun, Smash German Forces"

Surely this was no German newspaper. The price listed at the top was *Elastic—from zero to infinity.* It called itself a "bulletin of patriot propaganda to be distributed with regular irregularity and submitting to no censorship." At the bottom, advertisers were told to hold their money for better times.

"Where did you get this?"

"From Edward."

"He *gave* it to you?"

Jonah shook his head. "No, he doesn't know I have it. I swiped it out of his pocket once when he had a pile of them."

The issue was dated nearly a year ago, the office listed simply as an "automobile cellar" with the unlikely contact address of none other than the German Kommandantur right here in Brussels. "This is pretty old. Do you know if Edward is still involved with this?"

"Sure he is. He doesn't bring them home anymore; otherwise I'd have a more recent copy. I follow him sometimes, but I always lose him."

She folded the paper and handed it back to him. "I'm afraid you should burn this. It's dangerous for you to have."

"I keep it hidden."

"But if it's found, you could be arrested, you and your mother and Viole and Albert. Edward, too."

He took the paper without looking at her.

"Does Albert know you have this?"

"No! And he won't find out, either. You promised."

She shook her head. "No, I won't tell him, and I won't tell anyone else. But what are you going to do? Keep it and worry you might get everyone into trouble, or get rid of it and sleep easy at night?"

"But I've already had it this long. It's never been found so far."

"I'd say you've been keeping the angels around you busy then, and maybe it's time to give them a rest. Please, Jonah? You must have it memorized by now if you've had it so long. Why keep it?"

He started to speak, held back. His face splotched with red.

"Because I want to be part of it, like Edward. Everybody says the ones who print this paper are the saints of Belgium. Heroes."

She was sure of that.

"I have an idea. Why don't you and I take a walk to the edge of the park? I saw they're growing potatoes there now, right here in the city. If we can get close enough to a bush or tree, where people would never think to grow something, we can dig without attracting too much attention. Then, when the Germans are gone for good, you can go and retrieve it as the keepsake you want it to be. But if it's found, it won't cause trouble for anyone in particular."

"I guess I could, if I had something to keep it in, to keep the squirrels from getting at it, and the rain. I'll go find something and we can do it right away, before Mother or Edward get home."

Isa waited in the parlor while Jonah went in search for something to protect his treasure. Myriad thoughts coursed through her mind. If Edward was still involved in an illegal newspaper—something that had been circulating for at least a year—he was in greater danger than she thought.

"I'm ready!" Jonah held the folded paper in one hand, a small metal tin in the other. "My father gave this to me when I was little. It's a bank, but it's been empty a long time now. I've wanted to bury this ever since the Germans came through once looking for tin and metal. I've stuffed cloth in the slot. See? To protect my paper."

"Well done," she said as they walked out the door. "One day all the coins you used to help your family will be replaced—and doubled. God has a way of doing that sort of thing when we use what we have to help others."

"Think so?"

"Oh, Jonah," she said, catching his eye, "I know so."

6

We must, therefore, be silent as seeds, fiercely united and longing for that day when from our homeland soil grows our own true voice once again.

La Libre Belgique

"I tell you, I was followed."

"Lower your voice." Edward scanned the park. His unease was mirrored in the trembling young courier at his side, only Edward was better at hiding it. "Sit on the bench. Breathe easy. Look ahead."

Beyond stretched one of the few parklands not entirely overtaken by German army officers, one given to the people to grow potatoes in the hope of keeping their hunger at bay. A few civilians did what people used to do before the war—"taking the air" after their midday meal—but Edward doubted many were Belgian. Civilian clothes didn't mean they were Belgian.

"All right," Edward said, once they were seated. "Can you talk slowly now? Don't look at me. We're just enjoying a bit of sun, remember?"

Peripherally Edward saw the young man turn stiffly to face the potato beds. He breathed deeply, twice. There couldn't be more than a few years' difference between them, but nearly two years of working against the Germans had a way of growing Edward into the age of his disguise.

"Is he still following you?"

The man—Tomsk—shook his head. Edward knew his name, but such knowledge didn't go the other way around. "I lost him in the Quartier des Marolles."

"There! But how would you know you were followed with so many soldiers at the Palais de Justice? Are you certain?"

"I'm certain."

"Then you'd best leave what you have with me. Don't go home for a few days. What section of your route have you left undelivered?"

"The north end of Quartier Léopold."

"Here." Edward slipped a key from his pocket and placed it on the middle rung of the bench. "This is the key to an empty flat on Rue Avalon, number 219, advertised to let. Create no noise nor smell of food. Don't use the lights while you are there. Do not even let the floor squeak beneath your soles. Leave the key inside when you go. Return here in two days. I will contact your family, see if your home is being watched. If so, you must go over the border. If on the other hand you are safe, I will tell you simply to go home. Do you understand?"

"Yes. Yes, sir. I'll do as you say." Tomsk reached out to pick up the key, but his hand shook so much that Edward doubted he could do such a simple thing.

"Breathe easily, man." His tone made Tomsk withdraw his hand, the key still sitting there. "Do you have the issues yet to be distributed?"

Tomsk leaned forward, his jacket falling open. Inside he wore a harness something like the one Edward often wore, designed to hold a few hundred sheets of thin paper, divided into packets of fifty to be given to various distributors in the city. Edward saw those Tomsk had were each neatly folded into their envelopes. One was identical to any other—and therefore likely to cause suspicion if seen.

"Wait for those two men to pass," Edward whispered, eyeing two men walking by not far off. "Then take off your jacket and harness together with the issues inside. Leave it here on the bench between us. Pick up the key at the same time. Then wait a moment, take a breath, and go."

Edward waited until Tomsk had reached the edge of the park before glancing at the abandoned jacket. When he stood some moments later, he tucked it over his arm. He would deliver those left, because as Tomsk's supplier, Edward knew each and every "subscriber" on his list.

He often performed various tasks vital to the paper, delivering finished prints or finding blank paper to be used on whatever press they could employ. He'd even written an article or two under the pseudonym Bespawl, a name he'd chosen from a poem he once read because it meant "to spit." And each word he wrote was meant to do exactly that, directly into the German eye. But even now he had no idea of the editor; he simply passed on his articles to the man who supplied him with the copies he distributed, and somehow they found their way to the innermost secret circle.

Edward delivered the last of the papers; broad daylight was sometimes the best cover of all. Leaving the luxurious appointments of Quartier Léopold was easy for him, even now, when all of Belgium was united. Fleming and Walloon. Rich, poor, and in-between. Despite the temporary equality among most Belgians, Edward remembered his place, and Upper Town wasn't it—such a place was Isa's.

Still, he couldn't stop himself from passing her old home. As expected, it was still occupied.

Descending the streets to Lower Town, he returned to the park he'd left behind some time ago. He wasn't sure what caught his eye first—the shadow of a slight, crouched boy or the woman in peasant garb so obviously trying to hide him. Curiosity made him slow his pace, but anger quickened it when he recognized the two faces.

"Have you both entirely lost your minds? Jonah, what are you doing?"

Jonah popped to his feet, his hands covered with dirt, fingernails black. On his face was a look that flashed between surprise, fear, and then relief when he recognized Edward. "N-nothing."

"Well, Edward," Isa greeted him. "What are you doing coming from that direction? I didn't think you liked my old neighborhood."

He ignored her, noting the obvious guilt on his brother's face. "What have you been doing? You can't plant a potato under a bush."

Even as he asked the question, he saw Isa move back, casually stamping on whatever Jonah had been burying.

"Looking for dropped coins," Jonah said.

Isa looped her arms with both of them. "Come, Edward, let's all start walking. We've been in one spot long enough. We'll be perfectly honest, shall we, Jonah?"

His brother looked horrified, but Isa's smile was so easy Edward nearly couldn't resist smiling along. People smiled so rarely anymore, it was as if they'd forgotten. Probably she would forget too, after she'd been back for a while.

"We were burying a treasure. One we'll dig up after Belgium is ours again. And it will be someday. We're finished now, anyway. So shall we go back to Viole's and have lunch?"

"What treasure?" he queried. "Not the flute?" Some of Jonah's horror landed in Edward's gut.

"No, no, that's back in my satchel behind the cupboard at Viole's. Although," she added, "I think perhaps we should find a better place for such a valuable instrument. I have just the spot for it, once I'm living in my home again."

He nearly harrumphed over that silly notion but thought the better of it and stopped midstride. "What *were* you burying, then?"

"Not to fret. Jonah's old tin bank, for safekeeping. He thinks the Germans might go house-to-house looking for tin and metal and didn't want the bank your father gave him to be requisitioned."

"So you buried it in broad daylight?" He shook his head at Jonah. "You both could have gotten into trouble if you'd been caught."

"But we can't go out after dark, Edward."

"And we weren't caught." Isa's voice was as untroubled as always. Here, in the middle of occupied Brussels, she sounded as if she hadn't a care in the world. It irked him. "So, what were you doing in Quartier Léopold?"

"I went past your old house. Still occupied by German troops, so you might want to rethink where you'll be living."

Her smile hadn't the sense to dissipate even the smallest bit. "I went to see Brand Whitlock today, and he's promised to help."

"Ambassador Whitlock will see you in your house again?"

"He didn't promise, but he'll try."

Edward smirked. "Of course he didn't promise. What do you think he is, Isa, a miracle worker? He's a good, decent man who probably had a hard time saying no to his old friend's daughter. You had no right to put him in such a spot."

"I have a right to my own house, haven't I? He's just doing his job, protecting American interests. Believe me, if Mr. Whitlock didn't want to help me, I'm sure he wouldn't."

"I think we'd better come up with another place for you to live just in case he can't achieve the impossible."

Isa raised one brow. "Such as . . . wherever you're living?"

"No. I was thinking you might be more comfortable with an old neighbor or another friend of your parents. Anyone come to mind?"

She cocked her head with a teasing smile. "Most of them went with King Albert when the royal court left the country."

"Why don't we just take you to see Mr. Whitlock and he can arrange for you to follow that path, right out of Belgium."

WHISPER ON THE WIND

Instead of being offended, she patted his arm. "I wouldn't dream of deserting you now, Edward."

He sighed, soft and brief, then set a brisker pace.

"Halt! Halt!"

Edward stopped and saw that the others did too, in the same step. His heartbeat quickened, and he looked around hoping to see a soldier calling attention to someone other than them.

There was no one.

Slowly, Edward pulled his arm from Isa's and slipped his hand around hers. He took Jonah's hand as well and the three of them leaned together on the *pavè* as one. For a moment he was tempted to thank God he'd just rid himself of his contraband, but the thought ended there.

"You will show your papers, please."

Edward saw Isa scramble to get her papers first and stuff them under the nose of the stern German soldier. He was broad shouldered and strong, despite his thick glasses that no doubt guaranteed his position in occupied territory rather than at the front.

"And you?" He eyed Edward.

The soldier looked at his *Passierschein*, perhaps less closely than Isa's, and when he handed them back, he didn't even address Jonah, who still stood nearby but, Edward noticed for the first time, had not produced his identification.

"Very well. You may go."

Edward was the first to turn away. He thought he'd gotten used to these searches. Blast Isa; why did she have to be here to see things like this, anyway?

After they turned the corner, Jonah laughed.

"What's so funny?" Edward asked.

"I didn't have my papers!"

Edward eyed him. "And you find that funny?"

"He didn't ask for them, did he?"

"He's right about that," Isa said with a grin. She winked at Jonah. "I thought you were going to give those angels a rest?"

"What is that supposed to mean?" Edward asked.

"Only that I've been important to God lately," Jonah said.

Isa tousled Jonah's hair. "I couldn't agree more."

⟡

They reached the home they shared with Viole and her husband by noon, although Jonah left them before that. With so many school days interrupted for one reason or another—German raids, imprisoned teachers, lack of supplies—Jonah was one more Belgian with too much time on his hands. He disappeared when they passed a house he said belonged to a friend.

Noon was one o'clock German time, the clock having been changed shortly after the invaders arrived. Other than for the trams and trains, no Belgian seemed to pay attention to the change.

Genny and Viole sat on stools just outside Viole's home, busy making lace. Isa watched, amazed as their fingers nimbly chased thread bobbins through a maze of pins protruding from a stiff, round pillow inset with a patterned cylinder in its center, each with a set on her lap.

"Genny! I didn't know you made lace."

She laughed. "I don't, at least not well. Viole is the expert. She's been trying to teach me for years."

Viole looked up. "It's the only way to make a bit of money these days now that your American ambassador's wife arranged for lace makers like myself to make my own designs. We've had only this one grace since they came, those dirty Germans."

"Go on in and have a bit to eat," Genny said without looking up. "There's fresh bread on the table."

"*Fresh* bread?" Isa repeated.

"The CRB provides the flour to the baker," Genny explained. "And he sells to those who can afford it or accepts the *bons*—you know, the tickets—of those who can't."

Isa shook her head. That the Committee for Relief in Belgium had set up a process to sell bread wasn't what shocked her. "In England they're only selling bread that's at least twelve hours old. I came from America to England, and from there to Holland—"

Viole broke in. "We don't want to hear about that, *mademoiselle*. Why do they sell old bread there, anyway?"

"Because fresh bread makes one eat more."

The others laughed, loud and long, starting with Edward.

"Oh, Miss Genny," Viole said after a moment, "I know you've blood as English as it comes running through your veins, but those Englanders you left behind can be a silly lot, can't they?"

Isa was glad they seemed cheerful, although she wasn't convinced the British were as silly as all that, especially when people were hungry there, too.

Edward led the way inside, and Isa followed him.

"You didn't laugh," Edward said once they were in the kitchen.

"I don't find starvation funny."

He faced her, and she felt her heart skip a beat at his sudden, unexpected attention. "We don't either," he said softly. "But if we can pretend we're handling our hunger better than others, well, so much the better."

"Aren't you forgetting something, Edward? You're a British citizen."

"For all practical purposes, I'm as Belgian as they come, especially now." Then he added, "Like you."

Isa's heart danced in her chest. This was the first friendly exchange they'd had since she'd returned.

Isa accepted the bread and cheese Edward cut, even though she wasn't hungry anymore. Being alone with him always robbed her of her appetite.

"Don't you have anywhere you must be?" she asked. "A . . . job?"

"The hotel is gone. Where would I work?"

"I don't—"

He leaned forward. "The Germans control everything. Everything. And so we stand in the food lines rather than work for them."

"I'm sorry."

"Sorry? For me?"

She nodded. "I've never known you to be idle. It must be difficult for you, this forced unemployment."

He didn't reply, but she was unwilling to let the topic go. Surely he trusted her enough to let her know what he was involved in?

"You've always liked to work. How must you pass your days, then?"

His gaze lingered on hers. "Isa," he said at last, "I wanted to tell you something I should have said this morning."

She couldn't help but smile. "Please don't scold me for going out alone."

He shook his head. "No, not about that, although you should *not*. And I don't consider Jonah an adequate escort, either. He didn't even have his papers."

"Well, I had mine, which clearly state I belong in Brussels. In fact, I'm not to travel outside of the city, so I must belong again, at last."

"Blast it all, Isa, you make it sound like Brussels is paradise. Those soldiers think they can occupy every part of this city, own anything or anyone in it. I don't want them to get a glance at you, or one of them might decide to try to own *you*."

"Edward—"

"As a matter of fact, when you leave here, I want your promise that you'll wear the hat you had on the other night. Yes." The volume of his voice increased when she opened her mouth to speak. "That awful hat, that dark, dowdy, peasant cap. And a coat, and for heaven's sake keep your eyes averted. Look at the ground instead of any soldier. Do you understand?"

She gave a slight nod, not looking at him. "Like this?" She kept her eyes down, and when he failed to respond to her exaggerated example, she laughed. "Oh, Edward, you're so solemn when, at least for the moment, all is well. Is that what you wanted to say to me, to give me instructions for when I go out?"

"No." He sighed. "What I wanted to say was thank you."

"Why?"

He leaned into the table, bringing his face closer to hers and taking her hands in his. "You were childish, naive, downright foolhardy to come back. But," he added when she tried to pull her hands away, "you were also brave. I've never wanted to admit that a little slip of a girl could be so brave, but I can't deny it anymore. Thank you for wanting to bring my mother out of this place. I wish she would agree to go."

Now she held tight to his hands. "We both know the way to get her to do that."

"I haven't given up trying to convince her, and neither should you."

"We won't leave you behind."

"You've made that clear."

Isa studied his hands—had he forgotten he still held hers?

"It's generous of you to offer your jewels," he said. "I'm sure they meant a lot to you."

"Not so much," she whispered.

"You said your father gave them to you."

"They're more useful here."

His hands pressed more deeply into hers. "You confuse me, Isa. You always have. Why should you use your father's gifts for us?"

Growing up with so many visits to Edward's home, she'd only rarely been alone with him, and those occasions had been more rare as they grew older.

"Every year, my father presented me with one of those rings. An expensive item to pacify me." She gave him a lopsided smile. "Charles used to tell me the gifts were because our parents felt guilty about not spending time with us and we should take advantage of it. Bribes, of a sort. I suppose my brother received his own share."

He let go of her hands and leaned back in his chair. Her fingers felt cold without the warmth of his. "Yes, well, all those engagements at the palace and the queen's garden parties and endless dinners do have a way of taking one's time. Your parents were busy."

He said it with nearly as much scorn as she would have herself. "Exactly. Not like you, working so hard on your studies and going to the university so young. I'm sorry it burned. I know you wanted to be a professor there someday."

"Who told you that?"

"Your mother."

Edward didn't deny it. "Even though she wanted me to take my father's place. But it doesn't matter anymore because the university is gone along with my father's hotel. But you, Isa, now there's a different story. You were born into your parents' way of life, everything revolving around a social season that's been honored for centuries. When the war ends, you'll inherit such a life just as soon as you're old enough."

"Old enough!" Her hands lost the memory of how he'd held them so tenderly and clenched into fists. "First of all, Edward Kirkland, I already am *old enough*. I'm to be eighteen later this year, and that's plenty old enough to participate in any of my family's wretched parties, if I wanted to. Which brings me to my second point: I don't want any such inheritance. I have no intention of being as self-satisfying, as silly, as shallow as my parents."

"How *did* you get away from them?"

"I left. Perhaps they haven't even missed me yet."

Edward's brows rose. "They don't know where you are?"

"I left a note that I would be traveling and not to worry."

"Not to worry over someone traveling to unknown places during an international war." That he didn't believe it was possible was all too obvious. "But your brother knows where you were headed."

She shrugged. She wasn't about to tell Edward how she'd manipulated, deceived, overpaid, and circumvented various government authorities to get where she was. How she'd deserted Charles in England when he demanded she return to America. That had been especially heartbreaking, considering he seemed so different from the last time she'd seen him, before the war.

Sometimes God's ways weren't so easy to explain. "I'm here, so God must want me right where I am."

Edward laughed outright at that. "So whenever we find ourselves outside His will, we can say it must be His will after all? Even when we've broken the rules? Why were you *ever* sure God wanted you back here?"

"The goal was always clear; only the details were messy."

"It doesn't surprise me in the least that you misinterpreted what His will might be for you. He's not often clear about that, and even when He is, it's not always pleasant."

"But He only wants what's best for us."

Edward stood, obviously wanting to end the conversation. Isa stood too, and he put his hands on her shoulders and smiled like an amused older brother might. "I can see you're convinced of all this, but I hope you—and God—will forgive me if it takes a bit more to convince me that this is where you should be."

Her voice abandoned her. He was so close she could breathe in the scent of the soap he used, mixed with something else, perhaps the glue that wrinkled his skin or the powder that grayed his hair. "The Lord loved His apostle enough to come back and offer His pierced hands to touch. He didn't rebuke Thomas for his doubt; He gave him a way to believe. Maybe He'll do something like that for you."

"I'm beyond doubt." He went to the door, avoiding further eye contact. "I have a few things to take care of before curfew later today. In fact, I probably won't see you until tomorrow. Remember what I said about going out, all right?"

Then he left, closing the door behind him.

7

ALLIES SMASH GERMAN SOMME FRONT

The Allies delivered a severe stroke against the German front along a six-and-a-half-mile stretch of the front lines. Our troops gallantly swept away German forces and gained their objectives.

La Libre Belgique

Edward sat across the table from the two people who had come to know him better in the past year than those who had known him a lifetime. Trusting each other with their lives forged a strong bond.

"Did you see him?" Edward asked. He spoke English even though his companions were Flemish and he spoke that language as if he'd been born Belgian, too. But English was preferred. These days, everyone spoke a language the Germans would least expect.

Jan Krains nodded. The straight line of his brow and matching taut lips were the closest thing to a frown—or a smile, for that matter—that Jan ever mustered. "The man has the restraint of a two-year-old in a candy shop. He's definitely watching the Tomsk place. He can hardly wait to pounce."

"What are you going to do?" Rosalie looked at Edward the way she always did: intently, raptly. As if he had all the answers.

He let air out of his mouth slowly and eyed the room around him instead of them. It was cheerful, like Rosalie, with embroideries and small tapestries on the walls, light wood side tables and two chairs near a settee in front of a fireplace off to the side. Upon each chair was an embroidered cushion, featuring the design of an iris. Everything was sturdy and polished, neither sleek nor of costly design yet warm and comfortable. "We'll follow the examples set before us. Get Tomsk out. As for those of us still here . . . that's where we must be careful. Tomsk was cautious. How was he found out?"

None of them had an answer to that.

"If he were seen distributing, they would have arrested him on the spot, with or without more evidence." Edward shook his head. "No, he must have been named or implicated by someone else, either a German spy with suspicions or someone held at the Kommandantur."

He stood, preparing to leave. "Be careful," he told them. "Each of us has been seen with Tomsk in the past month, so we may be under suspicion too."

Rosalie's brows rose. "Aren't you staying?"

Edward shook his head. "I want to check the Tomsk home again. And I need to see someone about acquiring some paper, if I can get the money for it from my contact. Are you staying, Jan?"

He nodded. "I don't take the risks you do."

"I'm not going far."

Rosalie followed Edward to the door. "Take care." She put her hand on his arm. "Edward."

He turned to her expectantly.

"I must ask. How is your young friend, now that she's home?"

He put on his hat. "I wouldn't say she's exactly home, since she's living in Quartier des Marolles and not Quartier Léopold, but I'd say she's still foolish enough to be happy she's back."

"Are you happy she's back?"

He put a hand on the doorknob again. "My mother is happy to have her here again."

"And you?"

"Why do you ask? She means nothing to me either way."

"I thought you've known her since she was a child. Like a sister?"

Explaining why Isa Lassone had never, ever, stirred brotherly affection in him would take far more time than he presently had.

"Good night, Rosalie. Curfew, you know. I must go." He pulled the door shut before she could protest.

It was raining and he tugged the cap tighter to his head, then walked down the narrow artery too fast for the caution he usually took after curfew. He slowed, blaming Isa for the lapse. He shouldn't be thinking of her at all. She was here and there was nothing he could do about it. And while he was relieved neither one of them had been caught with the letters and newspapers she'd brought in, he was done worrying about her anymore. If she starved along with the rest of Belgium, so be it.

Suddenly he stopped. His thoughts had kept him from concentrating on his surroundings. He thought he heard something. Edward slunk into the shadows, waiting.

A cat shot by and he wondered if that was all it had been. He waited longer. In a moment he heard something else, the sound of German voices.

He understood what little he could hear, something about the cat and then a laugh and a joke about how everyone hadn't minded eating the stray dogs and old horses the army hadn't taken, but nobody wanted to try the cats. Another responded that they were too scrawny nowadays anyway, so why bother. When the sounds faded, Edward moved out of his hiding place. The church steeple was within sight. It was too late to speak to his contact tonight, but being at the church would put him in exactly the right spot to do business at first light.

Safely inside, Edward let the quiet of the sanctuary calm his nerves. He hadn't visited church so often his entire life, not even in the days when he wanted to go.

He walked deeper into the sanctuary to lie on the hard wooden bench. It wouldn't be the first time it had served as a bed, and no doubt it wouldn't be the last.

⁂

Isa lay in the dark. Beside her, Genny slept. Isa dared not disturb her rest, though that's exactly what she wanted to do. All evening Isa had shared Genny with Viole, Albert, or Jonah. While it was wonderful under any circumstance to be with this woman who for so long had been Isa's mentor and friend, she'd wished for time alone and hoped tomorrow might be different.

She wasn't sure at first, it was so quiet, but soon she realized Genny's breathing no longer had the steady rhythm of sleep.

"Genny?" she whispered.

For a long moment Isa heard nothing, not even breathing. Then Genny turned and gave Isa a smile. She could see little in the dim light from the single, high window in the room but could tell Genny had been crying, in spite of the smile.

"I thought you were asleep," Genny said.

"I thought the same of you."

"I'm sorry if I interfered with your rest."

"What's the matter?"

Isa saw a tear, suspended just below Genny's eye, slip down a slanted line to disappear into her honey blonde hair. Genny might be old enough to be Isa's mother but was still a beautiful woman. Her eyes were more green than the greenish gray she'd given Edward, and larger. Though her face had a hint of maturity with the barest shadow of a line here and there, she had the high cheekbones, full mouth, arched brows, and symmetry of natural beauty. But Isa saw a sadness she'd never seen before. At least not in Genny, who'd taught Isa to take joy in God's creation.

"Now and then I miss Jonathan unbearably. Do you know, the last time you were in my care, Jonathan mentioned how lovely you'd grown to be, and how . . ." Her voice quivered and she paused, pressing her lips closed. "How he wished you were our daughter. And he credited me with some of your loveliness."

"If I do have any loveliness, it was you who modeled it. He was right."

"He would be glad you've returned. In spite of everything, he would be glad, because he knew you've always brought me joy."

"I miss him too. How can you do it, Genny? How can you live here among the Germans who took his life?"

She raised a finger to shush her and shook her head, wide-eyed. "No, no, Isa. You mustn't give in to that. Hatred will only hurt *you*, not them. Believe me, I've learned the truth about that."

"Because you've hated them, too?" Somehow facing her own sin of hatred would be easier if Genny struggled with the same thing.

Genny leaned back and rested her arm along her forehead. "I don't like myself when my thoughts are so full of hate, and I doubt you would either."

"I know little of what's happened here, to you and to Edward and Jonah. Can you tell me?"

"It's difficult . . . to speak of it, even after two years. But you have a right to know." Genny's eyes squeezed shut, and when they opened again, two new tears rolled to the side. "I should start before the Germans ever came, if you're to fully understand. After that day your parents came to our hotel for you, to bring you out of Belgium, Edward and his father had a terrible argument. Edward wanted to return to England and enlist in the British army. He was so sure war was inevitable and feared Belgium needed to be protected. My

Jonathan believed Germany would respect the treaty and not violate the border. We knew Edward didn't want to join the army because he believed in a cause. What cause was there to believe in back then? Until Belgium was invaded there was no reason to think anyone should take up arms. By the time Edward tried to join the Belgian army, after we'd heard about the attack on Liege, it was already too late. No arms left, too much chaos. We should have left, gone back to England."

She pressed her fingertips into her eyes. "That night, the night they came to Louvain, we all stayed inside in hopes they would just pass through. But . . . oh, I don't know. There was so much confusion, and those soldiers were so young. Some people say there were two regiments of Germans, and they came upon each other thinking they were Belgian soldiers and that started the fighting. But the Germans claim armed civilians—snipers—fired at them. That's what they said when they forced us to leave the hotel, that someone had fired from an upper window. It wasn't true; how could it be? We had so few guests by then, and none of us had any guns. The mayor had requested all private arms to be turned over, to prove to the approaching Germans that we wouldn't resist."

She took a steadying breath. "We were marched out to the street while they took what they wanted, then set fire to the inn. Do you recall Martin, one of our most frequent visitors?"

Isa nodded. No one could forget Martin, the son of wealthy university patrons who was all grown up but in his mind still a child. Talkative, sweetly annoying in his lack of social manners.

"The noise outside frightened him and he went back inside. Jonathan—he ran after him. There was so much confusion, because the Germans didn't know Martin's ways. They thought he was going to get a gun, to defend the inn. Martin and Jonathan were both shot."

Isa wiped away the wetness on her face. "How awful for them. For all of you."

"There was nothing any of us could have done to stop them. And so while the fire raged and the Germans looked on, the rest of us went to the church to hide. The next day Edward left, to go and see what was happening. I begged him to stay, to keep hidden, but he went out anyway. I didn't see him again for almost five months."

She quieted, as if words were too heavy to utter until she regained her strength.

"Jonah told me Edward was taken away. To a work camp?"

"Yes, so many young men were rounded up that day. But a miracle happened, one Edward refuses to see."

"What kind of miracle?"

"They were brought back on a farm cart. It stank of animals. Seventeen men in all. Half of each man's head was shaved, the other half a tangled mass from top to beard. They looked awful, degraded. Edward was wounded on his shoulder, I think from a bayonet, although he never told me. It smelled so foul, and he was so feverish and weak. We had no medicine, no quinine, nothing. I could do nothing but watch him die. And pray."

Isa wiped away yet another tear and watched Genny do the same.

"But God heard those prayers and blessed us both that day. He healed my son and gave him back to me for a little longer." She turned to Isa then, and a smile glistened through her moist eyes. "It was a miracle, Isa. Of the seventeen who returned that day, Edward was the only one to live." She sighed. "The Germans think he died, and I never went to the Kommandantur to tell them differently. They expect all the men between seventeen and fifty to report regularly. But I think they've done enough to him. That's why Edward wears that disguise. His identity did die. Gourard even produced a death certificate for him, and I took it to the Germans." She put a fist to her lips, pressing against the quiver Isa saw nonetheless.

"Oh, Genny," Isa said and hugged the older woman. "Thank God, oh, thank God his identity was all that died."

"I do thank Him, Isa, every day of my life. Every morning I wake up and thank the Lord for sparing my son. Only . . ."

"What?"

"The Lord healed his body, but something inside of him is still infected. His spirit has shriveled up with hatred of the Germans. Sometimes it seems he even hates God for taking away his father. At least for taking him when He did, when their last words were so harsh. He won't speak of God anymore, and his Bible is here with me."

"God hasn't let go of him."

Genny pulled Isa to her. "I know."

Isa clung to Genny, with hope and desperation in equal measure.

8

Contrary to what the FOREIGNERS would have us believe, for every German victory there is an Allied victory. We must pray for the balance to tip in our favor.

La Libre Belgique

Major Johann Maximilian Gottfried von Bürkel let the breeze carry the sheer curtain aside, affording him a clear view of the street below. What had he expected? That they would arrive in royal style? in a vehicle or a carriage?

Perhaps not, but neither had he expected the owner of this impressive city villa to be dressed in rags. Who could tell which one he was supposed to watch? But why bother, anyway? The little group arrived as one insignificant mass, huddled close as they approached the entry porch.

He turned away as they left his line of vision. With only one crutch he was still nimble, easily making it to the nearest chair. He sat and placed the crutch with its mate, near his one remaining foot, heaving a sigh between resignation and disgust.

The war had taken its toll on everyone, including those who had once lived in such a grand home. His eyes took in the burgundy and gold room he'd called his own for three months now, with its brocade draperies, silk wallpaper, and carpet spun right here in Brussels. Only the very best.

He hadn't expected more than one of them but hardly cared which was the owner. Whoever she was, the Germans intended to keep an eye on her. He wished he could care about the things the army wanted; at least that might seem familiar. Instead, the thoughts that consumed him these days were far from armies and killing and German objectives. The future often filled his mind, but an eternal one rather than a German one.

A moment later brought the expected tap at his door, and he called his permission to enter. He used French, the language that came with the few servants left in this home.

"Pardon, Herr Major, but our Mademoiselle Lassone has returned."

He caught the pleased look in the middle-aged woman's eye and dismissed it as sentimental. "Very well. I intend to remain in my room. If she wishes to see me, she may announce herself. Otherwise, I shall give as little attention to her as I hope she will give to me."

Max watched the servant close the door. He settled back in the comfortable leather chair. He listened. At first he heard nothing, but then it came. The sound of feet on the stairs and then voices. He hoped they would pass his door without pause, and when they did, he was surprised at his own disappointment.

He should have gone back to Germany after he left hospital. But for what? For whom? His sons were gone, both of them killed within months of each other, before this vile war knew its first anniversary. And their mother . . . she might as well be gone, too. He knew she was safe where she was, cared for by the nuns in the convent where she'd lived as a child. There was some measure of comfort in that, whatever comfort he could find amid the fact that she no longer knew him. Grief was a powerful force, more powerful than her memory of him.

"Well," he said to himself, "I never did like fighting those hall stairs, so now I shall stay to myself." He looked around the well-appointed sitting room, seeing the bedroom through the open arch nearby. "It's not such a bad prison, really."

"Oh, Clara!" Isa said to the housemaid who opened the door to her old room. Walls covered in shades of green silk spun with a multitude of leaves, flowers of yellow upon the draperies, a combination of both in the coverlets and multiple pillows gracing her bed. "I used to think this old room was a prison, but now it's one of the most wonderful sights I've ever seen." She went to the wardrobe and flung open the doors. "And look! All my things are intact. Not even touched. Genny, isn't it a miracle?"

Genny, who'd followed, nodded with a smile. "Yes, Isa, that it is. After what I've seen in the last two years, I'd say it's nothing short of a miracle."

"But they never came inside the house in those first awful days," Clara said. "They came right down the street, like a line of gray ants, all marching in step." She made the motion of spitting, but nothing came out except her sentiments toward the occupying soldiers. "They only ransacked a few of the houses in this quarter, the ones owned by English and French. I do not know how, *mademoiselle*, but they knew which houses were owned by whom. They marked certain ones with chalk: *'Nicht plündern.'* The German houses and most of the neutrals. So your home has been safe all along. We were very much relieved; we didn't know where we would go if it was burned, like Louvain and the other towns. But I am so happy to have our *mademoiselle* back home. We did not think we would ever see your family again."

"That very well may be true of my parents, Clara, but *I'm* not going anywhere. Not after all I went through to get back. And now I want to take a bath and then get dressed in some of my own clothes. Will you help me?"

"Yes, and Henri will make sure the water is hot in the pipes."

Isa put a hand on the maid's forearm. "Henri is still here?"

"Of course, *mademoiselle*, where else would he go? He's too old to become a soldier, even if he could speak. I'll fetch him."

Isa was eager to see the one servant who, without a word spoken, had always been able to make her feel welcome. "Just one more thing, Clara," she called. "Are Mother's things still in her room?"

Clara's smile froze and she broke eye contact. "The rooms your parents shared have been occupied this whole time. Did they not tell you before you came today?"

"They said a wounded Major has been living here."

"Yes, he is the latest one to live here. He lost part of one leg in the war. A short time after he came here to stay, he ordered all of the personal items removed from the rooms he chose. At one time there were many officers here, but never in your room. Most of the rooms are intact, but your parents' clothes are in the attic."

"Perhaps you could show Genny where they are. I'm sure she can use my mother's clothing."

"No, Isa," Genny protested, "I couldn't possibly."

"Why ever not? We hardly need to feed the attic moths, do we? Besides, I'm sure the gowns are too out-of-date for my mother anyway. And see if there's anything of my father's or brother's that Edward could use. I doubt we'll have any luck for Jonah, though. He'll have to keep wearing the charity."

"I'm afraid Edward won't accept. He's uncomfortable enough going to the soup kitchens."

Isa looked at her. "You don't think he would see this as charity? Not from *me*!"

Genny nodded, her eyes sympathetic.

"I'll ask him about it later. When he learns we've been able to come here to live, he may want to wear something new." She turned back to her wardrobe. "Who could resist such clothes?"

❧

"You must tell me the worst of it, then, Clara."

Genny and the housemaid were in one of the guest rooms that, aside from a bare spot on the wall where a painting had once hung and an emptied dressing table, was still warm and inviting. The Hotel Cerise had catered to wealthy patrons exactly like Isa's parents, and so Genny was accustomed to the finely crafted furniture, the expensive floor coverings, the best linens Belgium had to offer. Things Genny often wished she didn't enjoy quite as much as she did.

"You must tell me what has gone on here since they came. And if there is anything I need to tell Isa."

"The silver is gone. An officer boxed it and sent it to Germany." Clara sighed. "And do you remember the vase *madame* had in the foyer? Monsieur Lassone always told us to be mindful of it because it cost a fortune. Well, I no longer have any such worry because a clumsy German broke it to a thousand pieces. With his bayonet!" She tried covering her laugh with one of her hands. "I later heard the soldier who broke it was sent to the front. Imagine that! All but a death sentence over a silly vase."

Clara had brought the clothing belonging to Isa's mother, boxes and cases and piles simply wrapped in linens as protection from dust. There were more dresses than Genny had seen in one room since she was a child at her grandmother's elegant London home. Many were evening dresses with lace or a multitude of decorative buttons, close fitting and with the V-neck that had been denounced in the pulpit and by doctors as unhealthy. Well before the war, when they spoke of such mundane things as fashion.

Genny chose a modest dress of dark blue damask with a tapered skirt and a loose tunic worn atop it. The high collar and simple cut made it the most sedate item she could find.

Clara brushed Genny's hair into a loose knot at the back of her head. It had been such a long time since anyone had helped her dress that she'd forgotten how nice it was to have someone fuss over her.

"There doesn't seem to be much missing from the bedrooms. Perfumes perhaps, a few paintings."

"The Major told the other officers to treat it well. Truthfully, having the silver sent to Germany seemed to surprise him. He accused the other officer of theft. Yet the other one insisted he sent it to the army headquarters, to be used 'for da goot off de Vaterland!'" She laughed at her own impersonation.

Genny didn't laugh. Finished dressing, she eyed herself in the mirror. The dark gown fit surprisingly well, flowing in softly shimmering folds to the tips of her shoes—shoes that were just a trifle large but soft as slippers.

"Tell me about this Major, Clara," Genny said. "How will it be for Isa, having to share her home with a German?"

"I would spit upon the floor if I didn't have to wash it."

"He's bad, then?"

"He is German, is he not?"

Just then they heard a commotion—a crash and a male voice raised in anger. Genny flew to the hallway, waiting for another sound to direct her to its source.

"It is the Major," Clara said, but she appeared to be in no hurry.

Then Genny heard a boy's voice and she sprinted so quickly she ran out of one of her shoes, not bothering to retrieve it.

"*Du Esel!* You are like the baby just learning to walk. Balance! *Nein, nein.*"

"Jonah!"

Genny stood in the doorway, shocked to see her youngest son with a knapsack draped on his back, full to the brim with weighty books. He appeared to be trying to walk along the footboard of the bed, a narrow walkway at best, all the while balancing yet another book on his head.

When Jonah turned to his mother, the book tumbled to the floor, joining another that must have already fallen. Yet her son had an unmistakable smile on his face.

"Oh, hello, Mother." He jumped to the floor and picked up the books, turning to the man who stood on crutches on the far side of the room. "Don't think for a moment I don't know what *du Esel* means. I'm no dunce, and I'll prove it to you."

He attempted his balancing act once again, with one book on his head, one on each open palm, and the knapsack still in place. It would take more strength than Genny imagined he possessed to keep everything in place and balance on such a precarious path. But he did the deed, then took the books in one hand and purposefully tipped the other from his head to land in one palm.

He hopped back to the floor. "I told you I could do it." Then he slipped the burden from his back.

The Major looked mildly pleased. "Try that on the planks of a muddy wooden trench and see how long you can keep your footing."

"Jonah, come with me now."

The soldier looked Genny's way for the first time since she'd entered the room. Even slightly hunched as he was because of the crutches, the man still stood taller than Genny. He had that Aryan look about him—light hair, blue eyes, stalwart even with his obvious disability, solidly built.

"Permit me to introduce myself," he said in perfect French. "I am Major Johann Maximilian Gottfried von Bürkel. Your son found his way into my room quite by accident, and we struck up a conversation about conditions at the front. I was merely trying to enlighten him."

"I assure you, Major, an eleven-year-old boy has no need to know of things at the front."

"Mother! I'm nearly twelve."

"A boy, nonetheless, *madame*, who may one day see for himself."

"I pray not," Genny said with barely moving lips. She turned to Jonah. "Come, Jonah. I believe you've disturbed the Major long enough." Then, with a hand on his shoulder, she directed him to the door.

"You will not be able to hide him behind your skirts forever, *madame*," the Major said, but he spoke to her back, since she was already halfway out the door.

Genny ignored the horrid words but took one last glance as she left the room. To her mortification she saw his gaze scrutinize her, resting at her feet, one clad in nothing but a silk stocking. She tried to keep her footing even as she slipped from the room, hoping she was out of his line of vision before that gaze could return to her heated face.

"Jonah, you are to stay away from that man."

"Suits me," he said. "He was full of himself, trying to prove he was so much better, even with only one leg."

"What did he do?"

"He had the books on his back and kept other books on his head, as if it were nothing even with those crutches."

She might have dwelt on the image of someone so disabled doing such a thing, but Genny heard her name called by a frustrated Isa.

"Go downstairs, Jonah," Genny said to her son. "Clara is going to show you where the school is, and I'll be taking you there tomorrow."

"Tomorrow already? Can't it wait until next week?"

"No. Go along now. Wait for Clara downstairs, and she'll tell you about it; she's been tending children from this neighborhood for years now."

Genny and Clara found their way to Isa, who stood in the center of her room. Her damp hair was pinned atop her head, and the fragrant scent of honeysuckle and lavender wafted from the adjoining bathroom. She stood with her arms outstretched at each side, looking down at herself with nothing short of disgust. Her feet were shod in soft leather slippers that were clearly too small, and the dress she wore—a disaster.

It was a lovely gown of silk, damask, and *mousseline de soie*, in a dark shade of forest green, perhaps the darkest gown she, too, could find. But her feet were in plain view, her arms barely covered by sleeves that reached a rather odd length somewhere between her wrist and elbow. The bodice was askew, and when she turned around to display the full extent of the miserable fit, it became clear that those buttons would never close while Isa's body was inside.

"Every one I've tried is worse than this," she exclaimed. "How can that be? It's been just two years! I feel like Alice through the looking glass. Or Gulliver in Lilliput."

Genny cocked her head with a rueful smile. "Two years of significant growth, evidently." She stepped closer, lifting the material to see if there was any give in the bodice area. "Clara," she said over her shoulder, "would you get that purple day dress, the one I was going to try next?"

"Not my mother's—and purple! I don't think I should wear any color with Belgium overrun."

"It will be better than this." Genny nodded encouragingly to Clara, who quickly disappeared to follow orders. "And it's a dark purple, almost black."

Isa flopped to the divan near her wardrobe and reached out to stroke one of the gowns still hanging within. "I was so happy to see them all." She expelled a long breath. "Oh, well, I couldn't have worn the majority anyway, they're so festive." Then she suddenly laughed.

"All right, let me in on the secret."

"Only that I shouldn't have been surprised Edward always thought of me as a child. I guess while I was gone, my body caught up with the rest of me." She looked at Genny with raised brows. "I wonder what it will take to make him see that."

Genny reached down and removed a strand of light golden hair that had strayed to Isa's face. "So, you still hold him in a special light?"

"Of course! Why shouldn't I?"

"I thought perhaps you might have outgrown your infatuation with him."

"If it were an infatuation, maybe I would have. Do you ever outgrow love?"

"Not if it's nourished."

"And I can't help but nourish it."

"I meant from both sides, my darling. From your heart—and his."

Isa looked away. "He still sees me as too young." She held up the edge of her dress and smiled. "But now even my clothes say I'm grown up, and I intend to make him notice."

Genny couldn't recall the first time she'd seen the way Isa felt about Edward. Her feelings seemed to have erupted the moment she'd met him. With him several years older, Genny's automatic response had always been caution.

Now, though . . .

Genny had once wondered if Edward would wait to marry until Isa caught up, and if he did, she always knew she would welcome Isa as a daughter-in-law as easily as she'd welcomed her as a surrogate member of the family.

Maybe Isa's dreams would come true after all. Genny knew one thing: if that ever happened, Edward would have little choice but to work out his faith; Isa would have nothing less.

Still, Genny wasn't the kind to interfere, even if she might be rooting for Isa in a way she never seriously had before.

Clara returned with the purple gown, a style reminiscent of the Gibson girl with a lacy bustline and swirling skirt. Isa's once-spindly body now filled the lines of her mother's gown.

Surely Edward would notice that without either Genny or Isa herself saying a word.

9

Excellence,

   . . . As for annihilating *La Libre Belgique*, don't hope for it; it is impossible. It will ever be beyond your grasp because it is nowhere. It is a will-o'-the-wisp, rising from the graves of those whom your compatriots massacred at Louvain, at Tamines, at Dinant; and it haunts you. It is a will-o'-the-wisp, rising from the graves of the German soldiers who fell at Liege, at Waelhem, and on the Yser, who now see the base designs of domination for which they were sacrificed under the pretext of defending their country.

From a letter written by **La Libre Belgique**
to His Excellency Baron von Bissing,
German Military General-Governor of Brussels

Edward rubbed his eyes and for a moment the burning increased, followed by a yawn and an instant eye watering. He'd been here for the two hours leading up to dawn. And no one, absolutely no one, had been up or down this street on which the Tomsk family lived.

He should leave, go back to the church, and find a pew to sleep on rather than greeting the dawn out here. Raids he'd known of in the past had come in the predawn hours, and with the sun would most likely come another day of relative peace. Father Clemenceau could find him fresh clothes. He could take a bath. He'd have to see Rosalie again to touch up his makeup anyway—

Something jingled, then clopped. Edward pressed back into the shadows, though he could still see the house he watched. Not even a careless milk cart would be so bold with noise.

Horses pulling a wagon laden with a half-dozen soldiers came into view, and neither passengers nor driver made any attempt to quiet the ruckus. Once the wagon stopped, soldiers clanked and pounced to the pavement, pulling rifles from their shoulders and bounding up the cement steps on hobnail boots. They pounded on the door.

Edward's fists clenched at his sides. They wouldn't find Tomsk, but they would find his parents, who would no doubt be carted off in that wagon, for questioning at the very least. If Tomsk had followed instructions, they would have nothing to say. But the fear they must face with such an ordeal . . .

Edward slipped down the alleyway, beyond the shadow of the house that had hidden him these past hours. His heart thudded nearly as loudly as those German boots at the Tomsk front door a moment ago. He battled the urge to run. Not only was curfew still in place, but any sudden movement was easy to spot.

Careful. Careful.

Sweat pricked his neck and underarms. He slunk from shadow to shadow, heading not to the church and safety but somewhere else. He had to know.

Seven blocks. He'd counted them before; there was no need this time. Six of those seven blocks were as still as this side of dawn should be, but when Edward reached the last, he slipped into the shadows again, as far into the darkness as an arcade shop alcove would allow.

There they were again . . . soldiers crawling along the line of shops like ants on honey, with the main dollop none other than the news shop Edward frequented, one that secretly doubled as a main supplier of *La Libre Belgique*.

His eyes burned again, this time from tears he wouldn't let fall. He made not a sound, not even when bolder rays of sun pushed away the shadows surrounding him. He crouched to the ground, knowing he should leave, get as far away as he could. But his limbs refused to move.

He knew where he mustn't go: Rosalie's. It was one of the dangers in having an address; one could be raided. Undoubtedly it was too late to warn her anyway, this being another example of simultaneous German raids. It was lucky they'd delivered the most recent issue, because even if her home was raided, they would find nothing.

He should go to the church as he'd planned. It was safe there. Maybe.

But instead, making sure he wasn't followed, Edward eventually found his way to the back of the Lassone mansion, a place he'd once convinced himself he'd never see again, at least not from any closer than the street.

He would visit one last time and never come again.

Edward let himself in. A rack for hats and hooks for shawls were just inside the door, hidden from view of the rest of the kitchen by a wall with an arched entryway. For a moment he stood quietly, looking back outside through the glass embedded in the center of the door. He'd taken pains to be sure he was safe but didn't want to take further chances.

Despite the early hour, low voices and the gentle clattering of dishes drew him the rest of the way into the kitchen. It was an ample room with vast work spaces, a sink with indoor plumbing beneath a window overlooking the garden, and many shelves—a room topped with open beams where he remembered copper pots had once hung. Those hooks were empty now.

And there, at the smallest of the tables, sat his mother and Isa. He saw they weren't dressed like peasants anymore. They fit this house . . . perhaps not the kitchen, but the rest of the mansion.

Seeing them, safe and together, brought him the calm he craved. "Let me see. Something is wrong. Two mistresses of a grand home, quite at home in the *servants'* quarters?"

"Edward!" Isa sprang to her feet, but when he put a finger over his lips, she stopped both sound and movement.

"You have Germans in this house," he said. "How many?"

"Just one. Upstairs. He isn't likely to hear us."

"And why is that? Has he no ears?"

She laughed. "No, silly. I was going to say he cannot be lurking nearby. He doesn't often manage the stairs because he has a foot missing from the war. He hasn't left his room for the two days we've been here."

"And servants? Has he any of his own?"

"Only Clara and Henri are here, and they were with my family before. Belgians as true as any other."

Edward let his gaze travel the length of her then, unable to help himself. She was all Lassone again. "Well, you're looking quite your old self, aren't you?"

He didn't expect her frown, especially not when he had to fight to keep himself from staring at her.

"My old self? You mean, the way I looked before I left Brussels, before the war? I haven't . . . changed?"

He shook his head, wondering why she looked with distress toward his mother. He tried to salvage his remark. "You know, quite the Upper Town attire and all. You too, Mother."

"Sit down, Edward," his mother said, and he had the distinct feeling he was missing something between the two of them. "Clara has managed to maintain a connection with one of the farmers from the country. She has a rather steady supply of eggs, thanks to the funds Mr. Lassone left for her. She's made an egg pie that'll bring you right back to the days before the war. Sit and eat."

"I cannot stay, Mother. I came only to urge you one last time to take advantage of what Isa has done and leave Brussels. I can make the arrangements immediately, and you can be in Holland by tomorrow morning."

But his mother wasn't listening to him, not a single word. She was already on her feet, dishing out the eggs.

"Surely you can stay long enough to eat a little? Real food for once, and not from the food lines?"

With the plate in front of him and the smell so enticing, he could barely hang on to his refusal. He must go, find out if anyone else he could trust remained free. He shouldn't have come here at all, except that he'd wanted to see his mother and Jonah, even Isa, as much as he wanted—no, needed—them to go.

He swallowed hard, his mouth watering.

"Sit, Edward."

And then he did because the eggs were just beneath his nose now, and he knew he could do nothing for anyone else. He would eat, he would convince his mother and Isa to leave, and then he would find out who was left.

To his own shame he enjoyed the eggs more than he should have allowed. He'd forgotten when food stopped being something to look forward to but rather something to be endured in order to keep going. Meatless broth, dark bread, or hard cheese, and no variety. When the committee for relief did have shipments—soup or real flour for better bread—Edward, unwilling to have his false identity scrutinized too closely, rarely took advantage of what they had to offer. Instead he relied on the generosity of the church, the affection of Rosalie, or benefactors surrounding *La Libre Belgique*.

But the taste of the food couldn't quite overcome his shame; he was free while others were in danger. . . .

He swallowed hard, but just then Isa smiled at him and everything else, even the taste of the eggs, faded away. She looked so like the portrait he'd once seen of her in this very mansion, done when she'd turned thirteen by Frans van Holder, who painted all the rich, upcoming debutantes in Belgium. At the time, Edward thought the artist had made her look too old, too grown-up. But now he saw what the artist must have seen. Isa had grown into the promise of that portrait.

He'd always thought her lovely. Now her light hair was gathered back in an informal braid, and despite the shawl she wore to keep away the early morning chill, he could see the curve of her neck and shadows along the rest of her that hadn't been there the last time he'd seen her dressed to her station in life, things only hinted at in the portrait.

He wanted that beauty to disappear, the blue glow of her eyes to dull, that welcoming smile to dim, the tilt of her chin to look proud instead of happy, the gold in her hair and the redefined lines of her body to be forgotten.

Imagining her as she used to be, always above him, with parents and a brother who lived as if the world had been created solely for them, always above even the clientele of his father's elite inn, Edward was reminded of all the resentment.

"You'll be staying here with us, won't you, Edward?" Isa asked. "There's plenty of room, and the Major told Clara he doesn't want to see us any more than we want to see him. There is so much more space here than with Viole, and I think perhaps Albert might welcome it if you didn't come around."

"You should stay," his mother put in.

But he was already shaking his head, pushing away the eggs altogether, what little was left. He wouldn't eat another thing until they agreed to go. "Neither of you listened to what I came here to tell you. You must leave, both of you and Jonah, at once. I can make the arrangements and—"

"Why should we leave now, when I've been given back my home? And I have legitimate papers, too, that match my passport."

His mother, next to him, put her hand over his. "You could easily stay here, Edward."

"As what? Your fifty-year-old son, when you're not yet forty-five? You know I can't."

"Perhaps as my brother, then."

"No, Mother. This disguise only works because I've never been taken note of by anyone who matters, never looked at too closely. I can't live under the same roof as a German who might get a good look at me. Day after day."

"Then perhaps you should come up with some other identity," Isa suggested. "Someone your own age, but unfit for service."

"I suppose I could sport a fair rendition of the village idiot without much trouble."

"Perfect! You could live here and no one would pay you any attention whatsoever."

"I was anything but serious, Isa. I cannot stay, and I don't have the money or the time to build another identity."

"What do you mean? All any of us have is time. And I have the money."

"She's right about that," his mother said. "Why don't you give it some thought?"

For the barest moment he was tempted to tell them just how dangerous it was for him, for them, to remain. Tell them what had happened that very morning, that even as he'd enjoyed those eggs, the parents of one of his coconspirators were being interrogated at the Kommandantur. Perhaps held as hostages until the Germans were convinced Tomsk was not in hiding but in fact over the border, beyond their grasp. They could, at this very moment, be subjected to who knew what by an army capable of nearly anything if they thought it might serve their purpose.

But that would mean breaking the one rule he'd vowed always to keep. Never giving those he loved any information for which they might be questioned.

He needed to leave, and right away. Pushing himself from the table, he stood. He had only one argument left, one he'd wanted to use from the moment he'd first become involved with *La Libre Belgique*, only his mother had still needed him too much. Now she had Isa. "If you stay, then all I can do to make you safe is to sever all ties. Starting at once."

"Edward!" Now his mother was standing as well.

Isa grabbed his forearm. "You can't do this to—to your mother. Or to Jonah. Isn't life hard enough for them without you withdrawing?"

"I'll do what is best for all of us." Edward stepped back, beyond Isa's touch, heading for the door.

"Edward, wait," she said, following him. "Curfew is over for this morning. Can I walk with you a bit?"

"I don't want you on the streets, Isa," he said. He glanced at the way her dress fit her so well. "Even less so now."

"In my vast experience as a woman—" she spoke with a twinkle in her eye—"I've noticed men are far more respectful of someone dressed the way I am than of a peasant."

In spite of the naiveté he knew she still possessed, she was right.

"Yes, talk to Isa," his mother said. "She'll convince you not to stay away, won't you, Isa?"

"I'll do my best."

Edward wanted to refuse her company; he wanted to tell her to stay put. Instead he said, "Wear a hat."

She found a scarf on a hook near the door and wrapped it over her hair, pulling her shawl tighter. Hardly enough to hide that she was no longer a child. At least her hair was out of sight.

Outside, he led her around to the front by way of the *porte cochère* that extended from the house over the lane to the carriage houses behind. The sun shone and the air was cool but dry. They walked down the pavement away from the house, heading toward the edge of Quartier Léopold.

"I have a confession, Edward." She looked somber, almost afraid. He'd seen her face a half-dozen guards at checkpoint stations, totally unruffled even though they carried contraband. What could *she* be afraid of? "I know why you want us to leave, why you think it's dangerous for those around you. I know about your involvement with *La Libre Belgique*."

10

And so we must remain united as we await the day of liberation from the FOREIGNERS in our land. Time is but temporarily on the side of these FOREIGNERS so long as we remember we are Belgians, all, and they shall never have the best of us because of that.

La Libre Belgique

Edward's expression quickened Isa's breathing. It wasn't suspicion; it couldn't be. Her heartbeat went wild, especially when he started to turn away as if to leave her alone on the street.

But he turned back and took her arm, entwining it firmly with his and steering her away from her home. "You're mistaken, Isa. I've heard of the paper, of course—who hasn't? But I'm not involved with it. I do wonder, though, where you heard such a story. Care to enlighten me?"

She stopped. "I can't. I've promised not to. And it doesn't matter, does it? What matters is that I can help."

"Spoken like a true patriot . . . or a spy trying for a confession."

His tone remained light yet the words were incredible. He couldn't believe her a spy, trying to beguile something out of him, to be used against him? *For* the Germans? It was too absurd to imagine.

Not after she'd brought in those letters and newsprint, which was no doubt to be used in the very paper he worked on.

"In any case, even if I had something to do with that paper, you speak as though one person is responsible for it. Anything on that scale would have countless people involved."

"Then you can use more help! There is something in my home for you—"

"More diamonds?" His condescending attitude was inconceivable, making him like a stranger.

"No. Listen to me. Don't be angry that I can't tell you how I found out about your involvement with the paper. Let me help!"

He laughed as if that were the end of their conversation.

"Don't you want to know what I can offer?"

"No, Isa, I don't. What I want is for you to forget all of this nonsense and whatever it was you were told."

She hadn't been back for long, but she knew people didn't stroll the streets of Brussels anymore, even in Quartier Léopold. And they certainly didn't stop to have arguments in broad daylight. But she squared off anyway.

"I won't have you shut me out, Edward. And I won't have you thinking I would ever, *ever*, bring you harm. It doesn't matter how I know about the paper; I just do. So let's discuss how I can help. There is a room in my parents' house that no one in Brussels knows about. No one except Henri and me."

He studied her a moment, as if interested in asking details, but instead leaned forward and took her arm again, walking.

"Will you let me show it to you? Perhaps you can use it to store papers until they can be distributed, or *print* papers, or . . . I don't know what you need! Only know that this location is there for you if you need it."

"A location right under the nose of a German Major. Now that's what I call ingenious, Isa. Who would ever suspect?"

"Yes, that's entirely the point. What German raid could possibly take place in the residence of a German soldier? It's the safest place in Brussels." She pulled back on his arm and he slowed at last. "I know you're involved with this paper, whether you admit it or not. You don't actually think I've learned that from some *German* source and that I would somehow use this against you?"

He sucked in air, letting it out with a shake of his head. "No. But I would like to know your source. Gourard, back in Holland knew, but I cannot believe he would say something to you, unless he thought you could use the knowledge somehow to persuade me to leave Belgium."

"Please don't ask, Edward. I would tell you, but the person who told me is dear to me, and I can't betray a confidence." She tried to smile, to coax one out of him as well. "Isn't this what you need in a conspirator? Someone who knows how to keep a secret?"

He nearly smiled, she was sure of it, but before she could be certain, he drew her onward.

"So, what is your answer, Edward? Will you let me help?"

He turned and started to speak, but his answer was lost in a sudden burst of noise and confusion. At once he lifted Isa from the ground and into his arms, thrusting her against the stone of a nearby fence, holding her immobile. Clattering hooves, men shouting and running closer . . . then past them. Isa saw nothing. Edward held her close, pressing them both to the enclosure.

As fast as it came, the sound disappeared. She saw little with Edward hovering close. But she was in no hurry for him to let go.

Although somewhere down the lane she could still hear the commotion, clearly the danger of being trampled under runaway horses and soldiers was gone. Yet Edward still held her, for the longest moment, as unmoving as the brick wall behind them. Then his hands slowly slid from the makeshift shelter clasped above her head to glide down around her waist.

The tempest was inside of her now. Was this really happening? Was he really holding her, his face so near her own? If she moved her face toward his, surely his lips would find their way to hers.

She had no chance to find out. Once again the street around them erupted into noise, though with measured horses' hooves and calmer German voices. But she didn't want to acknowledge them. She wanted to pretend nothing was near except Edward.

He moved away and she stopped herself from pulling him back.

"We should go quickly," Edward whispered.

She moved to follow, wishing he would keep her hand, but he didn't. She wasn't bold enough to slip her arm through his, even though she'd done it casually a dozen times before. Just then any touch seemed fraught with more than it had ever meant in the past.

Before long Edward delivered her back at the gate of her home, where he stopped. The gardens were mainly vegetables instead of flowers these days, but there was still a granite bench under the beech tree near the tall stone fence. She wished he would take her there and let her ask him if he'd felt anything in the flurry of that moment on the street.

But he seemed so eager to leave she wondered if that moment had happened at all.

"Edward, won't you come in? see for yourself what I'm trying to tell you about?"

He shook his head. "I can't."

"Why?"

"If you and my mother insist on staying here in Belgium, then I won't be back. It's the only way to keep you safe."

"Without even seeing the room? It's the perfect place, exactly what any secret could use."

His hands were on her shoulders so quickly it startled her, his eyes boring into hers, but neither the touch nor the look was any-thing she'd imagined. "No. I won't have it. I won't have you involved in any of this. Do you understand?"

She shook her head and tears stung her eyes. "But, Edward—all right if you won't use the room. Promise me you'll still come here. Without knowing if you're safe or not . . . I've lived that way for nearly two years. Please—"

"No, Isabelle."

He'd never called her that before, but she welcomed the newness of it, as if he'd realized at last that she should be called a name more befitting a woman than a child.

"Edward, please." She'd never begged before, never imagined herself begging him or anyone for anything. But pride was trivial compared to what she wanted most. "Tell me you won't stay away. That you can't stay away."

Edward let her go and stepped backward. He opened his mouth, but nothing came out. Then he turned, pulled up the collar of his jacket and pulled down the brim of his hat as if to hide his face, and walked away.

11

Only German folly exceeds the lack of discretion to which they routinely adhere, as shown by the most recent mistaken arrests.

La Libre Belgique

"That should do it," Edward said to Father Clemenceau, rolling two slim sheets of paper, content for another issue of *La Libre Belgique*. The second since the mass arrest.

At least seven of their conspirators awaited trial at St. Gilles prison, just south of Brussels proper, held for these last two weeks without contact. Between Edward and the priest, they had found only three other remaining links in the organization. Jan and Rosalie, by some miracle, had been completely ignored in the most recent round of arrests. Another main supplier survived, who had provided most of the content for the copy now in Edward's possession.

It would be Edward's job to get it to the printer.

This was not the longest but was perhaps among the more important issues. The edition from a week ago might have been more vital, following so closely after the arrests, its existence enough to dim many smug German smiles. This second issue would be a needed boost to the morale of every Belgian who fretted over the upcoming trial, and that was just about everyone in Brussels. The paper had survived, no matter how many people they arrested.

Edward handed the rolled sheets to Father Clemenceau while reaching under the table for a walking stick he used for just such an occasion. Turning it upside down and twirling off the tip, he tilted it toward the priest, who slid the papers neatly inside. Then Edward replaced the tip, reached for his suit coat and hat, and with a swift farewell was on his way to the printer Father Clemenceau had persuaded to run one more issue. The printer had not been easily convinced, and after this edition they must find someone else.

Nothing new there.

Edward walked down the street at a brisk though unhurried pace. He did nothing to call attention to himself, keeping his gaze straight ahead. It was three o'clock and even during peacetimes the streets would have been quiet, but now they were near desolate apart from soldiers.

He would have liked to take the tram to shorten the distance to the printer's but decided that would bring him too close to Germans. So he kept walking, using the enameled stick as though he'd done so a great many years, not because he needed help but because it was an appendage that showed the style of a successful businessman of the age Edward meant to portray.

***

Max von Bürkel sat, eyes closed, as strains of "O Day of Rest and Gladness" drifted from the hall, filling the room with melancholy. Somewhere close by, someone played the flute. He knew the words that accompanied the melody weren't meant to bring sadness but rather comfort. Yet they brought him only pain. Both his sons were buried somewhere south of here, in France. The music, so long absent from Max's life, brought them to mind with stinging clarity.

He retrieved his crutch with some difficulty and hobbled to the door, opening it and letting the last notes strike him like invisible bullets.

Just as he thought he might walk toward the sound, the melody ended and new music floated in.

Another hymn. He could not hear "A Mighty Fortress Is Our God" without thinking of his mother—*"Ein' Feste Burg,"* as she knew this hymn. For a moment the pain eased as he remembered his mother. He'd lost her, too, but she had gone to a peaceful rest, eager to meet the God who created her.

The memory of his mother faded, replaced again by his boys, and pain shot through him anew. He suddenly wished to join his wife, a thought that hadn't crossed his mind since she'd left him upon word that their second son had been killed. He thought of her now, not because she would welcome his company or even wish to grieve with him. No, he wished he could be enveloped by the church as she'd been. At the very least, there were no decisions to be made where his wife now resided, no news with which to deal. One didn't even have to talk, except perhaps to God. And everywhere she turned, she must be reminded that this was not all there was to life, that something else lay ahead. A place with God where, despite an egregious lack of training from their father, perhaps his boys had found a way after all. Certainly there was hope for that; a battlefield was just the place to find God.

Max had found Him there.

He'd been groomed to have allegiance first to God and then to family and country, but somehow it had gotten twisted through the years, with allegiance to the fatherland demanding the most, the best, the deepest in him. But now . . . his gaze fell upon the Bible that had come with this room.

It was his only comfort these days.

Max returned to his chair, leaving the door open, letting the music water his dehydrated spirit.

Genny rounded the upstairs hallway and headed toward Isa's room. So, she had not imagined it. The music came not from the music room but from Isa's own bedroom.

Genny stopped, savoring the sound filling the air. How sweet it was after so long a silence without any music to remind her of her soul. She knew the piano was available to her in the Lassone music room just down the hall but hadn't the heart to play. Now she stood quietly, letting the fruit of the instrument refresh her. How long it had been since she'd heard any loveliness.

Part of her wanted to go inside Isa's room, but she didn't want to interrupt. If music was a salve to Isa's recent sadness, it was a balm to Genny's weary spirit. She let herself bask in it awhile, leaning against the hallway wall, eyes closed, as inevitably the music erased her worries in prayer.

She didn't know how long she stood there, but at last she opened her eyes. Perhaps she could sit at the top of the stairs and listen to the rest—and find Clara, who would probably enjoy the music as well. Genny quietly made her way toward the stairs.

As she passed the Major's room, she couldn't help but notice his open door. She found her noiseless footsteps slowing and her gaze traveled within. There he sat, in his large chair in the middle of the room, one crutch held in his lap as if he might use it at any moment. She would have hurried past when she noticed his eyes were closed, but something caught her attention. He sat directly in the light from the open curtains. Perhaps that was what gave it away, the sunlight revealing an odd darkness to his lashes, which otherwise matched the fairness of his hair. And a tiny sparkle glistening just below one eye. A tear?

Was he in pain? Perhaps he'd tried getting to a standing position because he needed something.

Everything inside of her wanted to ignore what she saw. Perhaps she could send Clara to him, just to make sure his needs were met. But Genny's feet wouldn't carry her away. Clara had made her feelings about the Major clear; whatever pain he felt would certainly not be alleviated by her—at least not quickly. And so, swallowing something between repulsion and caution, she stepped into the doorway of the Major's commandeered room.

"Did . . . you need something?"

He didn't seem to hear her at first, and to her mortification she thought perhaps he'd fallen asleep. What was she doing, looking in on him in his private quarters?

Then his eyes opened and he stared at her. Not in pain, at least not that she could tell. Rather he looked at her with something else, an intensity of the sort one found only when lost to the world around and present somewhere else, immersed in thoughts that lifted body, soul, and spirit away. But it was soon replaced by something like confusion when his gaze stayed on hers, almost as if he'd forgotten who she was.

"I—I'm sorry," she said, suddenly aware she'd interrupted his own enjoyment of the music. "I didn't mean to disturb you. I saw your door was open and thought perhaps you needed something."

He was still staring at her, rather regardfully, as if observing her closely. A tingle of discomfort wound its way up her spine.

"No," he said at last. "I was simply listening. Tell me, who is playing?"

"Isabelle Lassone."

"Ah, the owner of this villa. I have yet to meet her, if I am to meet her at all. She plays well. Do you know if she plays Mozart?"

"Isa is very accomplished. I'm sure she can play a great many pieces."

"I should like to meet her, I think. And you as well, *Fräulein* . . . ?"

"*Frau,*" she corrected automatically. "Mrs. Genevieve Kirkland."

"Ah, yes, young Jonah's mother. You have a healthy son, Frau Kirkland."

She looked at him, finding his observation odd.

He must have guessed what she was thinking. "I mean only that you should be proud of him. He is young yet, but he will have a good future ahead of him. He's strong and smart and quick-witted. The future will be run by such as him."

"Yes, I am proud of him, and I look forward to his future in a free Belgium."

For a moment she wished she'd choked back her words, and just as instantly she prayed a prayer of forgiveness. How true that the tongue was untamable! Insulting a German soldier—let alone an officer—was punishable by fine or imprisonment. How many placards had been posted around the city to remind her of that?

Suddenly the Major laughed. He possessed straight, even, white teeth and he looked far younger with a broad smile on his handsome Aryan face. If no offense was taken, perhaps she could remove herself from his sight and he'd forget she existed. Forget that they shared a roof. Forget that he was the conquering Major and she but a minor flea in the way of a German-run future.

"*Ja,*" he said after his laughter dwindled away, "there will be plenty of room for all talent, too. We Germans welcome such. You will see."

"Then if you don't need anything . . ." She let her words fade as she took a little step backward. Much to her embarrassment, his gaze left her face to take in the rest of her, stopping at her feet and perhaps, she thought, seeing if she had on both shoes this time.

"Thank you."

The two quiet words made her pause. "But I've done nothing."

"You offered to see to my needs. Clara is obviously reluctant, and the nurse who comes now and then . . . she is well-trained but has enough to do without one more patient on her roster."

Every sensible part of Genny's brain cried a protest to this man's gratitude, to his presence here in this country where he wasn't wanted. How easy it would be to hate this German, like all the others. Effortless. He still wore a uniform, of sorts, a blatant reminder of the invaders who had killed her husband.

Yet wasn't God still in the individual? Not in the army as a whole, but in each and every man who welcomed Him? Belgian, English, French, and German, too?

No. Not in those who made up such an army.

She backed away. Without another word, she fled down the hallway and the stairs, sure he would not be able to follow.

12

We submit this issue with best regards to our most avid reader, Military General-Governor Freidrich Wilhelm Freiherr von Bissing. As you now hold in your hand that which you have tried suppressing by recent arrests, perhaps you will admit you hold innocent Belgians against their will.

La Libre Belgique

Edward found Rosalie waiting at the usual spot, in the shadow of the cathedral of Saints Michel and Gudule on Rue de la Chancellerie. It was a familiar spot between the long walk to Rosalie's home in Lower Town and the letter boxes they'd each been assigned in Upper Town. It was a walk they both knew well, although Rosalie probably best. They passed Rue de Loxum toward Place de la Monnaie where, before the war, Rosalie used to practice her artistry on the faces of famous actors and singers. Now she used her talents only on faces like Edward's, seeking anonymity instead of fame.

Since it was safer to walk in pairs, they'd often met at this spot an hour before curfew with enough time to spare getting back to Rosalie's. After a day of clandestine deliveries, seeing Rosalie used to bring comfort. It meant another day of offering hope to an oppressed population through the paper. Staying free to work again.

But lately her company brought less comfort.

She greeted him with her familiar smile—perhaps, he thought, a little too eagerly. Many times during this same walk he'd looped her arm through his, or they'd laughed as often as they dared without drawing too much attention to themselves. Not today; he walked silently at her side, all the way back to her home. He hadn't been there since the day after the arrests, had stayed just long enough to assure himself she wasn't among those taken. Since then he'd slept like a vagabond on one church floor or another or in abandoned flats to which he had the key thanks to his connections through *La Libre Belgique*.

Jan was expected at Rosalie's, but her house was dark and cold. Edward tried to light a lamp after finding there was no electricity. He followed Rosalie to the kitchen, where she bent over the stove to heat a kettle.

He withdrew the bread he'd received earlier from Father Clemenceau, taken from the top, visible layer of his specially sewn bag. The bag offered two sections: one compartment for the bread or other such innocuous items and another barely noticeable beneath that, except for at the seam from which he could pull one page at a time, empty now of more than fifty copies of their news sheet. Rosalie had sewn a dozen such bags, each used by couriers for the secret newspaper.

Rosalie brought a pitcher of water and cups, filling each. She took a seat then, watching him all the while.

"I'll see Father Clemenceau tomorrow about more paper," Edward said. "Have you thought any more about a replacement for the St. Michel distributor?"

"Yes, the boy Felix told me about before leaving for the border will work. He's willing."

"Do you know anything about him?"

"Nothing more than that Felix recommended him."

"Let's hope we can trust that, then." Edward stood to retrieve a knife from the drawer where he knew Rosalie kept them and set about cutting the bread. "I'd like to write another article about the difference between true justice and what's happening under the Germans. Or perhaps we should let the topic of the arrests die with the issue we just finished and go on as if nothing has ever happened. That would chafe them more, don't you think?"

"Yes."

Edward handed her a piece of the bread. He cut another slice for himself.

"Edward. Sit."

He obeyed.

"Shouldn't we talk?"

"We are."

"You've kept yourself so busy these last days I've barely seen you. And when I do, you can't even bring yourself to look at me anymore. Did I do something to offend you?"

"No, of course not. What could you have done?"

"Nothing. I've done nothing."

He sent her a smile that had always soothed her in the past. "Then nothing is changed."

She set aside her bread, leaning forward. "But something is. You're more distant than ever."

He stood again, to retrieve the plates he should have brought when he cut the bread. He gave one to Rosalie and kept one for himself. "Every month there are new arrests, Rosalie. Our turns are bound to come. Now is not the time—"

"Yes, yes, I've heard you say that before, only everything around me and everything inside me says differently. We're alive, Edward. Every day we should live as if it were our last, instead of hoarding it."

Hoarding life? He was willing to bring the battlefield right here to Brussels in the form of joining others who worked on an underground press, to help inspire the whole of Belgium toward the hope that one day their occupiers would be shut out, pushed back, made to pay for their crimes. He was willing to spit in their collective eye as no one with a real identity would dare. Yet here he sat with one young woman, afraid to tell her he knew what she wanted but had found he had nothing to give after all.

"I won't tell you how to live, Rosalie."

A moment ago it had seemed she was the stronger of the two, pressing him to speak when he didn't want to. But with those few words she seemed to shrivel, her shoulders drooping, her eyelids wilting.

She offered a smile but the corner of her mouth trembled and he remembered why he found her so attractive. Strength and weakness all at once.

"You're too comfortable with me. I've always thought so," she whispered. "Unlike me. I'm far more uncertain around you." She set her bread on the plate and rubbed her hands together, looking down at them. "I suppose I should find someone who cannot possibly wait for better times to be with me."

He reached for one of her hands, but she withdrew it before contact could be made.

"Rosalie? Edward, are you here?"

Jan's voice had never been more welcome. Edward called to him.

"Look!" Jan waved a paper in front of him as he neared the table, and even in the dim light of the open wood-burning stove, Edward could see excitement in Jan's normally cool eyes. "It's another issue, same number as the one we issued right after the arrests. I've been trying to track it down all afternoon, and all I could learn was it came from right here in Brussels. There are others left out there besides us."

He held another *La Libre Belgique*—similar in style and set, but not their own, issued as if in correct succession. Edward had to do little more than read the first line of the top article to know it was legitimate—illegitimately legitimate, as it were.

Jan was nearly smiling. Knowing they weren't alone was heady indeed. But Rosalie didn't smile, and Jan hardly seemed to notice.

13

Beware the German wolves wearing civilian sheep's garb.

La Libre Belgique

"I told you, she will not see you."

"And I tell you again, she is the one to decide."

"If you don't leave this minute, I'll have you removed. And I'll contact the Kommandantur in the process."

"You want them here no more than I do. Now go. Get your mistress."

Isa heard the voices at the kitchen door just as she stepped past the doorway from the dining room. Clara's impatience was obvious, and although the man spoke excellent French, he did so with a decidedly American accent.

"Clara?"

She saw the servant stiffen, turn her head slightly, then slam the door. But the man on the other side evidently did not take offense. He knocked a moment later.

"What is going on?" Isa asked.

"A man—a stranger—says he wishes to speak to you, but I do not trust him."

"Why ever not? Who is he?"

"A stranger; that's enough!"

"Oh, Clara, let the man in."

"I dare not!"

Isa pursed her lips. It was uncommonly early, just past nine. But sleepless nights worrying over and missing Edward ended sooner when she rose early and kept herself busy with whatever household duties she could find. She passed Clara and opened the door.

"Oh, *mademoiselle!*" Clara hurried from the room.

The man in front of Isa wore civilian clothes and was not much taller or older than Isa herself. He was handsome, with chocolate brown hair and eyes that matched and a sudden smile that showed slightly crooked teeth—indeed, his only apparent flaw, which made him all the more disarming.

"What can I do for you?"

"You're an American!" He spoke in perfect English.

She nodded. "How did you know?"

"I'm from America, too. Ohio, ma'am. Cincinnati."

She raised her brows. "But how did you know an American lives here?"

He pointed to the paint on the cement stairway leading up to the door, a blight on the once-pristine exterior. "*Nicht plündern.* You're one of the few houses around here without the comings and goings of a bunch of Jerries." He looked around as if nervous. "Say, listen, can I come in?"

Isa looked too, but behind her, wondering where Clara had gone. She saw no reason to turn him away. "We don't have much food, but we have bread and tea. Would you like some?"

"Yes, ma'am."

She stood back to let him into the kitchen, where he took a chair as she moved to the cookstove to light a flame under a pot of water. Then she retrieved two mugs from a cupboard and went into the pantry for the bread. Back at the table, she set about cutting several slices and glanced at the young man sitting before her.

"Why are you here, in Belgium?"

He hesitated. "We're alone?"

She nodded, handing him a piece of bread.

"I came over with the Canadians," he said. "I think it stinks what the Jerries did to Belgium, and so I joined up to fight. Got all the way to the front. Trouble is, I got separated from my unit. We were fighting over at Ypres." He pronounced the town as if it rhymed with *wipers*, and Isa had to catch her bottom lip to suppress a rude giggle. He certainly *sounded* American!

The young man looked suddenly serious as he set the uneaten bread aside and leaned forward, running his hands over his face as if rubbing away what he saw in his mind. When he looked at her again, his eyes were wet, the rims red. "I've been hiding out for months now, blending in here and there. But I have to go back. My men need me."

"Your men?"

"Well, the men I was with. I'm not an officer or anything. 'Course you couldn't even tell I'm a soldier in these civilian clothes. I stole 'em off somebody's clothesline. But even though I'm just a private, I'm a pretty good shot and I don't want them to think I deserted. I've got to get back."

"Then what are you doing as far behind the lines as Brussels?"

He leaned back in his chair. "I couldn't just walk back to the right side, you know? So I kept going, getting as far away from the fight as I could. As I figure it, I'll have to go all the way up to Holland and rejoin the Allies from there. They can put me wherever they want, so long as I'm fighting again."

It was a sound plan, and he seemed sincere, especially since his English was so natural.

She added tea to the hot water and let it sit, watching him

eat his bread. He did so slowly, as if he'd been raised in a proper, polite home.

"Why should you want to go back? It's not as if you've deserted. Certainly you have nothing to fear of your name being tainted."

"I've got to go back, ma'am. It's a point of honor. And I sure don't want to be caught by the Jerries."

"I see." She poured the flavored water through a sieve to collect the loose tea fragments. Then, offering him the cup, she looked directly at him. "I wish I could help you, but of course you know I cannot."

"What?"

"Just because I'm an American doesn't mean I know how to get out of this country."

"But—but you haven't been here from the beginning, have you? I've been watching all the big houses around here for weeks, and it seems to me you just got here."

She frowned. "Perhaps, like you, I've been in hiding. Germans were living here until a couple of weeks ago."

He shifted in his seat, taking a cautious sip of the hot liquid. "Yeah, sure. Nobody wants to help out a soldier, not with the Jerries ready to pounce on anybody who does. But I heard talk about how an American just showed up one day and moved back into her big house. They said you left the country before the war, and now all of a sudden you're back. I figure you came in the same way I can get out."

"But I have no idea how to help you!" She leaned close to him, adding quietly, "And further, I should tell you there is a German Major right upstairs who might be very interested in your visit."

He seemed to pale somewhat, and for the barest moment she wondered if she was wrong. But even if she was, how *could* she help him? It was impossible. One thing she'd sworn to Gourard was never to reveal the names she did know to anyone other than those he directed her to.

"Perhaps you should go," she said softly.

Just as she spoke, a tall shadow approached the kitchen door and Isa knew without looking that it was Henri. No one filled a doorway quite like him.

"Shall I have my friend show you to the door?"

The young man looked from her to Henri and then back again. "But I'm an American like you. Why won't you help me?"

Isa had no answer, at least not one she could tell him. She had only to give one quick glance Henri's way and he stepped forward. The man nearly jumped to his feet and hurried through the kitchen door.

Isa closed the door behind him. "I hope I've done the right thing."

Henri put a hand on her shoulder, and when she looked up at him, he nodded.

It wasn't easy to accept his consolation. "But how can I know?"

He pointed to his heart.

"There was something . . ." She looked up at Henri again, almost surprised at her own realization. "It was the way he ate that bread, as if he wasn't even hungry. If he's been hiding, wouldn't he have been nearly starving? Everybody's hungry—except maybe German soldiers."

Henri nodded again, then went out the door as if to make sure the other man was nowhere in the vicinity.

14

Let us hope the hens lay their required number of eggs as demanded by the Germans, and the pigeons return to their cotes under the new German clocks.

La Libre Belgique

"Pull it tighter around each pin," Genny said gently as she watched Isa's attempts at lace making. They sat in the parlor under an oil lamp, the electricity out today. The room glistened under the old-fashioned lighting and Genny couldn't help but wonder if the surroundings were enhanced because of it. The blue seemed softer, the gold fixtures muted, the wood more lustrous.

Genny hardly felt qualified to teach anyone how to tat lace, yet it was one of the few things they could do to pass the time. Isa was a willing if not particularly brilliant student.

"If Viole were here, she would have you weaving through those pins in no time. Out of the chaos will emerge a flower or a leaf or something just as lovely. You'll see."

"The process is slow! It'll take me until Christmas to finish this panel." Just then Isa dropped the little bobbin from her hand, and she retrieved it with an exasperated sigh.

"Mademoiselle," came Clara's voice from the parlor archway.

"What is it, Clara?"

Clara looked over her shoulder at the stairway from which she'd just come. "It's the Major, *mademoiselle*. He wishes . . . he wishes to dine with the family tonight!"

"Oh . . ." Genny saw the dismay on Isa's face and knew it must match her own. But she also knew she mustn't cave in to her natural inclination. Nor must Isa.

Isa was already answering. "Tell him he is more than welcome to use the dining room downstairs, but as we're in mourning, we are dining simply and in the kitchen."

"It's been two years since Jonathan's death, Isa," Genny reminded her. "The period of mourning—"

"Lasts as long as we are occupied by the German army."

Genny raised a brow. "I'm sure that will be well received." She looked at Clara. "Tell the Major it's our custom to dine simply, as Isa said, in the kitchen. It is entirely informal and hardly worth the effort for him to join us. Nonetheless, if he insists—"

Isa rose to her feet, sending bobbins to tapping. "Genny! I cannot believe you would sit at the same table with him. After what they did."

How she wanted to scream, *I know! And I hate them for it! I hate him! Let him rot in that little room upstairs, day after day, alone.*

Instead, she attempted a smile but her lips quivered in the effort. "Isa, no one remembers better than I what they've done. I miss my husband each and every day. But would you offend a commissioned officer of the German army when the consequences might be worse than the task?"

Isa sank to her seat.

"If our Lord were here," Genny whispered, "what do you think He would do?"

Genny watched Isa's anger diminish to frustration, then reluctant acceptance, as her brow unfurled, her lips softened, her breathing eased. No less than the struggle Genny endured but was better at hiding.

Isa turned to Clara. "Do as Genny says."

"And, Clara," Genny called, "when you go back upstairs, will you tell Jonah to come here? I think we need a little family meeting before dinner."

"Yes, *madame*, only I do not think little Jonah has come home from school yet."

"Not come home?" Genny repeated, glancing at the anniversary clock on the table nearby. Past five.

Now it was Genny's turn to rise from her seat. She went into the hall and to the front door, stepping outside and looking up, then down the street.

"I'll take a look upstairs anyway," Isa said from behind. "Maybe he slipped by us when our heads were over the lace."

Genny came back inside as Isa returned downstairs. Isa didn't say a word, confirming what Genny already knew: Jonah wasn't home. Wringing her hands, she tried to remember the names of some of the boys Jonah chummed with, but only names from Lower Town sprang to mind. He hadn't been going to school long enough in this district for her to have learned the names of any new friends.

"I—I'm not sure what to do."

"Let's go to the school and see if he's still there. Perhaps he's been kept after for some mischief."

Genny grasped at the notion. "Yes. Only you stay here, Isa. Perhaps he'll show up at any moment. Someone may try to reach us here. Someone should be here."

"Yes, yes, of course you're right. I'll get your shawl while you get your papers."

Genny was already on the porch when Isa returned with Genny's black lace shawl. She accepted it as she descended the steps, hurrying to the street and walking as swiftly as she could without breaking into a run.

Even as her unsteady breathing echoed in her ears, she reminded herself of the same thing she'd reminded herself two years ago. *God still reigns.* But although the words tried to summon a sense of trust, her feet did not slow. *Not the Germans, not the Germans . . .*

She found the school dismally quiet, the back playground empty. But when she went around to the small school's entrance, she stopped short. Not a child did she see—only a half-dozen or more parents with looks of worry on their faces that no doubt matched her own.

"What is it? What's happened?"

"We've been waiting nearly an hour, but the schoolmaster isn't here."

Another woman nearby nodded. "All the teachers were gone before any of us came. The janitor said they left quickly today."

"The younger boys who came home said there were soldiers here," another woman said. Her eyes were wide, her mouth taut.

Just then someone strode toward them at a brisk pace. Genny didn't recognize the man, but the others must have because they all pressed in on him. Genny did so too.

"Schoolmaster Frode is still at the Kommandantur. I returned as quickly as I could. Several boys were taken to St. Gilles prison— now, now." He raised his voice over their onslaught of gasps, moans, and questions. "We're told they are all together and not in a cell but in an interrogation room."

"But *why?*" echoed the question from nearly every person near Genny, including herself.

The man shook his head and looked down at the pavement. "You will have to ask the Germans that."

The parents broke out in myriad questions, all of which rang in Genny's head. She wanted the answers too, but knew this man could offer none. She wanted to do only one thing: rush to St. Gilles and demand to see her son.

God still reigns . . . and loves Jonah as much as I do. . . . God reigns.

Isa sat on the couch, the lacing tools and pillows forgotten. She hid her face in her hands, pleading God's protection over Jonah. Prayers alternated with possible plans. If Jonah was missing, she must find Edward. Genny would need him. Jonah would need him. She would need him.

A shuffling sound came from the top of the staircase. She looked up but did not move. The Major. The interloper, the invader. She preferred not to think of him at all, wishing he'd continue to stay inside the room he'd commandeered.

She must learn to deal with this man. If only she could achieve the calm of Genny, the control of Edward . . . the love of Christ.

She watched as the Major came into view, one hand on the walnut railing, the other on his cane. The hand on the railing was white-knuckled. His head was bent, looking at the steps before him, obviously concentrating on what must be a new sense of balance.

She took a second look at his feet. . . . Two?

Staring unashamedly, she saw a matching pair of shoes, one that tapered into a narrow wooden peg beneath the cuff of his trousers.

No wonder he'd been ready to try the stairs. Isa held back a sigh. She would indeed have to learn to deal with this man if he was to be as mobile as any other.

Still, he was obviously uncertain on the stairs and she wondered if she should help him. Surely she should. She didn't want him to fall, did she? didn't want to be witness to such an indignity? And yet how many indignities had his army caused the Belgium she loved? While the struggle between God's Spirit and her own gave her pause, the man reached the final step and the moment of offering help passed.

The Major looked back at the stairs once, then around, at last spotting Isa. "Ah," he said congenially. "Fräulein Lassone?"

She nodded, stepping forward. He seemed not to have noticed that she had watched his unsteady descent rather than offering assistance. Or if he did, he hid whatever it made him feel.

"Clara said you dine in the kitchen, and as that is a most agreeable location to me, I've come to join you."

"I—I'm afraid dinner will be delayed," Isa said carefully. She wasn't sure what to say, how much to tell him.

Just then the door burst open and Genny stood there, flushed and breathless. "They've taken him! Oh, Isa, they've *taken* my boy."

Isa rushed to Genny. "Who's taken Jonah?"

"The Germans!" She spoke the word with unveiled disdain, and it was then Isa saw Genny's gaze travel beyond her to the Major. She lost what little color she had left in her fair face.

Her eyes met Isa's again. "You must go to your friend, to the ambassador. It isn't only Jonah, but several boys from the school. They've been taken to St. Gilles—St. Gilles! Can you imagine what in the world they could be doing, taking boys to such a place? You must go right away, Isa."

The Major hobbled forward. "Jonah has been taken to the prison in St. Gilles?" He was clearly skeptical.

Genny squared her shoulders and faced him. "Yes, Major. Even now I don't know details, except that soldiers marched the boys from the school. I intend to go there while Isa goes to the American ambassador to see if he might help."

"St. Gilles is not an easy place to visit," he said.

"What would you have me do? Simply wait, while my son—my *eleven*-year-old son—is held in such a place?"

The Major turned away, and Isa saw Genny's face fill with disgust as clearly as she felt it herself. But before a moment had passed, the German yelled for Clara.

Clara came into the parlor, but the Major looked from the servant to Isa. "The Kommandantur is a fair walk from the American Legation, but you must do it. Will you wait and deliver a message for me?" He looked at Clara. "I need paper. And something to write with. Quickly."

Clara scurried off, and Isa exchanged curious glances with Genny.

The Major turned back to them. "I cannot promise this will be of any help. But at the very least it will not hurt."

He limped to the nearest chair, and in a moment Clara handed him what he'd asked for. He scribbled a note, folded it, and wrote a German name on the outside. He spoke as he handed it to Isa. "Give this to anyone at the Kommandantur at the Hotel de Ville. Herr Lutz is known by all, and they will see that he gets this. Go now, and then on to the legation. Having your ambassador involved will not hurt. Hurry, Fräulein Lassone. Frau Kirkland cannot be kept waiting long for her son."

Isa hardly needed him to remind her of that, but she only rushed from the room, refusing to ponder the unmistakable look of compassion upon his face.

She ran part of the way, slowing only when she turned to the narrow, busy streets leading to the Town Hall in the market square. The number of soldiers increased along here, so close to their headquarters. She slowed; she'd left in such a rush, she didn't have her papers.

Countless soldiers milled the Grand Place in front of the Town Hall. From its side bled a line of people that wrapped farther down the nearest narrow artery than she could see. The entire square hardly felt familiar, though she knew this wasn't the only foreign army these walls had ever seen or the only foreign boots to echo from the cobblestones. She walked past the ancient guild houses, past the king's palace that had never housed a king, forcing a calm facade though her knees fairly quaked amid so many uniforms. She clenched her fingers on the note in a feeble attempt at stilling her trembling hands, looking no one in the eye, merely walking straight ahead toward the loveliest of Gothic buildings with its gilt belfry beneath the weather vane of St. Michel slaying the devil, below which blew the flag of Germany.

There was the wide porch, beneath no less than seventeen arches in a row. Inside, paintings of grand municipal authority seemed prostituted by those occupying the halls now.

A sentry stood in her way toward the great staircase.

"I have a message for Herr Lutz." She held out the note.

"And your name?"

"It is a message from Major von Bürkel. I am but the carrier."

"And your name?" he repeated more firmly.

Isa swallowed, squelching her fear that he would demand to see her papers next. She told him, and he went to a podium where he wrote it down on a clipped stack, asking her the correct spelling of *Isabelle*.

"Does this message require you to wait for a response?" He appeared in no hurry for her to leave—or to deliver the note he now held.

"No. But it is urgent that he see the message immediately."

"Very well." He eyed her once more. "I will see that Herr Lutz receives what you've brought." Then, unexpectedly, he smiled. "You may wait if you like. I have chocolate. I will share it with you."

Isa took a step back, shaking her head. "No, I must go home."

Then, without waiting for him to issue another word, she rushed to the exit.

She never looked back, although part of her was afraid he might come after her or send someone in chase. But when she was three blocks from the German headquarters where so many uniformed—and civilian—Germans lurked, she breathed a bit easier and picked up her pace. The legation was still several blocks away, back uphill from where she'd first come.

Isa tried the door but found it locked and rapped loudly. She had no idea what time it was, though she guessed it was only past six o'clock. She knocked again, this time louder, until her knuckles reddened and her heart thudded nearly as fast. At last she heard footsteps approach, and the door opened, but rather narrowly. Before her was a woman, tall of stature, with gray hair swept up into a bun at the nape of her neck, wearing a gown of dark brown. Though she looked regal, as if born to the legation and therefore an integral part of it, Isa had never set eyes on her before.

"My name is Isa Lassone and I must speak to Mr. Whitlock." She took a step closer to the door but stopped when the other woman made no attempt to open it wider. "Could you tell him I'm here?"

"Mr. Whitlock is not inside."

Isa glanced up at the flagpole rooted in the front yard, relieved to see the Stars and Stripes still flying. Other flags over other legations no longer flew—France, the United Kingdom, Australia. Only those who sided with Germany still flew their flags, and the few remaining neutrals like America.

"Where is he?"

"You've missed him only by minutes with another urgent matter. There's no other kind these days! The Germans are seizing young men again, and Mr. Whitlock is doing all he can against it."

"What! Taking them—where? To St. Gilles?"

"No, no—worse! Deporting them to Germany for work."

Isa fell back as if the words were an assault. "But not children! Surely not—"

"I'll tell Mr. Whitlock you were here, when he returns. Though I fear he won't be able to contact you until morning at the earliest.

I'm sorry, miss, but there are a great many others suffering, too, and Mr. Whitlock is only one man. He cannot hear every case, no matter how urgent. Good night."

Then she pushed the door closed, effectively shutting Isa out. She heard the sickening click as the door found its home, followed by the tumble of a lock into place.

Only acting would stop her trembling; only action would stall her tears. She must . . . what?

There was only one thing left to do. Find Edward. He might know someone who could help. At the very least he needed to know what had become of his little brother—particularly if the Germans were sending Jonah to a work camp the likes of which Edward had already known.

Rosalie. The name came immediately to mind. Isa could not remember any house number, indeed she hadn't seen one that night Edward had taken her there. But she remembered the neighborhood and would find this woman herself. Surely Rosalie would know how to find Edward.

The nearer Isa came to the far end of Lower Town, the greater her doubt grew. She might consider herself Belgian, but she was a stranger to this part of Brussels. The way she was dressed, in her mother's forest green day gown, hardly lent much help—and yet, if anyone suspected her of being a German spy, wouldn't they think she would have taken more time to look like one of them, to fit in?

She didn't have time to worry about such things. She wished she'd brought her papers, but going back for them would have wasted too much time. She must find Rosalie, and then Edward, and get back home to Genny. Genny! Surely she was more frantic than ever.

She'd forgotten how each narrow, cobbled street looked so similar. How one began only to end unexpectedly. She was sure she'd reached the right street until seeing the next, then equally sure that was the one.

Tell me what to do, Lord! I don't know what to do.

She paced the blocks, trying to retrace her steps from so long ago. She eliminated several streets as being too far from the edge and a couple by virtue of oddities she was sure she would have noticed that night: a little statue of St. Martin, a porch so long it traversed the length of three town houses. Surely she would have noticed the smells of the stables at the end of one street.

As usual, there were few people out, but two people she asked did nothing more than give her their backs. She walked the two arteries she'd narrowed as her choices. Both had homes in the center of the block with a tiny, square window that looked so familiar. As she neared despair of ever finding help, someone emerged from one of the buildings she watched.

"Pardon." She approached the blond young man on the steps. He turned to her abruptly with a look uncannily passive from one stranger to another. She continued in French, "I—I'm trying to find someone and I wonder if you might help?"

He eyed her. "Who are you?"

"Isa Lassone."

"It's clear you're not from around here. Who are you looking for?"

"A young woman, dark hair, petite. Her name is Rosalie."

If the name meant anything to him, he didn't show it. "What do you want with this person?"

"I need to speak with her. We have a mutual friend."

"And who is that?"

Isa folded her arms against his close scrutiny. "I'd rather not say."

"And maybe I would rather not say if I know this Rosalie."

"Oh, but you *must* help," Isa pleaded. "I need help for a child!"

He appeared unmoved. This dreadful war! It made everyone suspicious. Were children its latest victims? Her gaze left his face and went to the door of the home he'd just exited. What had she to lose by going to every door and asking for Rosalie?

She took a step forward, intent upon going around the tall man, when it suddenly occurred to her that he might be younger than he initially appeared. Though the skin around his eyes and ears was wrinkled, there was something familiar in the aging pattern. In fact, recalling Edward's disguise, she knew at that moment that he and Edward had at least one thing in common: their makeup artist.

The man stepped in her path in one quick, agile movement. One quick, agile, and *young* movement. "I think perhaps you should return to your home, *mademoiselle*."

At two steps closer she was certain. With one glance around to see that no one was nearby, she whispered, "You know this woman, don't you? I tell you, I mean her no harm. I must talk to her."

"Talking to people these days is dangerous. Even pretty young women. Perhaps especially so."

"But I need help. A boy has been seized by the Germans and Rosalie will want to know."

At least he looked curious. "Why should she want to know?"

"Because of our mutual friend. He has a brother named Jonah."

He didn't easily dismiss the name or her, that much was clear. He studied her a moment longer. "Come with me."

Isa was at his heels before he finished his last word.

She recognized the small, barren entranceway. The man entered the inner door without even a knock and Isa followed. Moments later a woman appeared under an archway across the comfortable room. Isa pushed the thoughts from her mind but they came nonetheless: this was Rosalie. The woman Edward depended on at least for his identity. Someone he trusted.

Isa stepped forward, but even as her lips opened, words faded. Edward entered the room behind Rosalie: the Edward she knew, without a trace of the makeup marring his skin.

"Isa! How did you get here? What are you doing here?"

She wanted to fly to his arms, but her feet were firmly rooted in the spot near the door. She was the outsider in this cozily relaxing home where he was so at ease with two people who were strangers to her. Even as he stepped fully into the room, she saw that he had a cup of something in his hand, which he set aside on the nearby table as he approached.

"What is it?" He was near her now and placed his hands on her arms.

His voice shook away her selfish thoughts. "Oh, Edward, you must come with me. It's Jonah. The Germans have taken him!"

"What? But why?"

"He was taken from school, they said to St. Gilles, but I've just come from Mr. Whitlock's, and I was told Germany is seizing young men to be deported to Germany for work."

He looked behind him at the man and Rosalie, then back at Isa. "We've heard they were taking men from the provinces and expected it here, too. But Jonah . . . it hardly makes sense. He's just a boy." He turned from Isa. "I must go."

Isa stepped closer to his back. "Yes! Your mother is trying to track him down. But, Edward, the Major . . . he mustn't see you as you are. He doesn't stay in his room anymore. When I left, he was with your mother."

"With her? What do you mean?"

"I believe he was trying to help. He sent me to the Kommandantur with a note."

Edward's face reflected Isa's skepticism. But they both knew the obvious: Edward couldn't go to his mother with a German Major lurking in the same room.

He looked at the other man as if seeing how inadequate were their disguises, even in the dim light of a home illumined only by candle. Suddenly he faced Isa again. "I need you to do something for me."

She nodded.

"I'll need money. What do you have other than the jewels? And do you still have immediate access to wherever you've hidden it?"

"I have five thousand Marks, and some Belgian francs, too—a thousand in smaller notes. And a one-thousand-franc note. It's safe in the room I told you about. No one could possibly find it there, I promise you that."

No time to see if any one of them found the amounts impressive—Edward was already leading her to the door. "Go back; retrieve a thousand in German notes, five hundred in Belgian francs. You must bring it here and return home before curfew. Will you do it?"

"Of course."

"I'm going to the church," Edward said. "Go now, Isa. And hurry."

She turned away and would have dashed, but Edward held her back. For a moment he simply looked at her. "Be careful."

She smiled and nodded. Then flew from the room.

She ran nearly all the way, slowing only when footsteps neared, fearing to be stopped with a demand to check papers. But God had sent her peace; He would do something to save Jonah, and He would do it through Edward.

15

Let us present a strong, united, yet peaceful resistance as we await the day of our deliverance. In this way we prove the vast inferiority of what they call German *Kultur*.

La Libre Belgique

Genny sat beside Major von Bürkel in the backseat of the black motorcar driven by a young German soldier. The Major, beside her, had the grace not to look her way, for which she was thankful. Ahead, she saw only the black, white, and red colors flying on the little flags affixed to the hood of the motor. Colors of the Second Reich. Her head ached; her heart pounded; her soul prayed words her mind couldn't form.

Jonah was a spirited child, and she was fully prepared to believe he'd done something rash, even reckless. Yet whatever he'd done could not possibly deserve the punishment of imprisonment. He was a child!

She shrank to the farthest corner of the auto, feeling the very thing she told others not to feel. *Don't hate them, Jonah, because God loves even them. Don't hate them, Isa, because your hatred will only hurt your own soul. Don't hate them, Edward, in spite of all they did to you. Forgive them, as we've been forgiven. . . .*

She stifled a cry, imagining Jonah suffering some sort of German injustice even now.

What a liar she was, a fraud. She hated them, all of them, even this man beside her, for taking her husband, for burning her home and destroying her livelihood, for making Edward suffer as he had. And now for this.

God forgive her, she hated them.

And yet this was a man beside her, not an army. A man who seemed sincere in his efforts to help.

He'd said little since Isa had left with his note. When four other officers came to their door, Genny had nearly fainted of fear, certain they'd come to tell her Jonah's fate. Yet the Major had bid the men to enter. They had all seemed happy to see him, calling him Max, thudding his shoulder or back. He'd introduced her shortly after that, and everyone had been polite, offering formal bows, and one even kissed her hand as if they were at a soiree.

She'd wished them all away then, silently but fiercely, until one of them said "old Lutz" had sent them with a motorcar for the Major's use and to let him know he would check into the matter of Max's note.

Upon hearing of the car, the Major had glanced Genny's way, and as if they were suddenly the kind of old friends who could read each other's mind, he handed her the shawl she'd only just discarded and they went on their way. That seemed an eternity ago, but it must have been only minutes, for they hadn't been on the road long.

"Frau Kirkland," the Major said quietly, "I can ensure that you see your son, and I can have my friend Herr Lutz look into the matter, but neither I nor Herr Lutz can free him immediately. You do know that? That he's been taken here, of all places, suggests he's done something wrong. Something illegal."

She nodded, tearing her eyes from the flags on the hood to glance at him, then out the side window. Illegal according to German law, perhaps . . .

"It's a rather fragile web we've woven," he said softly, almost as if he spoke to himself. "We all do our jobs because we want to see our country victorious. We long for Germany to take its place among the great powers. Is that wrong?"

She peeked his way but he wasn't looking at her, either.

"We have jobs that seem quite separate, alien even, to other compatriots who serve our country." Then he cleared his throat and peripherally she saw him look her way. "That is why I'm unable to assure his freedom. Depending on the details, and upon the insistence and importance of his accuser, as well as upon the judge-advocate who hears his case, if one is to be heard, there may be nothing at all that I can do. In fact, were I von Bissing himself, I could do nothing unless those who are involved with the case allow it. It is all part of this web, do you see?"

She nodded again, although she didn't "see" at all. Justice was justice; why must it be so difficult to apply universally, rather than allow only a select few to decide? Was true justice to be found in any court in Belgium while Germans were here?

She kept silent, afraid she might say something to cause him to withdraw his offer of help. He had no real reason to offer such aid, she knew that. And she wasn't about to shun the precarious hand he extended her way.

At last they pulled up before St. Gilles. She'd seen it before, in passing. The turrets, the battlements, the arrow loops and perpetually guarded center gate. Only now those sentries were German. They spoke briefly to the driver. One flashed a light on Genny and the Major in the backseat while another examined their papers. Then they were waved through to an inner courtyard, and Genny heard the tires rolling over rough gravel before the vehicle halted. Here the driver exchanged a few words with another guard, who opened the door at Genny's elbow.

She found herself surrounded by the medieval battlements of the prison. With little more than moonlight to illumine the structure, it was as intimidating as any prison should be, especially one with so many years of service. Genny hoped it hadn't appeared so menacing by day, when the boys had arrived.

She exited the motorcar and waited for the Major. A soldier met them on the steps of an inner citadel. She watched Major von Bürkel move slowly, depending on a cane now rather than crutches. And it was then she noticed a difference: not one shoe but two, perfectly balanced, one at the end of each pant leg. How had she not noticed? When had this change occurred? In the dim light the only hint of his disability was in the careful steps he took. Genny paced herself to his gait.

Their footsteps echoed off empty halls. Soon she heard the noise of children talking—the first sound all evening that brought joyful tears to her eyes.

The room was large and dark, lit only by oil lamps set too high to reach without a wand, starkly devoid of furniture. In the center of a roughly tiled floor sat a circle of a dozen boys, all of similar size.

"Mother!"

Genny nearly tripped over the narrow hem of her gown to reach Jonah. For once he didn't pull away from such a public embrace.

"You're here!" he said into her ear. "Can I go home now? and my friends?"

Achieving a bit of calm for his sake, she shook her head. "Not yet, but soon. Very soon."

"What's all this about, Jonah?" the Major asked. "Why were you brought here?"

Jonah seemed to notice him for the first time. "Did you bring my mother here? Is that why she was allowed to see me?"

The Major said nothing, neither admitting nor denying the presumption. Instead, he said, "Answer the question now, Jonah. What's all this about?"

Jonah stepped away, folded his hands behind his back, and before Genny's eyes her son seemed to age a decade. He looked very much like Edward just now, taller and more mature, as if ready to accept whatever punishment was meted out.

"It was my idea," he said, chin held high, gaze straight ahead rather than at his mother or the Major. "I incited a mutiny against Herr Oberland, the music teacher."

Boys approached en masse, having stood the moment Jonah had but holding back until he'd spoken.

"No! It was my idea!"

"No! Mine!"

"It was a unanimous decision," Jonah said over the rest, "but if there is to be special blame for the instigator, I'm ready to accept it."

"Just what sort of mutiny did you incite, Jonah?" Major von Bürkel asked. "Was Herr Oberland harmed in some way?"

"No. We simply refused to enter his classroom."

"And why is that?"

Jonah stiffened, still staring straight ahead as if he were already a soldier. "Because he taught us nothing but German songs. We believe the rest of the world has music to offer as well. Some even better than Germany's."

Genny nearly cried out to cover the words before the Major could take offense.

But then she heard laughter, deep and pure and so unexpected she could scarcely believe it came from the man beside her. Yet it was the Major himself, so clearly amused she felt her knees go weak with relief.

"Yes, Jonah, you have a point." Then he became somber as he placed a hand on the boy's shoulder. "But you must do one thing, and that is to promise your mother you will not speak if officers question you as a group. Do you understand what I'm saying? For your mother's sake if not your own, you'll not say a word."

"But I—I've been elected spokesman."

The Major shook his head. "Resign the post, boy, as it's obvious everyone was in on the decision. Speak to a German officer only if questioned. Each of you. Do you understand?" He looked at the other boys, who still stood behind Jonah. "And for your own good, whoever answers will say the prank was aimed at this teacher because you don't like the way he combs his hair or because he has foul breath. Keep it to that and you'll be home by supper tomorrow. Do you understand? This is no time to make martyrs of yourselves, and that's what they'll do if you give them reason enough."

A few of the boys nodded. Jonah said nothing.

Genny put a hand under his chin, beckoning him to look at her. "This is no time to try conquering the army. Let the soldiers take care of that."

Still, he said nothing. She increased the pressure on his chin. "Jonah."

At last his gaze faltered and he looked down, nodding as he did so. "I was scared half to death I'd be shot."

With a low sigh Genny drew him back into her arms. "Well, now all you have to do is be silent unless asked directly to speak. And you'll be home in no time."

Genny looked around the room. It was chilly but not damp, and though it offered little by way of comfort, it was not unbearable. "I don't know how long you'll have to stay, Jonah. You'll remember you're never really alone, won't you? God Himself is right by your side. Always."

He nodded, his gaze meeting hers.

"All right then," the Major said. "Your mother cannot stay longer. We'll get word to the other parents that all of you are together and doing well, and that you'll be home in no time at all. So go back to your circle, and if you do sing, it'll have to be a song the teacher

144

taught you. A German song. That'll go well with the guards, and the tale of it will reach the dreaded teacher in no time and soften him up. You'll see."

Genny braced herself for a moan of protest, at least from her son, but even he showed wisdom and restraint, returning in silence to the circle. She didn't want to leave, but when the Major put a hand beneath her elbow, she knew she must.

She took a last look at Jonah as the door closed between them, and for the first time since the crisis began, she took a breath without trembling.

"Must they stay the night?" she whispered as they followed their escort back to the main entrance. "You heard it's nothing more than a trivial matter. Why must they spend any time here at all?"

"Evidently this Herr Oberland is a sensitive type. If he was offended, he'll have to feel the crime was punished."

"Surely that's already been achieved."

The Major lifted his shoulders. "The boys are fine, as you saw. No harm will come to them."

Genny knew she couldn't press the issue. "We must tell the other parents their boys are all right."

The Major nodded. "We'll go to the school. I'm sure we'll find someone there waiting to pass the word along."

By the time Isa let herself quietly into the back of her house, her lungs stung and her side felt as if a knife were embedded within. She hastened into the kitchen and found Henri at the door leading to the rest of the house.

"Oh, Henri, I need your help—"

He raised a finger to his lips, pointing to the door. She quieted, leaning her ear to the wood panel much as Henri had been doing a moment ago. Through the butler's hall came the definite sound of voices. Men. German.

And she needed her papers—from upstairs!

"Where is Clara?"

Henri motioned something she could barely decipher, even accustomed as she was to his way of communicating. A coat. She must have gone out. A prayer. Perhaps praying for help—or looking for someone to help.

It was no use. She couldn't send Henri upstairs; such an idea was too outrageous not to be noticed by the Germans. She must retrieve her *Passierschein* herself or risk another flight without them. But at least Henri could help with the other matter.

"I've hidden something in the cellar—in the special room. Will you go downstairs and bring me some of the money I've left on the table? A thousand marks, five hundred francs. And hurry!"

He nodded, then turned to the pantry door, the only access to the cellar.

Isa sucked in a deep, steadying breath. The sound of laughter pierced her. How could they laugh when men—and perhaps even boys—were being rounded up this very moment?

"Yes," she heard one man say, "and like Lutz, *you* would have me believing he's farther up the evolutionary scale than I."

Whatever that meant, the room erupted into more male laughter—a sound Isa hadn't heard in too many months to recall. She scanned the area for Genny but saw only uniformed men, each of them either smoking or drinking. What they drank, she had no idea. Nor was the Major present.

One of the men saw her and stepped forward, a Hauptmann by his insignia, and a well-decorated one at that. He clicked his heels and bowed formally before her, a young, clean-shaven man with well-oiled dark hair. His nose was not large yet it had a somewhat-pointed look to it. His chin, while not the jutting sort, had a precise cut. His cheekbones were well-defined, brows like two arrows emerging from the bridge of his nose. His eyes were dark like his hair—the searching kind, as if he saw more than most others. He looked at her now as if he knew her, and yet she'd never seen him before. She would remember if she had.

"You must be Isabelle Lassone, the American heiress who owns this home." He spoke French as naturally as he spoke German. "It is a pleasure to meet you, after having once lived under your hospitable roof."

Uninvited and unwelcome. She longed to refuse his hand but knew she could not. He let his lips linger on the top of her hand, and when he let go, she knew another battle against the desire to wipe clean the feel of his mouth on her skin.

The others introduced themselves, another Hauptmann, a Major, and the last a Rittmeister, all fit and strong. Only this new Major showed any sign that he'd been at the front, with a bandage on the side of his face and the scar of a laceration on the other cheek.

"Where is Major von Bürkel?" she asked.

"On a mission," said the first man, who'd introduced himself as a Hauptmann Rudiger von-something-or-other. "With another woman who lives here. Frau Kirkland?"

Isa nodded.

"They went to see about her son."

"To bring him home?"

He shrugged as if he didn't know. "That, of course, depends on his offense and the person bringing the charges."

Charges . . . "So this has nothing to do with what is happening in the provinces?"

The Hauptmann lifted one of those razorlike brows. "And what is happening in the provinces?"

"I've come from the American Legation, where they told me men were being rounded up and sent to Germany. I thought—"

The Hauptmann laughed. "You needn't worry, *Fräulein*; all we are doing is providing work for men who are otherwise unemployed. With generous wages! There should be no complaints."

She believed not a word, but it wasn't something she could argue. "Then Frau Kirkland's son isn't among those being deported?"

"How old is her son?" another soldier asked.

"Merely eleven. A boy!"

They laughed again. "*Ach*, he will be ready in a few years, but not yet. By the time he is ready to work, he'll know better what's expected of him."

"But if he isn't being rounded up with the men, why would he have been taken from his school today? They said several boys were taken to St. Gilles—to the prison there."

"None of us know," the Hauptmann said. "But Max will find out and set any wrong aright."

She wanted to demand what offense could be so great that an eleven-year-old child must be incarcerated in such a place but held her tongue. She only wanted one thing now, to retrieve what she needed and go back to Edward, to warn him about their house full of "guests."

"If you'll excuse me," she said as she backed away.

"But you'll want to wait for Frau Kirkland, won't you?" the same Hauptmann asked. "To see if she returns with her son?"

"Do you think there is a likelihood of that? that she'll be allowed to bring him home?"

"Once again, I cannot say. I wish that I could, for your sake."

"I am going to a family friend, one who will want to be here when she comes back—especially if she comes alone."

"Very well." He detained her a moment longer with a smile she was sure he meant to be charming. "But might I say, *mademoiselle*, that if you'd been in residence when I first came to stay, it would have taken the entire German army to have me leave?"

Isa turned away at the first polite moment.

She went up the carpeted stairs, to her room, and back down without stopping, carrying her *Passierschein*. She would have slipped into the kitchen without a word, but the Hauptmann caught up with her just as she entered the butler's hall separating dining room from kitchen.

"I would be happy to accompany you," he said. "It's getting late, and although I cannot offer my car—Max has that—my company will ensure your walk will go unstopped."

As tempting as a guaranteed unhindered journey sounded, to accept his offer was ludicrous. "No thank you," she said. "It's not far, and I'll be back shortly."

He opened the kitchen door for her, holding it wide until she passed. She didn't look at him, just entered the kitchen and never turned back, waiting until she heard the door close behind her. She went to the pantry.

Henri was just behind the door. He looked at her closely as he handed her the money. Then he pointed to himself and to her, but she shook her head. "No, Henri." She tucked the precious cargo away. "I'll be all right if I go alone. That is, if I go quickly!"

Once again she ran most of the way, slowing only when she heard voices or footsteps ahead or behind. This time she didn't have to search for the right townhome. Edward's friend approached her at the end of the street.

"Edward isn't back," he said, leading her to the right home. Rosalie was nowhere to be seen.

Inside, he offered her one of the chairs. "I would get you something to eat, only it's Rosalie's house and she doesn't have much in the kitchen these days."

"No one does." Isa looked around. "Is Rosalie here?"

"She is with Edward. My name is Jan, by the way."

He still watched her, and Isa wished she were bold enough to stare back. He was nearly as tall as Edward but somehow slighter, less handsome. Yet he was attractive with a somewhat-triangular face, the wide end at his broad forehead, his jaw tipping the other end.

"You are the one Edward's mother used to take care of, aren't you?"

She nodded. "Did you know Edward before the Germans came?"

"Yes. We were at the university together. We started together, though I was eighteen and he just sixteen. But then you would know that he started young, wouldn't you?"

"Yes, I know his parents are—were—very proud of him."

There was a long silence after that, and Isa could think of nothing to say that wasn't a question about Edward and Rosalie, where they'd gone, about the work they did that this man so obviously shared. About how closely Edward worked with Rosalie and if . . .

"It's generous of you to use your money to help Jonah."

And yet his tone hadn't sounded grateful at all; rather, he'd sounded curious.

"I would do anything for Edward and his family."

"You mentioned something interesting earlier," Jan said. "That you'd hidden your money in a room. What was all that about?"

"I brought with me what I could, in the hope of getting Edward and his family out of Belgium. But Edward won't go."

"Yes, I'm not surprised. Do not give up on him, though. There may come a time when he must leave at a moment's notice. And the room?"

"It's a room in my house where I've kept money and jewelry safe."

"How can any room be safe in your house with a German officer living there?"

"It's safe. It's very safe." If she wasn't so filled with worry over Jonah, she might have realized this opportunity sooner. "And it's available for use . . . should such a secret place be needed."

Just then they heard the door open and Rosalie came in. She took a packet from under her cloak, the size of a large textbook but soft, as if it were cloth wrapped in paper.

"Is Edward with you?" Jan asked.

"No. I'm to take the money and meet him." She turned her dark eyes on Isa. "Do you have it?"

She handed the notes to Rosalie without hesitation.

"You should go home now, Isabelle Lassone." Rosalie said the name as if it were a title. "Let Jan take you."

"Where is Edward?" Isa asked.

"He is arranging for a new *Passierschein*. I'm to bring him this." She held up the packet and the money. "He will come to your house as soon as he can. Expect Father Antoine tonight."

"Father Antoine?"

"He will say he is the nephew of Genevieve Kirkland, in case anyone sees the resemblance. False papers for a priest are expensive because their passes allow them outside after curfew, like doctors and Germans. Go now. His mother will want to know he's on his way. And I must go too."

She turned away but Isa caught her hand in a gentle touch. "Thank you," she whispered. *For keeping him safe, for helping him. I would trade places with you . . .*

Isa moved to the door and Jan followed, but she stopped him. "I can make it alone." She looked back at Rosalie. "Warn Edward there are German soldiers at the house. Four, without the Major who lives there now."

Then Isa hurried from the room.

16

Is there any way but war in this mad world of ours? A world where ill-advised, shortsighted, yes, downright maniacal generals are blindly worshiped? What other defense is there against such folly, except to fight?

La Libre Belgique

Edward walked up the half-dozen cement steps leading to the elaborate door of the Lassone home. Carved wood edged two intricately cut, frosted-glass panes that afforded the occupants privacy at night but sunlight during the day. It was an impressive door to an impressive house.

He twisted the bell next to the door and the chime sounded as bold as Edward himself needed to be if he was to succeed with this disguise.

A tall shadow appeared through the glass and the door swung open. Before him stood an officer roughly the same size as Edward, with slicked hair and an assessing gaze, even directed as it was to Edward in the one outfit that normally guaranteed respect. But too many priests had been arrested to let Edward believe the Germans held the cloth in any esteem.

"I am here to see Genevieve Kirkland."

"And you are?"

"Father Antoine, from the parish of St. Eugenio."

The German looked him over once again, finally stepping aside to let Edward enter. He, too, spoke in French. "I suppose you have identity papers?"

Edward nodded, patting the pocket of the black cassock he wore before he stepped past the soldier and went into the parlor.

The soldier came up behind him. "Then you don't mind if I look at them?"

"Oh!" Edward said, as if the question came as a surprise. "No, not at all." He fished for the papers, adding as he handed them over, "And may I say your French is excellent, Hauptmann."

The German inclined his head ever so slightly as he looked over the *Passierschein* and then returned them. "This is Father Antoine," he said to several other soldiers as he stepped around Edward and took up what had obviously been his wineglass. "And how do you know Frau Kirkland?"

"She is my aunt. I was given a message earlier this evening that she might have need of my comfort. I came as soon as I could from the bedside of an ailing parishioner. Is my aunt here?"

"No," the Hauptmann said. "But we expect her soon. So the messenger did not wait for you?"

Edward shook his head, watching as the Hauptmann looked toward the stairs and then toward the hall.

Another of the officers approached, distracting Edward's attention. He wore two pips of a Rittmeister. "Do you speak German?" he asked in his native language.

Edward found himself nodding before considering consequences. How bold this disguise made him, to be so honest before the enemy.

"You are young to be a priest," the Rittmeister said, and at that pronouncement some of Edward's boldness drained away as all four Germans eyed him now.

"God revealed my vocation to me when I was a boy. I went to the monastery for secondary school at sixteen." Which was partially true anyway. "I wasted no time to do the Lord God's bidding."

"He told you? Just like that?" said the Rittmeister, who couldn't have been much older than Edward himself.

"Not audibly, if that is what you mean. His word came by way of desire, as it often does."

The Hauptmann was clearly distracted as he stood near the butler's hall, but the discussion seemed to have caught his attention at least momentarily. "Desire?"

Edward glanced at the Hauptmann. He had yet to meet a German soldier he could like, but this one was especially irritating. "Yes. Desire, when within God's will, is a good thing. A motivating force."

"Please," the younger man said, "I must ask you, since you are a man of God. Whose side is God on in this war?"

The other three soldiers burst into laughter, and the Rittmeister beside Edward flushed a deep shade of red.

"Everyone knows God is on our side, Rolf," one of the others said. "Every soldier in the trench knows that. It's inscribed on his belt buckle!"

Nonetheless, the man at his side did not retract his question, and now all of them looked at Edward expectantly. He had his own ideas about this war, but common sense told him to keep those views to himself. Instead, he pulled his response from years of his father's tutelage.

"The Bible says God is the one who appoints the times to each nation and draws its boundaries."

"So whoever wins proves God is in their camp?"

"Not in the sense you mean. Who can say what corrupt nation He may use to a greater end?"

The young German's brows drew together, as if he was confused and dissatisfied by the answer. Edward decided to take the tack his own father would have used. "God is interested in the state of every man's soul. On the night before He was crucified, Christ prayed for His people to be united so the world would know God. He would rather we not fight to begin with."

Even as he spoke, Edward watched the Hauptmann. He was clearly obsessed with the kitchen.

Just then the front door opened and his mother stepped inside, a German Major shuffling in behind her. Obviously he was the one who lived here, yet he wasn't nearly as disabled as Edward expected. He had full use of a wooden appendage filling in for his missing foot.

Edward hurried to his mother's side and put his face close to hers as if to kiss her in greeting. But instead he whispered one word: "Antoine."

In that very moment she flung her arms around his neck and half laughed, half cried, "Antoine! How glad I am you're here."

"Yes, Aunt Genny, I came as soon as I could. What news is there of my young cousin Jonah?"

She looked at the Major beside her. "Major von Bürkel arranged for me to see him. Jonah is well, and we have reason to hope there will be no trial."

"Trial! What sort of crime did the boy commit?"

"Oh, nothing really," his mother said. As she removed her shawl, the Major took it from her.

"Boys being boys," the Major added.

To Edward, his mother and the Major suddenly seemed of another world, one where it was hardly odd that an Englishwoman of Belgian residence should be so familiar with the German soldier beside her. He took his mother's hand and led her from the Major's side just as Isa burst from the butler's hallway.

"Genny! Where is Jonah? What's happened to him?"

His mother put an arm around Isa and smiled away the fear on

Isa's face. "I came from St. Gilles. There are a dozen boys there, and from what I saw, they are not being mistreated—except they must sit on a hard floor and spend the night."

"But what happened? Why was he taken there in the first place?"

The Major spoke before Edward's mother could answer, looking at his fellow officers. "Do any of you know a Herr Oberland? He was brought from the homeland to teach here." He spoke in German, and Edward wondered if he knew they could all understand him—he, his mother, and Isa too. "He is the music teacher at Jonah's school. Evidently he's rather zealous in his appreciation of German music, and the boys wish to expand their musical education a bit beyond the German horizon."

All the Germans in the room laughed. Laughing was as easy as breathing to them. And why not?

"I've assured Frau Kirkland that our friend Herr Lutz will settle the matter by tomorrow." Then Major von Bürkel looked at the Hauptmann. "Perhaps you could see that he does."

The man drew his gaze from Isa's profile. "Yes, of course. I shall not sleep until the matter is settled satisfactorily."

"Very well," the Major said. "Then as I see it, the evening is at an end. You may take your leave, boys."

They seemed none too eager to do that, yet they set aside what little was left in the wineglasses and prepared to go, taking up their shiny helmets. As they bid Major von Bürkel farewell, they admonished him not to let too much time pass before they heard from him again. Then, at last, they were gone.

The Major was not as tall as Edward, particularly leaning on his cane the way he did. Edward watched him as he struggled to a chair, where he closed his eyes. When he opened them, his gaze was directed at Edward.

"I don't believe we've been introduced," he said. "Pardon me if I do not rise."

"Of course," Edward said. "My name is Father Antoine Marcellan, of St. Eugenio Parish here in Brussels. Madame Kirkland is my aunt."

"Ah." He rubbed his eyes. "I'm terribly sorry. It's been quite some time since I've been outside my room, and as much as I might have wished to leave it earlier, I'm finding myself pining for it now. I'll take a moment to rest before I conquer the stairs."

Edward took that moment to study his mother. She'd told him consistently not to let hate get the best of him, even though he believed to the core of his soul that she hated them too. And yet, just now, as she looked at this soldier, he didn't see what he'd always seen before in her eyes. Something was different.

Soon the Major began to struggle again with his cane and then made his way from the room. He paused as he passed Edward's mother and briefly touched her forearm. "I know this has been difficult, Frau Kirkland, but I beg you to try sleeping tonight. You've seen that your boy has not been harmed. I promise you, he will be returned."

"Promise, Major?" She sounded as skeptical as Edward felt. "How can one part of the web you mentioned guarantee anything for another?"

"Well said. I suppose I spoke out of compassion. Suffice it to say, then, I shall do everything in my power to see that your son is returned as quickly as possible. It's already in the works, so to speak."

17

The latest injustice committed by the German Imperial Army is that of the seizure of our young men and the unmitigated gall of their leaders to expect us to provide them with lists of names of those whom they may seize! Stand firm, fellow Belgians, for truly the Germans are revealing to the rest of the world what a barbarous, unconscionable race they are.

La Libre Belgique

"Did you hear something?"

Isa lifted her head from the cradle of her arms resting on the kitchen table, but all she'd heard was Genny's voice. Her gaze fell on Edward, who was sleeping on the floor with his back against the wall.

Then Isa heard it. "The door! Edward!" Her call or the act of scrambling to her feet awakened him and the three rushed from the kitchen. Isa could see through the glass that it was already morning, and the sun shone behind two silhouettes on the other side. One of those silhouettes was roughly the size of Jonah.

"It's him!" She fairly sang the two words.

Genny pulled open the door and Jonah was in her arms.

"I apologize for the early arrival," came the familiar voice of the

Hauptmann who had been there last night. "But I assumed you would want him back as soon as possible."

He was an intrusion upon the moment, and Isa refused to look him in the eye despite his gaze on her.

"Thank you for bringing him to us," Genny said, still holding Jonah.

At last Jonah stepped back, no doubt seeing Edward in the vestments of a priest.

Edward pulled him away from his mother and spoke before the boy could utter a word. "So, young cousin, how was your night in prison? You realize this will be quite a tale for all of your friends?"

"Most of them were there, and now they're angry with me because their parents are angry with them."

"Well, you can tell your own children about it, then, someday when you have them."

Edward led him away, no doubt to brief Jonah on his new identity.

Isa slipped her arm through Genny's. Then, remembering they weren't alone, she glanced again toward the Hauptmann, who lingered in the doorway.

"I was glad to be of assistance," he said. "And if I may say, I continue to be at your service. If you need anything, simply ask for me at the Kommandantur."

"Thank you, Hauptmann . . . I'm sorry," Genny said with a little laugh. "I'm afraid in all of the commotion last night, I don't recall your name."

He clicked his heels in a formal salute. "Hauptmann Rudiger von Eckhart." But during his introduction he looked from Genny to Isa, where his gaze remained.

Isa looked away.

"I must go," he said, "but I hope I may call again—to check on the progress of our Major von Bürkel. Some of us feel his recuperation has gone on long enough, and we hope to persuade him to come to the Kommandantur a few hours a day."

Genny glanced up the stairway at her left. "I doubt he's up and about this early, Hauptmann, but I will see that he's told of your inquiries."

"Very well. Then I wish you good day."

He bowed again, once to Genny and then to Isa. "Good day to you, *mademoiselle*," he said softly and then, at last, took his leave.

Edward had rejoined them just as Isa closed the door. "I'm glad he's gone," she said.

"Where is Jonah now?" Genny asked.

"In the kitchen with Clara," Edward told her, "who is no doubt feeding him more than whatever portion you're each allowed."

"I'm going to see that he's all right and then put him—and myself—to bed. I suggest the two of you get some sleep as well, after such a long night."

Isa nodded, but she no longer suffered the fatigue she'd felt a while ago, trying unsuccessfully to rest in a chair, still worrying over Jonah. And now here she was, alone with Edward. Adrenaline spread from somewhere in her middle, shooting out to her limbs, tingling her fingers and toes.

"What we should do is properly thank God Jonah's all right. When Mr. Whitlock's clerk told me about the deportations . . ." She shivered, pretending leftover worries to be the cause of her jitters.

He nodded.

"Hmm . . . you didn't deny God's involvement in bringing Jonah to safety. Have you come back to acknowledging His existence, after all?"

He grinned. "Must be the effect of the new disguise."

"One that will allow you to visit now, since even the Major knows you as part of the family."

"This doesn't change anything, Isa."

"It could. I could show you the room right now."

He stepped closer. "You did the right thing in coming to me, and I'm grateful for the money. But I want nothing to do with that room. And furthermore, don't use any more of your money; you'll need it for when you leave."

"When we all leave, don't you mean?"

He didn't answer but took his leave by way of the front door.

Edward went straight to Jan's. Since the most recent arrests, Jan had taken a new address and with that yet another identity: he was now a baker for the CRB, a profession that made him practically exempt from German interest or attention.

Edward made sure no one was around when he entered the seven-story apartment building. Some of his clothes were at Jan's, and Edward needed to take at least one set of street clothes with him to the church, where he would spend much of his time from now on. But he couldn't very well nap on a pew bench dressed as he was, so perhaps he'd snatch a few hours of rest at Jan's before asking Father Clemenceau where he was to quarter himself in his new identity.

Jan was just emerging from his bedroom, fully dressed as if ready to go out.

"Going somewhere?"

Jan straightened the collar on his shirt as he spoke. "I was about to look for you, actually. Is there news of Jonah?"

Edward rubbed his eyes as he removed the three-edged black biretta from his head and loosened the cincture at his waist. Then he started on the buttons . . . all thirty-three of them. One for each year Christ was on earth—even Edward remembered the symbolism of that. But at the moment thirty-three buttons seemed too much trouble. All he wanted to do was change his clothes and get some sleep.

"Jonah is home. I'm going to sleep a couple hours, if you don't mind."

Jan didn't reply, only stood in Edward's way. Edward looked at him expectantly, too tired to be annoyed.

"Last night Isabelle Lassone mentioned a room in her home where she'd hidden her money. When I asked about it, she said it was a safe room."

Fatigue no longer outweighed annoyance. His pulse picked up. "Nothing is safe with a German Major living there."

"Exactly what I thought," Jan said. "But when I asked her, she seemed certain—"

"It's out of the question." Edward stepped around Jan to go to the empty bedroom.

"Why? What kind of room is it? How big is it?"

"It's nothing."

"I want to see it."

"We can't use it, Jan. So just leave it."

Jan looked at Edward with a snort. "I didn't know you thought so little of the paper. A paper you said you'd give your life for, if it came to that."

"I said I would give my life, not anyone else's. That's where my *mother* lives, Jan. Do you think I'd put a press under her roof? Would *you*?"

"I know what I'd do. I'd let *them* decide."

Edward shook his head, turning away and continuing with the buttons.

Jan circled around. "Why not? Don't they have a right to decide what they'll risk and what they won't? Isn't Belgium theirs, too? Or do you make all the decisions for them, the way you've done for Rosalie and me?"

"If ever I've made a decision, it's because one needed to be made, and neither one of you seemed inclined to do it."

"Is that the way you see it? Fine. But you're not even giving them a chance."

"The simple act of asking puts pressure on them to make what they *think* will be the right decision. It's unfair to expect them to sleep above an illegal press or comp room."

"It's no greater risk than you've taken." Jan took a step closer so that his eyes were near level with Edward's. "It's their decision, Edward. Not yours."

Then Jan turned away, heading toward the door.

"Where are you going?"

"To Rosalie's."

Now it was Edward's turn to head Jan off, though it took some doing to move quickly with unfamiliar priest's garb hampering every step. "This matter is closed. No need to talk to Rosalie about it."

"Too late," Jan said with a crooked smile. "I did that last night after you left. And I'm afraid you've been outnumbered. She agrees with me."

He opened the door and left.

With a moan of purest frustration, Edward refastened the few buttons he'd loosed, retied the cincture around his waist, and placed the biretta back on his head. If they were going to confront Isa with a proposal about the room, he intended to be there. First.

"*Mademoiselle. Mademoiselle.*"

Groggy, Isa opened her eyes to see Clara just inside her bedroom door.

"Clara?"

"I am so sorry to awaken you, but Monsieur Edward—that is, Father Antoine—he insisted."

Isa sat up, rubbing her eyes so they would open. "Edward? He's back?"

"He's downstairs. I told him you were sleeping—"

"That's all right, Clara. I'll see him at once."

"Yes, *mademoiselle*." She helped Isa to dress.

Minutes later, Isa passed the Major's room slowly as she moved toward the stairs. Satisfied that he must still be asleep, she made her way quietly to the first-floor parlor.

"Edward?"

He turned from the window and came to stand directly in front of her. "Jan and Rosalie are coming here to talk to you."

"Why? If they need anything for the paper, it's certainly all right—"

Edward shook his head, going back to the window and peering through a slat of the shutter as if looking for someone. "You talked to Jan about the room."

She nodded, but even as she did, she saw his anger. Someone else might not see it; surely his voice was reasonable, his manner calm. But the narrowing of his lips and the inability to look her in the eye gave him away.

So when he turned to her and grabbed her by the shoulders, she was not surprised. "How could you do it, Isa? With my mother living here, and Jonah? I thought you loved them too."

"I do!"

"And so you're willing to risk their lives? Because of your own naive wish to be some kind of Belgian hero?" He kept his voice low but the harsh tone made up for the lack of volume.

"No, of course not! I only thought—"

"You couldn't possibly be thinking correctly if you've even considered such a foolish thing. Shall I tell you the names of those who've been arrested, deported to Germany, or sent to the firing squad in connection with this? Do you think your father's money will make you immune? Hardly. In German eyes, we're all equal—equally worthless, unless our lives, or deaths, further their regime."

He let her go, looking again out the window. "They'll be here shortly, and when they arrive, you'll refuse them. You'll have Clara send them away at the door because there must be no possible connection between this house and them. Do you understand?"

"Edward," she said softly, "I know you want to protect your family. And if you think it's too dangerous, then perhaps your mother and Jonah might consider returning to Viole's. But it's not really your place to protect this house or your mother or Jonah. Or me, for that matter, if that ever occurred to you. It's God's. We're all in His hands, not yours. So is *La Libre Belgique*."

Now his face reddened and then turned hard. "Maybe you're willing to trust a God who obviously cannot—or will not—step in when the world's gone mad, but I'm not."

"You cannot discount the Lord. Your faith is still in you, if you would just listen to it."

He said nothing, but his level gaze frightened her. Was he not in the least ashamed to have spoken so harshly against the same God he himself had once introduced her to?

"Why is it acceptable for you to take risks, but not anyone else?"

"It's the degree of risk. This is your home, Isa. You wouldn't have any hope for defense if evidence for involvement with the paper is found."

"When you first decided to help distribute this paper, didn't you ask yourself how far you'd be willing to go? if it was worth it?"

"Of course."

"Don't you think others have the right to do that too?" She put a hand on one of his. "Before I ever returned, I knew what I wanted to do. I love Belgium, Edward. It's more home to me than anyplace else, and right now it's sitting under an army that's trying to stamp out everything I love. All of Belgium wakes up every morning to a foreign army telling her what to do. They've stripped the factories, stolen money from the banks, requisitioned everything from copper pots to wool. The only thing left to us that the Germans can't control is what we think—and so it's words they fear, because they know as long as the spirit of Belgium is alive they haven't really conquered us or our faith. The only way to keep that spirit going is to keep the *paper* going. It's worth every risk."

He stared at her as if he'd never seen her before. "You don't have to convince me, Isa. I've lived with it for two years, and I decided a long time ago it was worth *my* life. But is it worth yours? I can see you're better informed than I realized, that the outside world educated you more thoroughly than I thought possible. But have you really considered it, or are you just playacting? Your money, your name—even your faith—won't get you out of trouble if trouble comes."

"I have no doubts."

"Isa, Isa, you answer too easily."

"No, Edward. You're too careful."

He clutched her hand that had touched his so lightly. "If you'd ever heard the firing squads at Tir National, you would know there is no such thing as being too careful."

The bell at the door made Isa jump. She reminded herself that it was just a bell, not the guns of which he spoke.

Edward turned back to the window. "It's them. Jan and Rosalie."

"But how did they know where I live?"

Edward walked toward the door. "Rosalie knew. She thought it was funny to deliver the paper here when it housed German soldiers—especially when we had headlines about German losses."

He reached the door just as Clara emerged from the butler's hall. "I will answer it, Clara. And they won't be staying, so you're not needed . . . thank you."

He waited until she'd turned her back, then glanced up the stairs as if to make sure no one lingered there and opened the door.

Jan stepped inside first, facing Edward. "I thought you might return here."

Edward didn't lead them farther inside. He leaned against the open door and faced Jan and Rosalie. "I've told her what you want," he said. "I've also advised her to turn you away."

Jan and Rosalie now looked at Isa.

"I'm willing for you to use the room," she said slowly, looking at Edward even though her words were directed to the others, "but on one condition. That Genny and Jonah return to where they were living before I returned."

Edward shook his head. "What, then, will you tell the Major when I or either of these two come round? Without 'Aunt Genny' here, even I have no excuse to call."

"The room is accessible from the back of the house. The room the Major uses is in the front. If you're careful, you won't be seen."

"Agreed," Jan said. "Now, can we see the room?"

Isa nodded, leading them toward the butler's hall and into the kitchen. Clara was at the sink, scrubbing dishes.

"You must listen for the Major, Clara. I'm taking Edward and his friends to the cellar, but I don't want the Major to know."

"There is nothing down there anymore, *mademoiselle*. If it's wine you're looking for, you must ask that Hauptmann who came here yesterday. I saw the label myself, one of your father's own bottles!"

"Please, Clara, just listen for the Major."

Edward was at Isa's elbow as she led them through the near-empty pantry to another door at the back of the shelf-lined room.

"You see how foolish this is?" he whispered. "Someone must be on the lookout for him whenever anyone is here. And if we're caught, everyone in this household will be suspected, even Clara."

"Then we'll have to trust her to help or give her the option to leave."

"And go where? That she's been serving Germans this long suggests she has nowhere else to go."

"She has relatives in the country; she's stayed this long only because of the money my father left her."

Isa led the way down the stairs to the cooler air of the cellar. Despite the button she pressed to illuminate the room, it was like a cave. The temperature varied little through the year, with its depth and massive brick walls.

She was glad the electricity worked today, although there were oil lamps nearby just in case. She saw instantly that the cement floor was dustier than it had ever been when there was a reason to come down here, when bottles filled the empty latticework or when the shelves were crowded with barrels of cooking material. Her mother had always ordered enough provisions to host a generous party at a moment's notice.

She stopped to let the others appreciate just how safe her room was. "Look around you. See if any of you could find the entry to the room I'm offering."

They all took the challenge, spreading out to various walls. She watched Edward poke and prod, Rosalie tap, Jan bend and stretch in search of some handle or crack that might lead to another room.

Edward faced her. "Very well, Isa. You've convinced us it isn't easy to detect. That doesn't mean a German search party with picks and sledgehammers won't find it in a few moments if someone tips them off."

"But who could? If only the four of us know about this room? And Henri, and I guarantee he won't say a word."

If Edward was amused, he gave no indication. "So where is it?"

Isa had his attention and wasn't eager to lose it but moved toward the hidden door. "I don't know the entire history of this room. I'm sure Henri knows. And my father knew about it." She knelt, reaching beneath the lowest shelf, ignoring spiderwebs that might have given her pause had she not had such an important audience. She withdrew a long, sturdy rod that was undetectable without reaching under, then upward. "There were tools left behind that my father told me were diamond-cutting equipment. Evidently the former owner of this home was doing something he didn't want anyone else to know about."

Holding the rod steady, she stuck it through the latticework, scraping the brick at the back until finding the small hole into which the rod perfectly fit. Tilting it upward, she pushed until the barrier on the other side fell from its holding place. Then, after returning the rod to its hiding place, she pulled on the end of the shelf that served as a handle.

Even when Henri had first shown her and Charles the room—he'd decorated it to resemble an American West battle fort to surprise the children—she'd been able to push open this door once the iron bar was unlatched. She'd always thought it something of a miracle until Henri had shown her the latches and how they were counterbalanced.

The air was just as cool inside the room, and Isa found the switch plate to reveal its size. It wasn't especially large but was perfectly square, with sturdy cardboard painted like the logs of a fort still tacked to one wall. Equipment left by the former owner was pushed off to the side—a tall, sturdy table held small hammers and Indian ink brushes and oil, dops and cast-iron disks. In another corner were the things her parents had given her and Charles when this was their hideaway. A tea set, a miniature boat Charles had built inside a bottle, a chair for reading when Isa grew older and Charles had abandoned the solitude of the room.

The interior walls were brick, even the back side of the door. She'd felt safe in here, where no one could hear her, where only books and games awaited. Unlike Charles, she'd always welcomed being alone.

Jan stepped off the room's measurements, then reached for the ceiling to judge its height. He even knelt on the floor as if to judge the flatness. It was concrete and smooth.

"A press will fit," he announced. "We don't even have to prepare a foundation; this floor will serve. We won't have to remove anything if we take the legs off that table and lean it up against the wall." He looked squarely at Isa then, brows still level but excitement in his eyes. "I know you realize the risk, but I wonder if you realize how important this is to us. You probably haven't any clue the trouble we've had finding printer after printer. This will save the paper."

"I want to help," Isa told him but was unable to keep her gaze from Edward for long.

If Jan was excited, Edward looked somber in the opposite extreme. Rosalie stood quietly by, saying nothing. Isa wanted to be exhilarated at the prospect of being involved in the same cause, but her heart was too heavy in light of Edward's obvious disappointment.

She wanted to assure him this was the right thing to do. It was a matter of trust, and not only for her to trust the same people Edward himself trusted. It was, perhaps above all, a matter of trust in God. And it might be the best way for Edward to rediscover the trust he once had too.

"You realize, Jan, if a press is found here, it's a death sentence for Isa?"

"Edward . . ."

Isa's protest was overrun by Jan. "You see how secure this room is."

"Is it? With a German Major upstairs?" Now Edward turned to Isa. "Is it soundproof? Even if it is, what about the odor of a gas-run press? or the scent of ink? or the supplies we'll have to traipse in and out of here?"

Rosalie stood at Edward's back. "You've said over and over that all we need is a press of our own. Now you have it and won't take it. I don't understand."

He gave her only his profile. "How would we even get a press down here? Even in pieces, the casting would weigh hundreds of pounds. What do we do, just carry it in and expect no one to notice? And where do you suppose we can get such a press anyway? They're not exactly an item the Germans allow to be traded these days."

"I know of one," Rosalie said. "De Salle's. He refused to print any more issues, but he hinted he would sell the press. He hardly uses it anyway with the Germans constantly raiding his shop."

Edward looked as though he would stalk from the room, but he took only two steps away before turning back to Isa. "Think this through. If a printer is caught producing something illegal in his shop, he can at least say he did it for the money, that it was simply another job to him. But if the Germans find a press where one ought not be, a press whose type is cast and whose blocks represent none other than the newspaper they most want to destroy, they'll know they have the heart of the organization. There would be no defense, none whatsoever. And that would mean the firing squad to anyone responsible for it. This is your house, Isa. That would mean you."

She couldn't let her gaze waver, even if the surety behind his words cracked her resolve. What if it did mean her life, after all? Others had been caught. She might want to think of the Germans as bumbling when it came to detective work, but of course they weren't. Even in recent days, rumors had gone around of more arrests. What if she were found out? Was this press worth it? Or was it just "a scrap of paper," like the treaty the Germans had broken between their country and Belgium?

No. And that was where the Germans *were* bumbling. They thought that words could be meaningless, that they had the power to decide which were important.

"I know what it means, Edward. And it's worth it to me."

Edward stepped back, looked once more at the room, at Isa, at the others. "Very well."

He went to the door, holding on to the edge and waving them all out. "We cannot stay to discuss the details here. It's close to midday, and the Major may leave his room soon if he hasn't already. You'll have to go upstairs to check before the rest of us go out the back."

She nodded, then went up the stairs, all the while her heart spinning in her breast.

She'd won.

And Edward couldn't call her a child anymore, not after she'd made a decision of this importance.

18

Take heart, beloved Belgians. Though the firepower to the south and the west constantly reminds us of those laying down their lives, it is a fight for right, for justice, for freedom. One we will surely not lose.

La Libre Belgique

Isa closed her eyes, allowing every thought, every emotion, every memory of the past or concern for the future to dissolve into notes floating up to heaven. Her mind sang the words of the Lord's Prayer in silent accompaniment to the music emerging from the flute at her fingertips. *"Our Father, which art in heaven, hallowed be Thy name. Thy kingdom come, Thy will be done . . ."*

Between the words of her prayer, Edward's warnings replayed in her mind—and those from Genny, too. How dangerous it would be to house a press in one's own cellar, how the Germans wouldn't make allowances for her age or sex, how she would be as liable to stand before a firing squad as any other person found with such damning evidence beneath their roof.

If found, she'd argued that morning against all of Genny's pleas. She trusted the room's secrecy. Moreover, she trusted God.

How easily she'd claimed her faith. But was it faith that made her so sure this was the right decision? Or was housing the press merely the means by which to gain Edward's attention and trust, to work with him shoulder to shoulder, united against a common enemy? to have him see her as a peer rather than a child? Because, truly, she wanted all of that every bit as much as she wanted to be part of that paper. A noble paper, a worthy tool against German oppression. Worthy of . . . one's life.

She played a lilting melody despite the growing weight in the pit of her stomach.

Thy will be done, Lord, in my life. But was it His will? How could she know? The words echoed from her soul even as the notes from her flute eventually faded—until a voice nearby broke that line to heaven.

"That was excellently played."

Isa opened her eyes. She'd forgotten even Genny was there and hadn't noticed the Major join them at the parlor's threshold.

"Thank you." Curt words, accompanied immediately by a stab to her conscience. Scarcely a new breath taken between prayer and sin. *Forgive us our debts, as we forgive our debtors. . . .*

"I heard you playing and came down to hear better. I hope I'm not intruding?"

Genny stood, offering him her chair. "Of course not. Please, sit."

But Isa began to dismantle the instrument.

"Finished already? I came too late, then."

From behind the Major, Genny shook her head, something near a scowl on her brow.

Must she entertain a German soldier? "I can play another."

"Might I make a suggestion?"

Isa waited, still unable to spare him a glance.

"I heard you play 'O Day of Rest and Gladness' not so very long ago. I wonder if you might play that again?"

She played and the words of the hymn filled her mind in a silent serenade to the Lord, taking her away from the Major's presence, away from Brussels, away from Belgium and all its mighty troubles. Away, especially, from the fear that had begun to take shape inside. Instead she stood at the threshold of heaven, lost in the gift of music. If she was to trust God at all, especially now, she needed never to forget what prayer could do.

"Thank you," the Major whispered, and Isa looked at him at last. She did not smile, but neither could she look away—until he smiled and she thought she should offer a polite one in response. Instead she took apart her flute.

The Major leaned forward on his cane, still seated, and looked from Isa to Genny. "I was going to send your housekeeper to you with some news, but as I was lured by the music, I decided to discuss it with you both myself."

Isa glanced at Genny beside her as the Major reached inside his jacket pocket to withdraw a piece of paper.

"I received this earlier today." Unfolding it, he looked it over as if reading it again. "It seems Hauptmann Rudiger von Eckhart would like to bring Herr Lutz here for a visit. With all of the excitement from the other night, I never did get a chance to thank my friend for his help, and Hauptmann von Eckhart wishes to provide me that opportunity. He wishes . . . he wishes to bring him for dinner. Here."

Up until the last part, Isa had thought the Major perfectly at ease.

She exchanged a glance with Genny. Did she feel what Isa did? Horror? Disdain? Repulsion? How could she *not*?

Isa stood. "I'm sure if you would like to use the dining room, Clara will not mind serving you there. Although, as you know, we have little food for entertaining."

"Headquarters will send something for your maid to prepare. But I'm afraid you don't understand, Fräulein Lassone. Hauptmann von Eckhart's note expressly states his desire that you—and Frau Kirkland, of course—share dinner with us."

Isa spun around to Genny, effectively turning her back on the Major. Genny stood, pulling Isa close as she turned her around so they both faced the Major again.

"I'm sure the Hauptmann will understand our reluctance to sit at the table with officers of the occupying army?" Genny asked. "After all that has taken place?"

The Major rose with what appeared to be relative ease, as if he'd been practicing the use of his cane. "Perhaps, for the evening at least, we might put aside current events and share a meal as those who have the unfortunate role of living through such difficult times. Merely as individuals."

"Individuals, Major?" Genny said. "You mean, as people without loyalties to our own countries? In all honesty, I'm not at all certain either party could do such a thing, even for one evening."

"Yes, I suppose you are right about that." He looked down at the floor. "I was rather looking forward to forgetting quite a bit for one evening. The war, the shortages, the heartaches. The guns in the distance. I wanted to forget. That's all." He looked at Genny again. "That's all it would have been."

"Of course," Genny said slowly, "I would like to thank Herr Lutz."

Isa started to voice the obvious, that no thanks were necessary because a boy should not have had to endure a trip to St. Gilles over such a frivolous offense, but Genny still held her hand. Isa squeezed it.

"Perhaps it might be easier," the Major said, his voice growing confident, friendlier, "if you knew Herr Lutz isn't a soldier but an adviser, and so doesn't wear a uniform. He was something of a mentor to me in my younger days. Sharing dinner with him would not be unpleasant."

Genny ignored yet another squeeze to her hand, so Isa stared hard at her, willing their gazes to meet. But it was as if Isa weren't there.

"I think we might be able to share dinner. Let us know which evening it will be, Major."

Genny let go of Isa's hand and walked from the room. Isa hurried after her, and once they closed the kitchen door behind them, she stepped in front of Genny with folded arms. "You agreed to dine with them!"

Genny went around Isa to the stove. "I'm heating water. Would you like some? It's chilly today, isn't it? Some hot water will help. We're out of tea again."

"How could you, Genny? How could you share a meal with them, as if they're some kind of . . . of *guests*?"

Genny went to the sink beneath the window but didn't look out. Isa watched as the older woman closed her eyes and, after a moment, turned. She wasn't smiling, but she didn't reflect a bit of Isa's outrage.

"It's the right thing to do."

"Treating those who overran Belgium like we *want* them here? How is that right? Besides, I don't want a bunch of soldiers coming around here now that I'm going to be—" she lowered her voice— "you know, *involved*."

"Better they come around now than in a week, or the week after that, when you are, as you say, *involved*."

Isa had to admit that Genny's point was a good one. Better to get this meal over with sooner than later. "You may be right. If a meal is expected, then a meal they'll get—but that's all. This once."

❦

A fair evening sunset ended the crisp autumn day as Edward made his way to Isa's front door. From habit, he'd almost gone around to the back, but his new disguise afforded him the luxury due any guest, at least for the duration of his mother's stay.

Clara showed him in and directed him not to the parlor but to the kitchen.

"You know," he greeted Isa, who was seated at the table with his mother, "you could sit in the parlor as if you owned the place."

They laughed and Isa offered the chair closest to her. "The Major has never found his way back here. I imagine he's a snob, thinking he's too good to grace any kitchen."

Edward sat, ignoring the urge to admit he'd once thought the very same thing of her. He looked at his mother. "Has Isa talked to you about the . . . about things?"

Clara hadn't followed him, but his mother glanced toward the door nonetheless. "I know you are against this, Edward, and I agree with you. But Isa's determined."

"How soon will you be returning to Viole's?"

She didn't speak for a moment. "We talked about that. I've already spoken to Jonah, and he seems pleased. Some of the boys in this neighborhood still blame him for the trouble they were in when they were taken to St. Gilles. He's eager to return to his old friends."

"Good. But, Mother . . . I didn't entirely hear what I wanted. You are returning as well, isn't that right?"

"Of course she is, Edward. We talked about it this morning."

Edward noticed his mother's gaze shoot between him and Isa. Nervously.

She pursed her lips. "Actually, Isa, I've been giving that further thought."

Edward tensed. "What further thought is needed? None. I don't want either of you here, but Isa is as mule-headed as ever and won't leave. Now you, Mother—you have far more sense than she has, so I expect you to follow through and return to Viole's with Jonah. The sooner, the better."

Instead of nodding, or at least losing that somewhat nervous, somewhat-apologetic look on her face, his mother reached across the table and took one of his hands. "Edward—"

"No!" He pulled away before her hand had barely touched his and stood so fast the chair behind him teetered. "I won't have it. Isa's idea is foolish enough without endangering more lives."

Both women left the table to stand near him, so close he could barely think.

"Do you know what Isa said to me this morning, Edward? That it's God's position to protect us. Isn't this press something He would support? Doesn't Scripture itself tell us to bring comfort to those in need? And doesn't Belgium deserve—?"

"Don't talk to me about reasons to become involved, Mother. I believe in it too. But I also happen to believe you've given enough to the war effort—in the life of my father. Haven't I, hasn't Jonah, too, without risking your life as well?"

She laid a hand on his arm. "You're right, of course, but think of the day-to-day challenges. Isa will need all the help she can get to distract the Major from what's happening, not to mention that my presence gives you a reason to come and go as you please. And besides all that, with the way things have become . . . Clara tells me the Germans are taking men again." She turned away and clutched the corner of the table. "I won't stand by and watch women lose their husbands, their sons, the way . . ."

Then her shoulders wobbled and he could tell she'd given in to tears.

He stepped closer, bolstering those shoulders by drawing her close. "I know you have every bit as much reason as I do to want to keep this paper going, but it's too dangerous. I won't have you involved. I won't."

She pulled away, looking up at him, then stretched out a hand to Isa. "We'll do it together, each of us, a rope of three cords."

Edward accepted Isa into the three-way embrace, but their resolve did nothing to ease his fear. He could see his mother was as stubborn as Isa, and short of calling in the Germans, there would be no changing their minds. He couldn't fight both of them and Jan and Rosalie too.

There was no turning back now. He freed himself of them and stepped back with one last hope that words would come to make them see reason.

None did.

"I've spoken to Rosalie, who arranged for the sale of the press. They say it will be ready on Wednesday morning. So as I see it, I have until then to change your minds."

He saw a strange look pass over both women's faces.

"Wednesday?" Isa's voice sounded as uncertain as a child's, something he hadn't heard from her since her return.

He nodded.

"Well, as it happens," his mother said, "we're to entertain that evening."

"Entertain? No one entertains anymore. What are you talking about?"

Isa put a hand over Edward's, a warning touch if ever he'd felt one. "The Major has invited Herr Lutz here to dine. He is the German who helped to bring Jonah home."

"There, I told you this was a mistake! Especially if that Major will be inviting guests with any sort of regularity."

"Clara tells me he isn't prone to entertaining, and we've certainly seen no evidence of it."

"Yes, this is a onetime affair," Isa added.

"Well, there isn't anything we can do about it, is there? What will Clara serve him from a near-empty kitchen?"

"The Major said they would send something from the Kommandantur," his mother said.

Edward stroked his chin. Perhaps this could work in their favor. "So there will be people coming here during the day? If they're bringing in things for their dinner, perhaps they won't notice a few extra boxes and one rather large, heavy crate that *we* bring in."

"Oh, Edward." His mother's brows drew together. "Not in broad daylight?"

"Nighttime would draw too much suspicion, particularly from the Major himself. As they say, the best place to hide is under the nose of the *Polizei*. What time is this dinner to begin?"

"Eight o'clock."

"How many?"

"Two, that we know of," Genny answered. "Besides the Major, of course."

Isa touched his hand again, drawing his attention from the plans swirling through his mind. "But, Edward, you do understand that it's not only the Major who will be sharing this dinner? Your mother and I will be required to sit at the table as well."

One of his ears started ringing; he wasn't sure he'd heard her correctly. "What was that?"

Now his mother touched his other hand, and both of his ears began ringing. "Yes, Isa and I will be expressing our gratitude for Jonah's return."

His fingertips tingled with a rush of adrenaline, all he would need to thrust a fist into a wall or at a face. A German face. If only he could. "Who are his guests?"

"Herr Lutz and Hauptmann von Eckhart."

The Hauptmann's name defined which German face Edward most wanted to assault. He glanced at Isa. "Why von Eckhart?"

"It was he who sent the note arranging everything."

Edward had a fair estimation of why. Blast it all, why had she ever come back? "That leaves me with one option. Mother, best tell the Major that your nephew Father Antoine would like to join the party."

Then he turned toward the door. He didn't have time to spare if he was to set their plans in motion.

19

Rumor has it the Germans will stop the revictualing. Let them! And see what hunger in the bellies of already-oppressed Belgians will drive other countries to do in our defense. Keep heart.

La Libre Belgique

Isa glanced at the timepiece on her vanity. Nearly ten o'clock in the morning. She studied her reflection, marginally satisfied with what she saw: light hair pinned in a loose knot, a few tendrils tickling her neck, exposed by the wide, box-cut neckline of her gown. It was a burgundy day dress, trimmed close at the waist. She and Genny had decided to take special care with their appearance this morning—anything to divert unwanted attention from the delivery.

Swallowing the jittery burst of nerves that threatened to wreak havoc on her insides, she retrieved her flute and brought it to the music room just down the hall.

She stopped, as usual, near the Major's room to listen for any sound. The rhythm of labored breathing came through, something she often heard when he exercised. She'd caught a glimpse of him once when his nurse was there with the door open. He'd been on the floor with one hand behind his back as if counterbalancing the foot that was missing while he pushed himself up, then down, over and again. She guessed he was doing that now.

Isa found Genny in the kitchen with Henri.

"Good morning," Isa said, instantly noticing Genny's flattering gown, another Isa didn't recall her mother ever wearing. It was midnight blue, with a high collar and long sleeves, yet its modesty and simplicity of cut complemented her femininity and grace. Her hair, like Isa's, was up, braided and twisted at the back.

However, the entire look was compromised by her frown. "What is it?"

"It's Clara."

"What's wrong?"

"She isn't here. Her sister is ill, and Clara left to tend her."

The nerves inside Isa zeroed in on her stomach. "What?"

"She promised to be back in time to cook."

Isa spun around, looking out the kitchen window. "Who cares about that? Those Germans can send a cook along with all their goods; I don't care. Or cook it themselves! It's the delivery I'm worried about. We *need* her to watch for the sentries." Nothing could go wrong today. Nothing!

"I suppose we should have warned her instead of waiting until the last moment. Besides, she was bound to wonder about all of this. Perhaps it's best she isn't here at all. The less she knows, the better. I will sit alone with the Major. He'll stay for a piano performance without the flute. It's still music, isn't it?"

Isa took a deep breath. "All right." Then she caught Henri's concerned look.

He neared them, gesturing toward Isa to pray. Suddenly he seemed more concerned over her behavior than Clara's absence.

"He's absolutely right," Genny said. "It's a good reminder for both of us. We'll pray our way through this day, Isa."

Isa nodded and another quiver shot through her, this time of gratitude that God cared enough to have surrounded her with people to help her stay close to His side. Surely what they were about to do *was* the right decision. She needed to remind herself of that and tell Genny, too.

"Genny, just one thing eased my mind last night. If Edward really thinks God has abandoned Belgium, then when everything goes well, might he realize how wrong he's been? that he can trust God to protect us instead of trying to do it all himself?"

Nearly an hour later, Isa stood at the kitchen window alone, waiting for a delivery. Any delivery, German or otherwise. So far not even the goods for the dinner had arrived.

Clara had not returned, though she'd sent her nephew with a message that she would be home in plenty of time to prepare the meal for that evening. From her vantage point, Isa couldn't see far past the garden or down the alleyway. She saw trees, low bushes, the stone fence. The tops of other homes nearby.

And then, through the gently swaying, colorful branches of the beech tree, she saw the top of a wagon. It rambled down the narrow artery at a slow pace, far slower than the rate of Isa's heart. Not surprisingly these days, an ox pulled the wagon rather than a horse. Just as well; he made the load look light.

Getting the press this far had succeeded. That counted the mission nearly half-complete.

Isa saw the driver as he pulled the rig up to the gate. His face was darkened by a bushy beard streaked with gray, thick matching brows. But Isa would know Edward anywhere, from the curve of his shoulders to the length of his arms. Rosalie had outdone herself this time. No one would recognize this wizened old man as the young man Isa loved.

Edward coughed and spit on the pavement, then stepped down

with all the care of an older man. Isa could no longer see him then, but she did see Henri emerge from his room above the carriage house. She folded her arms in front of her, itching to go outside.

Oh, Lord, watch over us now!

Genny played the piano as she'd never played before. The act was as much a prayer as it was a production. Only by keeping her mind on the Lord could she banish the tremor making her nearly fumble every chord. Only by prayer could she remember the notes—notes she hadn't played in over two years.

She was grateful she hadn't needed to knock on the Major's door with an invitation. Genny hadn't liked that idea from its inception, less so when knowing she must occupy him on her own. He'd joined her not long after she'd begun, as if it had been his own idea to leave his room and find her just down the hall.

The hymn ended and she began another. Delivery of the press must be under way by now. Years without playing soon evaporated as her fingers found their way across the keys to the tune of "Nearer My God to Thee."

Isa stepped aside to allow Edward and Henri access to the pantry, each carrying a box. "Henri will take these down to the room," Edward said. "Then he'll help me bring the casting in if there's no one around. It's too heavy for either of us alone. You'll have to stand watch outside, Isa."

Isa made her way to the wagon. She looked both ways, seeing no one near. But when Edward turned quickly on his heel and motioned her to silence, she looked frantically around.

And then she saw him. A German sentry coming round from the back of the wagon.

"Where did all this food come from?" he inquired, first in German and then in broken French.

"Kommandantur." Edward's voice was raspy as he turned his back on the sentry and started lifting another box. "Just this one," he said to Isa. "The rest go to the courthouse."

"We are hosting Herr Lutz from the Kommandantur tonight." Isa, proud of imitating confidence she didn't feel, hoped the name would mean something. "We're expecting a second delivery any moment. Wine, you know."

The soldier lifted a brow, duly impressed. He raised a hand to lift the top of the box in Edward's arms, but Edward turned just in time to avoid the contact, as if he hadn't noticed the soldier's intentions.

"Just a moment." He came to stand in front of Edward and opened the box. Isa peered around him to see what he would find.

Potatoes.

He chose one and Isa held her breath, hoping they'd put more than one layer over the parts below.

The soldier tossed the potato in the air, catching it and taking a bite. Then he saluted with it and went on his way.

Edward took the box inside but Isa stayed, watching until the man turned the corner and was out of view.

Genny's fingers and arms tired, unused to the service she demanded. But she played another anyway, and by the end she knew she would have to rest or the Major would wonder what drove her to perform even when stiff fingers would not obey.

The last note stumbled from her fingertips, and then she glanced the Major's way, embarrassed. "I'm sorry. It's been a long time since I've played."

"No apology necessary," he said. "I've thoroughly enjoyed it."

"Thank you, but it must be for lack of hearing anyone truly talented lately that you could have enjoyed my attempt."

"Nonsense," he insisted. "You play very well."

She shifted her position and stretched her arms and fingers, sending the tingles away.

"You're tired." He motioned to the chair beside him. "Please, come and sit. May I fetch Clara for some tea?"

"No—I don't believe Clara is at home. She's visiting her sister, who is ill."

"Oh?" He appeared mildly interested, then concerned. "I wonder if tonight's dinner might be better postponed, then?"

"I'm sure we'll manage, even if Isa and I do the cooking."

"I would be flattered, except my guess is you'd rather have the evening over than prolong the inevitable. Is that it?"

She hoped honesty was worth the risk of offending him and nodded. "I cannot help but admire your French, Major. You speak very well."

He bowed his head briefly. "My grandmother was French and taught me when I was a child. Then, when I was a university student, I spoke nothing but French."

"In which language are you most comfortable?"

"German, I suppose. Yet in many ways I like French better. Its cadence, its rhythm. I count in French. I think in German." He shifted his whole body to face her, rather than just turning his head her way. "What about you, *madame*? What languages do you speak?"

"I was reared to speak English, of course, but my father was a great lover of language. He insisted we speak French and Flemish as well. My grandmother was Belgian."

"And which language do you prefer?" His voice was soft, almost intimate, as if they were discussing something far more personal than languages.

"Most of my life I've spoken English, until coming here more than ten years ago. I raised my children on English, and . . . well, it simply has more words with which to express myself more precisely. So, English, I suppose."

"Ah. A good reason to learn the language, then." He smiled. "And when you've cut your finger or stubbed your toe, in which language do you curse?"

The topic suddenly seemed to match that intimate tone and yet she found herself answering lightly. "I may struggle with other sins, Major, but cursing is not one of them. Not part of my language education, I suppose."

"Do you struggle with sin, Frau Kirkland? You appear a model of virtue."

"Of course I struggle like everyone else."

"But what are your struggles?"

She looked at him, amazed she wasn't walking from the room at such a bold question. Amazed she didn't want to. "May I speak freely?"

"Please."

"I struggle with self-pity because my husband, whom I loved, was taken from me too soon and unjustly. And I struggle with resentment because every day I must see German soldiers. I know that any one of them might have been the one who shot him."

The Major sighed, leaning back in his chair. "Yes," he said at last, "yes, I can see that would be difficult."

The topic had grown too somber, and Genny wished nothing more than to depart but knew she couldn't, not until Isa joined them.

She shouldn't have allowed their discussion to grow so sour.

"Would you like me to play again?"

"No." He smiled at her again as he finished the word. "I would like to hear you play more, and I hope that I might soon, but I'm enjoying our conversation. It's been a lonely recuperation, you know, with only a nurse visiting now and then to see that I'm still alive. Do you mind?"

She shook her head, confused because she meant it.

"You said you raised *children*, Frau Kirkland. More than Jonah?"

"Yes, well, I meant Isa as well, although she isn't my daughter." And then, because she was afraid he might somehow already know or could easily find out from Kommandantur records, she added, "And I had two sons."

"Where is the other?"

"He—he's no longer with me."

Glad he didn't press the issue, she searched for another topic, but when she looked up, he seemed to be thinking of something else, staring straight ahead as if his thoughts replaced the conversation he'd claimed he wanted to extend.

"I had two sons as well. Only two years apart, and so alike many thought them twins. Strong, tall boys. Handsome." Then he grinned. "Fair appearances skip—every other generation, I used to say."

"What happened?" But she already knew.

"It's what's happened to every family, on both sides, since the beginning of this war. All our boys will be gone if it doesn't soon end."

"Were . . . both . . . ?"

He nodded and she very nearly reached out to touch him but held back.

Suddenly he struggled to his feet, his back to her. He didn't move nearly as smoothly as he had lately. "Yes, well, this war is what it is. None are pleasant, so I've been told."

She stood as well, afraid he was ready to leave. "I'm sorry for your loss."

"Thank you." Leaning forward on his cane, he faced her again. He seemed to want to smile, but the effort in the small twitch to one side of his mouth seemed greater than the result. "It appears all we have to talk about is sadness. I'm sorry for that. I would have liked to know you apart from this war."

Her own smile felt odd on her face, awkward, almost shy. Things she hadn't felt in years. "I don't suppose we would have had much opportunity for that, would we?" She might have mentioned he could have been a guest at her hotel, but it only reminded her of what his army had cost her, so she said nothing.

"No, I'm sure you're right."

Just then Genny saw Isa at the door and wondered how long she'd been standing there. Her cheeks grew warm and she looked away, ashamed she'd been caught enjoying this man's company.

"Has Clara returned?" Genny asked.

"Yes, actually, she's just come home."

"Ah, so the evening is saved," the Major said.

Genny started to move toward Isa, intending to go downstairs, where she was expected to help in the kitchen. But the Major briefly touched her arm.

"Frau Kirkland." His voice was so quiet she leaned forward to hear better. "I wish to say one more thing, if I may?"

Genny looked at Isa, who waited. "I'll be down in a moment."

Obvious confusion ruffled Isa's brow. "Yes, well, Clara will probably need both of us. The Kommandantur delivered more than she expected."

Genny nodded but did not move, only watched as Isa turned and left.

"I don't mean to keep you," the Major said. "Just long enough to tell you . . ." He hesitated as if carefully choosing his words. "To tell you that when the war broke out, I was not with those who marched through Belgium. I was in Germany training new recruits. It wasn't until late '15 that I was reassigned to the front, near Ypres, where I was wounded. I came to Brussels only months ago."

She said nothing, just took a small step away, toward the door.

"I don't want you to wonder, *madame*," he said gently after her, "if I was that soldier, the one who killed your husband. It was not I."

20

It is said the German spirit admires bravery of the small against the great, that they hold in esteem the Spartans against the Persians, David against Goliath. Yet in Belgium, Germany has become the very thing she previously abhorred.

La Libre Belgique

Isa sat on her favorite chair in the parlor. Yet neither the plush cushion nor the fine Belgian fabric offered comfort tonight because she sat so stiffly she barely felt the padded flowery upholstery beneath her.

Sitting above an illegal press, even one not yet assembled, would have been bad enough. But the Major sat in another Queen Anne not far off, and Genny nearby. Edward as Father Antoine had not yet arrived, but he, along with the rest of their "guests," was expected at any moment. Fatigue from a day fraught with tension left Isa raw, as if the slightest jab to her senses would be too much to bear.

She nearly jumped from her seat when the ringer sounded. She'd instructed Clara not to leave the kitchen and so, praying Edward would arrive first, Isa hurried to answer the call.

Hauptmann von Eckhart stood tall and handsome, with a smile so easy on his face Isa could barely look at him. She had little choice but to step aside and let him in, along with another, older man at his side.

"Mademoiselle Isa Lassone, may I present to you Herr Stephan Lutz."

Isa received their stiff bows in greeting. Only the Hauptmann was bold enough to kiss her hand, but she'd prepared herself for that and did not pull away.

"I shall take your coats," Isa said, following the Hauptmann's lead with her usage of the French language.

"Is there no one serving this house?" Herr Lutz asked, also in French, as he unbuttoned his coat.

"Yes, but our housemaid is in the kitchen finishing preparations for our meal." Need she explain that no one had money to keep servants these days? That it was only Clara's loyalty—and whatever money she still had left from Isa's father—that kept her here?

Isa received their coats and went to the closet on the other side of the staircase, where she took her time putting things away. There was no hurry to join the others, at least until Edward arrived.

Genny and Major von Bürkel stood with the visitors when Isa returned to the parlor. The Major spoke in heavy, ugly German, obviously pleased to be reunited with his older friend.

Herr Lutz had a pedantic look about him, like a science professor who could name every law of physics but would be hard-pressed to remember a single student's name. He was of medium height, with gray hair too long at the back and a beard that needed a trim. Obviously too busy with other matters to tend to something as trivial as his own appearance.

In a bizarre imitation of prewar days, Isa watched the exchange of pleasantries as if this were another dinner party her parents hosted in this very parlor. Isa should be friendly and talkative if she was to play the role her mother had modeled all too often, but how could she? Her mother may have entertained people she secretly disliked, but surely she'd never hosted marauders under this roof.

It was near time to serve and Edward had not yet arrived.

"Have you enjoyed Max's company since you resumed living here?" the Hauptmann asked, now speaking in French.

Company! Isa stole a glance at the Major. *Max.* Such a different sound from *Major von Bürkel.*

"He's been very kind," Genny said.

Isa was glad Genny had answered for her. Her gaze went once again toward the door. Where *was* Edward?

Clara came to Isa's side to remind her the meal was ready to be served, and Isa knew she couldn't stall and in fact didn't want to. The sooner this was over, the better. Edward would have to join them in the dining room, whenever he arrived.

Among the goods delivered earlier that day had been several bottles of wine, one for each course of the meal and one for an *apéritif.* All, so Clara claimed, from Isa's own wine cellar. Clara had huffed and puffed all afternoon, in between oohing and aahing about all of the food, especially the fresh dairy.

She and Genny had planned a meal no one had dared dream of for the past two years. Isa had done what she could—which was little, having had no training—but had enjoyed tasting sauces, stealing crisp vegetables, breathing in the scent of fresh dinner rolls all afternoon. It had taken her mind, for a little while, away from fretting over what they'd hidden in the cellar.

Place settings beckoned on each side of the narrow table in the long, dimly lit room. The electricity had flickered all afternoon and so Genny suggested candlelight. Under its gentle glow glimmered china and plain flatware—the silver having disappeared long ago—upon an embroidered cloth, with hothouse flowers set in a small bowl in the center. Candle sconces on the walls made shadows dance behind each place setting. Only one seat, next to Isa's, was vacant.

Herr Lutz stared at the open spot. "We have set a place for those we remember at war?"

"A nice sentiment," Isa said, "but we are expecting one more guest. Madame Kirkland's nephew, Father Antoine."

"Father Antoine? A man of the cloth?"

Isa nodded. The German's face revealed little; she couldn't tell if he was pleased or disappointed to share the table with a priest.

"Yes, quite a young priest, this Father Antoine. I spoke to him the other night." The Hauptmann laughed. "He said God doesn't care who wins the war."

That statement raised Herr Lutz's bushy brows and Isa's too. She wished she could have heard Edward speak of God.

"He is a Walloon priest, this Father Antoine?" Herr Lutz asked.

Genny nodded. The false name Edward had chosen left little choice.

"Then he is loyal to the French. When Germany wins the war, the only way to hold on to his faith will be to say God doesn't care."

Prickles stiffened Isa's back.

"Since he is not here to explain the point," the Major said, "I suppose none of us can ultimately agree or disagree."

The ringer echoed again. No one had taken their seats, and so Isa excused herself and went to the door. She liked having a duty, especially one taking her from their guests, if only for a moment.

"Oh, you're here at last! We were starting to worry."

Edward took off his biretta. "I'm sorry. I was stopped yet again for a search."

"We've just gone into the dining room. I'll put your hat away."

They entered the dining room together. The others still stood near their seats and Isa made introductions as she showed Edward to his chair.

"I see I've arrived just in time to invite the blessing of the Lord,"

Edward said, and Isa couldn't resist exchanging a pleased glance with Genny.

Edward prayed a brief blessing, a prayer wisely free of reference to the war.

"Before you arrived, we were just discussing you, Father," the Hauptmann said as Clara served the meal. "And your opinion that God is neither Allied nor Central in sympathy."

"Quite the contrary, Hauptmann," Edward said. "I believe we all have a great deal of God's sympathy. We are, after all, quite pathetic these days."

There was the barest moment of awkward silence, followed by a laugh from the Major that others soon joined.

"With all respect, Father Antoine," the Hauptmann said, "why would God have sympathy? for that matter, even give us a thought?"

"The answer is simple." Edward turned to Clara and took a small portion of the first course of creamed scallops to his plate. "Love."

That seemed to catch Herr Lutz's attention. "That's a rather sentimental answer, even for a man of the cloth."

"Perhaps," Edward said, "but it's also scriptural, so I shall stand by my answer."

With Edward at her side, Isa found it easier playing hostess. "Tell me, Herr Lutz, how is it that a civilian like you finds himself working at the Kommandantur?"

"My capacity is as adviser between the military and civilian personnel."

"We were grateful for your help in having my son returned, Herr Lutz," Genny said.

"I was pleased to be of service."

There. As far as Isa was concerned, the meal could end immediately, purpose served.

"Where is Jonah?" the Major asked, as if he'd just realized the boy was not in attendance.

"Jonah has gone to live with a close friend of the family," Genny said. "He misses his friends and asked if he could return to his old neighborhood for a while."

"So you will be apart from your son after all," the Hauptmann said.

"He is only minutes away."

Edward raised his glass of wine. "A bit more accessible than St. Gilles, wouldn't you agree?"

The Hauptmann did not reply.

"And you, Hauptmann?" Genny inquired. "Are you in Brussels on leave from the front?"

He shook his head. "No, this is now my permanent station. I am needed here. My civilian background is in law, and I work at the Palais de Justice."

Herr Lutz patted his napkin to his moustache. "It is good of you to invite us here this evening. General Freiherr von Bissing is most eager to improve Brussels society, and it must start with those like you, models of the community."

"Then you may tell him, Herr Lutz," Edward said, "he would do best in that regard by stopping the deportations of men from the provinces."

Isa's prayer that no offense be taken was as quick as her glance between the two men proving offense had already been exchanged.

Herr Lutz twirled his wineglass between taut fingers, his gaze anything but amused. "There are a great number of unemployed men in Belgium, Father Antoine. Surely since you are exempt from either idleness caused by England's blockade or deportation itself, you can at least appreciate what the General hopes to accomplish? To spare Belgium more mouths to feed, to improve the economy by putting men to work? To make sure the habit of work is not lost? Idle hands are the devil's tools, as your brethren remind us."

Edward's fork lingered over the steamed potatoes. "As to mouths to be fed, English and American generosity has addressed that. Though for how much longer, who can say, if they determine Germany must take on the burden as punishment for deporting men. And as to improving the economy and addressing idleness, once the men may work for Belgium rather than Germany, you will find them eager to expend the last ounce of their energy."

"I understand your reluctance toward change. It will take longer than just a few short years for General von Bissing to be appreciated for the leader he is, at least by Belgians. Perhaps not until well after the war."

"I'm sure we all long for the end of the war," Isa said.

"Perhaps we should generalize our topic so as not to offend our hostesses." The Hauptmann glanced Isa's way first, then settled his gaze on Edward. "Tell me, Father Antoine, what inspired you to take up the priesthood? I myself have always thought of God as nothing more than an illusion."

"An illusion suggests one has seen *something*, Hauptmann. And as I've never seen God, I'm afraid I devote my life to Him based upon something even less than that: pure faith."

"Life itself points to an evolutionary process," Herr Lutz said, "one in which there is no need for faith, for man-made religions. Survival of the fittest is a cruel truth, as this war will prove."

"Do you mean to say war is some kind of biological experiment?" Edward asked.

"It can be broken down to that, of course. For the sake of the species, the less advanced must step aside for the superior. For example, if an engineer develops a machine that is more productive than the one it replaces, he naturally stops using the less-effective machine. So it is with man. The best should be preserved and allowed to

impose its orders and social organizations upon the less advanced—
to replace or, if need be, destroy them."

He spoke so matter-of-factly he could have been discussing anything. Anything, that is, except the societies of man—of people, of
families, of men and women and children.

"Well," Edward replied, "you've certainly fit man into a machine,
haven't you?"

"What more is he than that?"

"It's a rather lonely viewpoint," Isa said, "don't you think, Herr
Lutz? If man is nothing more than a machine, then what is it all
for?"

"For the propagation of the race, of course."

"With or without love," Genny said. "With or without God."

"Let me understand correctly." Edward leaned back in his chair.
"Whichever army wins this war will prove that army is on the right
evolutionary track? And the army that loses, being unfit, will be
destroyed for the *good* of the rest of us?"

"This is only natural, Father Antoine. Biological factors control
our destinies, not some distant god who tampers now and then
with the little toys he's made. It is, of course, biologically certain
that Germany will win."

"And if not? If the Allies win?"

The Hauptmann lifted his wineglass. "Then I, for one, would
rather die in the melee than live in a world so resistant to natural
law."

"Your views leave little room for human virtue," Genny said.
"If it is only the fit who are destined to survive, then what good is
virtue?" She looked at Herr Lutz. "Yet I know you are not without
mercy. You were quick to see the injustice regarding my son."

"Freeing your son was a military decision. I believe the way to win
this war is on the battlefield alone. Imprisoning children, deporting
women to work camps, sinking ships with civilians aboard—these

are not sound military decisions. We might as well do the recruiting for the Allies ourselves with such deeds."

"And deporting men, tearing them from their families?" Edward asked. "Using them in the war effort against their own countrymen?"

"As I explained already, inviting men to work is a sound economic decision. Men are needed for a variety of work in Germany. We Germans are not the first, nor I'm sure the last, to employ such methods."

"Have you heard of the painter Paul Gauguin, Herr Lutz?" Edward asked.

Herr Lutz nodded.

"This house once boasted a painting by him." Edward looked at the blank wall at the end of the room even as Isa glanced his way. All these years he'd been more observant of her home than she'd thought. "It used to hang there, but it's gone now."

"Are you suggesting someone stole it?"

"I mention him because I have read a little of his life. He left his family to search for what was called the 'noble savage.' The *natural* man, like the one to whom you refer with your biological laws. The one untouched by society's restrictions, who would, Gauguin thought, display the natural goodness of man, an unspoiled example of individual freedom from laws, from responsibilities, even from God. But all he found were cruelty of a different kind and more death. To his last painting, he was always in search of answers— from where do we come, what *are* we, and to where do we go? I think we all must ask ourselves these questions and ask God to help us find the answers. Because, after all, God *is* searching for those who seek Him, whether we believe it or not."

"I couldn't agree more," Isa said.

21

Some things are best kept at a distance. A German, for example.
La Libre Belgique

"I will get your things," Isa said as they emerged from the parlor a short while after dinner ended.

The tension had gradually lifted, or perhaps she'd only gotten used to it by the time Clara had served coffee—real coffee—and custard pie sweetened with *sugar*. She rounded the far side of the staircase for the closet in which she'd earlier placed their paraphernalia.

It was dark except for the moonlight shining through the window in the door behind her. Without lighting a lamp, she found the coats and the Hauptmann's helmet and gloves along with Herr Lutz's felt hat resting on the shelf.

"I will help you with those."

Startled, Isa turned to see Hauptmann von Eckhart. Instead of reaching for the items in the tight quarters of an alcove meant for a single servant, he stepped close.

"It's no trouble." She was determined to make the statement true. She held the heavy headpiece between them, only one thing on her mind now: returning to the parlor, which from here was both out of sight and sound.

But the Hauptmann gently pushed aside the helmet so that they stood with nothing in between. So close his breath skimmed her neck.

"I know how to obtain the painting taken from your dining room."

She gave a timid laugh, but it sounded strange, like someone else's. "It really doesn't matter, Hauptmann. I never cared for it."

His hand touched her shoulder, one finger slipping beyond the edge of her gown to graze the skin at the base of her neck. "It must be worth something, since the artist is dead and won't be adding to anyone's collection now."

She took a small step to the side, clinging to the cold metal helmet he'd refused to accept. "I do not care."

She took another step just as he grabbed her hand, and the helmet rolled from her arms, landing with a dull thunk on the hard wooden floor.

"I don't think you understand," he whispered, closing the gap between them again. "I could be of great help to you. See that you are always fed, always warm, always safe. I am offering you my protection."

"How very kind of you, but really, we're fine under the protection of the Hague Convention. We may not often enjoy the kind of meal we had this evening, but we're not starving. The CRB is seeing to that."

"Then, as a token of our friendship, I hope that I may call on you?"

"Friendship, Hauptmann? Conversation at the dinner table proved how different we are. Friends usually have something in common."

"Perhaps you can convert me to your beliefs." Now he had her by both arms, holding her in a grip from which she couldn't pull away. Not without a fight.

She glanced beyond his shoulder, wondering what would happen if she screamed. "I shall pray for that very thing. Unceasingly. Now if you'll let go—"

But he did not. Instead, he lowered his face, and as his mouth neared hers, his grip loosened while his lips came down on hers. Jerking away, she did what came naturally, without thought to consequence—she raised her hand to strike. The slap sounded sharp and definite just as shadows approached. From the corner of her eye, Isa saw the silhouettes of Edward in his priest's garb and the Major behind him.

The Hauptmann stepped back, his jaw hard, lips now taut. He bent to reach his fallen helmet and brushed past Edward, who barely had time to step aside, not acknowledging the Major, who looked on with concern.

Edward stepped toward Isa, placing his hands gently on her arms where the Hauptmann had held her a moment ago. "Are you all right?"

She nodded. "Yes, yes. He—he was rude, nothing more."

The Major stepped closer as well, his brows drawn. "He does not represent his regiment well. I'm sorry if he offended you."

The Hauptmann's regiment was part of *their* army. She wished them all gone . . . from the Hauptmann to von Bissing. That included the Major. "I hope the Hauptmann will not be back in this house."

"No," the Major said, frowning. "He will not be invited again."

Edward retrieved the hat, still on the floor along with the fallen gloves, then took Isa's elbow with his free hand. Only Herr Lutz stood at the door with Genny nearby.

Herr Lutz accepted his things. "Von Eckhart left in a hurry," he said in German to the Major. "Did he misbehave once more?"

The Major said nothing, but that seemed a satisfactory answer for the other man. Herr Lutz bowed stiffly Isa's way, thanking her for the evening. Then he left.

Finally the door closed and their "guests" were gone. Isa began a deep breath, but her gaze fell on the Major. Too soon for that breath of relief.

As if he'd read her thoughts, he moved toward the base of the stairs. But he turned to Genny before battling the sixteen steps ahead of him. "I wish to thank you—all of you—for an entertaining evening. I bid you good night, then."

No one spoke, and as he topped the stairs using the polished walnut railing, Genny turned away. She went toward the kitchen. "I'm going to help Clara," she said over her shoulder, as if leaving it up to Isa and Edward whether they would join her or not.

Isa followed, and so did Edward.

"Since I'm here," Edward whispered to Isa once they were well away from the Major, "I'll work on refitting the press. Send Clara out of the kitchen so she won't notice where I'm going."

That proved easy with so many abandoned dishes still left to retrieve from the dining room. Both Isa and Genny offered to help, and Edward was gone when they came back to the kitchen.

It was quite late by the time the kitchen was neat again. Clara thanked them for their help before excusing herself for the night.

Alone with Genny, Isa said, "I found it interesting that God chose Edward to defend Him tonight, didn't you?"

"He's not letting go, is He?"

Isa shook her head, looking toward the pantry door. "Will you wait up for him with me?"

"No, I'm tired. Go downstairs; tell him he needs to leave before it gets too late."

Isa had hoped for an excuse to wait for Edward, but this was better. A reason to join him.

So she went down the stairs, noiselessly letting herself into the secret room. Edward stood on an upturned crate above the main casting of what looked to be a bigger press than she'd expected.

"Have you ever noticed this little opening up here next to the light? What room is above here?" No greeting, just the question.

"The dining room. Or the butler's hall. I can't be sure."

"And above that?"

"That would most likely be the music room."

"I'd like to take a look there."

"What will you be searching for? I might be of some help."

"I have a feeling that opening might have served as some kind of warning system for those who used this room before us."

"Henri can show us if he knows."

Edward returned his attention to the pieces in front of him, having placed them in some sort of order. "We'll have to test for noise once we have it running, perhaps use mattresses to absorb the sound if necessary. Have you any extra that won't be missed?"

"I'd offer the Major's, but . . ."

Edward didn't laugh. He kept himself bent over the parts.

"There may be something in the attic. But, Edward . . . I wanted to tell you I admired what you said tonight. About God."

He didn't respond; she couldn't see his face at all.

"Did it ever occur to you," she said quietly, "that God is pursuing *you*, and that's why He gave you the opportunity to defend Him tonight?"

Edward stood to his full height, only an arm's length away and nearly as high as the ceiling while standing on the crate. He looked down at Isa with an expression she'd seen before, one that said she was pestering him. "Isa, whatever I said tonight wasn't because of faith. It was out of hatred. For them. I knew if I was on God's side, I wouldn't be on their side. I doubt God used me as a mouthpiece with that in my heart."

She lifted a brow. "I believe somewhere in the New Testament, St. Paul says he doesn't care why the gospel is being preached, only that it's being preached."

Edward ignored her and returned to his task, hovering above the press where he could reach more of its surface.

There was but one thing to do. Act the pest he believed her to be. "I don't know why God spared you from that camp when He let the others die. Maybe we'll never know. How can we know the mind of God? But I do know I'm grateful, and so is your mother. I don't think we could have survived losing you with so many years of our own lives left ahead of us."

Edward stopped what he was doing. She saw his hands become still, but he kept his back to her. "You worry too much about me."

"It isn't worry. It's sadness. Because I know that nothing . . . neither height nor depth nor any other creature shall be able to separate you from the love of God. . . . And it must sadden Him that you don't think Him worthy to be trusted anymore."

Nothing. No response, no interest in her words.

"Have you no fear of God anymore?" She rounded the press so she could see his face but still he didn't look at her. "Would you like to know what I'm beginning to think? That you're prideful. You think you can do a better job running things than God can."

His gaze shot once to hers, but he said nothing, only picked up a tool.

"You've backed yourself into a corner where your only company is pride. You *haven't* stopped believing in God. Only you're angry He didn't answer your prayers to save those other men from the camps. You're angry He took your father when your mother and Jonah—and *you*—need him more than you've ever needed him in your life."

Edward dropped whatever tool he'd held and it landed with a clank that made Isa jump. "You've spent some time guessing!" His eyes were black, brows trying to hide them in the fiercest frown. "It's actually worse than that. I believed in God because that's what my father taught me. He raised me on the pure milk of God's Word. He believed every bit of it. But do you know what else he believed in? Pacifism! That mankind could solve differences through things like the Hague Convention, not with guns. Spend our national money on social reform; give it to the poor—do anything except spend it on an unnecessary army. We all know now what a fool he was to believe that. Maybe he was a fool to believe the rest, too."

Isa stared, eyes wide, but didn't interrupt.

"He was wrong, my father. All those years he lived with the honor and respect of everyone who knew him—and he died like a fool. Shot in the street. And for what? Because somebody thought he was going for a gun? Who knows?" He gave a deep sigh, and Isa saw his hand tremble as it rippled through his hair. "All the things he did, Isa, all the righteous things he did, I tried to emulate. I was the best student at school from the time I wore short pants to the day the Germans burned the university. I was the child who always tried the hardest, helped anyone who needed it, played games fairly. And do you know why?"

"Because that's what your father taught you?"

"Yes, that's what my father taught me. But *he* did it for God's glory. I did it for my own."

He sank onto the crate now, so that Isa had to chase around the press again to look at him. Exhaustion wrinkled his eyelids. "You're right, though. I'm full of pride. Why do you suppose God would want any part of me? Somebody who doesn't even have enough faith to stand on it without my father right here beside me."

There was just enough room on the corner of that crate for Isa to sit beside him. "You said it yourself tonight at the dinner table. God pursues us. It's all in the Bible you won't read anymore."

Edward shook his head.

"Oh, it's okay for God to love the Germans but not to love you?"

He stood, leaning against the wall that, with the press right behind them, wasn't so far away. Suddenly he lost the frown and smiled. "How did things get so tangled, Isa? I've always been the one telling you what to think or do, not the other way around."

She stood, the pace of her heartbeat multiplying. "I'm all grown up now, Edward."

She thought his gaze slipped—or wanted to, for the slightest moment. His smile dimmed. "I can see that."

"Can you? And yet you've done nothing but treat me as a child since I've returned."

"I wish you still were. Children are less likely to attract trouble from the Germans."

"Edward, why did you follow me to the closet earlier? when the Hauptmann tried to kiss me?"

"Aren't you glad I did?"

"Of course! I just want to know why you followed."

"Because I saw the Major watching that Hauptmann with what I took to be mistrust, all the while the Hauptmann was watching you."

She smiled again. "Because I'm no longer a child?"

He ran both hands through his hair now and shrugged away from the wall, looking at the press again. "Yes. Well. I should be going; it's late, and I won't want to take advantage of using my passes after curfew too often." He neared the door. "Why don't you go up first, just to make sure Clara hasn't returned unexpectedly? I'll go out if the coast is clear."

Isa stared at him a moment, wondering what he would do if she simply kissed him. Would he slap her, the way she'd slapped the Hauptmann? Kissing was certainly a personal thing, and one ought not do that without an invitation. Having just suffered such an assault, she should be the last one to consider doing something like that now.

And yet she wanted to, if only to forever erase the feel of the Hauptmann's lips violating hers.

But she couldn't. Instead, she passed him and went up the stairs to make sure no one would see him leave.

Edward let out a breath the moment Isa was gone. What was he thinking? He'd very nearly taken her into his arms just now—in an embrace that would in no way resemble any number of hugs they'd shared in the past.

And what had *she* been thinking? Reminding him like a little coquette that she was all grown up now? Any idiot could see that. Certainly the Hauptmann had.

It reminded him of that day the horses in the street had made him throw her to the side; he had reacted in the way any man would, holding someone so lovely. He'd written it off as a by-product of feeling strong and protective of her at a point of danger.

But now this. It wasn't as if he liked her. Even if there were no war, he couldn't possibly entertain the notion of loving Isa. Her family was not to be tolerated, particularly that arrogant older brother of hers. He was no doubt having as much fun as ever, safe and free and far from any hint of war, sacrifice, or danger. Very likely never gave the war a thought.

And yet the truth was too obvious. Isa wasn't at all like her brother. She'd returned here because of Edward's mother. She'd sacrificed her freedom, whatever money she could smuggle in, her old way of life.

He doused the light, letting himself out of the room when he heard her quiet call from the top of the stairs. Now was most definitely not the time to become involved with anyone. He'd meant it when he said the same to Rosalie.

He certainly didn't need the distraction of one Isa Lassone. All grown up.

22

It is easy to laugh when one sees a German advocate employing what he calls "diplomatic dexterity."

La Libre Belgique

Isa tried to open her eyes, but only one obeyed while the other remained stubbornly stuck. She listened for a moment, thinking she might have imagined the pounding. It was, she could tell from her window, still dark. Who would be calling at this hour? It was far too hard to leave the warmth of her covers just to check on a sound. She rolled over.

But the sound increased. A shot of energy tingled through her veins, and her heart drummed with the pounding.

The press!

Isa threw the covers off and reached for her robe, forgetting her slippers in her haste.

How could she, even in sleep, forget that in this very house was an illegal press and *she* was responsible for it?

She ran from her room and passed the Major's closed door, hearing an angry grumble from within.

"What is that racket at this hour?"

215

Isa flew down the stairs. There she met Clara, disheveled and appearing every bit as stupefied as Isa felt.

"Oh, *mademoiselle*, I am afraid to answer! It is before curfew, and they say only bad news comes to the door before curfew lifts."

In the dark, Isa saw nothing on the other side of the glass door. She knew she had only one real option, and that was to open the door before it was broken down.

"Isa! No!"

It was too late to heed Genny's warning from the top of the stairs. Three soldiers loomed before her, guns held at their chests, helmeted and gloved as if for battle.

"Isabelle Lassone!"

Neither a greeting nor an inquiry, rather it was a demand.

"I am Isabelle Lassone." She'd meant to sound brave but failed.

"You will come with us."

Isa, too stunned to obey, did not move. Her feet felt bolted to the cold tile floor.

How easily those feet left the floor when the soldiers lifted and propelled her out of her house.

They let go at the curb, and the cobblestones felt colder than the tile beneath her bare feet, though not for long. They shoved her into the back of a wagon. She wanted to cry out, at least be allowed to get her slippers, but then she saw Genny, held back by the Major. The terror on Genny's face was a beacon through the fog of Isa's confusion, igniting the same terror in Isa—for herself.

"What's wrong with it?" Edward asked. "Is the theology sound?"

"Yes."

"Is the opposing argument unclear?"

"No."

"Then what?"

Father Clemenceau placed the paper Edward had written on the desk before him and removed the spectacles from the bridge of his nose to analyze Edward. "It's not the content, Edward. It's honorable, true to the faith, in every aspect intelligently written. And I believe each word. But no pastor would dare read it from his pulpit."

Edward spewed a sigh.

Father Clemenceau raised a supplicating hand. "Priests have been singled out by this occupying army as it is. Enough of us have been imprisoned for reading Cardinal Mercier's letters—our own church leader, written to his own flock—because he had the gall, so the Germans say, to encourage his flock to long for justice. But this . . . this is outright thumbing one's nose at the Germans. It all but calls them heathens!"

"The ones I know are exactly that."

"I don't doubt some are. But think, Edward. If any of my brethren were to read this from the pulpit, they'd be jailed. And will they take the risk for an anonymous author? I cannot ask them to risk their freedom—what they have left of such a notion—for this. I'm sorry; I cannot do it."

Edward shook his head, closing his eyes. He'd stayed up all night writing the piece, knowing the church was his only avenue to expose the current mode of popular German thinking. He couldn't publish it in *La Libre Belgique*. His connection to it might be exposed if he expressed the exact philosophy he'd heard at the dinner party.

He supposed he shouldn't expect anyone else to take a risk. Even if it was all true, even if it would stir the hearts of believers to know without doubt that the message on the belt buckle worn by every German soldier wasn't true—God *wasn't* with all those who'd issued those buckles. They'd thrown Him out.

"I will pass this around to some of my fellow priests," Father

Clemenceau said. "It explains much, and perhaps it'll help us to remember that God will prevail in the end. But of course it's also true that others on our side have abandoned God. Some of our own neighbors. Each of us handles grief in our own way."

Edward stood. He didn't want to think about that; far less did he want to discuss why some had abandoned God.

But he wasn't sorry he'd written the sermon, even if it would be read only by the close, trusted friends of Father Clemenceau. Edward wasn't sure *why* he'd written it, except the words had poured from his pencil and couldn't be stopped. It wasn't a reaffirmation of his old faith; rather it was a concise explanation of how some justified what they did. By making man a machine, not a creation.

Edward left Father Clemenceau's office, glancing at his wristwatch. Ten thirty in the morning. He would go to Isa's to finish reassembling the press. The risk was already taken, so they may as well use it to the fullest.

Isa sat on the cot, bare feet beneath her, holding closed the lapels of her robe. When they'd brought her through the prisoners' entrance to the Town Hall in the heart of the old city, she wasn't sure which she'd felt more acutely: fear or humiliation. Fear of the unknown; humiliation that she had been taken in her nightclothes and bare feet.

Thankfully, because of the early hour, there was not the usual long line winding around the Kommandantur and filling the nearby narrow street leading to the Grand Place. Petitioners would show up later to pay fines, request passes to be out after curfew, or acquire permission for travel from one province to another. At least she hadn't been required to withstand many stares.

Confined in the lowest level of the fifteenth-century building,

Isa felt the tower itself—so huge, so magnificent with its turrets and spires—weigh down upon her.

She wondered if the sun had yet risen. Surely it must have by now; it felt as though she'd been here hours already as she waited on her cot, eyes closed in a mixture of dread and prayer. She was one of many prisoners held in various cells in this large, dark basement, obviously not originally intended as a prison. Bars had been installed around a series of cots, and each appeared full. She had seen no other women.

"Vorwärts!"

Isa opened her eyes to see a guard marching two of her fellow inmates up the improvised corridor to the stairs, which she could barely see from her cell. Just at that moment she saw a familiar figure descending.

"Guten Morgen," Hauptmann von Eckhart greeted her.

Isa did not move from her cot.

"I see you've joined us at the Kommandantur." He clucked his tongue at her. "You know, all of this could have been avoided had you shown a bit more cordiality last night."

She turned her back on him. She cared neither to look at him nor to have him see her dressed as she was.

He laughed. "No harm intended." The whispered words might have been an endearment on another's lips.

She faced him. "No *harm* intended? You have me plucked from my bed to be arrested, and there was no harm intended?"

He laughed again, then offered what she could only call a pout. "You hurt my feelings, *Liebchen*. How else to show you the depth of my . . . interest?"

"I do not welcome your interest."

"There now, you've hurt my feelings yet again." He placed a hand on the bars that separated them. "I would think a person in your position might show more respect. Come here, *mein Herz*."

She must obey; she had no choice. Isa swallowed her humiliation at having him see her uncovered feet. As she slowly approached him, myriad thoughts crossed her mind. The Bible Isa loved said to bless one's enemy. Genny said hatred hurt the hater. And yet it grew in Isa anyway, in a new way. Not against an army, an evil, an idea. This hatred was personal.

"There is a way to end this. Last night you rejected my protection. What do you say now that you obviously have need of it? of me?"

She raised her gaze to him. "I haven't changed my mind."

She saw a muscle twitch at his jaw before he turned on his heel and left.

Edward took the steps up Isa's porch two at a time. The bell rang with its familiar stridence, but before the sound faded, his mother stood before him, a look on her face he'd seen before and hoped never to see again.

Before he could ask, she grabbed his arm and spoke. "It's Isa! She's been arrested."

All at once every ounce of his blood drained away and his heart deflated for want of fuel.

"Why? Not . . . ?" Dimly aware of the Major nearing them, Edward closed his mouth.

"We don't know. Not yet, at any rate."

"What happened?" Edward tried—and succeeded, he thought— to keep his hands and voice like the steady priest his vestments presented him to be.

"Soldiers came early this morning," his mother said. If he wasn't shaking, she certainly was, even as she paced back and forth. "It was before dawn. Pounding, pounding at the door. I was so afraid! It was like that first night, at the beginning of the war, when they came to the hotel. I rushed to the stairs, but I was too late to tell her not to answer." Tears fell down her cheeks, and she dabbed them with a handkerchief that already looked damp.

"It would have made no difference, Frau Kirkland," the Major said. "A closed door would not stop them."

"Then what happened?"

"They—they took her. In her robe! In a wagon." She gulped a ragged breath, but Edward could tell it did little to calm her. "The Major sent Clara with a note to the Kommandantur, but we could learn nothing. Except . . ."

"Yes, go on."

The Major cleared his throat. "Mademoiselle Lassone's arrest was arranged by Hauptmann von Eckhart. You witnessed, as did I, a rejection of his advances. Von Eckhart does not take well to rejection. We don't know what charges he's made. As far as I know, refusing the attentions of an officer isn't illegal. Yet."

That the Major thought the notion just as ludicrous wasn't lost on Edward, though he had no time or inclination to absorb what that meant. The Major was in obvious sympathy, and that was enough for the moment.

"Where was she taken?" Edward asked.

"The Kommandantur at the Town Hall."

Edward paced away. "All right." He turned to the Major, knowing he must be bold. "If I find the means, can she be freed by bribery?"

The Major's light brows gathered skeptically. "In another prison, perhaps. But the Kommandantur . . ." He shook his head. "No, that would mean embarrassment and the harshest punishment for the guards. It's the heart of our operations here."

"Can I get in to see her, at least? As her priest?"

He looked no more hopeful. "They watch these cases most closely. Only German chaplains or German priests are allowed."

"A message, then? Can we get a message to her?"

Now his brows rose. "Yes, I think I can manage that."

"And a dress," Genny said as she went to a drawer in the table in the parlor. "They took her in her nightclothes!" From the drawer she withdrew a sheet of paper and a pencil and handed it to Edward, then hastened up the stairs.

Edward barely hesitated as a flood of verses from the Bible came to mind, indelible from years of study and training. On the paper he wrote one he knew she would welcome, especially if it came from him:

The Lord thy God in the midst of thee is mighty; he will save, he will rejoice over thee with joy; he will rest in his love, he will joy over thee with singing.

Signing *Father Antoine*, Edward folded the paper and handed it to the Major.

"Blast this war," the Major said as he turned away. "Not even a telephone to send someone over."

But a moment later the same ringer that had brought Edward the last hopeful sound he'd heard now rang again. Genny was just coming back down the stairs, clothing folded over her arm. She hurried to reach the door, and there stood a German sentry.

"For Major von Bürkel." He handed her an envelope.

From behind her the Major spoke. "Just a moment, sentry." He tucked another note in with Edward's, sealing it in an envelope. He accepted the clothes Genny held out and folded everything together. "This is to be given to Herr Lutz only. Do you understand?"

"Yes, Major."

Genny closed the door, and both she and Edward watched as the Major tore open the envelope the young man had just delivered. He scanned the page. It was full-size, but Edward could see the contents were bleakly short.

"She has been charged with aiding and abetting an Allied soldier," he said. "Her trial is set for December."

Genny gasped. "Two months!"

Edward scratched his head, relieved the arrest wasn't somehow linked to the press but at the same time confused. "Aiding an Allied soldier?"

"Oh, my!" It was Clara's voice, and all three turned to her at the same time. She looked stricken, nearly hidden in the shadows of the hallway nearby. "I knew that day would haunt us."

Edward approached her. "What day?"

"Oh . . ."

She sobbed again, and Edward's impatience multiplied. "Speak, Clara!"

She wiped the back of her hand against her nose. "There was a young man here not so long ago. I knew we should not answer the door. I warned her. *Oui, oui,* I did! I've heard of spies, so bold to come right up to the door and pretend to be a soldier looking for a way over the frontier. Surely he was a spy!"

Genny put an arm around Clara's shoulders, but she looked closer to joining her tears than able to offer much comfort.

"What did Fräulein Lassone do for this young man who came to the door?" the Major asked.

"I do not know! I left the room in search of Henri, to have the man put from the grounds. But I do know she gave him bread. I saw what remained on the table after he was gone."

"A misconstrued act of charity," Genny whispered.

Edward looked at the Major. "She couldn't have helped him."

"It doesn't matter. If he was indeed an impostor, feeding him was all von Eckhart needed. The Kommandantur has a file on many houses these days. Especially," he added softly, "on the house of someone who reappeared as Fräulein Lassone did."

Genny sucked in another sudden breath, followed by a new supply of tears. "What shall we do? How do we get her home?"

Edward folded his arms. "If we can't bribe her freedom, can we at least bribe a quicker trial date?"

"I don't know. That depends on the amount of cash you have available."

Edward nodded, then left the house with the promise to return as quickly as he could. It wouldn't do to have the Major know there was a stash of valuables in the cellar beneath his feet.

But Edward wasn't going far. Henri knew where to get both jewels and cash.

23

From those who occupy the land of "poets and thinkers" came this debacle! They have created nothing so noble as their forebears hoped. Indeed, wherever they step, they perpetrate tragedy in blood and ruin upon land made sacred by our loss.

La Libre Belgique

"There he is. Let me go. Jean-Luc! Jean-Luc!"

Isa looked toward the commotion, the first time in two hours that she opened her eyes. She saw a woman, dressed in a simple but tailored gown of the bourgeois class—a bit tattered, perhaps, like most clothing in Brussels these days, but dark, like the gowns all Belgian women wore. A soldier held her but she managed to break free, scurrying at once to the cell down the row. A man met her with arms outstretched, bars hindering their touch.

"Ah, Jean-Luc! *Mon cher!*" She collapsed against the iron, whimpering.

The soldier pulled her away even as the man in the cell begged him not to hurt her. She fought him, and the soldier had all he could do to drag the woman across the floor—stopping at Isa's cell.

Another soldier appeared from the stairwell and helped shove the woman inside. The woman only cried, face hidden in her arms.

"Pierrette! Pierrette!"

Isa looked between the two of them. Finally the man's voice penetrated the woman's grief and she crawled to the edge of the cell to see the man calling her name.

"Be strong, my Pierrette! We are here together, and together we go. Together, Pierrette!"

She scrambled to her knees. "Yes, Jean-Luc! Together!"

Isa felt like a reluctant voyeur to witness such pain, affection, and intimacy all at once. Pity moved her, made her wish she could appeal to the compassion of those responsible for separating these two. But Isa knew she, least of all, could be of any help.

At last the woman sank to the floor and looked up as if noticing her surroundings—and Isa—for the first time.

"I wish I could offer you a handkerchief," Isa said, now that the woman seemed exhausted of her tears. "But as you can see, I'm not equipped to offer anything at all."

The woman brushed her face with her hands. She looked back at the cell down the row, and so did Isa. The man sat on his cot, similar to the one Isa occupied. They were too far apart to converse without shouting.

Isa stood, motioning to the single cot. "Will you be more comfortable here?"

The woman pulled herself to her feet. She was not heavy but rather solid, and her slow movement indicated perhaps she was unused to the exercise she'd put herself through—fighting the guard, shouting, and convulsive weeping.

"Merci." The cot sagged under her weight. "Oh, but there is only one!" She looked at Isa. "Perhaps one of us will be able to leave soon, with only one cot."

"Yes, perhaps." Isa thought the Germans more likely to bring in another cot than let either of them go.

"Why are you here?" Pierrette never looked at Isa as she spoke. Her gaze was riveted to the man down the row.

"To be perfectly honest, I have no idea what charges they will make up."

"Ah." The woman nodded. "Well, I've heard it doesn't matter if they have evidence or not. One German's word is all they need to put someone away."

Isa had learned that from Jonah's experience. "And you?"

The woman lifted her hands as if she didn't know either. "I cannot say."

"Do you mean they've brought you here for no reason? the same as me?"

The woman gave her a half smile. "I didn't say that. But there are many ears around here, yes? I've no wish to add to whatever crime they think I've committed. You see?"

Isa nodded, although the notion of someone listening to every word hadn't occurred to her. She looked around. The soldiers were out of sight but must be nearby. Only fellow prisoners were close enough to hear their words.

Pierrette gazed at Isa. "I see by the quality of your nightgown that you're a woman of some means. Or—" she winked—"at least kept by someone as such."

Isa shook her head. "I'm being held because I refused to accept the attention of a German officer."

The woman laughed, so different from a few inconsolable moments ago. "If that is all they have, they must be very clever to figure out a way to hold you."

Isa's heart raced. If they searched her home, they might come up with enough evidence to cast out all hope. Surely they had nothing against her yet. The Hauptmann's visit made that clear.

But even if they did search her home, she had complete confidence in the secrecy of that room. Complete.

"This is Monsieur Painlevé. He is one of the foremost Walloon advocates in Brussels."

Edward—Father Antoine—sat in Ambassador Brand Whitlock's plush office at the American Legation as the barrister entered the room.

Monsieur Painlevé was an older man, perhaps sixty, with graying hair and a smile that seemed as comfortable on his face as the pince-nez resting on his nose. "Monsieur Whitlock introduces me as if it were still before the war. As it is, I am nothing more than a prisoner of war. Same as you."

"Mr. Whitlock says you might help our friend."

"He's told me a bit about the trouble," Painlevé said, "but my help may be nothing more than to give you a better understanding of why I'm unable to help much at all."

Edward looked between the two men. "Can you represent her?"

"That depends. What is the charge?"

"They say they're holding her because she helped an Allied soldier. Evidently a spy came to her door posing as an Allied and she gave him something to eat. That is all."

He looked perplexed. "Usually such offenses are settled without an arrest. A fine, house arrest perhaps. But not imprisonment."

"There is more," Whitlock said, looking at Edward. "Tell him the rest."

"She slapped the face of a German officer—one who tried to take advantage of her. He's behind this arrest. She is held for no other reason than protecting her virtue."

The man waved his hand. "No, no, that is not the reason, Father. At least, that will not be the reason claimed in court. She has insulted a German officer. To them, that is enough. The reason behind that slap is irrelevant."

"This is ludicrous," Edward said, half to himself. He'd spent the better part of the last eight hours going from contact to contact, hoping to find someone able to work the bribe money he had ready. So far he'd come up with no one. The Kommandantur was as close to bribe-proof as the Major hinted. Edward had been forced to seek the American ambassador in hopes that a more traditional route might succeed.

"I have sat in on many cases in the German courts," Brand Whitlock said. "They're not completely without justice. And if anyone can help, it is Monsieur Painlevé."

Edward looked to the barrister for confirmation, which he seemed reluctant to give. "I will say this: justice can be met there, but it is met inconsistently. At times, the courts are nothing short of a laughingstock, if anyone can laugh these days. But you do have the good luck that your parishioner is being tried in a Brussels court. If she were sent to one of the provinces, say Hasselt . . . well, there would be little hope for fairness, I'm afraid."

"Is it possible for her to be sent elsewhere, even if she was arrested here in Brussels?"

The man lifted both hands. "With the German army, anything is possible."

Edward sank back in his chair. He'd come for help and received only more possibilities to worry over.

"In theory," the barrister continued, "the tribunals were set up to try cases that involved crimes against either the German state or its army. But over the past two years I've seen case after case of so-called crimes that can be found in no military penal code—not even a German one. It's what comes of unlimited power, unfortunately. The army *is* the law. Basically, if a German prosecutor wishes to do away with someone, he may ask for a certain penalty and have it granted."

"Then what are you allowed to do as a defendant's advocate?"

"Almost nothing. I am allowed to sit the case—a case, I might add, with which I am allowed no previous counsel. I am usually given the charges as the trial begins. I am not allowed to see clients before that. I am not allowed to bring witnesses for the defense—not that I could find any who would willingly put themselves against a German tribunal. Nor am I permitted to present any real defense with any sort of spirit. It would be viewed as lacking respect for the German court. I am not even allowed to wear my wig or court robes. It is a sham. But now and again the truth won't be suppressed, as Monsieur Whitlock has said. You can hope for that."

"Hope? No. That's not enough." He wished he could march to Isa's prison and demand she be set free, demand justice. But he was powerless in a city overrun by those whose definition of justice had somehow been forgotten. "Will you agree to take her case, whenever it will be?"

"Of course—but with one caution," Painlevé said. "There has been a rumor—a rather serious rumor—that the Germans will decree Brussels a Flemish province. Which means, among other things, that only Flemish will be spoken in the courts. This should not matter in a German tribunal, where they speak mostly German. But they may choose not to recognize my credentials since I am Walloon."

"Forever trying to separate the two," Whitlock commented.

The barrister nodded. "And wholly failing, as far as I can see." He turned his attention back to Edward. "Let me say this, Father Antoine: I am not so sure it matters who represents your parishioner, not as much as it depends on the whim of the court on that day. They may take pity on her—tell me, is she a pretty girl?"

Edward nodded.

"Then they may very well."

Edward stood. He intended to go back to the church. He'd heard about an *abbé* who might hold information about bribing

Kommandantur guards. He didn't like going to someone he didn't know firsthand, but desperation made him bold.

Whitlock followed Edward to the door, much to Edward's surprise. "Father," he said quietly, when they were alone, "if indeed you are a priest."

Edward turned to him expectantly. Brand Whitlock was a bit taller than Edward, lankier. He was known for his eloquence in diplomacy, but just at the moment he had a look of pure consternation on his face.

"Tell me one thing before you go," he said. "You've asked for my help before. As I recall in *that* case, someone was legitimately guilty, at least as far as German law goes. Have you gotten Isa involved in any of that?"

Edward knew his face went white; he couldn't stop the blood that drained away. So, Whitlock remembered Edward as one of those who had come begging mercy for earlier victims of *La Libre Belgique*.

"It's that way, is it? You've put her *life* in danger."

"While it may be my fault she's involved, it wasn't my idea. Have *you* ever tried to change Isa's mind?"

"Tell me truthfully. Do the Germans know about what she's involved in? Will that come up in the trial?"

Edward shook his head. "No! I tell you, this is all because of that German officer. She hasn't done anything other than refuse his advances."

Whitlock sighed. "As an American I may be on thinning ice with the Germans, young man, but they won't want to add another international incident by condemning one of my countrymen—a woman no less—to a harsh penalty over something as slight as either feeding a spy or refusing to kiss a German officer."

"I wish you could promise me that." Edward left without waiting for a reply. No one could make any promises these days.

24

Recall with me the era before the war, when England called for the peace of all Europe, and Germany called simply for neutrality. While today Germany points the finger at England with the feeble hope of laying blame there, is it not obvious the reason Germany wanted extensive neutrality? Did she hope others would not ally against her when she moved to fulfill her plan to expand? How long, O Germany, have you planned this war?

La Libre Belgique

"He was our only child," Pierrette whispered.

"I'm sorry," Isa murmured. Grief was no stranger in Brussels.

Isa dreaded having to spend the night locked in a cell. She'd guessed she must when they'd brought in the second cot, even though part of her had stubbornly hoped otherwise. But at least the Lord had sent her someone to talk to, someone to help speed the time if she wouldn't be freed soon.

Pierrette glanced at Isa. "Before we knew he'd been killed at the front, I'd have given anything to hear from him. I thought of him day and night, worried and feared. And then, when all those fears became real, I still wished, somehow, that I could hear from him. Crazy, yes? As if he could write to me from the dead!"

Isa remembered the letters she'd carried from Holland and the stories Gourard had told of soldiers with their dying wish to speak to their mothers in a letter.

"Perhaps he did try to write to you," Isa said. "I'm sure his last thought must have been of you, his mother."

"I'll never know."

"If only the Germans would let through letters from soldiers to families. Even a censored letter is better than nothing."

"I know some get through," Pierrette said, low. "Surely you've seen the placards of those punished for carrying such letters. Heroes, every one of them!"

Isa nodded. She didn't count herself among them, having done it only once.

Pierrette sighed. "Ah, we must hold dear our heroes, *mademoiselle*. Do you agree?"

Isa nodded again, thinking of Edward and all he'd done in the past two years.

"I would be willing to do anything for my countrymen. And I've done so little, yet that's why I'm here."

"Why are you here?"

"I heard one accuse me of counting trains and conveying information to the Allies. Imagine! How was I to have sent that information, even if I was doing such a thing?" Her gaze wandered down the corridor to the cell belonging, for the moment at least, to her husband. "Same for my beloved Jean-Luc. They came for him this morning when I was out. When I came home, they were waiting for me."

"But you said you've done so little for your countrymen. You have done something, then?"

Pierrette laughed and eyed Isa. "You ask a lot of questions, *ma petite*."

"Yes, I've always been a pest, so I've been told." According to Edward.

Pierrette laughed again, and it sounded so strange amid their surroundings that Isa studied her closely. *She's an odd one. One moment mourning her misfortune and the next able to laugh at light humor.*

"Tell me of yourself, *mademoiselle*," Pierrette said. "I know that you are not a workingwoman. I can tell from your nightclothes. You come from Upper Town, yes?"

Isa nodded.

"Were you born in Brussels?"

"America."

"Ah, I thought as much. Your French is excellent, though."

Isa said nothing.

"You are American, then. What are you doing here?"

"My father is Belgian. I am Belgian."

Pierrette brushed a hand Isa's way. "This is no reason to be here *now*. Why didn't you go to America before the Germans came?"

Isa looked away from the woman's obvious interest. Perhaps it was the surroundings or perhaps Pierrette's own words. Even if the two of them did share a cell, they were strangers. And no one talked to strangers anymore. Still, Isa could think of no possible reason not to be friendly. "We did—that is, my parents did."

"Ah, they left you? But you are so young! How could they do such a thing?"

Isa suddenly regretted her decision to talk. She couldn't very well admit they'd taken her along but she'd returned on her own.

"My parents have always considered me inconvenient." That much was true.

Pierrette reached across the narrow gap between their cots to stroke Isa's cheek gently. "*Ma petite*, how can a child be an inconvenience?"

How indeed? She'd wondered that herself.

"How has it been for you, living without your parents? Have they been in touch?"

"Now who asks all the questions?"

Pierrette shifted on her cot, looking straight up at the ceiling. "Perhaps we have something in common. We are both pests?"

"I haven't heard from my parents."

"But surely if they left you behind, they know where you are?"

Isa didn't answer. She'd probably said too much already, although she wasn't quite sure it was necessary to be so cautious. At least not with someone on this side of the cell bars. She leaned back on the cot, listening as Pierrette continued to talk of her son, of her husband, of how happy they'd been before the war. Isa found it comforting to hear someone speak about how life had been before. Pierrette told of their bakery and Isa's mouth watered to remember the *tartelettes aux fruits, brioches, cornets à la crème,* and how families used to come at teatime for the delicate pastries and to drink chocolate. But they'd closed along with the other bakers in September, unable to get flour even from the CRB.

Isa didn't speak, only listened, until all the noises around them grew still, and after a while Pierrette talked herself to sleep. Isa lay there in the silence, unable to stop wondering what God had in mind with this.

"You will put this on." The guard thrust familiar clothing at Isa through the bars. She heard shoes drop to the cement floor with a clunk and reached for them eagerly, scooping them against her chest.

Isa turned to hastily change, removing her robe and for modesty's sake pulling her dress over her nightgown. The guard, she noticed, made no effort to leave or turn away until she was finished.

"So," Pierrette said with a half smile, "either they have shown you a kindness or they take you to trial."

Isa caught the word. "Trial?"

"Will they try you in your nightgown, for all to see how they arrested you? I don't think so."

Isa smoothed out the wrinkles of the day dress. It was her mother's dark green with high neck and snug long sleeves. No doubt Genny had chosen it from among the others because it was modest yet fitting. It felt tight over the thin layer of her cotton nightdress.

Isa brushed her fingers through her long hair. "I wish they'd sent something to tie this out of my way."

Pierrette reached up, pulling a ribbon from her own unkempt hair. "Here." She handed it to Isa. "It may help."

"But I don't know if I'll be able to give it back."

Pierrette laughed. "Confident you'll be set free after the trial, are you?"

"Of course. Why shouldn't I be? I've done nothing wrong."

"I think the Germans will decide that."

Isa slipped her feet into the shoes. Something poked her toe from the tip and she hastily looked around to be sure she was unobserved before removing a small, crumpled piece of paper.

She recognized the handwriting immediately. Edward . . . comforting *her* with Scripture. That alone was answer to prayer.

She tucked the scrap of paper under her dress, noticing too late that Pierrette watched. The older woman smiled and looked away, without asking the obvious.

Prisoners were given no breakfast—not that Isa cared. She doubted she could eat, especially with memories of the vile meal they'd been served the night before. Some sort of oats. Colorless, tasteless. Tepid.

Soldiers soon returned and announced that Isa was to follow.

Before leaving, Isa turned to Pierrette, wishing her God's protection until the day the cell doors opened for her.

"If we make it through our trials—both of us—perhaps we shall see each other again someday, yes? outside this prison?"

Isa nodded, but her thoughts were already on what awaited her. She turned back to the guards and silently followed.

The courtroom was in the back of the Town Hall. The room might have been a small meeting hall, but for the purpose of a German tribunal it was swept clear of all unnecessary furniture or images of wealth or Belgian patriotism. The walls were bare, even the windows barren of drapery. An oblong table was left at the front, with two smaller tables facing the one ahead.

Few people sat on chairs toward the back of the room. She was taken forward and to the left, opposite those who faced her. Three men in military uniform sat at the head of the room, German officers of varying rank. To the right and behind one of the shorter tables with their backs to Isa sat more officers. They appeared to be in conference, oblivious to what went on around them or of her. At Isa's table was a man in a civilian suit. He was an older gentleman, reading papers in front of him so diligently he didn't notice her entry either.

She looked around, fully prepared to see Hauptmann von Eckhart, but he was not there.

Before long one of the three judges facing them called the room to attention. "Isabelle Lassone," he said. "You will stand before the court."

She did so.

"You have been charged with aiding an Allied soldier." The man looked beyond her to those seated at the back of the room. "Meinrad Hindemith, you will stand."

Isa saw someone rise. It was the young man who had come to her home claiming to be an American, though his hair was combed differently. Confusion made way for realization. So her instinct about him had been right after all. They were trying her for giving a stranger a piece of bread? How had von Eckhart found out about that?

"Step forward," one of the judges commanded.

Isa was about to move, but the man at her side put a hand on her wrist. She looked to see Hindemith stand in front of the judges.

"Is this the woman who gave you aid when you posed as an Allied soldier?"

He turned around to face Isa, taking a leisurely look at her. She remembered thinking he was a fine-looking young man, apart from the one crooked tooth, but now she noticed something he'd hidden before, more an attitude than tangible. He looked overly confident, puffed up.

"Yes, this is the woman."

"How did she give you aid?"

"She took me into her home and gave me food and drink."

"And did she offer help for you to find your way back to the Allied army?" another of the three judges asked.

At this the man lost a measure of that pride. "She was obviously in sympathy for me as an Allied, as proven by the meal she offered."

"But did she offer a path out of the country?"

He folded his hands behind his back. "No, but when I inquired how she returned to Brussels so suddenly, she was obviously hiding something. There is no doubt she smuggled herself into the country as a spy."

Isa opened her mouth to deny it, but the man beside her once again put a hand around her wrist. She looked down at him, every bit as bewildered as alarmed. Was he here to defend her or to aid the Germans with their charges?

"You may be seated," one of the judges said. "Isabelle Lassone, you will step forward."

Isa stepped around the table and took the spot the German spy had vacated. She held her chin high. If this was their strongest evidence, how much danger could there be? It was ridiculous, ludicrous to accuse her of something even their own witness denied.

"Is it true that this man, claiming to be an American fighting for the Allies, came to your door seeking help?"

"Yes."

"And did you offer him help?"

"He was hungry; I gave him bread. He was thirsty; I gave him drink."

The judge-advocate in the center merely raised one cynical brow. "So you are saying you would have done this for any stranger coming to your door?"

"Yes."

"And did you discuss helping him get out of Belgium to ultimately rejoin his supposed army?"

"He said that was his desire."

"And you did nothing to discourage this?"

"I don't remember what I said, only that I could not help him."

Another judge, the one on the right, spoke up. "How is it, Fräulein Lassone, that you vacated Brussels with your parents on the eve of this war and two years later showed up at your family home, demanding the soldiers billeted there be evacuated so you may live there again?"

"I wished to live in my own home."

"Yes, but where were you for those two years?"

"In hiding," she answered, truthfully enough. "From my parents. They didn't want me in Belgium."

"And do your parents know where you are since you've resumed residence in your family home?"

"I haven't been in contact with them." *Lately.*

"Have you been in touch with anyone outside of Belgium?" He spoke quickly as if to catch her off guard.

"No."

There was a pause, and at some length the judge in the center told her to be seated. He looked to the Germans seated at the table next to Isa's, and one stood to launch their case against the accused. Obviously she was an Allied sympathizer, one who did nothing to alert the proper authorities of an alleged Allied soldier at her very doorstep, thus permitting him to go about his proposed illegal plan. Not only did she hide this from said authorities, she willingly fed him, strengthening him to leave Belgium and rejoin the Allied armies. Thus, she gave sustenance to the enemy. Not to mention the suspicious circumstances of her sudden appearance at her family home. Where was she for those two years? Why had she chosen to return to that home? He doubted she told the complete truth, and therefore she was capable of treachery. She should not be allowed to leave until a penalty was paid.

Before any mention of specific penalty, the man at Isa's side at last stood to address the court. He might have looked rather scholarly if he wore the robes of an advocate or at least a uniform like the others in the room. But although his jacket was tailored, his suit was shabby from wear.

"Officers of the court," he began with obvious respect, "I ask you to be lenient with this young woman, whose only crime was to act on her Christian faith and feed a hungry stranger at her door. It is as simple as that."

He paused for such a long time Isa thought he might be finished. And while there might be wisdom in simplicity, she wondered if such a short statement indicated her case was on the extreme end of unimportance.

"As for the rest of the suspicions, these are unfounded and without evidence. She has said or done nothing to indicate her attitude as anything except that of a young Christian, without animosity toward Germans or the German Imperial Army. And might I remind you, with all due respect, that while she is the daughter of an influential Belgian family, she is indeed also an American citizen by virtue of her birth to an American mother in that country across the sea. A country that has done all in its power to aid those in need in this very country. I ask lenience, above all, because she is young and naive and did nothing more than act on her personal faith."

Then he sat down and the prosecuting German across the aisle stood again.

"This is all quite sentimental, Your Honors, and I for one have heard more than enough. This woman is obviously an Allied sympathizer, and as for being an American," he nearly huffed, "well, that means nothing anymore. Americans have had blatant disregard for our army for some time, while our people starve behind British blockades and the Americans do nothing to help. Everyone knows they sympathize with the British. That is why I ask this woman be taken to the prison at Vilvorde and held not less than six months, and since she comes from a family of wealth, be required to pay a fine of no less than ten thousand Marks."

Isa heard the request and her head spun. Imprisonment . . . six months. She vaguely heard the monetary fine, wondering if a buyer could be found with enough cash for the jewels she had left. *Six months.*

The three judges at the head table conferred. There was no jury, and Isa was not asked to speak. She could only wait for the pronouncement of her sentence.

At last the center judge told Isa to stand.

Innocent or not, Isa felt her knees wobble.

"We find the accused guilty as charged."

Isa's heart sped and something fiery spread through her veins: disbelief and fear unfurled. *Oh, God, oh, God, teach me what You have to teach me. . . . Help me to trust You!*

God's hand alone held her on her shaking knees.

"Further, we find the penalty requested fair." He took a long look at Isa. "However, the court has decided upon leniency. Two months or five hundred Marks."

Relief and disappointment came at once, along with sure knowledge of what must be done. To willingly pay the fine meant supporting their army, their war. And while she could barely tolerate the thought of one more night behind bars with filth and mice and inedible food, it was all too clear what she must say.

"I will serve the time." Her voice was a child's, not her own.

"No one asked you to choose," the judge at the left snapped. "It is entirely up to us when you will be freed." He motioned to one of the soldiers who had been stationed at the back of the room. "Take her downstairs."

25

It is obvious from the writings of the Prussian cavalry general Bernhardi that the Germans must assume the guilt for starting this war. They used their Press to convince the people that a "war of liberation" was necessary.

May I say we at *La Libre Belgique* agree with the general on only one point: the power of the Press to stir the hearts, minds, and will of the people.

La Libre Belgique

"I'm telling you, the sentence was lenient, and if you allow me to deliver the money quickly, they may very well let her go immediately. It will show her family's wealth—and that equals power."

Edward heard the words and might have been disgusted once again by the German *Kultur*. But only one phrase coursed through his mind: *"They might let her go."* He sat in the barrister's office, nearly a dozen streets away from the Town Hall, where he'd waited all morning for the lawyer to return after his court session defending Isa.

He reached for the money inside his satchel. He had enough, thanks to one of the jewels pawned from Isa's cache. Edward counted the money needed, handed it to the barrister, and kept what was left.

"Your parishioner was quite brave in the courtroom," Monsieur Painlevé said as he accepted the cash. "No hysterics, which they despise; no crying or pleading, which makes them less likely to be lenient. She even had the pluck to say she would serve the time rather than pay the fee." He shrugged. "That was perhaps not wise, but it is the way of patriots these days. Fortunately for your friend, they did not withdraw their leniency. You are lucky to know such a woman, Father Antoine."

The barrister hurried off, and Edward was again left with nothing to do but wait.

Eventually he paced the office floor, back and forth, back and forth, glancing at his wristwatch again and again. He looked out the window but could see nothing more than the lush green leaves on the poplar in front.

Edward judged it would take the barrister twenty minutes to walk to the Kommandantur from his office if he kept a brisk pace and wasn't stopped by some zealous sentry. How long to pay the fine? Would he have to stand in the endless lines? How long to determine whether Isa would be released immediately or made to stay longer? The barrister had offered hope she might be released when the fine was paid, but no promises. Never any promises.

And so Edward paced. But he did not pray.

⌖

"You should have smiled," Pierrette said. "I don't care how old some of these judges are, they won't resist the smile of a pretty young woman."

"Smile! How could I have done such a thing? I was petrified."

"Well, at least tell me you didn't act like some simpering girl."

Isa shook her head, at the same time untying the ribbon from her hair and handing it to Pierrette.

"I'll say well done, then."

Isa cocked her head. "Why do you know so much about the German courts?"

"Did I not tell you? My brother is an advocate."

Isa didn't mention that knowledgeable advice might have lent her a bit of courage earlier. "Will your brother help you when your case is called?"

"Ah, no! He's in Germany."

"Oh!"

Pierrette's gaze dropped to the floor. "He was deported."

Isa had only to remember the little she knew of Edward's experience to feel a wave of sympathy.

Pierrette shot her gaze briefly toward the guard at the base of the stairwell. "The next guard that passes this way may very well come for you, Mademoiselle Isa. To take you to freedom."

"Or Vilvorde."

"Vilvorde!" Pierrette exclaimed. "Who said anything about that place?"

"One of the prosecutors. It's where he wanted to send me."

Pierrette shook her head. "He was a mean one, then."

"Why? Vilvorde isn't so far away. Like St. Gilles."

Pierrette laughed. "Do you know what they are saying, *mademoiselle*? That occupied Brussels is paradise, the *Etappengebeit*—the military zone—is purgatory, and *Operationsgebiet*—northern France—is hell?"

Isa shook her head. She'd been so sheltered since returning she had not heard that one.

"Well, *this* place is paradise, St. Gilles is purgatory, and Vilvorde . . . that, *mademoiselle*, is hell."

Edward looked at his wristwatch again. Two hours since Painlevé had left. Edward had tried to prepare himself that it would take longer than expected, perhaps an hour—but not double that. Desperation brought a prayer to his lips. Maybe Isa *had* been brought back to Belgium to help Edward renew his faith. If so, he assured God He needn't let it to go any further.

No sooner had the prayer left his heart than Edward heard noise in the hall. He rushed to the door to find an unkempt Isa, looking slight in the oversize raincoat obviously belonging to the barrister.

"Isa!"

At once he took her into his arms. Forget any hesitation; two days of worry shot away everything but relief that she was all right. The wet coat around her shoulders fell unnoticed to the floor, and Edward's heart beat hard and fast, his hands trembling like a boy's. He held her close and steadied those hands by placing one on each side of her face. For a moment she stared at him, tilting her face upward as if she fully expected him to kiss her.

And so he did. Square on the tip of her nose.

"Oh," she said, trying to pull away, "don't look at me! I'm a mess. My hair . . ."

He didn't let go, keeping his hands gently yet firmly on each side of her face. "You are," he whispered, "the most beautiful sight I've ever seen."

He might have kissed her again, this time far differently, but he caught sight of the barrister looking on, arms crossed, staring without shame at the spectacle.

The barrister was the least of the reasons Edward needed to restrain himself, but he let go of Isa nevertheless.

"Well, Father Antoine," he said, ushering them into his office, out of the hallway. "I've guessed already by your concern these past two days that this parishioner is quite important to you. But perhaps you might think about how your actions could confuse a young woman such as Mademoiselle Lassone."

Edward faced the barrister. "Yes, yes, of course you're correct. I shall return her to my aunt, who is like a mother to her. You see, we're very nearly family."

The barrister picked up his fallen coat. Edward had the feeling they weren't fooling him at all. But Painlevé said nothing, only hung his coat on a hook behind the door, then went to his desk and deposited his leather case on top.

He eyed Isa. "This young man has been quite beside himself since you were taken. Why don't you stay out of trouble so we may avoid going through this again?"

Isa laughed. "I'd be happy to."

❧

Isa barely felt the pavement beneath her feet. Edward had said she was beautiful! She was free! He'd very nearly kissed her!

She slipped her hand into his as she'd done a thousand times, but he removed it and looped her arm through his instead. It was almost as intimate, although she supposed it was more proper for a priest to guide her through the streets this way than the other.

"Edward, thank you for all you did for me these last two days. You saved me from such an awful place." She would tell him later just how awful it had been, how the injustice of it all deepened her resolve to do the right thing with *La Libre Belgique*. But for now there was something else on her mind. "Did you mean it just now when you said I was the most beautiful thing you'd ever seen?"

He stared straight ahead so she couldn't read his face. "Freedom is a beautiful thing." The words tumbled from his mouth.

"Oh. So it's justice, not me, that's beautiful?" She ran her free hand through her hair. "I suppose you're right, the way I look now."

"You're beautiful, Isa, and you know it. There. I've said it again, so you can stop trying to get me to repeat it."

She smiled. "Others might think I'm pretty, Edward. I just never knew you thought so."

"Let's hurry, shall we? My mother's been pacing for two days now."

Genny left her chair for the hundredth time that day, walking to the front door and opening it to look up, then down, the street. Once again she saw nothing.

She returned to the parlor, where there was no view at all. The front windows were tightly shuttered as if the house were closed for the off-season.

"The swiftest carriage of justice comes with paperwork." The Major was seated nearby, cane discarded on the floor beside him. It was the second time he'd reminded Genny of the time it would take to free Isa, even if all went well. The second time that it did no good.

Earlier that day a sentry had knocked at their door with a message from Herr Lutz. He'd been able to arrange a swifter trial and had put in a positive word to one of the judge-advocates who would sit the case. But that, he'd said, was the extent of his power.

Then, more than two hours ago, that same sentry had returned with a second note. The Major read it quickly, telling Genny the happy news that the trial was over and there was a good chance they would accept Isa's fine without having her serve any time.

Genny wasn't sure if she detested or welcomed the Major's company. This was, after all, another debacle of justice from his army of cohorts. But a part of her, one increasingly difficult to ignore, was comforted by his silent sympathy. She told herself she simply didn't want to wait alone, but if that were true, she could have gone into the kitchen with Clara and Henri.

"Do I have your permission to speak openly?" the Major asked.

Genny looked at him, surprised by the question. She took her seat again. "Of course."

He leaned forward, clasping his hands and resting his elbows on his knees. Because she sat on the edge of her seat and his chair was separated from hers by only a small side table, their knees were not more than a foot apart. Having the Major suddenly so close made her want to move again, but she didn't.

"There was a Bible left in the room I occupy upstairs, and last night I happened to be reading the Psalms. One line stood out among others. It said, 'The Lord will give strength unto his people; the Lord will bless his people with peace.' You are, I assume, familiar with that passage?"

She nodded, somewhat distractedly. His words forced her to her feet again, to resume the endless pacing. How could he speak to her of the Bible when just the other night his friend—his mentor—had spoken as if God didn't exist?

She watched him from the corner of her eye. He unclasped his hands, rubbed his knees, and reached for his cane.

As he stood, she stopped pacing to face him. She was struck by his height, similar to Jonathan's, and yet he was so very different. Jonathan had been dark haired and full of youth, even to the day of his death at just forty-five. The Major was no doubt of similar age, yet his temples showed gray and his face was lined at the forehead and around his eyes. His eyes were blue, unlike Jonathan's brown, and though the Major's were still very clear, the creases at the corners gave them a look of experience and intelligence with his quiet reserve.

"I know that you have great faith, Frau Kirkland. You already know God is sovereign in all things and that He loves Fräulein Lassone. Be still and know that He is God; trust Him." Then he gave her a quick, almost-shy smile. "You may think it easy for me to say because I haven't someone I care for so deeply being held unjustly. But when that's all there is to do, just to trust Him because we've done all we can, shouldn't there be some peace at least?"

Genny didn't know when her breathing became erratic. "You are right, of course. Thank you." She started to turn away but changed her mind. "My husband was a man of greater faith than I, Major. If he were here, he would have said something like that."

It was the first time since Jonathan died that she'd spoken of him and felt only joy in his memory, not the sharp pain of loss that tore through her being.

"You were well matched in the faith, I think."

"Yes. But it was Jonathan who encouraged me to read the Bible, because he'd been reading it all his life and had learned so much. It was perhaps the greatest gift he gave to me. You seem to know the Bible as well, Major. And yet . . ."

"The men I call my friends—Herr Lutz, the Hauptmann—are not exactly similar in faith?"

She nodded, glad he'd finished what she'd been reluctant to say.

"Let me first say, only Herr Lutz could be called a friend. The other, by circumstance, has been a comrade. One I trust implicitly . . . on the field. As for Herr Lutz, he is a good man who cannot see past his own preconceived notions. He used to complain that some students could not be taught the truth because they wouldn't let go of their old way of thinking. Herr Lutz is this way himself now. I understand only because I used to hold similar beliefs."

"And how long ago was that?"

"Hmm, let's see." He looked up for the barest moment as if to calculate. "A matter of months, I'm afraid, although I once knew the Bible quite well, as a child with a child's faith. Before my friends—and the German army—taught me to think otherwise."

"But the music . . . you knew the hymns."

"I was raised in a proper German Lutheran church. I received fine training and knowledge, but unfortunately, not until the prospect of facing heaven or hell did any of it mean anything personally. When I came here, God reminded me of Himself through the Bible that was left in the room upstairs. I began reading it almost from the day I arrived.

"And then," the Major added, his voice low, nearly a whisper, "you came. With your faith so strong and real." He cleared his throat, then looked at the floor. "You have been a powerful example to me in your kindness despite what you feel about the German army."

She couldn't help but laugh. "Until today."

"No, today is no different from any other day. You're living through this war in a way that holds firm to your faith. You lost your husband tragically and clung to that faith. And today you are concerned for someone else whom you love, yet your faith remains strong. I've seen some lose their faith altogether. Or so it seems."

He frowned, and barely aware of what she was doing, Genny touched his shoulder, letting her hand rest there gently. In a moment he placed his hand, the one not leaning on his cane, over hers.

Just then Genny heard a noise, but she'd imagined so many today coming from the front door, she was reluctant to see if someone might be there. It had been so long since she'd felt a man's touch, so long since she felt a kinship with someone her own age, so long since she felt anything but grief and worry and hunger. . . .

"Genny. I'm back."

The quiet voice didn't penetrate at first, but Genny saw the shadows out of the corner of her eye. And there was Isa, disheveled and staring as if confused. Just behind her stood Edward.

Genny rushed to Isa's side, scooping her into an embrace and blotting out all the thoughts as to why Edward might scowl or why Isa looked so perplexed. It didn't matter. "Isa! Oh, I'm so relieved."

Isa laughed and hugged her closer. "It's over, the whole awful mess."

Edward stepped around the women to stand before the Major.

"Yes, and it is no thanks to you for having invited your friends, is it, Major?"

The Major stiffened. He said nothing.

"I trust we all understand that von Eckhart is no longer welcome here?"

"Of course," the Major said.

Genny neared her son, grateful the Major was the amiable type. No one used such tones with German soldiers, not even to one of lesser rank than he. "Perhaps we should have tea and welcome Isa home." She looked at the Major. "You'll excuse us for a little while? We'll go into the kitchen and be out of your way. Can I have Clara bring some here to you?"

The Major shook his head. "No. I was thinking of going outside this afternoon."

Genny led the way to the kitchen, where she immediately turned to Edward. "You were not only rude, your words were on the edge of foolish. He may not own this house, but the German army thinks it owns this city, and we cannot very well give any one of them orders, now can we?"

"I don't care," he shot back. "His recuperation is about finished, I'd say. Why doesn't he go live at the Kommandantur with the rest of his cronies? Or back to the front for all I care."

"Many houses have soldiers billeted in them. He isn't going anywhere."

"And why is that, Mother?" Edward's tone was pure bite.

Genny's pulse raced, but she didn't look away. She would not be cowed by her son. "Is there something you wish to say, Edward?"

"Yes, and God forgive me for saying it with anger. Do you know why some of the families of the boys taken to St. Gilles won't let their sons see Jonah anymore?"

Caught by surprise, Genny shook her head.

"Because you came with *him* to see Jonah." He cocked his head toward the parlor, as if aiming at the Major himself. "Because it was obviously your influence with a German officer that obtained their freedom. And just now when we came into the room, you hardly noticed us. I thought you were worried about Isa. Yet when she finally came home, you barely looked up."

Genny shook her head, thoughts swirling so fast she could make no sense of them. Pain shot through her temples and she rubbed them, closing her eyes. When she opened them, she saw that Isa had come to her side and that Henri and Clara had unobtrusively left the room. She took comfort in Isa standing beside her, but it was small comfort.

She took Isa's hand. "You know I worried about Isa. As for those at Jonah's school, I cannot be responsible for the malicious thoughts of others. I will talk to Jonah, assure him—"

"I've done that already, Mother."

"Then how can you speak to me in this tone of voice? The Major saw I was worried. He was a friend to me today, and I'll not apologize for that."

"A friend? One of *them*? A German occupier? Not to mention that he sat at that dinner table and let his friends say all they could against the faith you hold dear. He's one of them."

"No, Edward. He is a Christian, same as you and I. You'll see him in eternity, so you had better learn to look at his face without sinning."

Her words had some effect; she saw it in the softening of his brows, the look in his eyes. He turned to Isa, who had watched silently, as if waiting for her opinion or confirmation from her own observations of the man.

"I've been around the Major so rarely," Isa said, "but he's been nothing but a gentleman. If your mother says he's a man of faith, I see no reason to doubt it."

"Might I remind you that it was his note to Herr Lutz that quickened Isa's trial? We owe him thanks, Edward, not hostility.

He is not the embodiment of the German army. He is a man with loyalty to his country, same as we have to our own."

"Yes, and which is stronger? Loyalty to God or to his beloved fatherland? I'm not sure a German can be completely loyal to both."

"Maybe they're saying the same in Germany about us. Aren't we killing their sons, the same as they're killing ours?"

She saw in the sag of his shoulders that he wrestled with whatever anger wanted to linger. At last he looked at her again, his gaze softened. "I'm sorry I spoke in anger." Then he looked at Isa. "And I'm sorry I spoiled your homecoming. You're probably hungry, and I've scared Clara away. Let's get something for you to eat."

Genny and Edward served Isa, who ate heartily, describing in detail the noxious meal at the Kommandantur.

When she finished, Isa turned to Edward. "You must want to work on the press, after the time you lost waiting for me."

His brows drew together. "I hoped you'd rethink this whole idea. All I've done these last two days is realize how dangerous it is for you, for everyone in this household. So I've decided we cannot possibly use it. All I have to do now is find a way to get it back to the printer who sold it to us."

Isa was shaking her head before he'd uttered his last word. "Those hours I spent in prison and at the tribunal made me more certain than ever. The German police *look* like real police, meant to protect, but they can arrest people for no reason. And their courts—they look like real courts, but there is no justice there. It reminds me of what we read in their propaganda newspapers. On the surface it all looks reasonable. *La Belgique* and *La Bruxellois* look like real newspapers, but each article, each word, is carefully chosen to push their agenda. It's all a sham."

"Of course it is, but you realize, don't you, that your experience proves the Germans already suspect you because of your return? that they'll somehow be watching you and this house? No doubt the Major you both seem to think trustworthy is telling them your whereabouts on a regular basis."

"And so we'll be careful." She reached across the table to take his hand. "God chose when each of us would be born and how we'll make a difference in the world. Our chance is here and now."

Genny watched her son stare at Isa, willing him to convince her that he was right. Since Isa's arrest, having the press in the cellar frightened her more than ever.

"You seem more determined now than you were before," her son said softly.

Those were not the words to change Isa's mind.

"I'm willing to take the risk, whatever it is. To the end."

Edward lifted a brow. "The end? If we're caught, you know what end that will be, don't you?"

Isa nodded.

Edward put his other hand over Isa's, and hers disappeared beneath. "To the end, then."

Genny watched the two of them as they exchanged the pact. And shivered.

Part Two

DECEMBER 1916

26

GERMANY SEEKS NEGOTIATED PEACE

In a note from Berlin, Germany says to neutral governments that their war aims are won, but they, the Central Powers, "have no desire to enter into a discussion regarding the origin of this world war. History will judge upon whom the immense guilt of the war shall fall. History's verdict will as little pass over the encircling policy of England, the revengeful policy of France, and the endeavor of Russia to gain Constantinople as over the instigation of the Serbian assassination in Sarajevo and the complete mobilization of Russia, which meant war against Germany. Germany and her allies, who had to take up arms for defense of their liberty and their existence, consider this, their aim of war, as obtained."

London remains skeptical about the sincerity of any call for negotiated peace.

La Libre Belgique

"Did you read the copy on the peace emblems yet?" Edward asked Isa as she pulled out the boards to fill with block letters from the typesetting box.

"So the Germans want us to abandon the rest of the Allies and wear emblems in support of a separate peace?"

"'Let the prosperity of peace return,'" Edward quoted from memory. "No doubt they want us to believe King Albert would bend to the will of his people and, from the corner of Belgium he still controls, arrange for a surrender from us all. As if any of us could be fooled by the German plan. Peace . . . at what price?"

"A German-run future, of course. Isn't that what Germany plans?"

Edward held up the paper upon which the next issue would be printed. "Exactly why this paper must go out. And quickly, before I see a single Belgian wearing one of those patches."

"Isn't it interesting," Isa said as she took a letter from the upper case, "that the Germans writing *La Bruxellois* these days are bantering back and forth with this paper, which, at least officially and legally, they refuse to acknowledge exists?"

Edward laughed as he readied to clean the cylinders. "How much paper do we have?" he asked.

"I picked up more from Jan at the de la Quarrere flat. It's there." She pointed to the crate behind him, where another ream of paper awaited. "Only the paper variance and text type have hinted at all the trouble you and the others have had keeping this paper going since the start of the war."

He caught the smile she sent his way, along with a look of admiration. It was a look Edward had grown to savor over these last two months of having her working at his side, a look that made him want to take her in his arms, especially knowing she'd accept him.

He'd grown far too familiar with this battle but so far had not lost it. Instead he cleared his throat, the collar on his priest's vestments suddenly too high, too close. "Which reminds me. I can get more money from Father Clemenceau, but I doubt he'll be able to replace what we used from your fund last week to pay for the ink. Again. It seems we've done nothing but use the money you brought along. How much do you have left?"

She shrugged, turning back to the typesetting box.

"Tell me, Isa. What is left?"

"I—I'm not sure."

Taking the compartmentalized box of letters from her, he gently turned her around and tilted her face toward his. "You do know, Isa. Tell me."

"I have two of the gold nuggets, one of the jewels."

"And the cash?"

"Gone."

He'd known that would be her answer. It meant only one thing: they were likely stuck in Belgium, unless they could depend on the connections they had at the paper to help with an escape, if needed. But how could the financiers behind the paper help—whoever they were? Funds were always a problem.

"I'm sorry," she whispered.

"For what?"

"That I didn't bring more. My parents have so much, and we could use it."

He laughed. "I knew it wouldn't be long before you missed your parents' money."

She gasped and started what surely would have been a protest except he laughed again to convince her he'd only been teasing.

They returned to their work and continued into the night, until Edward heard Isa yawn again. Without a word, he went to the light switch. At the end of each day, they waited for the all-clear signal from his mother, who spent most of her time keeping track of the Major, distracting him when necessary.

The light was on. All clear.

As they went upstairs, Edward couldn't help but think of

the hours his mother was forced to spend with the German. It rankled him, and that she didn't complain only made it more irksome.

Edward was surprised to see it was past ten o'clock. He should have left earlier.

He barely made it to the front door before his mother joined them. As usual, she smiled to see him.

"You are both working too hard," she said.

Edward shook his head. "It's not work—well, at least not by most definitions."

"You're both getting too little sleep and too little to eat. But I won't say any more. Far be it from me to become an overprotective mother hen."

Edward put an arm around her shoulders. "Too late."

She poked his side with her elbow. "I know I shouldn't object. I've never seen the two of you so happy." She looked from him to Isa. "Clara told me something interesting today. She said she met someone at the CRB food line who said she knew you."

"Who?"

"Pierrette Guillamay."

"An old boarding school roommate?" Edward asked Isa.

"Well, a roommate, but not from boarding school. We shared a cell at the Kommandantur."

"Why was she arrested?"

"I don't know. She wasn't sure. Perhaps for counting trains."

"How did she know Clara worked for Isa?" Edward asked his mother.

"That was what was so interesting. Evidently Clara was shorted today. Something about the number of coupons she turned in not matching the amount of food she was given. When she returned to work it out, this woman was there with the same problem. They started talking, Clara mentioned where she worked, and the

Guillamay woman said she knew Isa. Actually, she came home with Clara in hope of seeing you."

"Pierrette was here?" Isa asked.

"Yes, but of course I told her you were out and I didn't know when to expect you. She stayed and talked with Clara for a while. The two seemed to get along quite well."

"Pierrette is the friendly sort."

Edward studied her. "I've heard of German spies posing as prisoners as an attempt to get fellow inmates to incriminate themselves or someone they know."

"She seemed authentically Walloon to me. Her French was excellent—and she lost a son in the war. Besides, she didn't ask too many questions and talked more about herself than questioning me."

Edward shrugged. "It doesn't matter anyway, I suppose, unless she turns up again and starts making a pest of herself, snooping around."

Isa laughed. "Oh, Edward, you are the worrier. I'm sure she's harmless. As a matter of fact, I'm rather sorry I missed her. She was good company."

"Oh? Ready to take her downstairs to help pass the day, are you?"

"A simple hello might have been pleasant."

Edward prepared to leave by taking up the coat he'd brought from the cellar. "Well, if she comes back again, just make sure that's all it is. There's a reason no one trusts strangers these days."

"Of course you're right. But don't forget she was a victim of the German justice system, same as me."

"Perhaps." Edward kissed his mother's cheek. "Good night, Mother. We're nearly finished running the new issue, so you shouldn't have to spend much time with the Major tomorrow."

Then he buttoned his coat and bid Isa good night, stepping into the freezing December air.

27

It is bad enough what German soldiers do to Allied soldiers, killing them. But what they do to us, the living civilians under their occupation, is appalling as well. They have eliminated our freedom and disallow our dignity.

La Libre Belgique

"I believe, *madame*, your fox is surrounded."

Genny looked at the carved wooden board between them, with her lone red peg entrapped by a number of yellow ones. Indeed, the Major's geese surrounded her fox, despite her best effort to keep it free.

"Let's see," she said, sitting back, "you've bested me at fox and geese, hoppity, even cribbage. I'm tempted to give up on games altogether and challenge you to something you couldn't possibly win. A lace-making contest, perhaps? I'm not very good at that, either, but I'm confident I might beat you there."

"How about something easier than that? a foot race?"

She caught his eye, wondering how he could jest so easily over his disability. But then, in the past weeks of keeping his company, she had learned a great deal about Major von Bürkel. Max, as he insisted she call him. It seemed silly to continue calling him Major after how close they'd become.

For weeks now she'd spent several hours a day with him when he did not go to the Kommandantur or to the hospital, where he worked with other soldiers nursing wounds similar to his own. Sometimes, like today, she shared his company even when Isa wasn't home and Edward was off on one mission or another.

Guilt only occasionally nagged her anymore for enjoying Max's company so much. Day after day, sharing stories of their children, of their own childhoods, of memories that made them laugh or nearly cry, it was easy to forget that it was her job to distract him. Easy to forget that was all she *should* be doing, all Edward expected her to do.

"How do you do it, Max? This war changed your life forever, your body, your future. And yet you go on."

"Have I a choice, Genny?"

He only called her by name when he was sure they were alone, and even then only rarely.

He stood, going to the window, looking out. "When I see those boys at the hospital, I think the ones who lost only a limb are the lucky ones. Those, like me, who weren't out there for very long."

Max looked at her over his shoulder, his eyes bleak. "What kind of world have we made for those who will be left? The world your husband and my sons knew is gone, I'm afraid. Perhaps forever gone."

Genny joined him at the window. They could hear the sound of the guns off in the distance, and only yesterday an Allied plane had been spotted overhead. No doubt trying to bomb the zeppelin hangars at Ghent. Genny had read in the German papers that a German plane had intercepted it and shot it down.

The street was empty now, but she knew, out there, armed soldiers still marched, parading through the Grand Place, tacking placards of new rules on ancient buildings, rolling cannons down the avenues as a reminder of their might. Surely it wouldn't forever be this way, where guns ruled behavior.

As they stared out side by side, Genny found herself unable to imagine a future different from the past she knew and missed, different from the present she resented.

Max put a hand on her shoulder as if whatever vision he saw was too somber to bear alone.

◌◈

Isa stood at the flat's curtained window, watching the street below for a sign of Edward. He was late.

She glanced behind her to Rosalie, who lingered nearby. She'd arrived precisely on time to pick up her share of *La Libre Belgique*, minutes after Jan left. There were not enough remaining copies for Rosalie to take all she needed, Jan having claimed most of what Isa brought.

Despite knowing Rosalie was as dedicated and trustworthy as anyone else in their network, Isa barely knew her. She never spoke to Isa, rarely made eye contact with her. On any occasion Isa was with both Edward and Rosalie, Isa had watched them for a sign of intimacy, something to indicate that their relationship was more than just workers sharing a goal worthy of their lives.

But there was nothing.

Shifting one of the only two chairs in the flat closer to the window, Isa sat. Transporting finished copies of *La Libre Belgique* was her least favorite task, taking them from her home to this flat registered to a fictitious William de la Quarrere. From here the newssheets would be available to various distributors like Jan and Rosalie, then moved to secret depots throughout the city. From each of those, copies found their way into letter boxes as far away as Antwerp and Ghent. And though the paper rarely totaled more than a couple of sheets printed back to back, transporting several thousand copies was no small mission. She had set out first, with a ream of copies spread evenly beneath her clothing. Edward was to follow with the same, plus an attaché case with concealed compartments.

She'd expected Edward to arrive shortly after she had, but she'd been here nearly a half hour with no sign of him. Worry soon took the place of the awkwardness of sharing Rosalie's company, and for a moment she wished they were friendly enough that she might voice her concern about Edward's tardiness.

Perhaps she'd become too lax in her day-to-day trust in divine protection. When was the last time she had coerced Edward into praying with her before they set out? How many days ago? Why had she let him go yesterday, and the day before, and now today, without prayer?

Oh, God, dear God, watch over him now.

"You love him, don't you?"

Isa looked at the other woman.

Rosalie gave a half smile. "You needn't say it. I can see that you do."

Rosalie was a Fleming, and her heavily accented French made her sound almost German sometimes.

She crossed her arms, and Isa noticed her long, graceful fingers. How many times had Rosalie administered Edward's disguises with those lovely hands? Isa was grateful his new identity didn't require such ministrations.

"But he hasn't accepted that love, has he? No, you needn't admit that, either."

Isa turned back to the window, wishing Rosalie had let the silence continue. She didn't want to hear whatever Rosalie had to say, even though part of her told her she must listen. Rosalie might not have known Edward for as long as Isa had, but she knew him. Well.

"Do you know the reason he won't accept love?" Rosalie hadn't moved, still leaned against the far wall, near the door. "He is consumed by this paper, by the danger it brings. Has he told you yet that this is not the time to indulge in love? in life? because death could be so close?"

Her words, each of them, stabbed Isa's heart. Did she and Rosalie have a bond, then? Both rejected by Edward?

She leaned closer to the window just as a figure caught her eye, one moving briskly but oh so familiarly. Ignoring Rosalie, Isa hurried to open the door, watching him enter from the street and take the stairs two at a time. Attaché in hand.

"I was beginning to worry." Her words sounded so breathless it could have been she who'd just bounded up the stairs. She closed the door behind them.

"Yes, I thought you might." He barely looked up, only thrust the case on the table and opened it. "Father Clemenceau needed several hundred copies and couldn't wait until later, so I went there first."

"I was wondering what could have kept you." She hadn't realized she was trembling and so near to tears. Results of worry or Rosalie's words. . . .

Where was she? Isa scanned the one-room flat, seeing that Rosalie had moved behind them, into the shadows. Edward hadn't yet seen her.

Edward took one of Isa's fidgety hands. Despite the cold outside, his fingers were warmer than hers. The radiators in the flat were unheated today; undoubtedly there was no coal for the boiler in the cellar.

"I thought you didn't worry?" Edward brushed away a tendril of her hair that had escaped the neat bun she'd twisted at the back. "You said God is protecting us."

"God, Edward?"

Isa had wanted to make the inquiry, but if it had been her, those same two words would have been hopeful, inviting. As it was, Rosalie's voice teetered between surprise and skepticism.

He turned to Rosalie, still holding Isa's hand. For a moment Isa was tempted to withdraw, even though Edward had held her hand before. Letting him hold it now, in front of Rosalie, seemed to say something it didn't mean.

"Yes," he said. "Isa spends most days reminding me to pray. And I must admit I haven't minded."

Then he did drop her hand, but not before sending an extra smile her way.

"I'm glad," Isa whispered. "Perhaps you're growing into your vestments."

Rosalie approached and took up the copies, already bundled, that she would conceal in her satchel. "You should consider the priesthood permanently, Edward." She looked at him. "It would give you a solid reason to refuse the women who fall in love with you."

She transferred that fixed gaze to Isa before stuffing the copies of the paper into her satchel, and then she left the flat.

Isa moved to busy herself by separating the remaining copies from the attaché while Edward removed more from beneath his coat. Additional distributors were expected, but neither she nor Edward needed to wait. She wanted to leave now, right away, before Edward had a chance to dwell on Rosalie's words.

He stacked the copies from his coat next to those Isa took from the attaché. "Did you and Rosalie have some sort of . . . discussion while she was here?"

"Barely. Why do you ask?"

"You didn't think it odd, then, what she said before she left?"

"For you to become a priest? Perhaps you should."

He laughed. "Me? With the history of my faith? I'm not even Catholic."

"Your faith never left you. You didn't acknowledge it for a while, but it's been there."

"Let's not discuss the possibility of my becoming a priest, shall we?

Let's discuss why she said that to begin with. To give me an excuse to refuse women who love me? She made it sound as though there were a number of them, so would you please direct me to such a line?"

She couldn't make light of the topic as he seemed eager to do. "Perhaps there are more women than I'm aware of, but as it is, I know of only two."

They stood not a foot apart, but a barrier filled that narrow space. If he refused to discuss this with any sort of sincerity, Isa would know she and Rosalie did indeed share that bond. Maybe someday Isa might thank Rosalie for making Edward face this topic once and for all. For helping them to get it over with, to know if Isa had anything to hope for or if she was just another woman, like Rosalie, whom Edward couldn't love.

If he said nothing . . . or turned away with a jest . . .

"Two?"

She nearly sighed with relief. So at least he would face it. "It's obvious, isn't it? Rosalie . . . and me."

"You, Isa?"

She wanted to scold him or run away because he surely knew but was making her say it anyway. "You know I love you, Edward. It's why I came back."

"You came back for my mother."

"And you."

"And Jonah."

"But it was you. Really."

Another long moment, as if that invisible barrier allowed neither one to move or to touch the other.

"Is this the wrong time for love?" she asked. "Because of the danger? Because it would make us less careful? Is the paper all we should devote ourselves to? Maybe you believe loving someone now would make the loss too great, unbearable, if one of us were caught."

"All of that is true. And more. It *would* be unbearable if one of us were caught, especially if we planned some sort of future together. What kind of future could we have, anyway? We're not at all fit for one another. You with your family, me with my university burned to the ground."

Edward stepped closer, breaking that barrier between them. "But I do love you, Isa. Your faith, your courage, even your stubbornness."

She looked up at him, pulse racing, light-headed. Caution tried to stop the race. "You—you love me? How? In what way?"

For a moment she was sure he would take her in his arms, finish this confession of love in the way she'd dreamed of often enough, with a kiss. Instead, he turned away, stepped back to the attaché, and put his fingers to the locks. "I love you. Let's just leave it at that, shall we?"

She'd barely heard the words between her heart thumping all the way up to her ears and his quiet tone. This was hardly what she'd waited so many years to hear.

"We can't leave it at that, Edward. Not until you define the kind of love you're talking about."

Suddenly he turned to her again and clutched her shoulders in a way that was anything but romantic. "I'm asking you to forget this, Isa. To wait. To go on as we were before."

"So you're rejecting me in the same fashion as you must have rejected Rosalie."

"What? Exactly what did she say to you?"

"Only that you won't let yourself love someone because it's too dangerous and now is not the time to lose your head."

"True, every word, and I have no right to let either one of us get carried away with anything but caution and concern for the paper."

She shook her head. "So I'm supposed to forget this? forget that you love me? that I love you?"

The pressure on her shoulders increased. "Isa, I saw sixteen men—good men—die at the hands of German soldiers. I should have been one of them. Since then I've seen a dozen people arrested, all because of this paper. Yet here I am, free. Why? Am I supposed to live as if something like that isn't just around the corner for me, too? ignore the danger, hope for a brighter future, when there isn't supposed to be a future for me?"

"How can you not deserve a brighter future? You've been careful. You were stronger than those who died because of the work camp. God has protected—"

"Stop! Isa, just stop."

And so she did, but she was no less confused than a moment ago. "I don't understand. You love me and yet you want me to forget that you do?"

"Nothing's as it should be; you know that. Before the war, you wouldn't have entertained notions of marrying someone like me, bound to be a professor of all things. And I . . . how could I ever fit into your family, with parents who waste all their time at parties and a brother who thinks I'm barely fit to tie his shoes? We're not facing any of that living the way we do now, but it won't be any less real when this war ends. And it will end. So we'll forget all of this until the last German has marched out of Belgium."

"No, Edward." She pulled on the sleeve of his cassock. "I won't ever forget your telling me you love me, even if this war did ruin the way it should have been said."

Then it was she who closed the gap between them and pressed her lips to his in a way that left no doubt as to the kind of love she felt for him.

⁓

Edward was helpless to stop himself. He drew Isa closer than she'd allowed a moment ago, so that it was no longer her kissing him but rather the other way around.

But even as he lost that grip on control, he fought his way back. This could not happen. He couldn't let it.

"Isa, Isa," he whispered as he pulled her away. "I can't."

"But, Edward . . ."

He stepped back fully, outside of her arms, away from her touch that addled his brain. He shouldn't have told her, shouldn't have admitted he loved her. Even though it was true. Even if it meant she would take it for a rejection, the same kind he'd given Rosalie. Even if it wasn't.

"I'm sorry. I love you, but I can't. Not now."

He grabbed the empty attaché and left the flat.

28

And so the cannons rattle over our streets, but it is not just our city they trample. They trample all that is good, all that is just, all that is right. We—each of us who passively resist—are living testimonies to what they have done. And for those whose blood has stained our fields where poppies once bloomed, we offer eternal testimonies.

La Libre Belgique

Genny breathed deeply and for a moment between slumber and wakefulness felt a smile on her lips. Jonathan lay beside her, whispering that he loved her. She enjoyed his kiss and raised a hand to caress his image . . . but the very act of lifting her arm broke the link to that place of dreams, and reality returned.

She turned to her side, clutching the pillow beneath her head. "Oh, Jonathan." And then her tears tumbled to that pillow.

Some time later she went to the pitcher and bowl and splashed icy water on her face. She combed her hair, dressed, straightened the covers on her bed, then faced the door but was suddenly reluctant to leave the privacy of her room. Heaviness made every effort greater this morning, a heaviness she was just beginning to understand.

Her affection for Max weighed heavier all the time; the larger that affection grew, the larger the burden.

She left her sanctuary and headed to the stairs, knowing she would pass his room on the way and listen, as she did every morning, to hear if he was awake.

But the music room door was already open.

"Genny!"

She stepped inside, where Max was just rising from his chair with the help of his cane. Before him was the table they used to play games, this time covered with a white cloth and set with tea, toast, and what looked like a tin of jam.

"I hope you don't mind," he said with that most disarming of smiles, the one that revealed the streak of shyness running through him. "I've asked your Clara to bring breakfast in here, enough for both of us. Will you join me?"

She nodded, even though the instant she saw his face, the image of Jonathan came back, so vivid from the dream.

Max held out a chair for her, then reclaimed his own at the intimate breakfast table. He didn't wait for her to pour tea but instead, like the host he was, poured for her.

"We have jam this morning," he said happily. "Straight from Germany."

She watched him finish serving her, taking a piece of the toast, spreading it liberally with the red confection, and handing it to her.

"Maybe," he said slowly as she took it from him, "when you've finished with that, you might tell me why you're downhearted today."

He seemed to have made himself a student of her, claiming it his business to guess her mood and the reason behind any fluctuation. While it was flattering to be of such interest to someone who obviously found greater challenges fascinating, it was also unsettling.

"I had a dream this morning." She sipped her tea. "I dreamed Jonathan was alive, here with me. I miss him."

She welcomed the sympathy in his eyes, grateful that her memories of Jonathan never ignited awkwardness between them.

"Dreams can be gifts sometimes," he said. "A visit with someone we miss."

"Have you had such a dream?" she asked. "Of your sons, perhaps? or . . . your wife?"

He'd rarely spoken of her, and the few times Genny had mentioned the mother of his lost boys, he had discreetly but quickly changed the subject. But she'd found herself more curious lately, for reasons she wasn't ready to explore.

"No," he said abruptly.

"Max," she said, setting down her tea, "we've shared so much in these past weeks. We've become friends, and I must honestly admit I've shared more with you than I have any other man except Jonathan. But I'm not sure you could say the same."

He lifted a skeptical blond brow at that. "Do you think I've been secretive about myself? After I've told you everything from my pettiest peeves to my biggest disappointments?"

"Only about one subject."

He looked downward, suddenly seeming as melancholy as she felt, and she couldn't help but wonder at the cause.

"You're right, of course. If I've guessed at some of your moods, Genny, you've guessed—and been correct—at more of mine."

He placed one of his hands on the table, thumbing the handle of the knife he'd used moments ago. "You once accused me of methodical thinking. And of course I'm guilty as charged. But there is a part of my life I haven't been able to put into any neat compartment, explored and understood. I mean you, of course. And my wife."

Genny's heart pattered in her breast. Why should it matter to hear him talk of his wife?

"The funny thing is, I've prayed about this nearly since the first moment I saw you standing at the door of my room." He looked up at last with a half smile. "Do you remember that day? You'd come after Jonah and somewhere along the way lost your shoe like the girl from the fairy tale."

She didn't respond. Couldn't.

"I suppose we should have discussed this already," he went on, "except that discussing it seemed to make the problem real, and I didn't want to acknowledge it. That's unlike me, I know, because I normally attack whatever challenge I'm faced with. It's why I'm so good at games, I suppose. But nonetheless, here it is. I think you've guessed, by now, what I'm getting at."

She wasn't at all sure, although perhaps in part because she didn't want to be. "You've hardly spoken of your wife, Max. I assumed you were a widower, else why wouldn't you have gone home for your recuperation?"

"Yes, that's a logical assumption. And perhaps I'm making something of nothing by telling you she isn't dead, that in fact she is very much alive and living in Germany."

Genny stiffened and didn't know why. Why should it affect her one way or another? And yet she couldn't deny that her insides went leaden, heavier than they'd been when she first walked into the room.

His chair was not far from hers since the table was so small. When she'd placed her tea down, she'd let her hand rest nearby, close to his. Now he put his hand over hers.

"We've become close, Genny, and friendships are always rather complicated between a man and a woman, aren't they? Even without a war going on, one in which we happen to belong to opposing sides. I don't know if it makes a difference to you that I'm married. It shouldn't, but somehow, to me at least, it does. Because of how close we've become."

Pulling her hand away, she tried to smile. "We're friends. Why should it matter if either one of us is married?"

"Yes, precisely."

"I wonder why you haven't told me, though." She strained to keep her voice light and easy. "Why you've said so little of her."

"I will tell you now if you want to hear."

She nodded.

"Käethe and I were married young. Too young, I suppose. I wasn't yet finished with my schooling. I was quite different back then. I was home from university and saw her during the Christmas holiday. We were both rather rash and foolish." He paused as if to skip over certain memories and shifted in his chair. "At any rate, she became pregnant and I hurried home from Paris to marry her. She returned there with me, and when I graduated and obtained a job, we lived off the generosity of my parents—who were all too happy to have us living in Paris, where no one would count the months from our wedding date to the birth of our first son."

Max leaned back, rubbing his forehead, closing his eyes a moment. "We were happy enough. We had Thomas, our first, then two years later, Karl. Then we moved back to Germany, close to family, and simply lived. We raised our boys together until one year we realized we loved our children but no longer one another. It's what comes of marrying too quickly, I suppose, and for the wrong reason."

He paused again, looking at her briefly, then away. "I've envied the memories you have of your husband. I know you loved him, and your love never dwindled."

"All marriages have an ebb and flow," she whispered. "Perhaps that's what happened in your marriage, and that original love can be recaptured."

"Käethe lived for her boys. Her boys alone. When they died, she found she had nothing to live for anymore." He leaned forward again, pushing away his plate, folding his hands where it had been. "Thomas was killed only days after Christmas in '14. Karl died two months later, and I went home to grieve, to be with her. But she was gone. Not physically, but inside. She didn't even know my name. The grief had taken her away." He paused again, breathing once deeply. "She lives in a convent now, where the sisters take care of her. I get a letter now and then from one of the nuns, after I've sent money, keeping me informed of her general health. She eats; she sleeps. That's all. She doesn't speak; has never asked for me; has never, on the occasions I've visited her, even recognized me."

Genny placed her hands in her lap, her heart aching for a woman she didn't even know, a woman whose life was so shattered and empty. "With the sisters, you say?" she asked quietly. "Surely they've tried to speak to her, tell her that even in the midst of her pain, God is there, grieving with her? Has she no hope at all of feeling God's love?"

"I don't know."

Genny leaned forward, never more sure of anything than what she was prepared to say. "You must go to her, Max, now that you've come to better understand God's love yourself. She needs to hear it, and maybe from you, she'll be able to listen."

"Ever compassionate, Genny." He frowned and looked away. "More so than me, I'm afraid. You're right, of course. I should go to her, especially now that I've discovered a faith that's helped me in so many ways. I should have thought of it myself. Perhaps I did, but . . ."

"But?"

He looked back at her. "But I haven't wanted to go. I haven't wanted to leave here. You."

They were words she wanted to hear, but she squashed the attempt her heart made to fly. "Then that is all the more reason for you to go."

She stood, leaving the breakfast uneaten. He stood as well, and at first she couldn't bring herself to look at him.

"I think it wise that we don't allow ourselves to be alone anymore, Max. I know that we're only friends, but there's been a sort of intimacy about our friendship that no longer seems appropriate." She looked up at him. "I'm sorry."

"No, don't apologize. It was all my own foolishness. I thought— I thought that I could be your friend and nothing more. But I was wrong. It's I who's sorry, Genny. And I am. Profoundly so."

She could think of nothing else to say, and so she backed away from the table, feeling the chair behind her. Awkwardly she stepped around it, each movement so tense she thought her bones might crack from being put to use in such a state. Somehow she made it to the door.

"Will you go out today, Max? Please? Away from here, away from this room? To the hospital, perhaps? Or . . . elsewhere?"

"Yes, Genny, I'll go."

29

The slave gangs will arrive here in Brussels, have no doubt. And to think the world once thought all of Europe so civilized.

La Libre Belgique

"Have you tried using the rice flour they're making these days? It's closer to white, at least."

"Ah, but the taste! We are known for excellence, for the lightness of our pastry, the flakiness of each layer." Pierrette shook her head in disgust. "We must not form our precious little tarts into tasteless lumps."

Isa laughed, enjoying the exchange between Clara and Pierrette. It was the first time in two weeks that she'd felt herself again, having been muddled by a haze of confusion. Edward loved her, but couldn't. He loved her. But didn't. He loved her and perhaps loved Rosalie, too, but not either one enough to conquer whatever ghosts he carried with him from the camp. Isa hadn't even told Genny because Genny seemed in a world of her own lately too.

Edward had been to the house only once, and that was to work the press. He hadn't directed a personal word her way, not even a hello or good-bye. And she waited, hoping all he needed was time to realize their love was real and vital.

Isa had found Pierrette's company a pleasant diversion, while Genny was once again reclusive.

"You did love your work, didn't you?" Isa asked now.

"But of course! Every artist does."

Clara, still at the sink, tilted her head to one side. "Artist? I thought you were a baker, same as your husband."

"Baker! Bah, what sort of term is that to describe fifty-two variations of pastry? And my cakes! Oh, if I but had the right ingredients, Clara, I could show you what an artist I am."

"You are certainly right about the rice. Here we are, nearly starving, and they send us something like that. Ach, it's hard to get down."

Pierrette nodded. "Yes, they should take pity on us."

"It's been hard for everyone, being unable to work," Isa said. "How is your husband?"

Her blue eyes sparkled. "It's why I came today! To tell you my good news—that my dear Jean-Luc was acquitted of the phony charges against him. He was let go only yesterday—think of that, after so long in those awful cells awaiting freedom."

"Two months! And that dreadful food."

"Oh, please, do not remind me!"

The ringer at the front door sounded and Isa jumped. Would she ever forget the day soldiers had come to her door? But then, would the Germans ever use the ringer instead of the butt of their rifles?

Clara wiped her hands on a towel, then hurried from the room.

"Tell me, Isa," Pierrette said, "what you've been doing since you were freed. Since we lost our shop, we've struggled to get through the days. Boredom is not easy, is it?"

"No. But I'm learning to sew lace, and I have Clara and my dearest friend here with me, so the days aren't so long."

"Ah, yes, Madame Kirkland. She is English, yes?"

"Well . . . yes, but she's lived here in Belgium more than ten years."

"And the Germans, they have left her alone anyway?"

"Why shouldn't they? She's done nothing wrong—even though they killed her husband."

"So she is a victim of them too. Those Germans. How I hate them!"

Just then Clara rejoined them, and Isa asked her who had been at the door.

"A sentry for the Major," she said. "Something must be happening to him. It is the second message this morning already!"

Max ran the *Passierschein* between his thumb and forefinger, refolding it and placing it on top of his few belongings. Arrangements had taken nearly two weeks, but a driver from the Kommandantur would come for him in a few hours, bringing an army-issue duffel bag to hold his belongings. Max would soon be transported to the train and on to Germany.

He looked around the room. He would leave it as he found it, with the single exception of the wear on the Bible that had been in perfect condition some months earlier. He would have liked to take it because it held much meaning for him, and obviously its former owner had no use for it. But he would find one of his own. Perhaps at the abbey.

Thoughts of his destination inevitably led to thoughts of his wife, which by contrast led to thoughts of Genny. If Max had learned anything by now, it was an ability to denounce personal desires for a greater goal. By sheer discipline of mind he concentrated on his duty, and that, coupled with prayer, brought him some measure of peace. Certainly he'd had none of that while spending so many waking hours wishing he were free to devote himself to Genny.

He sat next to his things. Silence again, something he'd forgotten during the days he'd spent with her. He would have to say good-bye to her soon, not at all certain his discipline of mind would be enough to get him through.

Genny read the first line of her book three times before absorbing its meaning. She should be grateful that Isa's home offered so many books from which to choose; reading had always been a favorite way to pass the time.

She'd been reading in the parlor because she could still perform the job Edward and Isa needed her to do: make sure the Major was well away from the kitchen or pantry. But Genny couldn't deny, if she was to be honest with herself, that she'd far preferred talking, playing games, sharing music, and generally *being with* Max to pass those hours.

Just then she heard noise at the front door, followed quickly by the ringer. This time Genny went to see who it was before Clara even made it out of the kitchen.

She opened the door to a stocky sentry. "I am here to collect Major von Bürkel."

"Collect?" She noticed the folded field gray duffel bag beneath his arm.

"Collect."

From behind her, Genny heard Clara's approach. "Will you tell the Major there is someone here for him?"

The sentry moved inside, sidestepping Genny. "I will follow."

Genny watched the two go up the stairs, wishing she had the right to go too.

She didn't bother returning to her book, knowing any attempt at reading was futile, at least until she knew the details of why Max was being "collected." She'd thought—hoped—the German army had refused his request to return home, since he spent so many of his days at the Kommandantur or sanitariums with recuperating patients.

Barely five minutes later she heard movement from the top of the stairs. Hurriedly she took her seat, picking up the book but not seeing a word.

She saw Max first. He looked toward the butler's hall, then toward the parlor, where his eyes rested on hers. He was dressed in a dark greatcoat, gloved, holding his shiny steel helmet under his arm. She stood and he approached after giving orders to the sentry to take his bag and wait outside. Clara closed the door behind the sentry, then looked at the Major as if ready to open it again for him. But when she looked in the direction Max stared, she left altogether.

Genny met Max in the center of the parlor. The lamp she'd used to read by only dimly lit a corner of the room. The shuttered windows of the parlor let in no light at all.

"I'm taking your advice and returning home at last." He offered a half smile.

She nodded, unable to speak. Unable, too, to stop looking at him, though she wished she could turn away in case he saw her wildly erratic breathing.

"I would have told you my travel was approved," he went on, "but word came to me only this morning. I hope . . ."

She waited for him to finish.

He started again. "Perhaps this seems abrupt since we've barely spoken these last days. I don't mean it to be."

She nodded again, silently calling herself a fool for being so speechless.

At last he took a step closer and with his free hand reached for one of hers. "Will you let me stand here blathering like a fool, Genny? Won't you even say good-bye?"

She tore her gaze from his to look at his hand, so strong, so much larger than hers as it tenderly held her own. "Good-bye," she whispered, so quietly she could barely hear her own voice. She dared not speak any louder and give away the tremble she knew he would detect.

She felt him take a breath as if to speak again, but no words came. He let go of her hand and turned to walk toward the hall.

"Max," she said, unsure she should say anything but unable to hold back.

He stopped immediately, facing her again. But he didn't step any closer.

She bit back the words she wanted to say—how she would miss him and wished he weren't going, how she would think of him while wishing he were still here. But she refused to feed this monster between them. Instead, she offered a quick prayer even as words began leaving her mouth.

"Love her, Max. Your Käethe. I've heard it said that sometimes the feeling follows the action. You have the discipline for the action; I know that."

He smiled, but she thought it was a rather sad smile. "Yes, discipline I have. That's true." He paused, started to turn away again, then looked at her with a larger smile, one that held the admiration she'd seen on his face so many times before. "Good-bye then, Genny."

"Good-bye, Max."

And then she watched him leave.

30

Once again the Germans have proven how shallow, how utterly worthless, their promises are. More men are being seized and sent to Germany—in cattle cars of all things. Even men holding cards allotted them by the CRB are being deported, and such men were once "promised" to be exempt from the seizures.

La Libre Belgique

Edward worked on the latest issue of *La Libre Belgique*, waiting for Isa to return to the room and finish typesetting the final page. They'd barely spoken since that day at the flat; he could tell she was waiting for him to say something. How was it that he felt so much yet could express so little? Could he admit his dreams of a future with her turned to nightmares under the sure knowledge that he didn't deserve any of this—her, happiness, life?

And so he kept silent because he couldn't understand what he felt and even less how to share it all with her.

Upon learning the Major had returned to Germany, Edward had expected his mother to be relieved, with one less enemy, especially one lurking in the house. Except she hardly looked happy at all.

And in the last few days a new nuisance had arisen.

"Is she still up there?" Edward asked Isa when she pushed open the door.

"I went out the front door on my 'errand' while Genny sat with her in the parlor so I could reenter the kitchen and come back down here."

"You shouldn't have taken the risk while she's still here."

"I don't know when she's leaving. It's getting late and we still have so much to do."

"I'm working on it," Edward said.

"And it'll take twice as long for you alone," she said. "All the depots are set up for noon tomorrow for this next issue. It must be done."

She didn't need to tell him that. She was every bit as conscientious about work as Edward himself. But he didn't like anyone taking risks—most especially Isa. Having Pierrette Guillamay around made everything a risk.

"I know you don't like her, Edward, but—"

"I never said I didn't like her."

"You don't trust her."

Edward glanced at Isa. "I trust few people these days."

"That's because you don't know her. She's a friend."

He shrugged. That didn't make any difference.

"I wish you would give her a chance. I think she might be of some help."

"Recruiting her for *La Libre Belgique*?"

"No. It's just that she's so bored since her shop closed. And she seems patriotic."

"That may be true. But more than a few people have been arrested for trusting the wrong person."

If she'd argued, he might have argued back, but she tended to her work again instead. A benefit of his confession of love? They hadn't argued since that day.

He left the press and stood before her. "I admire your capacity to believe the best in people. And I trust your judgment. Perhaps, if there is a way to check into Pierrette's past, we can do as you say. Invite her help."

She gave him one of those smiles he dreamed of, the one that said she admired him, his decisions, and everything he did to protect her.

It was all he could do not to take her into his arms.

Isa flipped her braid out of her way. Typesetting was laborious work, calling for patience and concentration, but she'd finished some time ago and Edward had the press running full steam.

Sometimes she believed she'd dreamed what happened in the flat. But he'd told her he loved her. She'd kissed him, and he'd kissed her back. All regular components in the long-held romance of her imagination.

And yet the results had been far from a dream come true. Since then they'd only worked harder, with an increased determination to make sure the paper was distributed. Safely, securely. And as regularly as possible.

One thing was certain: doing that demanded all the energy she had to give. And lately, that was considerable.

The press quieted and both of them set about bundling.

"Now whose stomach is growling?" Isa asked. He used to tease her about the protests her empty stomach made, but she'd distinctly heard his just now.

He didn't look up, just kept working. "Amazing how you can do that."

"Do what?"

He glanced at her with the first grin in two weeks. "Make your stomach noises sound like they're coming from me. What form of ventriloquism is that, exactly?"

She took a step away from the table that was strewn with paper and stretched to relieve a stitch in her back. "Let's go upstairs for something to eat."

"Better check the all-clear light first."

"Oh, I'm sure Pierrette is gone by now. She's never stayed this long."

"Isa—"

"You're so cautious! All right, all right."

They turned off the light just long enough to see that the all-clear light was not ignited.

Isa frowned, pressing the button to light the overhead again. "Maybe your mother forgot. Pierrette cannot still be here."

Edward shook his head. "She wouldn't forget."

"Maybe she fell asleep."

Edward lifted a brow. She could see he thought that a possibility. Sleep was all Genny seemed to do lately.

"I'll be quiet," Isa said. "If I hear anything from the kitchen, I'll come back out without being seen."

"I'll go."

"No. I know the kitchen better than you do and where to find what we'll need."

"All right." But he closed the two steps between them and put his hand gently around her wrist. "Be careful."

She nodded and let herself out.

Isa crept up the stairs silently, slowly pushing the door at the top. It creaked. She stopped. The sound had been slight, barely a scrape of metal on the hinge. The door opposite, to the kitchen, was still closed. She walked to it and put her ear to it, hearing nothing.

Turning around, she saw the bread wrapped in a cloth on the counter. Carefully opening a drawer, she withdrew a knife. She would take it down with her. The cheese was wrapped as well, near the bread. All she needed now was water, but to get that she must venture to the kitchen.

Placing both hands on the door, she listened again. How foolish she must appear, waiting for sounds that obviously weren't there. But Edward's constant caution had left an impression. She peeked carefully around the edge of the door.

Isa pitched herself back as if the door were on fire. Pierrette stood not four steps away. The other woman leaned against the sink facing the window, though it was dark and she couldn't possibly see out. What was she *doing* here all this time?

Isa tiptoed back down the stairs without taking the bread, careful to skip the squeaky stair. She let herself into the secret room, and Edward had only to take one quick look to guess something was wrong.

"What happened?"

"Pierrette is still here."

"Did she see you?"

Isa shook her head.

"Are you sure?"

"Yes. She wasn't even looking my way."

Edward frowned. "I wonder why she is here so late."

"I wonder the same."

"Still think you want to trust her?"

Isa took a deep, calming breath. "Oh, Edward, I'm sure we're both overreacting. I agree I'm not ready to trust her, but there was no harm done. I really do take your cautions to heart."

"That's good news. Surprising," he added, "but good."

Grateful for his attempt to lighten the moment, she nodded. "Let's finish up."

And so they did. An hour later they were tying the last of the bundles to be dispatched tomorrow.

"Why don't you try the light again?" Edward said after Isa's stomach growled louder than his once again.

"I think we should keep some food down here from now on." She turned off the overhead light and finally saw the smaller light next to it.

"Let's go," Edward said.

With the room securely shut off behind them, they were upstairs in moments.

Genny sat at the kitchen table alone.

"When did Pierrette finally leave?" Isa asked, taking a seat next to Genny.

"Fifteen or twenty minutes ago. She waited so long for you tonight, Isa, I didn't know what to tell her."

"What did you say?"

"That you were with a close friend and might spend the night. When I reminded Pierrette about sentries, she just shrugged and said she didn't mind taking risks because she has nothing to hide. I suppose that's how she ended up in that jail cell where you met her." Genny rubbed the back of her neck. "Isa, we should either tell her what you're really doing or end this friendship. It's nerve-racking."

"For me, too!" Then she told Genny how she'd seen Pierrette in the kitchen, apparently alone.

"That must have been when I was upstairs in the convenience," Genny said, looking a little embarrassed. "When I came back, she was still in the parlor."

"She was standing by the sink. But why come in here at all if you were visiting in the parlor?" Isa shook her head. "I don't like it, but I don't see how I can end the friendship, either. Wouldn't that be odd, for no reason?"

"You're a Lassone, Isa," Edward told her. "Snubbing people from Pierrette's class should come naturally."

She wanted to think he was making light of the topic, and maybe there was a hint of a smile in his eye, but Isa wasn't sure, so she looked away, uncertain. "In any case, the excitement is over for now, and the latest issue is complete." She looked at Edward again. "When will we have copy for the next issue?"

"Father Clemenceau said not to expect anything new until the end of the week."

"Well, at least I'll be available if she comes back tomorrow."

Genny laughed. "Oh, I think you can depend on that."

Edward was still frowning. "It'll probably take both of you to distract her so I can get those bundles out."

"Maybe she won't come," Isa said. "Since she stayed so late today, she may want to spend some time at home with Jean-Luc. He must be as bored as she."

But Isa could see neither Edward nor Genny appeared convinced that might be a possibility.

31

We Belgians have always valued our freedom, and yet what freedom do we have, living under martial law? Why must martial law be imposed when the armies are no longer at our doors and we have proven ourselves peaceable? Injustice—that is what we live under.

La Libre Belgique

Much to Edward's surprise, Pierrette Guillamay did not return the next morning. He wanted to think Isa was right, that the woman would spend more time at home with the husband she loved so much. But he couldn't convince himself not to worry.

It occurred to Edward as he finished packing bundles destined for different depots that he was fortunate. Despite being caught in the center of a military occupation, there were still things to be thankful for. The theme of the latest issue of *La Libre Belgique* was to resist working for the Germans because every job a Belgian filled left a German free to fight. Poverty wasn't so tragic as betraying one's fellow Belgian, it said, and far less a price than those who forfeited their lives.

Yet he and Isa were spared the boredom. They had work. The blessing of work, his father had called it. Without it, Edward would surely go mad.

Edward harnessed copies of *La Libre Belgique* beneath his clothing while Jan took the greatest amount all at once in a box of books
labeled for donation to the hospital. This particular box had a
false bottom in which were stowed nearly a thousand copies to
be delivered to the provinces, northward to Antwerp and eastward
to Liège.

Edward left the house with Jan and walked toward the ring road,
where Jan would go south and Edward north. Eventually Jan would
end up at Midi Station and Edward at various shops along the way,
familiar distributors all. Isa was to follow in another hour so they
wouldn't attract too much attention with so much activity from
her home. She would make two runs to the flat, where Rosalie and
others would pick up their copies.

Near the end of Avenue Louise, Edward saw Jan shift the bulk of
the weight from one forearm to the other. "Getting heavy?" At his
friend's nod, Edward added, "You carried heavier books than those
between buildings at the university."

"We're getting old before our time."

"It's the food—or want of it, I should say."

They would soon reach the point where they would split. More
people were on the street today, mainly soldiers enjoying a rare day
of sun despite the continued chilly January temperatures. "There
are too many sentries out today. I'll cross here. It's safer alone than
together, considering what we're carrying."

Jan nodded and Edward left him. For a little while they traveled
the same street in the same direction. At the ring road, Edward
turned to the right, sparing a quick glance behind him. Jan had
fallen behind, no doubt still feeling the weight of the books. He
would have to switch methods or at least get rid of some of the
legitimate books he carried.

The attention of a sentry who focused on Jan caught Edward's eye.
He stopped to watch, making himself an unexpected impediment

in the stream of increased foot traffic. Another man bumped into him.

"*Passen Sie auf!*"

A German civilian, so Edward only bowed a silent pardon.

But the contact loosened the harness beneath Edward's coat, and he knew he would have to right it quickly or risk leaving a trail of illegal newsprint in his wake. His nearest destination, a news shop, was nearly three blocks away. So he slipped inside the first café he passed, knowing all he needed was a place to stop and open the top of his coat, slipping one hand inside as if reaching for a wallet.

He ordered coffee he didn't want and did just that.

Barely five minutes later he returned outside and glanced back in the direction he'd last seen Jan. There Edward froze. A commotion had erupted, Belgian *Polizei* blowing their whistles—crowd control being their most trusted duty—and a swarm of German sentries buzzing beneath a swirl of paper blowing on a breeze.

Just beyond the edge of the crowd were the remnants of a crate and a pile of books trampled beneath German boots.

Edward hastened in the other direction.

❦

Isa locked the flat behind her, having completed her second run between home and this depot. Satisfaction was almost heady these days, with another issue complete. Working with Edward undoubtedly had something to do with the euphoria, but so did the importance of the job itself.

God had surely blessed her.

"Isa!"

She saw Edward at the base of the stairs and would have met him halfway but he was nearly at the top before she'd so much as turned his direction.

"What is it?"

"It's Jan. He was arrested." He looked around, behind her, above. "Come with me. Leave the key under the mat."

She did as he asked, following him out to the street. "I went to Rosalie's, and she's going to wait until tomorrow to come here for the pickup. She'll keep an eye on it between now and then. See? She's in that café near the window, where she can watch."

Isa looked in the direction he'd gazed, but not for long. He pulled her along faster than he'd ever allowed them to walk before.

"You have nothing on you right now, correct?" he asked as they walked.

"No. The last of the papers are upstairs, waiting for Rosalie and the others."

"Fine. I don't want you to go home directly. I won't return there for a few days. It's best if we wait and see, even if it means finding another printer for the next issue."

Isa wanted to feel his caution, because he was so clearly concerned, but didn't. "I know you want to be careful, Edward, and I'm sorry Jan's been arrested, but he would never give us away. What can we do for him?"

"Get another issue out to prove they haven't stopped us, that he's just a courier and not worth serious punishment. But not on the press in your cellar. We won't be using that again until we're sure the Germans can't trace anything back to you. I intend to see Father Clemenceau after I take you to a safe place."

The safe place turned out to be another abandoned flat, registered to yet another fictitious name. Edward did little more than open the door and tell her to stay put until he came for her; then he fled.

Being alone allowed the fears Edward left with her to ferment. The flat was barely furnished, with a table and one chair. It was just one of many homes left empty since the Germans had crossed the border over two years ago.

She was tempted to go to the window, to roll up the blind and let the sun spill into the room. But she knew she couldn't. All she could do was wait. And pray.

For the second time since Jan's arrest that morning, Edward arrived at Isa's home. The first time had been to take his mother to the home of Father Clemenceau's niece, someone without connection to either Isa or Edward himself. But by midafternoon Father Clemenceau had sent her home, something Edward had protested. The priest had said Edward was being too cautious, but was there such a thing?

Edward never stepped beyond the alcove in the kitchen of Isa's home. Caution had sent him to the back door, and now he was glad. Clara said Pierrette Guillamay had arrived over an hour ago and waited for Isa in the parlor with his mother.

He shook his head when Clara asked him if he would join them.

If their connection to Jan had been known, an arrest would have been immediate. But so far, nothing had changed. Rosalie seemed unaffected, too, and even the flat seemed safe. He'd taken the remaining illicit copies to the couriers himself, so now even if the flat were to come under suspicion, nothing would be found.

Which wasn't true of Isa's secret room in the cellar. If it were found, they might not discover any copies of *La Libre Belgique*, but there would certainly be enough other incriminating evidence, starting with the press itself. Block type of the paper's heading, a block of artwork mimicking a failed German zeppelin attack, a ream of paper awaiting the next issue. Illegal, each and every item.

So much for taking extra precautions. He'd come to ask his mother to join Isa in hiding. Now not only couldn't she go, but Isa would have to return.

"You should come home with me if you're so worried about us," Isa snapped as they walked away from the flat she'd been imprisoned in all day. She was tired, but more than that she was hungry. He'd left her in that barren flat the entire day, worry her only companion. "Meet Pierrette for yourself."

"It's best to give everything a few days more, and that would include not letting your friend know of any connection to me or to any priest."

Edward stopped at the end of the street. She would have continued on, knowing he would stay behind, but he caught her wrist.

"I'm sorry, Isa." He stroked her hand with his thumb. "For this whole, awful day."

His considerate tone brought the first light moment since that morning. "You're only being careful. I know that."

"But you're hungry and cross and it's my fault. It's only that I want you safe. You know that, don't you?"

She would have leaned into him, forced an embrace the way she'd always done her whole life around him, but knew she couldn't. Not out here in the late afternoon sun, and he in priestly vestments.

So she nodded and squeezed his hand before letting him go. Already her frustration was dissipating.

But not her hunger.

Isa made her way inside her home, seeing Pierrette with Genny on the two Queen Anne chairs, a teapot between them with only water in the cups. Genny welcomed Isa with the shortest glance, but even that was enough to reveal an extra shadow of worry in her eyes.

"Oh, Isa!" Pierrette sprang to her feet. "I hoped you would be home soon, and here you are. Where have you been all day?"

Isa received Pierrette's embrace even as she planned as vague an answer as ever to Pierrette's inquiry. "I'm glad to be back, actually. My friend was especially lonely today and bade me stay too long, only she hadn't much to offer. And I see we're out of tea, too."

Pierrette scurried back to her chair, where she'd left a little purse. "I have something to share. Look! It's a tin of meat. One of the soldiers gave three of them to my dear Jean-Luc, and he said to make sure to bring one here today. Isn't that sweet?"

Abandoning any disappointment over having to entertain Pierrette despite her lingering suspicions, Isa received the can and led the way to the kitchen. Since Clara was not to be found and Isa hadn't paid attention on the rare occasion they'd had canned food to know how one accessed the inside, she let Genny do it for her. Isa retrieved three plates, hoping there was enough to leave some for Edward, Clara, and Henri but knowing such a hope was futile. Oh, to have a bottomless supply, one she could send over to Jonah as well . . .

Between the meat and a small slice of tasteless dark bread, Isa chased away the worst of her hunger. Finishing with a long drink of water gave her a false sense of satisfaction, at least for a time.

Pierrette chatted on as always, even refused to take any of the meat. Yet when she asked for the second time where Isa had spent the day, Isa's misgivings resurfaced.

"I was with the wife of an old friend of my mother's," she said, thinking it best not to give a name, even a false one.

"It's only that you said this friend hadn't much to offer, and I wondered if there might be something we could do for her? Pool our food tickets? Perhaps Jean-Luc can get more tins. To help, yes?"

"That's very kind of you," Genny said, exchanging a glance with Isa.

"I'm surprised she hasn't enough if she lives around here," Pierrette continued. "Usually Upper Town finds a way to more food. Is she from around here, then?"

"No—not really very close at all."

"But you said she was a friend of your mother's?"

Isa nodded, wishing she were a better liar. "Yes, but through the diplomatic corps."

"Tell us about how Jean-Luc received the tins, Pierrette," Genny said. "Has he found a German with a heart for us, then?"

"Yes, oh yes, he made a friend in a guard from when he was in their custody. They are not all so bad, you know. But most of the Germans are terrible. Most would be only so happy to give you the peel, should they have a banana. Ah! How I hate them."

As Pierrette bubbled on, Isa glanced gratefully at Genny, glad to have had her help in diverting the conversation from Isa's supposed circle of friends. These days, that only extended as far as those within the circle of *La Libre Belgique*, and Isa sensed they both knew Pierrette couldn't be trusted with that.

By the time Isa and Genny walked Pierrette to the door, the frustrations of Isa's day had begun to subside. She stood arm in arm with Genny and waved at Pierrette from the threshold.

"What a day," Genny said.

"It's all over now. Tomorrow we can do as we please."

32

Immanuel Kant once said that war makes more bad people than it takes away. German Field Marshal Moltke has been quoted to say that war develops the noblest virtues of man. Certainly both cannot be right.

Germany has been forced to adopt Moltke's "truth" so that their young, sacrificed on the altar of war, may be said to have died in glory for the Fatherland.

La Libre Belgique

Isa awakened to pounding feet on the floor below. The sound echoed from the front to the back of the house. The parlor . . . the kitchen . . . the pantry . . . the cellar . . .

The cellar.

Clara burst in at Isa's bedroom door, clutching the collar of her nightdress to her throat. "*Mademoiselle*, they broke the door! Glass is shattered everywhere!"

Isa sat up. Clara's words, the sounds—a nightmare. Surely only that? A reenactment of the day she had been arrested, but not real, not anything that could harm her. Not really.

If they had broken the door, Isa would have heard them.

But that stomping—that was real. Too real to call a dream.

She pushed away covers that suddenly seemed heavy and all too warm. Other than that heat, she felt nothing, knowing if she faced a single emotion she would cave in to them all.

"Soldiers?" How calm was that word. She slipped out of her nightgown, thrust a dress over her head, and put on her shoes. She'd learned her lesson the last time.

Genny was already in the hall, still in her nightclothes. Her face ashen, eyes wide.

"Get dressed, Genny."

Isa went down the stairs. Her heart rate matched the beat of . . . something she could not place. Not boots on the floor or stairs anymore. It was the sound of something else, and it rattled the walls. The floor beneath her feet shook the nearer she came to the kitchen.

There, at the pantry door, was a German Feldwebel, spiked helmet atop his head, fully armed. So large and menacing she saw nothing but him.

Isa swallowed and pressed her shaking hands against her arms. "Is there some reason for all of this, sir?"

He said nothing, just turned his back and faced the door at the top of the cellar stairs.

She didn't have to see the cluster of soldiers in her cellar to know they were there. Isa's suspended heart plummeted. They'd been given away. She was flushed with more heat, primed for a quick sprint—a chance to escape, if she could slip out the back door. But through the window she saw guards posted in the yard. No doubt they came as a matching set, one for the front as well. Was the entire German Imperial Army on her father's property?

The pounding in the cellar demanded the pounding in her head and heart to match. She would be arrested, but what of Edward? and Genny? Even Clara and Henri were at risk simply by living under this same roof.

What had she done?

Footsteps ascended the stairs. They were not the frantic kind as if propelled by a discovery—they were too slow for that. Isa listened as they spoke in German.

"Nothing, sir."

"*Nein!* Do not tell me that, *du Esel!*"

She heard more footsteps, this time going down. She ventured a few steps closer, almost entering the pantry but daring no farther.

"Look, sir," she heard from below, "there are nothing but brick walls on all sides. The wine racks hide only solid walls."

"We'll see about that," the Feldwebel said, and then Isa heard more banging, hard and fierce, from one side, then another. Each strike shot hope and terror into her.

Low voices soon replaced the battering. She would have to step closer to hear better, but she couldn't gather the courage to move. Instead, she stepped back into the kitchen and waited for the soldiers to reappear. But even as she did, she offered up a prayer of thanksgiving for the silence. Silence, no celebration. The secret room was solid. Thank the Lord! Surely they were saved!

The Feldwebel returned to the kitchen, and she saw sweat glisten at his temples. She remained where she was, standing in front of the sink.

"You are Isabelle Lassone?" His voice was near breathless, no doubt from overworking himself with a sledgehammer below.

She nodded.

"You are under arrest."

Her heart did another somersault. But they'd found nothing!

"You will stay here until another officer comes for you with a cart. There are guards all around; do not attempt anything foolish."

Then he left.

Isa sat on one of the kitchen chairs, her head so light she thought she might faint. But she was no longer shuddering and took courage from that. She must remain clearheaded. Undoubtedly they would be back, but they would find nothing more. The room had held!

She folded her arms and put her head on the table with a silent plea for guidance. But how could she guess what they knew or why they suspected something in the cellar? They would go away if all they had were suspicions and could not find the room, wouldn't they? She and Edward could dismantle the press and take it away.

She shivered.

Genny came through the kitchen door, followed closely by Clara.

"What happened?"

Mindful of Clara's blessed ignorance, Isa chose her words carefully. "They were in the cellar, but they left. They said I'm under arrest, that they would be back for me."

Genny grabbed her arm and pulled her to the door. "Then you must go before they come back!"

Isa shook her head. "There are guards posted at the front and the back."

Clara burst into tears. "Oh, *mademoiselle*! What shall we do?"

Isa tried to smile. "I think they're only coming for me, Clara. Please don't worry."

"But, *mademoiselle*, I do not want them to take you back to that awful place."

Isa couldn't help but tremble.

Genny stepped to the kitchen window, looking out before turning back to Isa. "If it's just you they want, perhaps one of us could leave." She headed for the little alcove by the back door, where her coat hung. "I will go to Edward at the church. He'll know what to do."

Isa's heart raced. Yes, that way they would know if Edward had been implicated too. If Pierrette had betrayed them, she'd never met Edward. Surely that meant something? Nonetheless, it was too early to be out, even for someone not suspected of a crime. "I don't know," she called after Genny. "Curfew isn't lifted yet."

"I'll try anyway," Genny said.

Isa and Clara watched from the kitchen window as Genny opened the back door and stepped outside. The guard stood in her path, rifle poised across his chest. She produced identity papers, but he didn't accept them. She talked, but if he listened, her words made no impression. In a moment Genny turned around and came back inside.

Isa slumped against the sink. "I'm going downstairs to assess the damage," she said. She heard Genny and Clara step behind her but couldn't tell if it was curiosity or fear of being left alone that made them move together as one.

The cellar was in shambles, splintered wood everywhere and chunks of white brick chipped off here and there. Thankfully not even the scent of the ink could be detected through the dust.

Her eye went to the brick-lined door that opened to the secret room. Without the cover of the wine rack she could barely make out the edge of the door. She knew where to look for the small hole through which the lever on the other side was let down, but unless one was looking for such things, the wall appeared as solid as the others. She breathed a bit easier, seeing there was little possibility of the room being at risk.

"Well, at least we'll have some firewood," Isa said.

Genny sent her a nod and a faint smile.

Upstairs, Isa accepted tea. They stayed away from the smashed front door letting in an awful blast of wintry air, opting instead for the warmth of the kitchen. Isa let Genny brush her hair, as she'd done when Isa was little. Genny braided it down her back. Isa barely felt anything, welcoming the numbness again. It was all a dream, and soon she would wake up. She would tell Edward all about it . . . or maybe she wouldn't. He already worried too much.

Then they heard the sounds again: pounding feet, harsh German voices. Someone giving directions. Isa's heart sputtered and terror replaced the numbness. She huddled with the others as the kitchen door banged opened and soldiers marched through again.

So many? Surely one or two soldiers would have been enough for her arrest. But a half dozen arrived, a few carrying sledgehammers and picks, two carrying something she'd never seen before. Not a gun, yet deadly nonetheless, with something sharp protruding from the center, wooden handles on each side—like a little motor of some sort with a screw at the tip. The soldiers plodded through the kitchen, passing her by, going down the stairs.

The Feldwebel was the last to arrive. He walked past Isa, who cowered with the other women, as if none of them were there.

They'd already tested the wall with sledgehammers! Why try again? Something in the pit of Isa's stomach pulled her spirits to a new low. She wanted to cry out, demand they all leave, but knew no one would pay her any attention.

And then she heard the buzzing. Like a wasp, only louder. Deadly drilling.

No doubt right through the brick.

Sickness rushed through Isa and she ran to the sink and vomited. Genny, behind her, held back her braid as she'd done when Isa was ill as a little girl.

Isa threw herself into Genny's arms. "Oh, Genny, you know what this means! I . . . I'm so . . . sorry."

"Shh," Genny said softly, stroking Isa's head. "You've no reason to be sorry. We all did what we had to do."

"But Edward didn't want you endangered. It's my fault!"

Genny shook her head. "I remember all of us making our own decisions. I still believe in what you and Edward were doing. Don't you?"

Isa nodded, accepting the towel Genny offered. She wiped her face, the tears, her nose. Of course she'd believed in the importance of the paper. That was why she'd agreed to house the press. Mostly.

"We'll face the consequences, whatever they may be." Genny drew her close again. "But remember this, my little Isa: whatever happens, God is with us."

Isa couldn't find comfort in Genny's words. They might each have made their decision, but certainly Genny wouldn't have been forced to make one at all if not for Isa. And Isa had wanted to work on the paper because it was a sure way into Edward's life.

How could she hope for God's protection now, when she'd accepted the press for just as many selfish reasons as altruistic ones?

33

They have done their best to paralyze our voices, but we will not be silenced.

La Libre Belgique

Edward brushed his teeth and combed his hair, donned the black priest's garb, and grabbed his biretta. It wasn't much past dawn, but that was the best time to slip into Isa's home unobserved. He intended to spend the day watching her place, making sure it wasn't attracting any new attention.

But already the night had calmed his nerves. Even while his concern over Jan grew, having heard he'd been taken to St. Gilles, Edward was beginning to believe in Isa's claim that God really was watching over her. He'd spent a frantic day yesterday, but nothing had happened to either Isa or his mother. What good had his worries done?

Upstairs, he avoided the sanctuary as he usually did, for fear of running into a parishioner who might think him a real priest. Instead, he went to the exit in the back—except a tall shadow at the base of the altar caught his eye.

"Henri!"

Henri's face didn't need words. Edward grabbed his arm. "Is it Isa?"

Henri nodded and every bit of strength abandoned Edward.

"The press . . . it's been discovered?"

Another nod. Edward grabbed the kneeler nearby, the walls, the altar, the pew benches all spinning around him.

"They arrested Isa? and my mother?"

Henri nodded again.

Dread stunned him. Hadn't this very thing haunted him from the start? He should have had a plan, one he could count on now. Did he? His mind blurred.

Edward hadn't the faintest notion of what to do.

He stepped away from Henri, pacing one small track, back and forth, twice. "Money." He looked at Henri. "I suppose there are soldiers there, collecting evidence, dismantling the press."

Henri did not move. He must not know. "We didn't have enough left anyway. A couple of gold pieces, a jewel. That wouldn't bribe her way out of home confinement, let alone the Kommandantur."

He turned and paced again, knowing if he howled, it would shake the rafters. But he kept silent. *Oh, Lord God, what do we do now?*

He needed paper, a pencil. Action.

"Come with me, Henri."

The big man followed Edward to the small room just inside the narthex where Father Clemenceau left pencils and envelopes for giving. He tore open an envelope for greater length of paper, one he could fold back into shape when he was finished.

Leave Belgium. Take Jonah.

He didn't sign it; Rosalie would know from whom it came by the envelope.

Then he searched for another sheet of paper, this one without evidence of its origin. He found nothing, only the blank endsheet from a catechism. It would have to do; he tore it from the binding and scribbled a note in German.

"You must take this one to a friend of mine," he said to Henri, holding up Rosalie's refolded envelope. "And this one to the Kommandantur, to be forwarded to the Major who once billeted at Isa's. I'll give you explicit directions to Rosalie's—"

But Henri was shaking his head. He pointed to Edward, then started toward the door, motioning Edward to follow.

"I must reach the American ambassador, Henri. And you must get those messages off. Immediately."

Henri pointed to Edward's wristwatch; yes, it was early to see Mr. Whitlock at the legation, but Edward would find him somehow.

And yet Edward trusted Henri, and Henri wanted Edward to follow him. Edward didn't doubt the man's devotion to Isa.

"All right."

They left the church. Edward didn't look back, though he wasn't at all sure he'd ever return.

Henri led him through the old city. They never varied their pace. Edward's mind raced to all the things he could be doing, *should* be doing. Seeing Mr. Whitlock, imploring his own contact with *La Libre Belgique* for bribe money, trying to find someone sufficiently remote and disconnected to him yet willing to go to the Kommandantur to make inquiries about Isa and his mother. Finding a printer for the next issue was more vital than ever if he was to convince the Germans they hadn't found the paper's main source. Beside all that, Edward must establish a new identity. He doubted they would wait long before interrogating everyone who'd ever stepped foot inside Isa's house, and several Germans knew he had a connection there.

Henri took Edward to another church . . . no, it was an abbey. Well, at least they were walking in the right direction. The American Legation was on the same side of town.

Henri rang the bell at the gate, and after a nearly unendurable wait, a nun opened the lock.

"Henri, you are early today. I don't know if your mother is awake yet." She glanced at Edward and smiled. "I see you've brought a friend. Welcome, Father."

Edward barely managed a polite nod. His mind shouted to leave instead of entering this quiet, peaceful place. What was he *doing* here? He wasn't about to hide away, if that was Henri's idea. He had to do *something*. . . .

And what had she said? Henri's mother? This made no sense.

The sister led Henri and Edward across a courtyard and through a vast room with a low, beamed ceiling. They navigated corridor after corridor, dimly lit by candles held in sconces.

At last they stopped. The sister tapped lightly on a rounded door. Edward looked from the sister to Henri, who stared so intently ahead he looked as if by his sheer will that door would open.

And so it did.

A woman stood there, dressed in the habit of a novice. Her face and hands were wrinkled with age, but her eyes were still a bright blue.

"Ah, my son! *Mon cher*, come here."

Henri, so big and strong, would make anyone seem fragile. And this woman was nearly as tall as Edward himself. She patted Henri's back with spirit and then, at last, noticed Edward.

"Well, whom have we here, Henri?"

Henri lifted a hand, palm up, directed Edward's way, as if he were going to introduce him.

Edward spoke. "My name is Edward. And I wonder if your son and I may speak with you alone?"

Henri's mother gave a little laugh. "Oh, Sister Zehara is as mute as my son when it comes to secrets."

But Edward shook his head. "I'm not sure why your son has brought me here, but I believe it has to do with helping someone we both care about. She is in the kind of trouble it's better to have no knowledge of these days."

The old woman's smile faded as she looked from Edward to Sister Zehara. The nun nodded, then left the room.

It was a small place, sparsely furnished. No adornments, not a personal item to be seen.

"I can see you're troubled, young man, so you may as well get right to it. What is the nature of the problem?"

"Do you know for whom your son works?"

"Of course. The Lassone family . . . well, just little Isa now, since her parents left." She smiled as if anticipating Edward's question. "My son and I communicate via our own language—gestures and hand motions we've developed over the years since he lost his ability to speak."

"It's Isa who's in trouble."

"What kind of trouble?"

Edward hesitated, sending a quick glance Henri's way and receiving a nod, encouraging him to go on. It was even difficult to trust here, of all places. He told the woman the extent of it as briefly as he could.

She looked at her son and patted one of his big hands. "I know what you want me to do, Son. Go and get them."

Henri went to the dresser, opening the top drawer and pulling out a small pouch. He handed it to his mother.

"These have been my son's for many years, Edward," she said. "For as long as it's been since last I heard his voice. I've kept them for safety. Oh, I pull them out from time to time just to see the sparkle, but I can do without that." She finished with a frail laugh.

She emptied the contents onto the dark table, and before him were at least a dozen diamonds, all of various sizes. Yet the smallest was larger than any of those Isa had brought. "Where did he get them?"

"Our Congo, of course. Brussels is not the center of gems for nothing." She laughed again, as if the diamonds couldn't be looked at without such mirth. Then her blue gaze rose to Edward's. "Visit me when you have time someday, and I will tell you how Henri came to own this fortune—from the former owner of Isa's house."

"I saw the diamond-cutting equipment before we moved the press to the secret room," Edward said.

"For cutting diamonds pilfered and smuggled." She cast a gaze her son's way. "Yes, my son was involved for a time. But when he met our Savior, he mended his ways."

Then those eyes clouded as if the memories couldn't be had without pain. "He tried to quit honorably, even taking possession of these diamonds to barter his freedom. He nearly lost his life instead, but all they succeeded in taking was his tongue. He was left to die, but it wasn't Henri who faced his final judgment that night. It was the man who owned that home and every illegal diamond. God took him peacefully in his sleep, of a heart attack. Those left behind never came looking for the diamonds Henri took because they'd all taken shares of their own."

She sighed. "Who can tell how God works? If only we'd known that man would die so soon, my son would have been free and his tongue not lost. Except," she added, placing a delicate hand over Edward's, "he wouldn't now possess these diamonds, would he? For you to use."

"I don't—I don't know what to say, how to thank you."

Before the words were out, Henri pushed the entire pile Edward's way. He wanted to protest, to remind them there would be others in need too. But he couldn't. Isa's life was at stake, and Henri must know as well as Edward that it would take all the bribe money they had to find a way out of Belgium with her life intact.

Edward put the diamonds back into the pouch. "This will save Isa and my mother, too. There is enough here to set up a clear pathway out of Belgium. Will you come along?"

Neither even looked at the other before they both shook their heads.

"The Germans may start looking for you, Henri. Anyone associated with Isa's house must be known to them."

"My son will not leave Belgium," his mother said, slowly rising to her feet. "Not while he might help others still here."

Edward needn't ask details, having once known the same reason to stay. Before now.

"Use this treasure to free your family," she said. "And my son will do everything he can to help you all leave Belgium safely."

34

Allow me to count the German virtues:
Injustice
Tyranny
Dishonor
. . . to name but a few, and let us not forget their eagerness
for cruelty, behind which they hide their greatest weaknesses.

La Libre Belgique

Straw covered the cement floor but did little to keep down the stench. Isa looked at Genny. Her face, like Isa's, was bruised and swollen. Isa gently touched her own jaw; it was afire.

"How long have you been printing? How many times have you written illegal articles? How did you receive the rest of your copy, and from whom? To whom did you route it? How were you funded?" And on and on . . . until they'd battered her for a better result. But she'd refused to speak, grateful Edward had been so protective of what she knew, of whom she knew. Even if she'd wanted to talk, there was little she could have said. A name or two, a depot, a flat registered to someone who didn't exist. But she said nothing, not even any of that.

Genny knew nothing about the paper and must have been convincing in her honesty because her inquisition lasted two hours less than Isa's. Even Clara had been with them earlier, although only at the Kommandantur. When they'd been taken from the Town Hall, Clara had been set free while Isa and Genny had been taken to a wagon. To St. Gilles.

The ancient, fortresslike building shrouded with German flags offered no comfort. Isa knew Genny had been here with the Major to see Jonah. She tried to find strength in that, knowing Jonah had once walked this way and survived. Surely she could do the same.

Yet when she walked, her knees buckled, her feet stumbled. And the guard had taken no pity, as if he'd led so many this way he'd long since lost sympathy.

Their cell was far more secure than the cellar of the Kommandantur. Double the guards, various layers of bars added inside. The cell itself had wide stone blocks on three sides and heavy iron bars on the fourth. But the smell was familiar, only stronger.

Genny and Isa barely talked, fearful of those listening. And it hurt. Isa winced with the slightest jaw movement. After their brief, whispered comparison of interrogations, they fell silent, unable to offer much comfort beyond knowing they weren't alone.

Isa had begun working for the paper knowing the possible consequences. But no matter how many brave admonitions she gave herself, she was afraid. May God forgive her for not trusting Him, but terror accompanied every breath. She'd begun this venture without the pure intentions others held; hers had been mixed with the selfish hope of proving herself grown up, worthy of Edward.

How silly it all seemed now; how foolish that her motives hadn't been clearer, her assurance more firm. Had she ever been certain she'd been following God's will? If she had, she might better trust His protection now.

She heard Genny's soft voice next to her.

"'We believe in one God, the Father Almighty, Maker of all things visible and invisible. And in one Lord Jesus Christ, the Son of God, begotten from the Father, the only begotten, from the essence of the Father, God of God, Light of Light, true God of true God. . . .'"

Before long Isa joined in the creed that stated so clearly their faith, finding comfort amid her fear.

"It would be suicide for you to try anything before then," Father Clemenceau said.

Edward rubbed one palm absently over the back of the other hand. "January 27." He said the date as if somehow by hearing it aloud, it would sound better. Less than two weeks—but a lifetime—to somehow free Isa and then wait for the day of escape from Belgium.

The priest folded his arms. Sounds around them drowned their discussion, the noise of soldiers in the distance, civilians around them in the lines for bread. It was the only place in the city to hide in a crowd. They were dressed in the common fashion of the day: poverty. Tattered clothes, old shoes. Clemenceau disguised as a civilian, Edward no longer disguised as a priest. "If you are successful— and that, my friend, is a huge *if*—then you can depart on the boat we've already set up for my people. They've been busy over at Rue de Berlaimont with one arrest after another. Others are eager to flee because of the deportations. Rumor says the Germans still plan to deport men from Brussels, and every healthy young man in the city would rather risk flight than be rounded up for a work camp. The day we've chosen is important—festivities in honor of his Imperial Majesty's birthday will serve us."

"Yes, and the city will overflow with soldiers."

"It already does! You once told me yourself, Edward, the best place to hide is under the nose of a *Polizei*. You get them to the tug docked two kilometers south of the guard station on the Senne outside of Brussels, and my friends will get them—and the rest of you—to Holland."

Edward tried again but came up with no alternative. Nothing.

Get them outside of Brussels.

As easy as that.

His only choice was to succeed. Somehow. "All right."

Edward turned. He had much to do and not much time in which to do it. But first he must get back to work for *La Libre Belgique* and pray the others working for the paper had found another printer. The sooner they produced the next issue, the better for Isa and his mother. If the Germans thought for a moment they'd truly gotten the heart of the paper when they found the press in her cellar—the "automobile cellar," as they'd once named their imaginary headquarters—then the women he loved were doomed.

35

Was it not Shakespeare who said:
And on your head
Turning the widows' tears, the orphans' cries,
The dead men's blood, the pining maidens' groans,
For husbands, fathers and betrothed lovers,
That shall be swallow'd in this controversy.

La Libre Belgique

The guards woke them early, surely before dawn. Isa guessed the time by her own fatigue, without a clock, wristwatch, or even a window to gauge anything by the sun.

She and Genny had clung together in the corner through the night. From their cell she could see no others but guessed only women were nearby. They'd heard voices last night, and other than the guards', all of them were female. A few had talked freely as if they'd been there some time and grown used to the surroundings.

But how? How could anyone adapt to the dark, the filth, the dampness, the hopelessness?

A nun came through once, speaking in German, telling the prisoners not to worry, that God was surely there. But somehow, hearing the comforting words in German brought no comfort at all.

The guards, instead of delivering the kind of tasteless food Isa remembered from the Kommadantur, thrust canvases through the bars, with a roll of thread and needles for each cellmate.

"You will sew the rest of these as the example on top shows," the guard announced to Isa, then went on to deliver the same bundles to others.

"These are for sandbags," Isa said to Genny.

"We cannot refuse—"

"They can't force prisoners of war to do war work. It's against international law."

Someone gasped. Isa hadn't meant to be heard outside of their cell; she wasn't even sure of the source of her boldness to have said anything at all, even just to Genny. Except she recalled Edward once saying the Germans had enough reason to shoot him, so one more reason hardly mattered. How fitting were such words for her.

Another prisoner spoke up. "There is a law saying we don't have to do this?"

"That's right," Isa answered.

"She is correct." Another unseen voice echoed in the damp stone corridor. "One even the Germans must obey. They signed the Convention of the Hague too."

"You will be silent as you work, *Frauen* and *Fräuleins*." The guard's voice drowned out the women's chatter.

"Resist!" another voice farther down shouted.

"You will work!" the guard returned.

"We shall not do it anymore," someone called. "We shall not work for the Germans against our own sons at the front."

"Silence! I will have silence." The soldier marched the corridor, stopping at Isa's cell. "This is not against the law. As none of you are prisoners of war, it is perfectly legal to have you do this."

His face was so cold, his gun so near, Isa took a step back.

"Not prisoners of war!" one of the women demanded. "Then what are we?"

He never took his eyes from Isa, despite her silence. "You are criminals. Now get to work."

Isa didn't move but the standoff wasn't from courage. Fear made her immobile.

The objections stopped, the calls ceased, but based on the silence, no one had taken up the work, either. The guard took another step toward Isa's cell. "You are the one who started this, *Fräulein*. It is you who will set the example for the others, even if I have to *inspire* you."

His calm tone did nothing to lessen her fear. "If you beat me," she said, "I shall be of no use at all."

"True enough. I'll not beat you. I'll beat *her*." He pointed his nose Genny's way.

Bile rose in Isa's throat. Bruises inflicted on her the day before reminded her how mercilessly efficient the Germans could be with their punishment, even upon women.

Isa sat on the cot, taking up the first piece of canvas and the needle.

"She is a wise woman to put herself to work. Work will help you to pass the hours of your confinement. It is for your own good. I suggest the rest of you do the same."

The soft rustle of canvas, the gentle noise of quiet work began. After a while the guard stopped marching the corridor. And so Isa worked. She had never been good at sewing and took some comfort in finding no reason to improve.

Before long someone down the way began humming. A single voice soon joined in. Isa looked at Genny. They both knew the tune and added their voices.

"The Lion of Flanders," a song Isa had learned as a child.

The German returned and shouted his threats again, reminding them it was illegal to sing, whistle, or even hum songs that used to represent Belgium. He banged his rifle against the bars and one by one the voices fell off.

But not before Isa winced under her first smile of the day.

❧

Edward stared at the carpet, holding his head in his palms, elbows on his knees. How long had he waited while men paraded in and out of the American Legation? All looking as desperate as Edward felt, hoping to obtain cards freeing them from the German deportations.

But they weren't as desperate as Edward; they couldn't possibly be. He was losing his hold on time, losing his mind. He hadn't slept more than a couple of hours in the past two days; exhaustion muddled him. And yet he'd had to come again, to see if Brand Whitlock had found any hope of freeing Isa and his mother through legal means.

Whitlock had all the sympathy Edward could hope for from someone so important and had taken the responsibility to contact Isa's parents, without telling the Germans that he'd done so. He'd told Edward that although communication was limited and for the most part monitored, he hadn't yet heard from Isa's parents, but they would no doubt immediately petition Washington for additional help. Unfortunately, so far, they were all apparently powerless.

"Relations between America and Germany have been deteriorating for some time now," Whitlock said gently. "Even if I had all the time in the world—which as you can see from the state of things around here, I don't—the Germans wouldn't listen to me." He leaned back and suddenly looked old, tired, sorrowful. "I'm sorry. For Isa."

Then he stood, and Edward did too. He followed Whitlock to the legation door. "Tell Mr. Painlevé I am at his disposal if there is anything he thinks I can do. As long as I am in Belgium, I will do what I can."

Edward nodded, thanked him in a low voice, then left the building. He put his hands in his pockets. The air was cold, colder than he could ever remember, as the biting wind stung his cheeks. He let the weather dictate his pace, as even the soldiers did lately.

The streets were nearly empty, between the cold and the deportation cards that had been sent out recently to every unemployed man in Brussels. Edward did not see a single sentry all the way to Painlevé's office.

Painlevé shoved a piece of paper across the desk. "These are the names, as close as I can gather, of those I might be asked to represent. Isa and your mother are on the list."

Edward sank to a chair, knees weak.

Painlevé sighed deeply. "I suppose I should not even ask, but is this the end of *La Libre Belgique*, then? Have they gotten them all?"

Edward would have liked to grin but couldn't muster it. "The next issue is being printed as we speak."

The barrister could still laugh. "The German celebration dinner shall be rained upon for certain."

Edward had visited his contact early that morning. They knew about the celebration feast being planned for that evening: a banquet honoring those who had worked so hard to arrest the resistors producing *La Libre Belgique*.

One of the first issues off another illegal press was to be delivered to that very celebration, and another folded neatly into an envelope for General von Bissing himself—delivered to what everyone hoped was a deathbed since rumor had it he was ill.

"This is good," Painlevé said. "At least I will be able to show a copy to the judge-advocate tomorrow. They will know they have yet to capture the heart of the organization."

Edward's heart thumped. "The trial is tomorrow, then?"

"Which is unfortunate."

Edward sat forward. He already knew one reason to wish Isa's trial postponed—at least until he could smuggle her out of Belgium. She may be uncomfortable in a German prison, but at least they would have to keep her alive until tried. "Why unfortunate?"

The barrister's brows drew together. "Do you remember me saying so many sentences depend on the whim of the court?"

Edward nodded.

"Doktor Stuber is presiding tomorrow. His whims are never good."

Edward swallowed, afraid to ask the obvious. "Who is Doktor Stuber?"

Painlevé cleared his throat as if stalling to let Edward have one last moment of peaceful ignorance. "Doktor Stuber is a judge-advocate known for demanding the death penalty . . . upon men, upon women, even upon boys too young to be called men."

The last time Edward had been filled with this kind of desolation, he'd been standing over the rubble of his family's hotel and home. Maybe it was a leftover habit, maybe it was a faint memory of his father's wishes, but Edward was reminded to pray. He hadn't known what difference it would make and didn't now, either. All he knew was that day he'd refused.

This time, he didn't.

36

LA LIBRE BELGIQUE, SPECIAL EDITION, JANUARY 20, 1917

The immense Palais de Justice sits on a hill above the city, the most prominent of buildings in the most prominent of places, as if to say that justice watches over all. This building that once offered Belgian justice now flies the black, white, and red, flag of an occupying army. Lined around its walls are sandbags, and at each corner near the statues of Justice, Law, Force, and Royal Clemency now sits the black orifice of a great cannon, aimed at the very city the building itself was once dedicated to protect.

Inside the Senate chamber today began another mass trial of those suspected of involvement with none other than this paper, *La Libre Belgique.* Sculptures of great Belgian history tucked within carved mahogany panels overlooked the accused. They sat upon benches fashioned into semicircles, with bayonet-bedecked sentries at each end. Nearby, four Belgian barristers frantically conferred among themselves, having only just been given their cases.

Facing them all were the German judges in field gray, medals shining in the light. The bench at which they sat was covered in green baize, where rested their dark leather gloves and silver spiked helmets. The president of this tribunal sat in

the center: Doktor Stuber. For those *La Libre Belgique* readers who have not had the displeasure of meeting him, Doktor
Stuber has a look of cruelty about his grim-visaged face. *La
Libre Belgique* has it on solid authority that he is stern in public and demanding in private, critical of those around him,
insensitive toward others while secretly thin-skinned. To him,
everyone is either a superior or an inferior—there exist none
equal to him. Belgians are the latter of the two.

Prosecutors were to present their strongest cases first, no
doubt in a wish to begin with the harshest of sentences. To incite
the others to either tell the truth or face consequences of their
lies? Or simply for the iniquitous Doktor to watch the faces of
those who must follow sentences of severest magnitude?

They called the first victim. Isabelle Lassone.

A woman stood and stepped before the judges. She might
have been pretty once; who could tell? Her face was covered
with bruises, her loose, peasant-style dress soiled and shape-
less . . . and somehow familiar. This court has seen prisoners
brought in before wearing just such hideous garb. Her hair
might have been lovely some time ago, probably blonde if
allowed to be clean. Instead, much of it was shorn close to
her head, with oddly missed strands sticking out at peculiar
angles.

How thorough the prosecutors were to include altering the
image of the accused so as not to arouse unwanted sympathy
in the men who would judge her.

They recited the list of crimes she'd committed against the
Imperial Government: illegally housing the press and printing
La Libre Belgique, writing for *La Libre Belgique*, distributing
La Libre Belgique. Indeed, they accused her of being the very
core of the organization, the cellar of her residence reputed
to be the legendary "automobile cellar" that had for so long
produced the illegal newspaper.

Added to that crime, this Mademoiselle Lassone was

formerly found guilty of aiding an Allied soldier, at which time she was shown pity and given a light sentence of a mere fine. Most recently, while housed in St. Gilles, she incited a riot within the cellblock, refusing to carry out work generously provided in order for inmates to productively pass their time. She inspired others to sing a banned song of Belgian patriotism. She is, members of the court were told, a leader and a spark, one who inspires followers in her rebellious ways. For that reason alone, a harsh and memorable punishment must be granted.

Crime: *Verrat in einer Zeit des Kriegs.* Treason in a time of war. Proposed sentence: *Todesstrafe.* Death.

To her credit, this Belgian patriot swayed only slightly when the requested sentence was announced. No hysterics, no tears. She closed her eyes and stood stiff as if blocking out her surroundings. Other prisoners behind her appeared shocked, afraid, timid. Just the sort of reaction the virulent Doktor Stuber undoubtedly craved.

The defense barrister stood. *La Libre Belgique* was still in operation, he claimed while balancing passion with caution. Despite the accusation that this woman was at its core, a new issue had been found only that morning. A nimble hand had pinned a copy to the sentry just outside the Palais de Justice door. Nor was there evidence she'd ever written for the paper. The Allied soldier, the spy to whom she'd given aid, had himself admitted she didn't offer to help him flee the country.

The barrister finished with a plea for leniency of the court, reminding them that she was an American citizen by virtue of her mother and her birth in that country. To condemn one of their own to death now, when an apparently endless number of American men might soon be called against Germany, would only inspire them to their arms all the quicker.

Doktor Stuber need barely have listened. It is the way of German justice to see only one damning fact at a time. After all, Isabelle Lassone's home housed the infamous automobile cellar. (*La Libre Belgique* offers this with a grim irony, as our surroundings are untouched, our paper still free, our voice undiminished.)

And while the Germans prove once again the sham of their justice, *La Libre Belgique* will mourn the shortened life of yet another lovely young patriot.

Those German citizens filling the streets of Belgium who knowingly support the continued injustices perpetrated by their country are guilty, at the very least, of criminal blindness.

La Libre Belgique

37

Edward stumbled on the pavement. A nearby sentry looked his way and Edward turned, afraid of attention. He walked. Not slow, not fast. He no longer felt the cold, didn't care when the wind stole his hat. He paid no attention to where he headed. Inside his head spun a whirlwind.

Though he'd spent the morning spinning more productively— seeing to final details regarding distribution of *La Libre Belgique*'s special edition—with that finished, Edward could no longer push away the truth.

A death sentence. Firing squad.

The words echoed in his head, over and again with the same result. Death.

Nausea accompanied each vision of Isa at the hands of the Germans, sent to Tir National like the others.

He didn't even have the comfort of going to his mother or to his friend Jan—both sentenced to labor in Germany. His mother for three years' servitude, his friend deported to a work camp.

And so he walked. He must move, must clear his mind of images too ghastly to withstand. One step led to another; it didn't matter where he went.

At last, the twin towers of the cathedral loomed overhead. He should go inside and pray. He should plead with God to save her, and maybe somehow . . .

Edward kept walking. He couldn't feel his fingers or toes. His jacket was not enough to ward off the chill. Yet he couldn't stop. He didn't know where to go.

He could go to Rosalie's abandoned home. She'd gotten safely away, and Jonah too.

But Henri hid at Rosalie's, and Edward didn't want to face him. He couldn't tell him. Not yet.

The bells rang at the chapel he shared with Father Clemenceau. He hadn't meant to come here; he hadn't been back since Isa's arrest for fear of being arrested as well. The one time he'd met the father was under cover of a crowd, and neither had been dressed as priests. Now Edward found he didn't care about the risk. He made his way into the sanctuary.

Walking slowly up the aisle, Edward stood before the altar. But he did not bow.

Instead, he folded his arms and stared at the crucifix.

"Edward! What's happened?"

His voice was so soft and compassionate that for the barest moment Edward felt a childish response: he wanted to burst into tears. But instead he turned to one of the seats and sank onto the unyielding wood. He spoke quietly, telling the priest about the sentences.

"I don't know what to do." Edward swallowed again. He knew only one way to steady his emotions, and that was through anger. An anger that came from the core of him. "I know one thing I'm *finished* doing, and that's praying. I tried that before, Father—and everybody I prayed for is dead. So I'm done asking God for help. His kind of help I don't want."

The priest's perpetually friendly face altered only slightly in raised white brows. "So you think this is all God's doing?"

Edward leaned forward in his chair. "All I know is that two years ago when I returned from the camps, I prayed for the men I was with. They died. I was the only one who didn't. And now the people I care about most in this godforsaken world are the ones in trouble. Am I supposed to pray for them now? So they can die too?"

"It's your fault, then, that whomever you pray for God singles out to die?"

It sounded ridiculous even to Edward, yet he found himself nodding. "Yes, that's exactly what I mean. He's cursed me with life while others—those He brings into my life to love—He takes from me. What kind of jest is that, Father? What kind of God do you serve?"

The father frowned. "A loving one. Do you think God owes you an explanation of why He's allowed you to suffer? Do you think He must give you an accounting? We speak of God Almighty. And I will say to you what He said to Job: 'Where wast thou when I laid the foundations of the earth? declare, if thou hast understanding.' Were you there, Edward, when God created the world? Why should He explain anything to you?"

Edward couldn't speak, not even to offer a defense.

"God never told Job why He let him suffer," the priest said, softer now. "But don't doubt that God is God, Edward, and that He hears each word you utter, knows each thought. His plans may never be revealed to you fully, at least not in this life, but it's not yours to question. You must accept the sovereignty of God and trust in His goodness even when everything around you feels the opposite. He will bring glory to Himself through you, Edward, if you let Him. And as our Creator, isn't that the greatest gift He can give?"

Edward's head was empty and lost, his heart leaden. He had nothing without those he loved. Without Isa. His mother. All his worry, all his caution, had done no good.

He was powerless. And if he could not turn to God, his Creator, then where else could he turn? God was God, and Edward wasn't.

Edward was just a puny man whose effort to protect everyone had failed. He was without the right to challenge his Creator. It would be like holding his palm against the wind to try stopping it. Impossible.

"There is one more thing, Edward," the priest said gently. "Your girl and your mother need you now more than they ever have before. They need you to be strong in all ways: emotionally, physically, and perhaps most importantly, spiritually. Depend on God for your strength, and He will see you through. You can be certain there is a higher purpose for all of this. I promise you that because He promised it first."

Your girl . . . Isa, my girl.

"I'm sorry," Edward said, so low he wasn't even sure Father Clemenceau could hear. But it didn't matter. He wasn't apologizing to the priest.

Isa didn't see Genny after the trial. She saw her only as she was led from the Senate chamber. Their gazes met for the briefest moment, long enough for Isa to see the anguish in Genny's eyes.

Isa was taken outside without a coat, herded to the back of a foul-smelling wagon. Someone said, "Vilvorde," and that made her look up, wondering if some measure of evil glee would accompany the acknowledgment of where she was being sent. Hell, Pierrette had called it.

The castle prison at Vilvorde.

Maximilian von Bürkel hobbled up the stairs of the building on Rue de Berlaimont. He counted them in French because if he didn't occupy his mind, he would curse each one. He wasn't sure what method he would use to keep himself from cursing once he saw von Eckhart.

At the correct door Max strode past yet another sentry, faintly surprised by his own dexterity, barely needing the cane. Perhaps fury was the greatest source of strength and balance.

The sentry had no chance to offer an objection, if he'd been bold enough to make one. Von Eckhart was at his desk and looked up with a smile at Max's sudden appearance—a smile Max wanted to smash from his face.

"Tell him to shut the door behind him," Max said. How calm he sounded, deceptively so.

Von Eckhart nodded to the sentry and the man backed out.

"Max! This is an unexpected pleasure. I thought you'd gone home to Käethe."

"I'm back."

"Oh? And how is she?"

Max never took his eyes from von Eckhart's. "I want to know about Genevieve Kirkland and Isabelle Lassone."

"Oh, so you've heard about our most recent arrests? We haven't entirely stopped that foul paper, but we're closer than ever, I promise you that. And I suppose I should really thank *you*, Max. If it wasn't for you, I never would have met your Fräulein Lassone or continued having her shadowed by my informant."

"Don't give me credit for your false arrest. I came here to clear up this nonsense."

"False arrest?" He laughed. "You're too late. The trial was two days ago, and they've both been found guilty. With plenty of evidence, I might add. Do you mean to tell me you never once heard that press running in the cellar? smelled the ink?"

"I can guarantee that Frau Kirkland had nothing to do with it."

"There I must disagree, my friend. Surely she knew; she was one of them. In all probability she was the distraction to prevent you from finding out about the whole thing."

Max's jaw clenched—even if that was a scenario he'd already considered. "You said the trial is over. I came straight from the train. Tell me Frau Kirkland's sentence."

Von Eckhart stood. "Ten thousand francs. Three years' penal servitude."

"Either, or?"

"Both."

For the first time since entering the building, Max's anger failed him. He looked behind for a chair and, seeing one, sank into it.

Von Eckhart came around to the front of his desk and sat on the edge closest to Max. "Look, old man, I didn't know you cared for the woman. I thought when you went back home, you'd found out about the press but didn't want to be the one to betray them. I know you're the loyal type."

Max barely listened. *Three years.* "Is she still in Brussels?"

"Frau Kirkland is at St. Gilles. She won't be moved until after the Kaiser's birthday. Everything waits until the celebration. Did you know we're going to have cameras? Filming the Grand Place with cheering civilians, so happy to wish their benevolent new leader a happy birthday." He laughed again. "Of course, those civilians will be Germans and not Belgians, but who will know? Fortunately for us, cameras do not record the sound of German voices."

Max stared at von Eckhart. "There was a fine assigned. I've heard rumors about such matters. If I offer to pay that fine . . . along with, shall we say, an extra incentive . . . might they agree to pardon the rest?"

Von Eckhart sucked in a breath. "I don't know. The press was found under the roof where she lived. The sentence was light, considering that."

Max sprang up, fighting for balance with his cane. "I tell you, she never touched a copy of that blasted paper."

Von Eckhart wasn't afraid; Max could see that. But he knew von Eckhart respected him, or had once, and Max had never been more earnest in his life.

"You can vouch for her whereabouts, I assume?" von Eckhart whispered. "Day . . . and night?"

"Think whatever you like, but get her out of there."

"Not so fast, my friend! I need to see some money first."

Max turned away. After receiving Father Antoine's note, he'd gone to his family home, where he had money hidden in a vault. But it had dwindled considerably, evidently drained by Käethe before she went to live in the abbey. He had barely enough to cover the initial fine—in Marks, but he doubted von Eckhart would care.

Max handed over what he had. "Consider this the first installment. Tell me what more it will take, and I will get it."

Von Eckhart took a moment to count it, then looked up at his old friend. "Double this and she will walk out with you."

"I want to see her," Max said.

But to that von Eckhart shook his head. "That would not be wise if we're going to alter her sentence, old man. For now it's best we keep this between you and me."

Max had no leverage. He must accept what he could get. He headed to the door, hearing von Eckhart retreat behind his desk.

"You know, Max, you're lucky you know me. I'm not normally so agreeable. But for you, well, exceptions can be made."

Max never turned around.

38

Does it do any good to shut your eyes against danger? No, my fellow Belgians, we must be awake, alive, alert to all that is around us and not listen to the falsehoods spread by the German propaganda.

La Libre Belgique

Edward ran the streets for three days between the American Legation, Painlevé's office, and most recently, the back of a cardboard factory, where he once again met Mr. Jocosa. That was not his real name, but Edward knew no more of the man's actual identity than Jocosa knew of Edward's. Even so, the two became well acquainted. Recommended by Father Clemenceau, it was the mysterious Mr. Jocosa who knew which soldiers were safe to bribe and which to avoid. When he learned Edward wanted to gain the freedom of no less than three prisoners—one even sentenced to death and held at the prison in Vilvorde—he laughed. He only accepted the challenge after Edward produced one of the largest diamonds in Henri's collection, promising more.

Edward received word on Jan first. Jocosa told Edward that Jan would be on a train bound for Germany with other prisoners condemned to deportation. Jan was to be shuffled from one car to another at Aix-la-Chapelle at the German-Dutch border, where he would have three minutes of freedom. If he was recaptured after that, it would be his own undoing, but it was the best offer Jocosa could get. Some of the soldiers welcomed such games, betting their own skills against the prisoners', all for the money and love of a battle of wits.

Edward trusted Jan's wits to get him safely to Holland.

The news Jocosa brought of Edward's mother baffled him. The guard through whom all bribes were channeled in that block was reported to have acted oddly. He easily took the money but already had a plan for her release that differed from the one Jocosa proposed. Far simpler, though it involved an officer, which usually guaranteed success but was normally more expensive.

Nonetheless, Jocosa said Edward's mother would be free before the end of the week.

Isa's release filled Edward's mind every moment of the day. He'd already funneled thousands of francs Jocosa's way, to no avail. He'd gone back to Mr. Whitlock and Barrister Painlevé so many times he was sure they tired of him, yet neither offered any hope. Painlevé had been the one to tell him where Isa was being held and that he wasn't sure if it was good news or bad that her sentence had been delayed until the twenty-seventh. Normally such sentences were carried out immediately, but in honor of the Kaiser's birthday they would dispense with the traitors as part of a dawn tribute to their leader.

Edward rejoiced. It gave him more time. But it also added an unwanted element: with so much emphasis on the celebration, anyone in the German army connected to the sentences was beyond reproach. Dutiful, dedicated, devoted to the Kaiser. Unapproachable with a bribe.

But Edward would not give up—and wasn't about to let Jocosa give up either.

Max took the few steps up to the front door slowly. The frosted glass that once had been framed within the carved front door lay in shards on both sides of the jamb, letting the cold January air howl into the hall.

Glass crunched beneath his shoes as he stepped inside. The open, deserted home in a desperate society had fallen prey to looters. There was nothing left. The blue upholstered furniture was gone, the once-bright carpeting now more black than gray. No light fixtures, no brass knobs on any of the doors. Indeed, even one of the doors was missing between the parlor and the butler's hall. But there was no damage to the structure except where fixtures had been ripped from the walls. It looked like a house ready to be let, except for repair and cleaning.

Max went to the kitchen, through the pantry, and down the stairs to the cellar. He saw piles of wood and bricks, gaping holes in three of the four walls. Two led to dirt. The last was the largest hole, large enough for him to step through.

There was no press but there were remnants of crumpled paper and a few cylinders left behind. He'd believed the report, but something inside had spurred him to see for himself.

Was this why you spent so much time with me, Genny? to keep me distracted?

But he found it didn't matter. The truth was, he loved Genny and would do anything to free her, including using the last of his savings and selling a ring that had been in his family for three generations. He didn't regret doing it, even if Genny had felt nothing for him. He'd never expected anything from her. How could he? He still had a wife. One to whom he must return, even though she couldn't remember his name.

Max left the secret room, picking up the longest lengths of wood he could carry, scraps of what had once been wine racks. He had no nails but hoped to find some. As thoughts of boarding up the front door blossomed into the idea of moving back in, at least for a few days, Max found himself climbing those stairs with the agility of a whole man.

Isa lay still on the cot, her back to the bars. She breathed steadily but was far from sleep. In the past three days she'd used slumber as an escape, and God had granted her the blessing of rest.

At last she turned on her back and stared at the low, curved ceiling. This was the crudest of the cells she'd been in, the most isolated. She was surrounded by cold, damp cement; it had the feeling of a hole in the earth. Water dripped from somewhere, but she was the only living being, other than the occasional passing rat, to inhabit anything within hearing range. Two sets of bars separated her cell from any other she'd passed when first brought in. There were no windows, no electricity, no plumbing. Just a cot and one thin blanket. And a bucket.

Guards changed every twelve hours. One sometimes sat between her cell and the next set of bars, close enough so she could hear him move, far enough so she felt the isolation more sharply.

Of the guards she'd seen so far, only one had looked her in the eye. He'd even managed to produce the blanket and bring her tea with the tasteless gruel yesterday. He'd also spoken to her, telling her he'd enjoyed her song the night before. It was a hymn she'd sung while hoping to banish the absolute silence and to invite the presence of God.

She had thanked him politely, the way Genny had taught her no matter the source of such a compliment. And then she watched him go, to be replaced by one of the others who blended in so well with the gray walls surrounding them.

Since then she had lain on her cot, nearly unmoving. Praying the numbness would last. Until the end.

"He's left messages in every parish in Upper Town, trying to find someone who knew Father Antoine."

Edward turned his full attention to Father Clemenceau, who had sent for him through various connections, not one of whom would know how to find Edward if the chain was broken. New identity papers were stuffed in his pocket: he was now Faas van Folkvaror, the son of a wealthy Dutch shipbuilder.

"What rank did you say this officer held?"

"Major."

Edward's heart sped. "But he wouldn't leave a name?"

"No. He said if Father Antoine wanted to see his aunt again, he should come to the Lassone residence."

Edward made a hasty track to Isa's. He didn't listen to his own cautious nature. It could be a trap. After all, Father Antoine had been at the Lassone residence countless times while the press was there. Surely he was suspected as well; that was why he'd taken the trouble to change his identity. But something told Edward this was one German Major he need not fear.

The door was boarded, glass swept to the side. Edward knocked and it sounded hollow inside. He knocked again, hearing nothing and fighting to hang on to his hope even as it sank. Pivoting to look around, he half expected armed guards to appear. But the front garden, the street, the neighborhood, appeared deserted.

At last he heard an uneven footfall approaching the door. Edward breathed easier. He hadn't been mistaken.

When he opened the door, Major von Bürkel looked at Edward, obviously perplexed, then surprised, and finally pleased.

"Major," Edward greeted.

"Come in out of the cold," he said, stepping out of the way.

"Though I can't promise it's much warmer in here. Come to the kitchen. I've lit the stove at least."

Edward followed, seeing Isa's home devoid of its former splendor. It might have rankled or pleased him once, but the loss seemed trivial now.

It was indeed warmer in the familiar kitchen. The table was gone and in its place stood a smaller version and two plain wood chairs.

"I found these tucked in a corner of the garage. Evidently the looters missed that spot."

Edward took a seat, and the Major produced two cups, hot water, and tea. What might have once been awkward for Edward now seemed ordinary, that he should sit at the same table with this German officer.

The Major looked at Edward as he poured. "I see you aren't a priest, but you aren't her nephew either, are you?"

Edward shook his head.

"I thought as much, to be perfectly frank. I thought the resemblance too strong. Is she your mother?"

He nodded. "How do you know she will be freed today?"

"Because it was I who arranged it."

"You . . ."

"I don't know all that went on here," he said with a glance toward the pantry door, "but I've come to know your mother. She doesn't deserve to be in servitude and certainly not in prison."

Edward nodded again, taking a sip of the hot beverage.

"I will be returning to Germany soon," the Major went on. "I wasn't sure she would know how to find you, so I hoped you would get my message. And so you have."

Edward eyed the older man curiously. "Isn't this quite a switch for you? dangerous, even, for you to show us such kindness? knowing what we've done?"

He shrugged. "Not dangerous. Foolish, perhaps, though my career in the army is over anyway." He patted his injured leg. "I serve a higher General now."

"God?"

The Major laughed at Edward's expression. "Is it so surprising?"

"I . . . no. My mother once told me you followed the same God. I am indebted to you for helping her."

"No. Don't be." The Major stood, going behind his chair and leaning on it rather than on the cane still hanging on the edge of the table. "Your mother will be here soon and I think it's wise that only you be here to greet her."

"You don't want to see her? Even though you came here to help her?"

The Major started to speak but at the last moment held back, looking away and shaking his head.

"What shall I tell her?" Edward asked. "Shouldn't I tell her it was you who helped her? She'll want to see you, to thank you."

"No, she needn't do that. When this is over, when she's safely away, tell her . . . tell her I couldn't see her again. Some good-byes are too difficult to do more than once."

Edward wished he could put a hand to the Major's shoulder, tell him that he understood, as incredible as it seemed to share such an unwanted bond. Saying good-bye to Isa would be unendurable.

But Edward didn't know how to share that bond, and so he folded his arms and regarded von Bürkel a moment longer before speaking. "You're going back to Germany, then?"

"Tomorrow. I'll spend the night at the Kommandantur. There is a cot folded away in the pantry. I spent last night here. But it isn't adequate for you and your mother. You must find another place to stay or somehow replace the missing furniture. I can fairly assure you the secret police have no interest in her—or this place—anymore."

Edward said nothing about his plans to take her across the

border as soon as he had Isa at his side, and to keep her well out of sight until then.

The Major took up his cane as if to leave, and Edward's pulse sped. He'd scoured the city looking for help, and here before him might be his only chance. If he could ask.

"Major . . . you've helped my mother. Is there anything to be done for Isa?"

He leaned on his cane, shaking his head slowly, sadly. "I don't think von Bissing himself could change it now, were he well enough to intervene. He's quite ill, so I've heard."

The pulse that sped went along faster, hotter, through Edward's veins. "They have no more right to murder Isa than they did when they took the lives of all the others accused of treason. Treason! Tell me, Major, how is it that Isa is accused of treason when it isn't her own government handing down that sentence?"

The Major looked at Edward and the implacable facade that Edward had seen covering the older man's face a moment earlier softened. "Don't you see? There's nothing that can be done."

Edward shook his head. "No, I don't see that at all. You freed my mother. Why can't you do the same for Isa?"

It was a childish question, even Edward could see that, but it was one he couldn't help but ask.

The Major turned away. "It's impossible. She is being guarded by the most loyal German soldiers. Everyone in Brussels awaits the upcoming celebration. Not a bribe on earth could make a difference now."

"Can you get me in to see her?" Edward demanded. "At least that much?"

The Major looked surprised, then thoughtful. He rubbed his forehead again and studied Edward. "Do you still have your cassock?"

39

Have no doubt, my fellow Belgians, were Christ in our midst today, He would surely fight for a definitive end to this war and look with sorrow on every injustice.

La Libre Belgique

"Thank you," Isa said breathlessly. A Bible, paper, and a pencil. She looked up from the gift to the guard who had just handed it through the bars. He was blond and Aryan, with a broad forehead, blue eyes, stocky build. Then she added in German, "*Danke, danke!* You've no idea what this means to me."

"You speak German, *Fräulein!*"

She nodded.

He pointed to the Bible. "Because of your hymns, I thought you would like that."

"Oh, I do!" she assured him. "The days are long here."

When he started to turn away, Isa spoke quickly. "What's your name?"

He turned back to her. "Franz."

She smiled and held out her hand. "I'm Isa."

He diverted his face slightly and did not take the proffered hand, but somehow it didn't seem like arrogance holding him back.

She did not withdraw her hand, watching him closely. "Franz?" she coaxed. "Will you not shake my hand?"

Slowly, his hand rose to take hers, but briefly.

"That wasn't so bad, was it?"

He smiled, not letting his gaze meet hers.

"Franz," she said, "maybe you could sit and talk to me a bit. Would it bring trouble to you if you did?"

He looked behind him, then shook his head.

Isa watched as Franz moved his stool from the farthest edge of the intermediate room to sit close to the bars in front of her. And then she started talking. She wasn't sure what compelled her, except several days of silence. She knew once Franz left, she had no chance of talking to anyone, and so, even to her own amazement, the uniform he wore, the country to which he was loyal, the army he represented, suddenly made no difference. He was just a boy, not much older than herself, who could smile and show kindness. And she learned of his family: a sister and parents who loved him and wished the war were over. Just like countless Belgian families. She did not sleep on the cot at all that night. Instead she talked the entire length of Franz's shift.

She could do all the sleeping she wanted tomorrow.

"Guard."

Max's voice was neither stern nor commanding; rather it was composed and quiet.

Nonetheless it was enough to send the dark-haired day guard swiftly to his feet, so swiftly that the stool flew out from under him and hit the wall with a crash before tumbling to the floor.

"Sir."

"I wish to see the prisoner in cell twenty-five."

Max watched the discombobulated soldier scurry for the key. His hands fumbled with the lock; then Max stepped into the intermediate cell. The moment he saw Isa, he was grateful he'd put off Edward until later.

Though she stood and appeared strong enough, with something of a dim smile on her face, she looked repugnant. Her hair had been chopped away in chunks, her eyes faintly purple beneath those blue pools. Her bottom lip was cracked and slightly swollen. And her dress, if a rag could be called that, possibly came from another inmate by the way it smelled.

He stood before the bars. *"Fräulein."*

"Guten Tag, Major," she said. "I'm very surprised to see you."

Aware of the guard behind him, Max chose his words carefully. "I learned of your sentence. I am sorry."

His sorrow did not seem to penetrate her steady facade. "Do you know the sentence for Genny?"

He offered her a smile. "She is free. Safe and well."

Her eyes closed. Against tears of relief?

"But for you," he began slowly, "I have no authority to alter things. I do promise you fresh water to wash with, a change of clothes. The German army can extend that much."

"Thank you," she said softly.

Amazement washed through him. There she stood, unemotional and calm, utterly collected. He was unsure he could achieve the same under similar circumstances. And he'd come to comfort *her.*

He started to turn away, but she moved forward ever so slightly. "Do you have scissors or a knife?"

Every soldier had an army-issue knife. His own was in his pocket. "What would you do with such a thing?"

She moved a hand to one of the dangling strands of her hair in the first self-conscious move he'd seen from her. "Cut the rest of my hair."

Max pulled out the knife.

The guard behind him moved closer, keys at the ready as Max handed her the tool. What did he think she would do? Attack him? Take her own life? Max swallowed an unexpected lump, hoping he'd read the situation correctly.

Slowly she raised the sharp edge toward her head, but it never came close to her throat. She sliced away the odd lengths that stuck out between shorter cuts like some kind of foolscap. When she cut away the last strand she could reach, he couldn't say she looked very much better with the hair so closely shorn, but at least she no longer looked like the jester of old.

"Did I miss any?" she asked.

Max took the knife, motioning her to come closer, for indeed she had missed some in the back. He did what he could, straightening the ends until—from behind at least—she looked like a boy. But it would grow back. . . .

He caught those words meant to comfort before saying them aloud. It wouldn't grow much before the twenty-seventh.

For the first time he saw sadness in her eyes, perhaps a reflection of the despair he suddenly felt for her. He wanted to leave, to hide from the injustice about which he could do nothing. But instead he stayed put.

"May I tell you of an observation I've made, *Fräulein*?"

She nodded.

"When I was recuperating, before you and the others came to live at your house, I spent much of my time at the window, watching the birds that live in the trees nearby. I watched them hunt food, build nests, squabble. But sometimes they simply fly, as if that's the thing they most enjoy. It's as if each little bird found the gift God bestowed upon him and flies just to thank the Creator that he can. But—" he lowered his voice—"if he senses danger, he no longer floats along with the wind; he turns abruptly and flies into it. It gives him height, sends him higher, faster, to do what he must. He flies *into* the wind.

"Do you know what I learned from that? I learned when we're in trouble, we should let those troubles carry us higher—closer to God Himself, who is never unaware of what we face. The wind—or our trouble—isn't necessarily our foe if we let it take us closer to God. Somehow, like that little bird whose flight itself brings Him glory, He'll let us bring Him glory, too."

Her gaze had not left his face, and he knew he had her attention. When he finished, she started to bite her lip, then winced from a forgotten bruise and tried to smile.

"Thank you, Major."

Max turned to leave but remembered something else. "Oh, I nearly forgot." He withdrew the pieces of her flute from his inner pockets. "I found this in your home." He didn't tell her about the looters, that the flute was nearly the only thing they'd missed. "I thought you might like to have it."

"Yes!" She reached for it eagerly. He was glad he'd brought it since it returned the smile to her face. "Thank you."

And then he left. He had much to do before he let Edward come.

40

**LONDON ESTIMATES GERMAN CASUALTIES
IN THE MILLIONS**

. . . *La Libre Belgique* acknowledges the upcoming birthday
of the German Kaiser. Certainly the Kaiser has impacted the
world, and an acknowledgment of the date of his birth is only
fitting. But what can be said of the man who erected an altar
of blood and iron upon which were sacrificed those millions
of soldiers?

May this birthday be his last.

La Libre Belgique

Edward kept his eyes on the Major, praying he didn't do anything to
give himself away. That he spoke German was perhaps as vital to his
disguise as the cassock he wore. Condemned prisoners were allowed
to see priests or chaplains, but only German ones.

He wasn't sure how the Major knew his way so easily. The
prison was huge and cavernous and the way was dimly lit by covered torches placed here and there, sending shadows along the
low, arched ceiling. Countless smells assaulted him, the best of
which was simply mold. The worst he didn't wish to name. He
heard sounds now and then, coughing or banging, an occasional

shout. No talking, however. Not a single calm, conversational tone to be heard.

At last the Major stopped at what appeared to be a solitary dead end set apart from other cells. The Major said nothing. The guard, a dark-haired man not much taller than Jonah, though considerably older, stood at attention the moment they approached.

"Sir."

Edward, still standing behind the Major, saw little and had to fight the impulse to peer around him in search of Isa. But not wanting to give himself away, he waited.

The guard unlocked the bars and a moment later Edward followed the Major into an inner holding cell. At last his gaze found her. The cell was barely lit by a single torch just outside the bars. She was sitting on a cot, and in her lap was an open book. It appeared to be a Bible. When she'd looked up at the guard opening the outer lock, Edward noticed her shorn hair and bruises, but her posture was healthy, her eyes alert. As she caught sight of him, he saw the beginning of an astonished smile.

Setting aside the Bible, she stood and neared the bars, her gaze locked to his.

"You will allow the father to go in with the prisoner," the Major said.

There was a slight hesitation, but even Edward knew a German private wouldn't defy an officer. He was inside in a minute, fighting the urge to take Isa in his arms.

"He'll hear her confession now. Come along, soldier."

They left and Edward grabbed Isa to him, hot tears stinging his eyes. He pulled her away just long enough to look at her again, seeing her face was wet with tears too.

"Isa, Isa," he whispered and kissed her. He was gentle, mindful of the bruises that marred her lovely face. He brushed a hand over her short blonde hair, his other hand still at her back. The linen blouse was rough—though surprisingly clean—beneath his touch. She was the first thing he smelled that didn't offend the senses: no familiar perfumed soap but clean nonetheless. He'd been angry with the Major earlier when he said he must go alone to see about getting Edward in, but now he wondered if the Major was the one responsible for Isa's being the only clean spot in the place.

Edward put his hands on her shoulders and looked her in the eye. "I'm doing everything I can to get you out of here. Mr. Whitlock is working on it too. We're even petitioning Pope Benedict to intercede on your behalf."

Her brows rose. "I'm not even Catholic!"

"Yes, well, we have plenty of friends who are. We're petitioning through Father Clemenceau. My mother is helping in any way she can."

"Your mother? Have you seen her, then?"

"Yes, thanks to the Major." He glanced over his shoulder in the direction the Major had disappeared. "He's not so bad, really, despite his lineage."

"He's a son of God," she whispered.

"And so am I," Edward whispered back.

Her blue eyes swam with tears again. "Edward . . ."

He nodded. She hadn't misunderstood.

"Oh, Edward!" She held him close, murmuring nearly incoherent words. "Thank God! I am at peace."

Edward smiled, remembering Father Clemenceau's words. She needed him to be strong spiritually most of all. . . . He was glad he'd been able to show her he was at last.

Still, he needed to be honest. "I've been trying to figure out why God allowed you to be put here instead of me. Isa, you live His love like a reflex. Even now, in this place, you haven't turned away from Him like I might have done. I think some people need His protection more than others because we just aren't strong enough in our faith."

"He sends me so much of His love." She glanced down at the Bible on the cot, leaving the circle of his arms to retrieve it. "Do you know whose Bible this is, Edward? It's Edith Cavell's. She was the English nurse who helped so many men find their way across the border to freedom. She helped my brother, Charles. Have you heard of her?"

Edward nodded; he'd known his share of guilt about her too, since he'd directed more than one man to her network when it existed. Charles Lassone being among the men she'd helped was news to him.

"Her Bible is full of notes and praises. She must have meditated night and day before . . . well, until she died. It's quite an example to follow, and somehow God intervened to get this to me."

Though she held the book like the treasure it was, his heart weighed heavy at the thought of the nurse standing before a firing squad. Edward pushed away the image of Isa facing the same fate.

"Isa." He bit the desperation in his voice, too late to call it back.

She folded the Bible to her chest and placed her free hand across his lips. "No, Edward. Don't say anything except that you love me. I couldn't stand anything else."

He held her against him, fighting tears. "I do love you, Isa. I always have even though I tried to ignore it. Now I know what a fool I was to hold that back, to wait until it's too late. I'm sorry."

"You did what you thought was best for both of us. Don't be sorry."

"I want to marry you."

The sound of her laughter was like music. "I've wanted to marry you since I was seven years old. But whom would you care to invite to this sacred ceremony? Will the guard be enough or did you want General von Bissing here too? Or maybe we could wait until the Kaiser is in town . . ."

But she didn't finish. His arrival would be the day of her execution.

He drew her close and felt her tremble. "I came here today to give you hope, to tell you I'm working on a plan to free you."

He rested his forehead on hers, but she didn't respond.

"I love you, Isa. I would spend every moment here at your side if they'd let me."

They heard the Major clearing his throat, and Edward stepped away at the approach of the guard.

Edward left Isa with a smile he knew must have seemed grim, but it was the only one he could muster. As he walked away, he secretly vowed that nothing, *nothing*, would prevent him from stopping her sentence—or he would join her in heaven trying.

"Marry her! Of all things," the Major said. "It's out of the question."

They talked in the kitchen of Isa's home, the Major seated while Edward leaned against the sink. "At the very least it's out of the question because I suspect you plan something else. You don't want simply to marry her. You think you can break her out of there, don't you?"

Edward's silence was enough to confirm the truth. He'd expected some resistance to his plan to visit Isa again, but not such a quick, flat denial.

"It's too dangerous. Any attempt would be downright foolhardy."

"Which? A wedding or trying to get her out?"

"Take your pick; either is equally foolish."

"I don't think you understand what I'm saying," Edward said patiently. "What I am saying is that I intend to get her out, and if that attempt works, all the better. If it doesn't, well . . . it won't matter."

"And I'm saying it does matter. You're a young man, Edward. What about your mother?"

His mother, who at this very moment hid at Rosalie's, protected by Henri. Praying, as Edward did, for a way to save Isa. "My mother is a woman of faith, Major, as you know. I've made it clear to her I would rather live in the next world with Isa than without her in this one."

The Major shifted in his seat, folding his hands on the table. For a long moment he said nothing, and Edward didn't know if that was a good sign or bad.

At last the Major shook his head. "There is only one way to do this if you're determined to go through with it."

Edward stood straight as if at attention. "How?"

"You won't like it."

"Tell me."

The Major came laboriously to his feet to stand before Edward, leaning on his cane with both hands. "Wait until the day of her execution." He held up a hand to still Edward's protest. "When they transport her from the prison at Vilvorde to take her to Tir National. It is the only way."

Edward shook his head. "I won't wait that long. To the day? No, I won't have it."

"*You* won't have it? Young man, I don't see that you have any choice."

The Major was right. And yet to wait until the last minute, with no time for a second chance . . .

"If you think we have more than one try at this, you're quite wrong. Either we get it right the first time or we die in the effort. That's it."

It was as if the Major could read his mind. However, one word caught Edward's attention. "We?"

Major von Bürkel rubbed his eyes before looking again at Edward. "I'm tired of this war," he said quietly. "I no longer believe in one side or the other. I am loyal to God, to justice. And," he added with sudden color to his cheeks, "to your mother. Isa is important to her." He cleared his throat and added gruffly, "My career with the German army is at an end. I might as well go out doing something I believe in, the same way I went in. In any case, I'm the only chance for help you're likely to get. You must tell me everything you've been thinking. What resources you have, if we might be able to use any of them."

"I have money," he said, "and Henri. You remember Henri."

"The giant gardener?" He nodded. "Yes, we can use both."

Isa let the last note rise softly from her flute until it disappeared, leaving behind only peace. All in the hands of God. She needed that reminder. She needed it nearly every moment of every day.

"That was very good, *Fräulein*," Franz said from his stool outside her cell. "Maybe you're tired now. I will get you some water."

Isa nodded, watching him go to the barrel in the corner of the outer cell. It had been three days since Edward's visit, and ever since she'd expected him to miraculously show up at any moment with a legitimate priest at his side, to somehow perform a secret marriage ceremony so she would go to heaven married to him. It was the only dream that had gotten her through those days, but as each passed, it became less real, less hopeful. Tomorrow, just after dawn, would be too late. She had known it couldn't happen; hadn't she told him so?

Why, Lord? If I am to join You in heaven tomorrow, why not allow one last earthly hope, to marry the man I love? Is it too much to ask?

Only the knowledge of His presence, His peace, eliminated her self-pity. She'd read Jesus' prayer in the garden of Gethsemene over and over, praying with the Lord: *Let this cup pass from me: nevertheless not as I will, but as thou wilt.*

She was learning how deep the definition of *trust* must go for it to mean anything.

Franz handed her a cup of cool water.

"Franz," she said, thinking if she was ever going to know, she must ask now, "I wonder why you're so kind to me. I've been found guilty of a crime worthy of death by the army you serve. Why aren't you like the others, who won't even look me in the eye?"

"I was like that once." She saw his gaze fall to the Bible on her cot.

"Do you know God, Franz?"

He looked at her somewhat vacantly and shook his head. "I know there is a God; at least that's what I've been told. But I don't think He's very interested in me. No," he said, "it's not God that makes me nice to you. It's her."

"Her?"

"Fräulein Cavell."

"Edith Cavell?"

Franz nodded. "I was her guard, too." As he spoke, his eyes grew more vacant than they'd been a moment ago. "I wouldn't speak to her even though she was nice to me. Do you know, when I first came back from the front, she tended my wounds? That was long before they arrested her. They didn't know that, otherwise they wouldn't have assigned me to guard her. And she didn't remember me. Too many patients, I suppose. But I didn't say anything, either to my superiors or to her. I knew my duty, and I did it."

"Is that how you came to have her Bible?"

"It was left behind. The prayer book was taken by the chaplain. I don't know what he did with it. And the letters . . ."

"What happened to them?"

"They were commandeered."

"And then? Weren't they sent to those she thought of in her last hours?"

He shook his head. "No, *Fräulein*. They were destroyed."

Isa closed her eyes. She'd written more than one letter herself, so reminiscent of her diary. Letters to Genny and to her brother, Charles, to her parents and to Edward. Especially to Edward.

But now, to learn her letters would probably face the same fate . . .

Franz stood. "I vow to you, *Fräulein*, if you give me the letters you've written, I will get them out."

"Thank you, Franz." She swallowed hard, pushing away a sudden wave of terror, of fear, of helplessness. Such waves often came unexpectedly, washing through her body with physical force that dizzied her. In those moments she'd learned to steady her breathing, banish all thoughts, and pray. Dwell on the Lord. Abide.

Franz moved his stool away from the bars, back to where it normally sat when others were on watch. His shift was coming to an end. The next time she saw him would be the last, when they would come at dawn to escort her to Tir National.

She was weary of the emotional battles. She wanted to lie down, to sleep, to escape from the doubts that gnawed at her faith, her peace, and her sanity. But instead a thought came to her that helped. She turned to Franz.

"Franz," she said gently, "tomorrow, after they come for me, this will be left behind again." She lifted the Bible. "Will you take it and keep it as your own? read it?"

"It's in English."

She'd forgotten the difference in languages. "Can you get a German translation? Look at the areas that are underlined in here and then read them in your Bible. Will you do that for me, Franz?"

He looked at her, then at the book, and at last he nodded. She believed he would do it. Honesty was part of duty, and that she knew he did very well.

41

You may smash our buildings, crush our bridges, destroy our men. But our spirit goes on.

La Libre Belgique

Dawn was an hour away. Edward sat in a wagon outside the prison. He hadn't slept more than a few minutes at a time all night and yet had no trouble staying awake now. He knew what would happen if he failed. He must not fail.

Edward's mother had been taken to the meeting place with Father Clemenceau. She, at least, would escape before the sun rose this day, even if the rest of them never made it.

The wind stung Edward's eyes and ruffled a bit of hair sticking out from under his spiked helmet as he held the reins on the horse before the wagon. He had to admit the Major was a formidable source. He was intelligent and thorough, forcing Edward to face all the possibilities—including killing another human being.

Edward had been amazed at the Major's willingness to be part of such a plan. He was bold, even ruthless. And yet that ruthlessness was tempered with caution. If all went well without any deviation, they could succeed without a shot fired. He'd wanted Edward to be prepared but made it clear he hoped his treason did not stretch to murdering his countrymen.

The horse Edward directed was one of the finest specimens left in Belgium, and it had cost a hefty chunk of Henri's money. The animal was worth every penny, as strong as any brewer's horse. Smaller, admittedly, but faster. And that's exactly what they would need if anything went wrong.

The wagon had once been a wooden flatbed, now fitted with iron bars so that it looked like a cage on wheels—something a circus might bring to town to show its most dangerous animals. But now it held Henri, the Major, and a coffin. The Germans were so very efficient.

He pulled up to the gate at the castle prison in Vilvorde. Despite warmer weather the day before, recent snow had been cleared to allow the doors to swing easily back and forth. The hooves made an odd tapping noise against the cobblestones. Edward had impaled nails into the very edge of each unguis to guarantee the traction they would need later.

The first test: Edward's uniform. Amazing what money could buy. Edward now wore the identity of a Vizefeldwebel, complete with the worsted braid on the overcoat collar to show the NCO rank. It was even a perfect fit. Finding one for Henri had been a bit trickier and more expensive. He was now a Feldwebel, and it had been decided that he would accompany the Major inside the prison to retrieve Isa. Edward wanted to be the one to go inside, but the Major had refused. He wouldn't take the risk of Edward being recognized after his visit as a priest.

The sentry at the door saluted and, as Edward anticipated, never looked him in the eye. He accepted the papers—papers the Major had taken such risk to obtain, stolen from none other than Hauptmann von Eckhart—and then opened wide the gate to let them pass.

So far, Lord. So far, so good.

Edward pulled up to the innermost curb in the yard where the Major and Henri alighted from the back without a word. They did not give Edward a glance as they went about the plan with military efficiency. And Edward took up his prayer again. It was all he could do, all he could think.

Keep her safe, Lord.

Isa heard the boots on the cement floor approach. If she'd been able to eat anything the night before surely she would have lost it now. The sound echoed in the predawn stillness along the curved ceiling, the metal bars. How soon that sound came. Earlier than she'd thought, but how could she know? Time had stopped mattering, as if she'd slept, then woke, and could no longer tell how much of the night had passed. She didn't remember sleeping.

She had prayed through the night. Between her prayers she'd wondered what she would feel after they tied the blindfold around her eyes. If she would feel each bullet or just the first. If this side of death would hurt.

But this morning she was strangely calm. She knew within a few hours she would be in God's presence. In some mysterious and unexpected way she found herself longing for the moment. Wasn't that the way it should be if she truly believed as she said she did? Why, indeed, would anyone choose to remain on earth when heaven beckoned? She remembered a verse from Hebrews: *Looking unto Jesus the author and finisher of our faith; who for the joy that was set before him endured the cross.* She too would endure death by the hand of others but soon know that joy.

This was the only difference between her and most who died. She knew the moment death would arrive. And her moment was soon.

Only when her hand happened across the letters she'd written did that calm threaten to shatter. Leaving those she loved was her source of pain. She knew life would be hard for them until that day they too came to the joy.

"Shutz."

The single word calling the guard started her heart galloping. It was time; it was time *now*. Could she face it without abandoning everything she believed?

She stood, gathering the letters atop the Bible. She must give them to Franz. Here was her comfort, knowing her words would reach those for whom they were intended. She prayed it would make it easier, not harder, for them to say good-bye.

Franz opened the inner bars. That lock had not been touched since the day Edward had smuggled himself in to see her. The iron hinges squeaked a protest when they moved.

"Franz." She looked at his sad countenance and handed him the goods. "Remember what I said about the German Bible. Don't break that promise, my friend."

He accepted the book and the folded letters on top. He nodded, then looked away. Did his hand tremble as he took the bundle? Hers were so calm!

There was nothing left to do except retrieve her flute. Music was a gift from God. She would go to her grave holding the instrument through which that gift had so often flowed. She also took the blanket off of the cot. Tir National was a good distance away, and she would have need of it, at least until she got there.

Then she turned for the first time to the soldier who would escort her. And nearly gasped.

Major von Bürkel. Now her heart hammered anew with confusion and something else. What was he doing here? She swallowed down anxiety and unbidden hope. Surely he was here as nothing more than a comfort, to offer a familiar face instead of the cold, impersonal ones of the strangers who would end her life.

Isa bowed her head, afraid her face might give something away. She followed him, the blanket clutched around her shoulders in tight fists.

Another soldier stood just outside the holding cell. A huge man. She would not have looked twice except that the presence of the Major made her curious about everything involved in her exit from this prison.

And then she knew, without doubt, that the Major had not come simply to comfort her in her last hour.

It was Henri.

Isa's knees weakened. Every steady thought was washed from her mind, and yet she kept still until the moment she had to step behind Henri and follow him out.

What were they doing? Risking their lives—for her? How could they? She alone was to die this day.

She heard little from the cells they passed, except occasionally someone said her name as a salute.

When she stepped outside for the first time in what suddenly seemed an eternity, she relished the fresh, cold wind. She was alive.

A cage sat on the back of a wagon, and she gave a quick look to the driver. But he sat with the traditional stiffness of most German soldiers, staring straight ahead. Were his shoulders as broad as Edward's? Should she even hope for such a thing?

Isa got in first, her gaze drawn to the coffin. She sat opposite it, even as Henri boarded and sat atop it as if it were nothing more than a bench. The Major followed with surprising ease and slammed the door shut with a bang.

The wagon lurched forward and she nearly lost her seat—not from speed but rather from her own instability. In a moment they stopped at the front gate. She wanted to talk to the Major, ask him what was happening, but dared not say a word. She would not do or say anything to endanger them.

The sentry at the gate waved them outward, and Isa watched as the driver slowed but never stopped. In the next moment they were outside the last set of bars that had separated her from freedom, except for the ones on this very wagon.

Prison torches fell behind as the driver flicked the reins for the horse to pick up the pace down the narrow, snow-covered street, the only road leading from the prison. On either side of the road were deep ruts, so that only the middle appeared safe to travel.

She looked at the Major at last, wondering if he might speak, but he raised a hand for her to remain silent.

Only minutes from the prison, headlights shot at them from ahead and the driver pulled on the reins.

"Halt! You will halt!"

Isa looked for the source of the command. At first she wasn't sure the driver would obey. A black motorcar with German flags affixed above its headlights stood crooked across the road before them, barring passage.

In a moment Isa saw the man who issued the cry. She held her breath even as, out of the corner of her eye, she saw the Major turn away, taking a seat on the coffin so Henri blocked him from view of the approaching man.

Hauptmann Rudiger von Eckhart approached, and he had a look of a madman. Or a drunkard.

"You are early! This was not to take place for another *hour*. What is the meaning of this?"

The driver spoke in a gravelly voice in perfect German. "Orders, sir. Only following orders. She's the first of three today."

"Yes, and it was to begin at dawn, and they were to be transported together. It is not dawn!"

Isa could not stand the sight of the Hauptmann shouting and standing there without even a coat. "It doesn't matter, does it, Hauptmann? An hour, more or less? What's that in a lifetime?"

"Fräulein Lassone!" He rushed to the side of the cage, pulling on it and shaking the entire wagon as if it would open. "It is unacceptable that the orders have been changed. You were to have until dawn—"

She nodded but couldn't guess if he saw her. Suddenly she heard the whip and the horse bolted forward. She flew along behind, this time unseated and landed with a thud over Henri's massive legs. The Major skidded beside her, except his wooden leg had caught in one of the bars and it swung him back to the edge of the cage like a life-size doll.

Fighting to regain her seat with Henri's help, she looked at the Major. "What is going on?"

He too was holding on, for the horse hadn't stopped picking up speed. "That's Edward," he said, taking one hand off the bars for the barest moment to point at the driver.

Isa's heart soared.

42

In the distance we hear the beat of the guns, sometimes slow, sometimes fast, sometimes steady. It is the heartbeat of this war.

La Libre Belgique

Edward shouted the horse to a run, the animal's footing sure on the icy road thanks to the nails. They dashed down the deserted, slippery streets in the cold predawn hour.

"Halt! Halt!"

Edward ignored the shouts. No simple command would stop him from his destination. Sentries scattered from their huddle around a fire barrel, some yelling to make chase. Edward slapped the whip again, harder when he heard the pop and whistle of gunfire. The foot soldiers were no match for the strong and agile horse Edward had paid a fortune for.

And then he saw the headlights. From behind the wagon, two beams illuminated the street and Edward heard an engine roar.

Shouts sounded—Isa's voice, then the Major's. In a moment the cage door banged open. With a quick glance, Edward saw two things: the vehicle gaining on them and Henri thrusting the empty coffin out the back. It hit the front of the motorcar with a whack, breaking one of the headlights and splintering to pieces as the heavy, unstoppable menace rolled over it.

Edward stood in his seat, cracking the whip again as they raced down the dark hill, nothing to light the way. But Edward saw the trees in the waning moonlight and counted them along the road: four, five, six . . . That was it. He pulled hard on the reins and the horse—an animal accustomed to the chaos of battle—turned instantly to the left. The horse maneuvered easily over the bumpy ground through the park, avoiding trees and bushes. Finally they approached the last hurdle, a low rise that bordered the road running along the canal's bank. Edward nearly lost his seat over the bump, but they reached the road—one von Eckhart's motorcar would be hard-pressed to find.

The nails affixed to the horse's hooves worked just as Edward hoped. Like a giant polar bear with claws on the ice, the horse might as well have been on one of the smooth roads of Belgium. Ahead, everything was clear.

Edward ventured a glance behind. No sign of the single headlight on the motorcar. Edward shouted the horse on to greater speed. The drunken Hauptmann wouldn't easily give up, and they had miles to go.

The narrow canals of Vilvorde and Brussels fed into the wide River Senne, now just northwest of them. Soon they would abandon the wagon and go the rest of the way on foot to meet the boat that would carry them to freedom.

Edward plowed through each set of sentries, grateful for their speed not only for those caged behind him but for himself as well. He'd left behind the ruckus of gunfire but sentries could be around any corner to offer more. No one on foot could follow, and there were so few motorcars in the city anymore, he had little need to worry over any but von Eckhart's.

The trees on each side of the road opened at the river.

And then he heard it . . . subtle at first, and then louder—the sound of a motor, soon followed by the light of one beam. The motorcar was nearly upon them.

Edward had no choice. The river widened along this route, with a walkway along either side meant only for foot traffic. It might accommodate them. . . .

He whipped at the horse, urging him where he obviously had no desire to go, so close to the water's edge and in such slippery conditions. Edward needed only to get to the rendezvous, and yet how could he with a German officer on his heels? Even a drunken one could give away the boat's hidden cargo.

The headlight behind bounced off buildings and trees.

"Henri! I'm going to stop. I need you!"

Edward pulled the reins, alighting before the wagon had even come to a stop.

"I'll have to face him. You'll have to continue on to the rendezvous. Get her there. Don't let anything stop you."

But even as Henri freed himself from the back of the cage to come around to Edward's place, the Major hobbled down as well.

"Go on, Edward. Go to your mother. I'll face von Eckhart."

"But he hasn't seen you yet! One look at you and they'll know—"

"We haven't time for this. Just go!"

Edward scrambled into the back of the wagon—not before seeing the motorcar hurtling toward them. Edward barked at Henri to hurry but there wasn't time. Von Eckhart tried a screeching halt, only to have the wheels catch on ice. The sole headlamp beamed one way, then the other; the black vehicle skidded until its back wheels left the road and the motorcar stopped with a metallic crunch, the underbelly teetering on the edge of the walkway.

It tipped upward, until it shone like a beacon into the sky.

Then it toppled over backward and was gone.

"Go, Henri!" the Major shouted behind them.

"No! Wait!" Isa called. "You're coming too, aren't you, Major?"

He still clutched his cane and shook his head. "No. Now go. You're free."

"I—I don't know how to thank you."

"There's no need for that. Go now; you haven't much time to make it to the rendezvous."

She reached out through the open bars, long enough to draw him into half an embrace, perched as she was above him on the wagon.

"Thank you, Major. I'll never forget—Oh! Major! Look!"

Behind him, from the edge where von Eckhart's motorcar had gone into the river, appeared none other than von Eckhart himself.

The Major turned to him. "Go now," he said over his shoulder again as he walked at an uneven—but quickened—pace toward von Eckhart.

But Henri, from the seat, waited for Edward's nod.

Without looking at Isa, Edward jumped from the back of the wagon. "Go now, Henri! Get her there."

The wagon lurched and Edward had just enough time to close the cage door once again.

"Edward, no! We'll all go together." Isa pushed the cage door; it wasn't locked, but the latch was stiff. "I want to stay with you!"

"We don't have time to argue," Edward called. "Keep going, Henri. Take her and don't let anything stop you."

Without waiting for a response, he ran toward the Major just as the wagon pitched forward.

His first glance at the Major spun Edward's head. He lay on the ground, his foot at such an odd angle he knew no one could withstand such pain. Until he realized it was the artificial foot, loosened from its proper position. The Major might have struggled to regain footing with the help of his cane if von Eckhart weren't hovering over him, shaking him by the lapels of his jacket.

Edward approached from behind.

"You shouldn't have stopped me, Max," the Hauptmann said. "I had to stop you, didn't I? Didn't I?"

"Now who's the loyal type, von Eckhart? Not me, but you."

"That's right! My loyalty is where it belongs—not to a woman but to our country!"

"Yes, but it's over now. You've done your duty, and I did what I needed to do. I'll face a tribunal, and you can play the hero."

"True enough!" Von Eckhart let Max go, stepping back and reaching for the gun holstered at his side. "You are under arrest."

The Major laughed. "That thing is soaked. What makes you think it'll work?"

"I think it *will* work, my friend. Not that I need it to overtake you."

Edward pressed the nozzle of his own gun against one of von Eckhart's ears. "Mine will surely work, Hauptmann," he whispered. "So you may drop yours."

The Hauptmann stiffened, then let his own gun fall, but before it reached the ground, he swung around. Edward took a blow to his jaw, aimed far more squarely and solidly than he would have thought possible from a man so deep in his cups. Perhaps the frigid water of the Senne had reinvigorated the man's senses.

Von Eckhart grabbed for the gun and Edward pulled back, caught by the force of the Hauptmann's lunge. His gun fell harmlessly to the ground.

Edward dodged a second punch and managed a single blow to the side of the man's head—a reflex action from the pain he'd already suffered. It was clear already that Edward's relatively sheltered upbringing by a pacifist father left him no match for von Eckhart's training, even marred by whatever alcohol he'd consumed.

Edward blocked yet another strike but his return missed von Eckhart altogether. He took a second swing and that connected, but he didn't move quickly enough to miss von Eckhart's fist to the same jaw he'd already hit.

Another swing—another miss. And yet von Eckhart went down. His head hit the pavement behind them with a crack and he lay there, unmoving.

Edward looked behind him, where the Major, still on the ground, held up his cane. He'd landed it to the Hauptmann's middle, who was just unstable enough to be knocked off-balance.

Edward stood over the fallen opponent, seeing he was unconscious.

He went to the Major, who was shifting his artificial foot back into position and tightening the straps. "You have no choice now, Max. Even drunk, he'll identify you. If you go back now, you'll lose everything."

"I already have," Max said.

"No. You haven't." Even as he spoke, he reached to help the Major up. "You're coming with me."

Edward shoved one arm under the Major's weak side and pulled him along. It wouldn't be long before guards from the prison found their trail or some street sentry caught up.

"Leave me, Edward," the Major said. "You'll never make it in time hobbled to me like this. Go."

"Shut up and run like we're in a three-legged race."

And despite his protest, the Major ran.

The boat wasn't large, little more than a tugboat.

But this boat was headed south, not north. Isa wasn't at all sure Henri had taken her to the right place.

"Henri," she said at the gangplank, "this can't be right. It's headed the wrong way. The North Sea is *north*."

Henri shook his head, pushing her forward but not stepping onto the plank.

She grabbed his arm, pulling him closer. "Aren't you coming?"

He shook his head again.

"But, Henri—"

Someone from inside the boat called out, "Get aboard!"

The voice, though quiet, held unmistakable anger. Henri pushed her again.

"I'll go," she said. "But, Henri . . . thank you. Thank you for everything you did to help me." She hugged him close, enveloped in warmth as his massive arms circled her. "I'll see you again. When this is over."

She might have said more, but the voice from the boat called again and Henri gently nudged her forward.

The boat looked empty. It was an old, sturdy tugboat with a tall smokestack shooting up into the dark sky. She climbed the gangplank quickly because it had no grab rails and she knew any pause would bring fear. Once aboard, she looked for the owner of the voice but saw no one.

"Go below."

She looked up. The voice had come from the bridge.

Isa glanced back ashore, but Henri had already disappeared. Confused longing ran through her. The city was behind them, the Brussels she knew and loved. She couldn't go back, perhaps not ever. And yet what lay ahead?

She found the portal leading below. Halfway down, she stopped. The entire belly of the tug was crowded with people all pushed together, mostly men, no doubt escaping the deportations or hoping to join the Allies. There was barely enough room for her, let alone Edward when he came.

Because surely he would.

"Isa! Oh, Isa!"

It was Genny, nestled in the furthermost corner.

Isa scrambled over limbs and feet, past smells and sounds, falling into Genny's open arms. Pulling apart proved difficult. They wedged together into the single spot Genny had vacated.

"Where is Edward?"

"He's coming." She told herself to believe her own words, otherwise she was sure both of them would scurry ashore. "We were separated from the Major, and Edward went for him."

"Max!"

"Yes, of course. Without the Major, I don't think—"

Genny trembled so fiercely Isa quivered with her, squashed together as they were.

"Are you saying Max has been with Edward? that he helped plan this escape?"

"He must have! The Major came to see me in prison, and Edward told me he was planning something. He didn't tell me who was involved, but it was the Major himself who came for me in my cell this morning."

"I . . . didn't know. I thought Max was in Germany." She looked at Isa, who saw both fear and fervor in her eyes. "And he's coming with us? over the border?"

"I—I think so. Why wouldn't he? How could he stay after helping me? He'll be arrested!"

Suddenly the engine roared to a start.

Isa's heart crashed against her breast. "We can't be going—not yet!"

"We should have left ten minutes ago." The voice came from one of the men on the other side of the ladder.

"That's right," another said. "We must get past the Brussels checkpoint before the sun is up or we'll be like ducks at the carnival, ready to be picked off."

"But there's someone else coming," Isa insisted. "We can't leave him behind!"

"And risk the rest of us? I don't think so, *mademoiselle*."

Isa struggled to her feet. Yet she didn't make it far. The two men closest to her shifted just enough to block the way.

Isa sank to the floor, sending an anxious glance to Genny. *Oh, Lord, deliver them now! Hurry them to us!*

Then the tug started to move.

43

Our resolve against the enemy must not melt in the German furnace. Be strong as we await our day of liberation!

La Libre Beligique

Every muscle in his arms, legs, and back threatened collapse, but Edward didn't give in. The Major moved nearly as fast as he, his body strong. Once they found a similar stride, they moved with surprising speed—fast enough to win any Sunday school three-legged race.

They stayed along the river's edge, which was blessedly deserted at such an early hour. It couldn't be much farther.

Then he saw the outline of the tug in the middle of the river. Heading, as expected, southward and away from the dock to reduce attention. Boats headed north—toward the border—were more likely to be subject to unexpected searches. So at least until they were well away from the nearest checkpoint, the boat would be heading south, toward them. The scheduled turnaround wasn't far before it would head away and out of Belgium altogether.

"Come on." From somewhere inside, Edward's strength increased, and so did the Major's—Edward felt it. Like angels prodding them forward.

"We'll have to swim toward it. Can you make it?"

Max withdrew his arm from Edward's shoulder and spoke as he removed his uniform jacket. He started to unhook his helmet but must have thought better of it, leaving the protection in place. "Member of the Berlin Swim Club for five years. Let's go."

He dove in and Edward rushed after him without taking the time to get out of his own jacket or metal helmet. He knew the water would be cold, and with the jacket loose enough, he hoped it would help and not hinder.

Edward nearly blacked out when he hit the icy river. The water pierced every fiber.

Someone from the high bridge of the tugboat must have spotted them; a Jacob's ladder appeared down the side. The Major reached it first and fairly hopped from one rung to the next, his upper body pulling him along until someone reached him and finished the job. Edward followed.

"You're late."

"Not too late, though. We've made it."

"You said there would only be one more. There's no more room below."

"Then we'll stay above."

But the sailor eyed the Major, who stood leaning on the gunwale. "Not him." Though the artificial foot was in place, the Major's wet trousers clung to the wooden appendage, revealing his handicap. "Go here. Stay inside."

He opened the door to a compartment at the bow, little more than a forepeak, in which were stored coiled ropes and hitches with barely enough room for anyone to hide.

Nonetheless the Major did as he was told, somehow fitting himself to the cramped quarters.

"What do I do?" Edward asked.

"Stay low. I can use your help, especially dressed as you are. Your uniform might buy us a moment if we're spotted." The man shoved a rifle into his hand. "I am Rémy," he said quickly, then looked toward the prow. "A guard station lies not far ahead. If they spot us, we may have to use these, but for now, keep out of sight."

The man crouched and Edward did as well. He waited, knowing there was nothing else to do but pray as the little boat chugged down the Senne, steadily picking up speed. Now northward, toward freedom.

A beam shone on the deck. Edward stood tall, hoping his German uniform would be enough to let them through.

A shout—German. "Halt!"

The tug rumbled on.

Nothing for a full moment, nothing but the sound of the motor growing louder in the dim hours of morning.

Something hit the smokestack with a ping, like the sound of a marble hitting a target. Edward ducked flat. More spotlights lit and gunfire exploded into the night.

The captain shouted to the engineer to give it all they had. Sparks from the guard station flickered in the darkness, and Edward saw Rémy and another man Edward hadn't seen before return fire.

Edward joined in. He knew how to handle the rifle thanks to a hunt he'd been on with Jan and his family during their university days, but that was the extent of his training. He hoped he wouldn't waste too much ammunition. And he'd never shot at a man before.

Even if his shooting lacked skill, it was better than sitting still. Time suspended in the flurry of battle. It must have been only minutes but seemed like an hour.

Then, at last, they were out of range. Edward sank to the deck, relieved.

"That was number one," Rémy said.

Edward wasn't sure he wanted to know but felt compelled to ask anyway. "Number one?"

The man spared Edward by not answering.

Heading northwest as quickly as they were, they would hit the Scheldt and be across the border before long. It was, indeed, the quickest way out of Belgium.

Edward wished to go below—to be sure Isa and his mother were there. To be away from the sights. Away from gunfire, if more was to be had as he fully expected. They were well out of Brussels, and at this rate not very far from being out of Belgium. But it was hardly free sailing in between.

He couldn't leave the deck, though, so he leaned closer to the man nearby. "Did any women board? One earlier, one shortly before you left the meeting place?"

He didn't answer at first, as if conversing at all was absurd. "A woman? Yes, one more. That makes four."

"Four?"

"And two children. Below. With the rest."

Edward leaned back, eyes closed. He had no gauge, nothing but his own anxiety to guess how far they'd come. Every passing moment brought them closer to the border, but he couldn't tell one moment from ten, one minute from an hour as he waited, prayed, for the sun to rise to prove time hadn't stood still.

Even as he prayed to leave Belgium behind, he knew the closer they came to the border the more likely was a return of firepower.

Soon he sensed the boat went even faster, though the engine sounded no louder. A look over the side told him the current had picked up. God was pushing that strong little boat as fast as it could go, increasing its power, hurtling it toward safety.

Suddenly Rémy jumped to his feet, going to a trundle chest at the stern. The other sailor stood as well. Rémy returned and gave Edward what looked like wire cutters, keeping another set for himself.

"You'll know what to do with these in a moment," he said, the extent of his explanation.

"Have you another?"

Edward spun on his feet. It was the Major.

But the man shook his head and boldly pointed to the Major's disability. "You wouldn't have the leverage. You'd be more help behind that, if you know how to use it." He pointed to the rifle Edward had put aside to accept the wire cutters.

Edward looked at the Major, who hadn't bargained for his own escape, especially when that might include shooting at his own countrymen.

Max took up the gun.

Edward looked down at the tool in his hand. It was the length of his forearm and sturdy enough for serious cutting. Meant to chop wire or chain?

The tug hit something invisible beneath the surface, and it resounded with a thudding chime from the hull. The men rushed to the gunwales and Edward followed. The first man picked up a long, hooked stick from the deck. It looked like a staff from the little girl in the children's poem with the lamb. He leaned over the prow and heaved. A chain came up with a jingle and a splash, and both Edward and Rémy started hacking away. Rémy cut through it in moments.

By the time they hit a second chain, another station was in sight, firing a hailstorm of bullets. Hauling in the chain left the one man most vulnerable, even leeward of the German storm. Edward and Rémy crouched until the last moment. Then cut, spurred on by the other to be the first to break through.

Another chain sank to the river's bottom, this time from Edward's slice.

From somewhere behind came rifle discharge, from another sailor—and from the Major.

At his comrades.

Edward hacked and hacked again with all his might.

The sailor with the hook wrestled with the fourth chain, yelling for help. Edward and Rémy dropped their cutters to lend aid; the chain was caught by something near the bank. On the count of three, the men gave it a heave-ho and it flew from its frozen restraints to swing directly around, broken from the embedded links. The three ducked at once. But the Major, still intent on the guardhouse, did not even turn.

"Major! Duck!"

But it was too late. The chain struck the Major's helmet, winding comically around the spike on top. In a flash it pulled the helmet away, jerking the Major along with it. He hit the side of the boat and the helmet strap broke, sending it flying and the Major, obviously stunned, to the deck.

Edward started toward him, but the German shook his head as if to shake away pain and then, spotting Edward, held up a hand.

"I'm all right," he said, then picked up his rifle and took aim again.

Seven times they hit a chain, pulled it in, chopped it through. Seven times one man risked his life leaning over the prow, providing the German soldiers with a living target while Max and the others covered for him. And seven times those Germans missed their moving target—or so Edward thought.

Until he saw the blood on Rémy's shirt.

"Hey! You're hit!"

But Rémy only shook his head, oblivious.

They were out of range again, beyond the last of the chains that had been scouted. Edward fell to the deck, breathing heavily.

"We've made it."

But the man who'd brimmed with bad news so far offered no hope now. What could be *next*? And not for the first time Edward wished he'd chosen to go by foot. Even if the Germans had doubled the electric lines at the border, it surely would have been easier than this.

Nothing for a blissful few minutes. Or perhaps it was hours; time was still foggy.

"Holland." Rémy, at his side, whispered the word as if he were looking at God Himself.

Edward gazed in the same direction. The sun . . . so it hadn't disappeared after all. There it was, finally shedding light on the eastern horizon. When had the light first appeared? Edward couldn't recall. He saw a windmill in the distance and his heart lightened. Holland—only minutes away!

Then Edward saw something else. A thick wire was strung just above the width of the river, straight in their path at the approximate height of the prow. Edward dropped the wire cutter, eyeing the origin of the wire. There was no cutting *that*.

It was bare electric. If the voltage was high enough, the dampness permeating the metal and wood boat would be enough to destroy them. If it hit the steel smokestack, it wouldn't even need the dampness to conduct its deadly current.

Orders from the tug's captain showed no cowardice. The engine blasted and in a moment shouts sounded from the right bank. Edward ducked, preparing for gunfire that always accompanied German cries. And yet it didn't come. He looked at the bank. Soldiers were there, all right, and they were armed. But they simply stood there. Watching the boat approach the wire.

And so did Edward; so did everyone else on that deck.

The wire disappeared below the line of the prow. Edward closed his eyes, preparing at the very least for a jolting shock.

But it didn't come.

The wire struck the boat and acted like nothing more than a rope holding back the powerful little tug. The engine raced and the boat slowed. It raced again and the wire pulled them to one side—to the left, away from the suddenly erupting bullet fire—but suddenly it didn't seem to matter. They hit a shallow spot and scraped the river's bottom. For one breath-catching moment, Edward thought they were lost in spite of the inadequate electric line. They were stuck in icy muck like a soldier caught in the mud of no-man's-land.

He saw a pair of soldiers run to the box from which the wire emerged. They must have been as surprised as those aboard to see the wire hit and do no damage.

But the tug still floundered, listing to the side. The engine chugged as the tug tried to reverse while the muck held fast. Then the tug reeled and they were wondrously free—headed into the line of German fire. The boat's pilot steered starboard, headed to Holland, the harmless wire caught beneath the tug's prow.

Edward looked back at the pair of soldiers bending over the voltage box. If they found the sabotage of the voltage box and repaired it before the boat pulled free of the wire, that would be it. He spotted the wire cutters: metal from tip to grip. The voltage might be too low to conduct through the damp wood of the prow, but he wasn't sure a direct hit with metal would be as ineffective. Yet, if that would save them . . .

The tug engine still churned, struggling against the taut wire. He started toward the prow, but just as he picked up one of the wire cutters, something else caught his eye. The pole holding the wire tottered in its place, and the two soldiers below were already looking up. The tug kept swaying against the wire attached to that shivering beam and in a moment it crashed down, barely missing the two soldiers below.

The suddenly unconfined wire sprang upward in a mad dance across the river, away from the prow. Abruptly the engine of the tug roared with freedom, with one last burst and a rapid pitch forward.

Then the clink of bullets hit the smokestack again and everyone plunged to the deck. But it ceased in seconds.

Dutch guns protecting their side of the border covered them now.

"Full speed ahead!" Never had a captain's yell been so heady, so full of gusto.

Unabashed cheering rose from every corner of the ship, then from Edward himself—and the Major. Only when they burst into song did Max grow quiet beside him, perhaps not knowing the words of the Belgian patriot hymn "La Brabançonne." Still he smiled, leaning against the rail.

The deck flocked with people; men's strong voices lifted the song ever higher. Edward sang but his eager gaze sought just one face.

First he saw his mother, smiling and crying. But even as she waved at him, he saw her gaze drawn to the Major as he stepped forward, using the Allied rifle now as a crutch.

At last Edward spotted Isa and fought his way through the celebrating passengers to grab her to him, holding her tighter than he'd ever held her before.

"Come with me," he said but knew she could barely hear him over the joyous singing echoing from every direction.

He took her hand and led her to his mother's side and, without a word, directed both of them portside of the small tug. The Major followed.

Hands still joined with Isa's and his mother's, his mother holding the Major's, Edward dropped to his knees. Needing no further invitation, they sank to worship beside him. With the victory songs accompanying their prayers, the four paid homage to the God who had saved them.

Edward barely noticed the songs fade away. At last he opened his eyes and looked to see the other refugees aboard.

Each one on their knees.

44

On this day, the 27th of January, Germany celebrated the birthday of His Imperial Majesty, the Kaiser. In their newspapers, German propagandists proposed the reason there was not a single shot fired in Tir National this morning to be the sympathy and affection the Kaiser holds for the Belgian people. Even for those Belgians who, like errant children, have yet to learn not to test German leadership.

But *La Libre Belgique* has it on reputable authority that it was Belgian ingenuity and bravery that stopped the executions this morning. Perhaps this very newssheet will be held in the hands of at least one of the formerly condemned, who escaped yet another of the injustices the German army attempted to perpetrate.

La Libre Belgique

Land had never felt so good, although Max hadn't made enough voyages to give him the means for comparison.

Holland.

Neutral ground. Neither Allied nor Central.

His gaze shifted southward, where a while ago occupied Belgium had disappeared. Around him refugees hugged and cried, and some still sang.

Edward had taken Isa ashore ahead of him, and Genny was with them now. The three of them clutched one another, unashamed of their tears. Dampness clung to his own eyes, too.

But as glad as he was for them, something else pulled at his heart.

"Max," Genny said, holding out her arm to invite him into the group embrace.

He joined them but kept both hands on the wooden handle of the rifle at his side.

"There are soldiers there," Edward said, shading his eyes from the sun. He pointed to a tent, outside of which sat a table and Dutch soldiers, obviously taking information from those who had just disembarked from the tug.

"Go," Max said.

"They'll help," Edward said. "All of us." He started to lead their little group forward, and Max watched them take the first steps.

Max stayed where he was.

Isa turned to him. "You—you're not coming with us?"

She was shocked, he could tell, but even with only a peripheral glance, Max could see that Genny was not. She knew him better than he knew himself.

"I will see you again, all of you. Someday, God willing."

"But where will you go now? You'll need help! You need us!"

He smiled at Isa, at this young woman whose roof he'd shared, who because of his army had suffered so much. Max touched the hand she extended, one he was sure she would have used to pull him along if he'd let her. "No. I'll say good-bye now."

"But—"

Instead of joining her protest, Edward touched her arm. Max had been sure in the last few days that he'd earned the young man's acceptance. Perhaps he'd believed what Max had said about the difficulty of good-byes and didn't want to extend the argument or the good-bye. Max himself had only suspected the truth before; now the reality sliced through him.

"You're a brave girl, Isa Lassone. A brave young woman, I should say. Edward is fortunate to have your love."

Edward stepped closer. "That's certainly true."

Then she had her arms around Max's neck. "I would have liked to know you better, Major. And now I'm afraid I won't have that opportunity."

He patted her back and pulled away. "Maybe someday. I hope so. Finding the Lassone family in Belgium will be easy enough, if Belgium is ever free again." He stole a glance toward Genny, and he was sure he saw her nod. "And if . . . if Belgium is annexed by Germany, then I will look for the Lassone family in America, should I ever travel so far."

"Baltimore, Major. The Lassone family of Baltimore. You won't forget?"

"No, I won't forget. Baltimore."

Edward stepped forward, extending a hand. Max grasped it.

"I don't know how to thank you, Max."

"No need. I did what I had to do."

But Edward shook his head. "No, you did more than that, and I'm grateful. I'll be grateful for the rest of my life."

Then he put his arm around Isa again and started to lead her away.

Though he barely let himself a moment ago, Max looked at Genny fully now and couldn't take his eyes from her. If Edward spoke again, or if Isa made a last farewell, he did not hear them.

"Genny."

"Max."

"I cannot go with you; you know that."

"But you can't go back. You mustn't."

"No, not yet. But when I can. Somehow."

"And in the meantime?"

He once again looked toward the distant border. "I'm a traitor, Genny. A traitor to Germany."

"But you aren't! You fought against injustice. You did what you thought was right."

He stiffened. "I shot at men wearing my own uniform."

"Yes! To save us—all of us! How could you have done anything else?"

"I could have stayed. I should have."

"And been arrested yourself."

He would have admitted that was what he deserved but knew she would only challenge that, too.

"It won't be easy, going off on your own," Genny said. Somehow he knew she wasn't referring just to facing the German army again, but to all the rest. To Käethe. To his own disappointment over all he'd once served and believed in.

"I'm not sure life is supposed to be easy, Genny. After a life of ease, one might be surprised to find God's there at all."

She nodded, tears catching light in the corners of her eyes, a tremulous, brave smile on her lips. She'd never been lovelier.

"Genny," he whispered, "there is much left unsaid between us. But it must be this way. I shall have to return home eventually. Or send for Käethe. I don't know which, subject to what charges I may face." He attempted a smile but felt only half his mouth obey. "I suppose that depends on who wins, doesn't it?" He touched Genny's chin with his thumb, looking at her intently. "I admire you greatly. I hold you dear. I'll not say more because I'm not free to do so. I ask only one thing."

She said nothing, gazing at him.

"That if I am ever free, I have your permission to find you."

She offered a laugh that sounded more like a sigh, nodding her consent. "Max, I won't ever forgive you if you don't find me. Promise me that you will."

He nodded, then placed a kiss on her forehead, not daring anything more.

He knew he would have to walk away because it was he who couldn't have her, he who wasn't free. He who needed to settle and mourn not only this, but the death of his allegiance to the country of his birth. Time alone could resolve all of that.

He took one step back, then offered a smile. He'd never had a confident smile, and this one wasn't any different.

But it was all he had to give just then, and he preferred her memory of him to be that and not the sorrow that made such a smile so difficult. Leaning upon the makeshift crutch, he turned and walked steadily away.

He could not look back.

This war reveals the utter failure of such a notion as armed peace. Man has yet to discover a way to prevent war.

La Libre Belgique

Epilogue

Isa Kirkland sat in the front parlor of her parents' grand home, amid the noise of an end-of-the-war party. Celebrations had erupted all over Baltimore but none more festive than her mother's. Perhaps few participants elsewhere had as much to be grateful for as Isa and her family.

But that wasn't the only reason this was one party Isa welcomed. Her parents had spent more time in the last year with Isa and Charles than away from them, ignoring countless social obligations. Even now, with guests still pouring in and filling the many rooms of their elegant home, the family stayed intact here, in the smallest parlor of the house.

Across the room were her brother, Charles, and his wife, Julitte, Charles in concentrated discussion with Edward. Genny and Jonah were here too. Jonah was nearly as tall as Isa these days. And the newest addition to their family, a son recently born to Charles and Julitte, gurgled and giggled on a blanket in the center of the room.

Isa could barely tear her eyes from the child, knowing in a few months' time his cousin would be born. Even animated talk about the armistice couldn't command her attention.

"You look like you have a secret," Genny whispered, next to her on the plush brocade sofa.

Isa felt the warmth of a blush. "Maybe I do."

"You've never been a tease, so you must want to tell me."

"I do. I will—we will. I was just waiting for a lull in the noise."

Isa's gaze landed on her husband, whom she'd loved nearly all her life. He laughed over something Charles said but caught Isa's eye and sent her a wink. Edward and her brother had become as close as brothers themselves, much to Edward's surprise—and to Isa's glee. In the year and a half since they'd joined forces to create one of the most popular newspapers on the East Coast, the two had spent nearly as much time with each other as they had with their wives.

Isa glanced at her friend, her mentor, her mother-in-law, all in one. "Genny, I know it hasn't been easy for you these months since we've moved here. But I'm hoping if we surround you with enough family, you'll think of this as home."

Genny brushed Isa's cheek. "I once told you that where you are—and Edward and Jonah—that's where I'll call home. I haven't been unhappy here."

"But not really happy, either. So far from your memories with Edward's father . . . and Max."

Genny looked away as she always did when Isa whispered his name. How long would Genny wait for him? It had been nearly two years without a word.

"I'm happy, Isa." But the sparkle of a tear in the corner of one eye belied Genny's words. "The war is over; Jonah will not be called to service. The world is safer than it was just yesterday. And you, I suspect, are about to give me another reason to be thankful. What more could I ask for?"

Isa wanted to say Max's name but feared the single tear in Genny's eye might be joined by others if she did.

"Come now," Genny whispered. "Catch the eye of that husband of yours again and have out with this announcement. I have a hug just waiting to be shared."

✦

"Are you sure this is it?"

Max von Bürkel did not move from the motorcar, one he'd hired with its driver at the Baltimore dock. The importance of the question made him forget, for the moment, to be proud of having learned the English language, though he imagined his accent must be heavy.

"Yes, sir. That's the address you gave me. The gate is open. Do you want me to drive you up to the door? I can make it past all of these other motorcars."

An open gate and countless other vehicles should not be an impediment to one more visitor, yet it was to this one. Those vehicles no doubt belonged to invited guests, unlike Max. Perhaps they celebrated the end of the war, a war in which he'd been their enemy. The lane curved to accommodate several tall trees, but even so he could see the size of the mansion befitting such grounds. Brick, three stories, tall windows. As spacious as only America could offer.

Was she in there, his Genny? If not, anyone who lived in this Lassone estate could surely tell him where to find her.

He cautioned himself again about calling her "his Genny," but no matter how many times he told himself otherwise, he'd never listened to his own best advice. It had been nearly two years. Two years since he'd left her, sneaked back into Germany and to his wife's side.

The first had been a year of visits, a year in which Käethe had gradually come to know him again, in which they had become friends again. A joy he never would have known had he not done what he knew he must and honored the promise he'd once made to his wife. A promise Genny herself had reminded him to fulfill. So he'd returned to her, loved her.

But Käethe had never come home with him. Had she sensed the truth, even though he'd never admitted that his heart resided elsewhere? Perhaps, if they'd been given enough time, he might have convinced her to come home with him. They might have lived contentedly at least, as friends.

Instead, when the influenza gripped the convent, Käethe had been among the first of its victims. One day Max had been there with her, handing her his kerchief when she'd coughed. And the next day she had died, before he even knew so many were sick.

Somehow the sickness had spared him. It was random in its choice, taking nearly half of the nuns and those who tended them. And though Max had been a regular visitor, he'd never developed so much as a sniffle.

That had been six months ago. All those months he'd waited, and not just for the war to end, though Germany had grown so desperate that he'd known the people couldn't support it much longer. Max had also waited for guidance from God.

Eventually he'd gone to the officer who had once commanded him and revealed his crimes, confessed his treason. And waited again. Surely he deserved whatever punishment was deemed necessary.

But it never came. The army was in such chaos, throwing every man to the guns, that Max's crimes were forgotten. Germany had more troubles than it needed without punishing one more of its own from within.

Amid rumors of the end, Max had no desire to stay, to wait until the army caught up with its punishments. Nor did he wish to watch the soldiers return—not to victory parades but in defeat.

His destination had been decided long ago.

And yet . . . was he meant to be here? What would Genny need with him after so long? Particularly if she lived here, with a family that had so much?

Nonetheless, he would let her decide if she wanted to see him or not. He'd promised to find her, and so he would.

"To the door," he told the driver.

Because Max always honored his promises.

Author's Note

All characters in this book are fictional except for Brand Whitlock, the American ambassador to Belgium during this period of time. Doktor Stuber is inspired by Doctor Stoeber, the German judge-advocate who sentenced Nurse Edith Cavell to death. *La Libre Belgique* (Free Belgium) is an actual newspaper that began printing in the year 1884 under the name *Le Patriote* (The Patriot), started by two brothers, Victor and Louis Jourdain. *Le Patriote* stopped circulating after the August 1914 German invasion, refusing to submit to German censorship. In 1915 the paper reemerged clandestinely under the direction and financing of Victor Jourdain and his friend Eugene van Doren as *La Libre Belgique* in order to give hope to an oppressed population. After the war, it retained the name *La Libre Belgique* and is still in circulation today. Apart from the quotes opening chapters 5 and 9 and the Berlin letter excerpt cited before chapter 26, all other "quotes" contained in this novel from *La Libre Belgique* are the imagination of the author but strive to convey the message represented by this paper in its form during the German occupation of Belgium.

About the Author

Maureen Lang has always had a passion for writing. She wrote her first novel longhand around the age of ten, put the pages into a notebook she had covered with soft deerskin (nothing but the best!), then passed it around the neighborhood to rave reviews. It was so much fun she's been writing ever since.

She is the author of several novels, including *Pieces of Silver*— a 2007 Christy Award finalist—*Remember Me, The Oak Leaves, On Sparrow Hill, My Sister Dilly,* and most recently, the Great War series. She has won Romance Writers of America's Golden Heart award and American Christian Fiction Writers' Noble Theme award and has been a finalist for the American Christian Fiction Writers Book of the Year award, the Inspirational Readers' Choice Contest, and the Gayle Wilson Award of Excellence. She is also the recipient of a Holt Medallion Award of Merit.

Maureen lives in the Midwest with her husband, her two sons, and their much-loved dog, Susie. Visit her Web site at www.maureenlang.com.

Discussion Questions

1. Isa and Edward are willing to risk their lives because they believe in the power of words to inspire, restore, and give hope. Share an experience where the written word has impacted you so that you felt differently after you read it.

2. Isa is naive about the state of affairs in occupied Brussels, even surprised when she learns the Germans have taken over national landmarks like the Palais de Justice. As Americans, we've been blessed to never have to confront an infringement on our freedom. What everyday activities do we take for granted that might be taken from us if we were ever occupied by foreign troops?

3. Isa and Edward express different ideas about how to interpret God's will. Isa claims it must be God's will for her to be there simply because she has made it safely. Later, Edward tells a group of Germans that God revealed His will by way of desire. What are the merits and the flaws in each of these interpretations? Why do you think God's will is sometimes hard to figure out?

4. Throughout much of the story, Edward doubts that God can be in control when life is so chaotic and unfair. Have you ever turned from God rather than turned to God when you don't understand why bad things happen around you?

5. Genny tells Isa: "I don't like myself when my thoughts are so full of hate, and I doubt you would either." But when

Genny is with Max on the way to St. Gilles, she admits to herself that she hates every one of them, even the one at her side. Share a time when your outward appearance, words, or actions vastly contradicted your inward emotions. Was that good or bad? How did you handle it? Is it possible to redirect one's emotions? How?

6. Have you ever considered which side God would be on in the wars throughout history? How do you think God feels about war in general?

7. After Isa agrees to house the press, she realizes she might have endangered all of them just to get Edward to notice her. Have you ever convinced yourself you were doing something solely for God, depending on His protection, when underneath you had mixed motives? What made you realize that?

8. During the dinner party discussion between the Germans and Edward, one of the sentiments expressed is that God may exist but can hardly be concerned about the details concerning mankind. Edward assures them God is concerned, because He loves all of us. How would you respond to this sentiment? Do you think Edward is right? Is God concerned with every decision we make?

9. Edward admits he was never sure whether his faith had been his own or simply handed down to him from his father. Have you ever wrestled with whether your faith was your own and not simply something you "inherited" from your family or culture? How did you resolve this uncertainty?

10. Genny informs Edward that he'd better learn to distinguish Max from the army he represents because Max is a Christian and they'll have to spend eternity together. Have you ever struggled with your attitude toward a fellow Christian who differs from you in some substantial way? All emotion aside, how do you think God wants you to handle your relationship with this person here on earth?

11. Have you ever felt helpless in a situation where anger seemed to be the only emotion you could decipher? When Edward thrusts his fist at God, Father Clemenceau reminds him that God doesn't have to justify Himself to anyone. Has anyone ever given you this sort of spiritual slap in the face, to remind you of your place and that God is God and He can allow what He sees best in order for us to know Him best?

12. When all seems lost, Isa accepts her fate. How do you think she might have handled her sentence if she didn't have faith that there is more to this life than the number of years we spend on earth?

Turn the page
for an exciting preview
of book 3 in
THE GREAT WAR
series.

Travel to postwar Germany, where a
young soldier returns home, only to
find he no longer has one he recognizes.
When family friends ask him to go to
Munich to find their daughter who has
run away to join the political scene,
Christophe agrees . . . not realizing it will
change the course of his life forever.

Available spring 2011

1

One step, then another. He'd started out with his eyes forward, chin up anyway, but somewhere along the journey, his gaze had shifted; all he could see now were the tips of his boots.

Christophe Brecht was inside German territory, the train having taken them back over the border, away from the trenches that had marred France for the past four years. The ground his boots pounded belonged to the fatherland.

Home.

The only sound was that of his men marching beside him—not that their tread could be called marching. Most looked as tired and worn as he, barely able to take that next step, still covered from boots to knee in the mud of no-man's-land.

He looked over his shoulder again. There were shadows back there. Not of men, but of . . . what? He didn't know.

Did any of them remember how it was when they marched—yes, really marched—in the *other* direction? Songs echoed from every avenue, praise and flowers showered them from smiling women, and proud pats resounded on the back from fathers and old men.

He told himself to look up again. He could see far down the road. They'd been made to get off the train on the outskirts of the city, not far from Christophe's village. So he shoved away old thoughts of how this day was supposed to be. No victory parades to greet them, no flowers. No woman to kiss him now that he was home. Just silence.

He stared ahead under the bright sunlight. His vision was clear, something the army had taken advantage of when they'd trained him to be a sniper these past two years. Most likely many men beside him couldn't see as far as he could—the series of signs on poles before them with splashes of red, in flags, in backdrop. Political signs he hadn't seen the likes of since before the war. Back when people still talked about such things, when the German voice wasn't the single one it had turned into during the war.

Then he saw it. An older poster, a bit tattered in the wind. The Kaiser's face, easily recognizable with his moustache and uniform. A call to arms.

Christophe tore his gaze away, to the sky, back to his boots. He'd answered that call; so had each of those who trod at his side. A call that had ended this way.

Rumor had it the Kaiser had fled Germany. Good riddance. But somehow having him step down, even in disgrace, wasn't enough. If what they said about the armistice was true—that Germany was to blame for the war—then the world hated them. Hated all of them for how the Kaiser and his cronies, both aristocratic and military, had pushed them into this war.

Hated them almost as much as Christophe hated himself for all he'd done while in it.

His pace picked up before he knew it; blood pumped as wildly as it had during any fight with the British or French, either in offense or defense. He reached for a rock and hurled it at the Kaiser's image. It landed with a thud directly between the eyes.

Another rock, then more, along with a grunt here and there, a muffled cry. Were they his? No. A few men broke ranks and hurled themselves at what was left of the poster.

All his life Christophe needed something to cling to. His parents, a schoolmaster, the church, his commanding officer. In the trenches, other soldiers. And Christ.

Hate filled him now, and he clung to that.

Christophe held back another rock in his hand—no need to throw it; the poster had disappeared.

"And so, fellow Germans! The calendar may say autumn, but in fact we are in the springtime of Germany. The winter of an unjust war is behind us. New life buds for all of us. Are there storms in spring? Yes, but the squalls bring us the energy we need for change. We can build our country anew and model for all—for ourselves and for our neighbors, with the world's eye on us—that we speak as one voice, a voice of men, of women, *all of us* together."

She barely paused, although the crowd was already beginning to cheer. She read the same fervor on every face; it was like a wave passing over those gathered, binding them together, uniting them. All of them, no matter what walk of life separated them beyond this crowd, now—together—were one.

"They'll hear us speak of protecting and not exploiting our fellow citizens. They'll hear of our compassion for those in need, feel it in the plans Jurgen has for Germany. We'll no longer be stomped by the yoke of a monarchy or under the oppression of warmongers. We will be free—yes, really free—to live in the peace our men fought for. Peace! Freedom! Fairness!"

Annaliese Düray reveled in the jubilation, in the immediate approval of her call. They outmatched her voice, which was a considerable thing because her voice was bigger than she was—especially on this platform. Hands raised, she lifted her cry even louder, momentarily proud of the timbre she'd inherited from her onetime schoolmarm mother. Not strident like a screeching woman but mid-toned, boisterous, easy on the ear even at this volume. "Peace is ours! And so is the future! If we rally behind Jurgen!"

"Anya . . . Anya, come along now."

Leo Beckenbauer's arm went around her waist and he ushered her from the crowd. Two others carved a path between the brick wall of the *Apotheke* behind them and the crowd before them, and off they went, the exuberance still echoing in her ears.

"Did you see them, Leo?" she called, breathless. "And more were coming! We should stay. . . ."

But he pressed forward and there was little she could do except follow, with Leo next to her, Koby and Ivo in front, and Huey behind them. Each one was a brother to her—united not by blood but by something deeper—a passion ardent enough to stir all Germany toward a better future.

And sometimes they were nothing more than bodyguards.

They skirted the few people who followed by turning into a narrow passage between the back of the *Apotheke* and the shop next door. Only four blocks to the back of the butcher shop Leo's father once ran, their temporary headquarters for those whose ideals about the future matched their own.

Not a block from headquarters, Annaliese heard the echoes and cries of yet another rally—led by a voice she recognized as one of her competitors. In her neighborhood?

She barely had a thought gathered before Koby and Ivo left her in Leo's care. Koby was an ironworker and Ivo a bricklayer, as tall as they were stalwart. It would take little more than a word from either one of them to disperse a competing crowd in their territory.

"I could have stayed this time, Leo," Annaliese said once they entered the back of the darkened shop. Though the kitchen hadn't boasted a single slab of meat or even the stingiest of sausages in well over a year, the slight residue of blood and spices still tickled her nose when Leo closed the door behind them, leaving Huey outside to watch the entrance. The everyday energy in the butcher-shop-turned-party-office superseded any excitement these walls had known before or since it closed as a butcher shop—although it had been quite some time since Leo's father had died, and along with him his shop.

Leo went to the pump and filled a pitcher, taking a glass and filling it with water for Annaliese. "You know how Jurgen likes it; you keep their thoughts on our message while he's gone. When he returns, that will be the time we spend more freely with them. Keep them wanting more. Wanting him and his message."

Annaliese knew the orders; Jurgen would return from Berlin tomorrow to the crowds she kept warm in his absence. Of all the voices struggling to be heard these days, it was Jurgen's that attracted the biggest response from nearly all corners of their broken society. He liked to tell her she brought the women's voice to him, but Annaliese knew better. People came because they wanted to see him, to hear his voice, to witness the spark in his eye as he promised them what they wanted most of all. Each came with one need or another, but Jurgen had the answer, no matter the question.

"Oh! It must have been delivered while we were gone." Annaliese scooped up the package left on the wide butcher's table. "And just in time for tomorrow's council meeting."

Ripping away the string and paper, she held up the jacket for Leo to see. It was exactly as she'd told the tailor to make: broad across the shoulder, with a touch of padding to make those shoulders appear fully capable of holding the world's woes, just as he needed. And not black, but blue—dark, though, because anything too bright would be out of place in their tattered world. Yet blue would cast his elegant eyes in the best light, and if one looked closely enough reveal the hope that came with such a color.

But Leo was shaking his head. "He'll look like a capitalist."

Never mind her own father had worn such a suit once, and he

the definition of capitalism. She shook her head. "He will look the way every man wants to look," she said. "Strong. Fatherly yet handsome; a leader."

Leo aimed a skeptical brow her way. "Fatherly? I wasn't aware that's how you viewed him."

Jurgen was old enough to be her father—or very nearly so, she guessed. But no, that wasn't how she or any woman in their movement saw Jurgen; she was fairly certain of that.

Yet she ignored the comment. It wasn't the first time Leo had tried coaxing free her infatuation with Jurgen. "It's important that he not look like a military man, even if we do want the military behind us. We've seen enough leaders in uniform. And he won't wear the top hat of a capitalist, either, or the shoes of a monarch. He'll wear trousers like anyone else, only this jacket will show he has the means to take on another's burden without needing the excesses of an exploiter."

"Yes, well, he's doing that, isn't he?" Leo fingered the sleeve, then looked at her. "Well chosen, Anya. You're young but smart; I've said so right along."

Annaliese smiled at the praise, especially coming from Leo. Jurgen might be the one to receive public praise for their campaign—or the blame from those who disagreed—but anyone who worked beside them knew whatever Jurgen believed, Leo believed first.

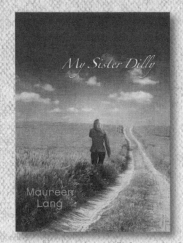